The Way By

A Faire Tale

Holly Walters

ISBN13: 978-1-959350-37-8

Set in: Fairybells 36/38pt, Georgia 11pt, Extra Ornaments QCF 41pt

For Frieda
Because you believed

"Some day you will be old enough to start reading fairy tales again." – C.S. Lewis

Chapter One

In 1806, or so goes one peculiar version of the tale, there was, in the Bodleian Library of Oxford, a regular library patron of the most unusual sort. A young girl, with a mess of braids in her uncombed hair, would arrive upon the doorstep each Friday, turn herself thrice in circles on the fourth stair of the Radcliffe Camera, and once satisfied would commence with a fast-paced kulning.

The ancient Swedish herding call, with its roots left moldering somewhere in the Nordic medieval age, was once used for its special high-pitched sound and thus its capacity to communicate with animals and creatures through very far distances. Having then finished her song with a series of signature lilting half-notes, the girl would then race up the remaining stairs, enter a side room set aside for the housing of "curiosities," and promptly vanish. Years following her last appearance in the fall of 1836, then as a grown woman of some remarkable stature, her memory devolved into a reasonably famous ghost story – which is to say that several successive generations reimagined her as an unmarried ingénue pining for her lost love; in this case, an Oxfordian scholar who chose the life of a clergyman over the adoration of a fetching lady.

But as truth would have it, such a ghost never actually troubled the neo-classical halls south of the Old Bodleian, nor had any apparition ever caused so much as a neglected page to turn, made one unaccounted for footstep to sound out in an empty room, or made the hair to rise on a single studiously bent head. But, despite this one minor inconvenience of fact, the girl enjoyed a distinguished reputation as one of the most oft referenced causes for academic failure in all of South East England.

That her real name was Mary Elizabeth Toft and that her disappearance directly coincided with the opening of the London and Greenwich Railway was never discovered. She did, however, leave behind a rather strange, hand-written, commentary on *The Private Memoirs and Confessions of a Justified Sinner,* which for many years remained unnoticed in the narrow spaces between two shelves pressed together in the early religious fiction section of the upper balcony.

In it, she wrote of a demonic antagonist Gil-Martin "*....as a rather curious fellow; a homicidally egotistical Virgil who, despite taking his companion Wringhim on a confessional tour of his own internal hellscape, assures the doomed man that no sin can come from one chosen by God. It is just this manner of corruption to which we, the Waysmiths, must be most vigilant.*" She went on to say, "*Wherein we encounter such monsters inclined more to simply cut out and devour a man's heart than discuss the exegesis of Scripture, should we chance to meet the fiends whose evil is so cleverly masked by pious declarations of virtue, we cannot but see the hands of the duplicitous Faire at work.*" This it read, until it too disappeared; pilfered by an uncommonly observant individual for the posterity of a similar story yet to come.

That story began in the early spring of 2016, when the Hearthcraft Community of Massachusetts received an unexpected guest in a long-practicing matron by the name of Evelyn Bel Carmen. At the first congregational meeting she attended, Madam Bel Carmen rose from her appointed seat and addressed the gathering. She began by complimenting the Mother House for its dedication to Pagan Witchcraft and listed the many rare and exceptional books that the community had managed to procure over the last decade.

As the main house was also located just outside of Manchester-By-The-Sea, just a few miles from Salem, she also took such an occasion to mention the region's famous history and to convey her empathy to the victims of the abominable witch trials. She then hinted that it was no mere impulse to her in coming to Massachusetts or to know of the existence of such a company of practicing witches. Those who adhered to the orthodoxy of British Traditional Wicca, she reminded her audience, were better respected than their more free-form counterparts and that a careful attention to their henotheistic roots would certainly result in a finer comprehensive understanding of the nature of magic than any hidebound dedication to Biblical dualism might supply.

Many nodded at this, as though they understood any of what that meant. Madam Bel Carmen then said that she had studied for many years and knew all manner of esoteric details regarding the history of magic and its influential if secretive practitioners. Given her deeply invested interests in her own Benin ancestry and the lineages of Black witches from which she knowingly descended, she also continued to read new publications upon the subjects of polytheism, pantheism, animism, and monism; on the definitions of witchcraft cross-culturally, on esbats and sabbats and controversies erupting over the Wiccan Rede.

She had even made prudent contributions to selected volumes, especially when they involved the subjects of evangelism, Dahomey spiritualism, and the African Diaspora. But as she stood before the assembly, she wondered aloud as to why writers who spoke of the machinations of the Fairest (to which she made an aside as to the modern pronunciation of "fairy") in the dealings of the everyday world were so readily dismissed. Why was it indeed that treatises that took these entities more seriously than cookery and thievery, or those that described the hidden peoples with broader gravity than the usual barely concealed derision, could be left on shelves scarcely elevated over fiction?

Madam Bel Carmen wanted to know, she said, why the covens of the East Coast no longer held their practices accountable to the ancient pacts though they continued to profess their continuity with the theology of Diana, Airdia, and Cernunnos, of Cuchulainn, Conall Cernach, and Nuada Airgeadlámh, and of the divine syncretisms of the Aziza, Yaksha, Mogwai, Tien, and Menehune. Names, she noted with concern, that were now merely entries on a list with nothing else behind them. Letters and spellings debated over but the substance forgotten.

In short, she asked to know why Americans so dismissed the Fae. What she did not know, of course, was how truly commonplace the Fae actually were. But the question was one that had not been put to the leaders of the Hearthcraft Community with any seriousness before. Aside from a few favored motifs in jewelry and personal dress, fairies remained relegated to child-like symbols and bedtime stories with only the odd professor of various literatures to raise the level of conversation beyond the whimsical.

Even then, to take the ontological existence of such creatures any more sincerely than the purely symbolic risked labeling such a person as the victim of Hollywood movie-making, or worse yet, a dimwit. Regardless, the attendant members of the community took the question with some measure of surprise and with the swift realization that they could not offer a united answer. In short, they weren't entirely sure.

The High Priestess of the Hearthcraft Community, a middle-aged woman she knew only as Amelia Cosmos, who had mastered the complicated upswept bun that curled her greying temple locks into an elegant symmetrical double-spiral, turned to Madam Bel Carmen and pointed out that the question belied a problem of available knowledge.

"It ignores the fact that such ancient traditions as you mention have not been recorded with any confidence as to actual mythologies and experiences, rather than the Victorian fabling most publications that we know of are really drawn from. Most of these works are playful nonsense, as you must see. You cannot seriously claim, for example, that Robert Kirk's *The Secret Commonwealth of Elves, Fauns and Fairies* is based on some real events with anything approaching honest inquiry. You wouldn't stand before us here and make a case that Middle-earth or Narnia, no matter how convincingly portrayed, are iconic of real wizards and mythical beasts or that Shakespeare was being entirely literal when he penned A Midsummer Night's Dream? My dear Ms. Carmen, if, as you say, we should continue to take pride in the fact that we are better respected among the new pagan traditions, shouldn't we also endeavor not to sully our reputations with fantasy, no matter how personally affirming they might be?"

A younger woman with rheumy blue eyes and the telltale scar of a cleft-palate interjected (whose name was Lua, or Loa) that she didn't think it a reasonable question. Furthermore, at risk of offending others who might identify with available fairy emblems, Madam Bel Carmen shouldn't have traveled so far to ask it in the first place. Fairies were simply too much of a risk when it came to outside inquiries and that even the mention of the term was more likely to invoke images of Tinkerbell and Cinderella's Fairy Godmother than anything of any legitimate importance.

Simply put, fairies were for entertaining children while the Fae were a subject of real study, but because the former was so much more popular than the latter, the reputation of witches couldn't afford to yoke itself to what amounted in the national consciousness to consummate bunk. Any practical study was destined for collegiate basements. It was the providence of humanities dissertations and New Age book publishers, and if the topic was particularly lucky, the relative imaginative safety of a good novelist.

The young woman then finished her stream of consciousness with a flustered fadeout, regarding Madam Bel Carmen with a look that she hoped would adequately convey her frustration with the current discussion. She wanted so very much to show her learning through a critical position, but at the same time, not completely distance herself from just how much she enjoyed beautiful tales of elves and sprites free of intellectualism or, to be honest, practicality.

Madam Bel Carmen sighed.

Arguments ensued. Unfortunately, as is true in the gathering of any people known to be experts in their respective fields, no consensus could be reached as to who professed the correct view on the matter, though a multitude of opinions were voiced as to who professed the wrong one. A number of the women found Madam Bel Carmen's question to be an intriguing one and soon began to debate amongst themselves if the problem might be more one of popular representation than anything having to do with the actual scholarship of magic worlds.

Emerging from this discourse, a stately woman by the name of Alice Guthrie, graced with a naturally pleasant smile and the impeccable prosody of a poet, publicly lent her support to Madam Bel Carmen by way of posing the thought that perhaps the real controversy at issue was whether or not one was referring to "the" world or to "a" world.

To explain, she went on to summarize her thinking as to how "fairy" might either be thought of only as a metaphor in the imaginative sense or if a more sober examination of the literature should be undertaken with an eye towards building an evidentiary case. Even if they all remained agnostic about the actual existence of the thing in question. As the resulting exchanges became more heated and Amelia Cosmos once again attempted to reassert control over the proceedings, Alice drew Madam Bel Carmen to the margins and whispered her most intimate concern.

"Please do not be put off by this, Ms. Carmen." She said. "I'm sure you can see that there are many positions at stake here alas, many of which must take into consideration far more than just academic progress. But, if you would be so kind as to humor me, to what do we owe such a question? Have you uncovered something new? Some lost message or diary that we all might see? Do you come on the behalf of another?"

For her part, Madam Bel Carmen was moved by Alice's sincerity and it was to the credit of such an earnest lady that she did not find herself more crestfallen than she might have been. "It was never my intention to start a fight, Ms. Guthrie," she whispered in return. "But I had hoped to win the community's favorable leanings before I revealed my motives."

But as neither Madam Bel Carmen nor Alice Guthrie were particularly inclined to be easily discouraged in their endeavors of interest, they soon rejoined the conversation with a mind towards steering the final outcome. What followed was a raucous, though not especially spiteful, foray into the possibilities of folkloric studies given the question at hand. On one instance, however, after an especially biting remark from Amelia Cosmos, Madam Bel Carmen was called upon to defend her position.

"Our guest today," said Amelia, "seems to be implying that this community ought to regard all folklore as objective truth! There are a great plenty of respected academic journals now dealing with the revelatory studies of fairy tales and it is not the role of this gathering to intercede. Since the publication of Bettelheim's *The Uses of Enchantment*, each of us here has had to navigate the throngs of pedestrian adolescents clamoring to alter themselves into mindlessness and believe in fairies. I, for one, am not going to see our character become an object of ridicule."

Madam Bel Carmen remained seated at the side of Alice Guthrie, a disconcerted look weighing her brow. "Very well then. I had not intended to place this fine assembly in such a position of fear and mockery. But I say to you all that this issue is not at rest, and if there are magical practitioners of a serious mind and brave enough in their inquisitive constitution here in Massachusetts, I shall find them!" It was here that she left the meeting and was not party to what came after.

The budding friendship between Alice Guthrie and Madam Bel Carmen, however, did not end with the meeting of the Hearthcraft Community. She soon invited Ms. Carmen to her house just off of Tappan Street for a dinner of New England clam chowder, a slice of corned beef, boiled potatoes and carrots, and the finest apple cider cake in living memory. It appeared that Alice dwelled comfortably in the company of her two children; John, a dashing nineteen-year-old sailing enthusiast and Fiona, a sixteen-year-old track star contemplating state schools on the furthest side of the West Coast she could find.

As Madam Bel Carmen knew very few people in the area and had not yet had the time to gain enough seniority in any of her club hobbies to garner long-term associations, she was grateful for it all. After her first visitation, she also came to learn that Alice Guthrie was a rather talented pianist who favored the contrapuntal keyboard works of Bach and the sonatas of Beethoven and Schubert over the innovative cycles of Messiaen or Chopin. As such, she always kept a worn copy of "Hammerklavier in B Flat Major" on the piano bench, more as a meaningful decoration than an invitation given her impeccable memory of the piece.

She also had interests in learning Spanish, but after a few failed attempts at using language tapes in her car years back, she simply talked about it as an amiable possibility for the future. In fact, it was following one such conversation regarding the difficulty of training one's mind to wield new words with any manner of functional use that Alice suddenly announced that she thought Madam Bel Carmen herself to be just what she wanted to see in a modern witch: thoughtful, curious, educated, and kind. Though, she did also remark that she worried that such moderate approaches rarely had the effect of changing the stubborn status quo.

The confidence between the two women continued into the subsequent weeks. Within a short time, Madam Bel Carmen was spending two to three afternoons, and just as many evenings, in the company of Alice Guthrie, either at her house on Tappan Street or having luncheon in one of the many restaurants along Cape Ann. In the event that the Guthrie children were hosting friends, which was not uncommon in the summer months, Madam Bel Carmen and Alice would shut themselves away in the back rooms to discuss the pressing question that had now come to consume them both – was the serious scholarship of fairies a real possibility?

Unfortunately, though their conversations often went long into the night, fueled by endless cups of Alice's favorite rooibos tea, they could arrive at no solid solution for introducing the idea to either the academic establishment nor the leadership of the local pagan groups. It would seem that their thoughts to take into account Fae as persons in their own right, as actual creatures of Nature buried under enough layers of cultural allegory, symbol, and trope as to be rendered invisible, could only be met with disdain. It would have been easier to simply invent a new god and open up shop to sell another religion.

Alice Guthrie, however, was a proud and energetic woman whose own mother had often referred to their maternal family lines as Latina but by way of the Vatican. Meaning that much of their mobility and Hispanic ancestry followed notably Catholic roads that had directed their feet and not so much their hearts. But as a result, she always liked to be doing something. Even if she could not yet foresee a use for her projects, she felt the vital drive to carry them out anyway. For this reason, she often had on hand any number of potentially useful and artistic elements, from bottled essential oils, hand-rolled beeswax candles, and dried herbs for potpourri or tea to half-finished quilts, driftwood carvings, and bags of collected seashells.

The present task, however, was to gather the primary sources, texts, and other information that might be needed to design a suitably convincing plan for mounting a new academic discipline, or at least causing a schism in a current one. In many ways, both women delighted in the comparisons they were able to make between their own ventures and the quests of the hero and heroines of the stories they enjoyed. Solving riddles in the face of impossible problems, searching for lost knowledge in dark, forgotten archives, and occasionally turning up a small treasure here and there to further encourage their efforts.

It was not surprising then, when Alice began to liken their work to the salient points of the Hero's Journey. Holding aloft a copy of Joseph Campbell's *Hero with a Thousand Faces*, she remarked that any real expedition into comparative mythology should pay homage to the rules of the story as set out by the structure of fairy tales themselves. She meant here, to find the story by becoming it.

Meeting Madam Bel Carmen's confusion, she further remarked that, seeing as the both of them had already fulfilled the call to adventure (quite necessary to begin any tale according to Campbell), the next step would be to meet a great mentor before crossing the threshold and setting out into the mystic world, however it was that would come about.

Ultimately, what Alice Guthrie meant to propose was that it might be time to go somewhere where they could consult someone. Setting aside quickly that she did not mean a return to the Hearthcraft Mother House (which she was happy to label as the "refusal" part of this particular monomyth), but that she was growing concerned that they were stuck. If nothing else, a fresh point of view on their work so far should be enough to get them going again.

She also had quite the mind to burst into some poor lecturer's office and demand a few hours of their attention, but she was forced to dolefully confess that she did not know any and had no idea who it was that they should ask in the first place. Madam Bel Carmen consoled her friend's palpable despair, and without admitting any prior knowledge or intention, told her where they might begin.

Madam Bel Carmen had come to Massachusetts in search of a certain litterateur. Her diligence of study and dedication had only, in her mind, ever really paid off in one respect, and that was the day she had chanced upon a small book, *Lostwith Notes: The Truth (Without Permission) of the Way By Stumble*, by Somerset Sayer. The author of this remarkably obscure work lived a reclusive life somewhere near Yarmouthport on the Cape where, it was rumored, she almost never left her house (save for the occasional local café appearance) and spent the majority of her days curating rare and unusual books along with a collection of macabre sketches.

Following a learning conference celebrating the 320th anniversary of the Salem Witch Trials in 2012, Amelia Cosmos had actually penned a letter to Somerset Sayer, then a well-known folklorist, inviting her to participate in a panel regarding Medieval and early modern witchcraft for the Hearthcraft Community's workshops on pagan practices throughout history. Unfortunately, her reply, though phrased with the utmost politeness, was unequivocal.

My dear Ms. Cosmos, she saluted, *It is with great honor I received your invitation to speak at the upcoming Salem conference on magic and witchcraft, but I am afraid that I am quite unable to attend at this time. My schedule such as it currently is, remains choked with obligations I cannot neglect on any account. Also, I fear that my on-going absence from public scholarship is likely to render any thoughts I might provide irrelevant to the progress of learning your conference seeks to undertake. I wish you my best, of course, and offer my regrets. Sincerely, Somerset Sayer.*

The conference planners of the Hearthcraft Community had each reviewed the response, and more than one felt obliged to comment on the unusually artistic handwriting of the missive, noting the straightness of the down strokes on each letter followed by wide flourishes for both upper and lower curves. She also apparently was in the habit of using a typeset-style small "a" rather than the typical manuscript small "a" common to American cursive. Then, though with some disappointment at their inability to draw a notable scholar to the event, they dismissed the folklorist from their thoughts. But Madam Bel Carmen had seen the invitation list from the conference purely by chance, in the folder of one of the committee planners, as she had also attended the workshops on the history of magic by the same invitation.

She said to Alice Guthrie: "I think we should begin in the place most likely to yield as many new sources as we have not yet seen, or may not have recognized given what we have studied already."

To her mind, surely the connections and perspectives of an experienced scholar could reveal some new avenue of exploration. Madam Bel Carmen thus proposed that they should send a letter to Somerset Sayer whereby they would come to some appointed meeting place and conduct an interview regarding her research publications.

Aside from *Lostwith Notes*, Somerset Sayer had also had previous publication successes with *Apprentice Alice: Practical Applications for Hobart's Constant, Baba Yaga Enters a Pelican into Evidence,* and *Hansel and Gretel Had It Coming*. And so, heads bent together over a college-ruled notebook, they wrote the letter, and using their subsequent corrections and marginal notes as guidelines, drafted an email which was sent at promptly half past three that afternoon.

They waited on the reply for only two days, much to the surprise of Alice Guthrie. The short response, in a little less than four lines with both a polite salutation and curt valediction, expressed curiosity upon receiving their message as well as a comment on the serendipity of their timing. It would seem that Somerset Sayer was currently engaged in a research project at the Physics Research Library on Oxford Street in Cambridge and would be happy to meet them should they be willing to travel there.

She then provided a number at which the two women could reach her and an address where they were to call on her, preferably on the afternoon of the 15th around 2pm. With Madam Bel Carmen's resulting enthusiasm, Alice Guthrie found herself gripped with some trepidation. The wording of the reply was amiable enough, but she couldn't shake the feeling that something more sinister lay behind the visitation agreement. It wasn't that she thought Somerset Sayer to be malevolent in any overt sense, but that there was a subtle disdain to the tone of the message.

It did not, however, dampen her desire for further discovery and she thought that, despite any possible hostilities that might arise, she would go at the appointed time and glean from the exchange whatever she could. At that moment, she was also reminded of the old Theosophical adage, "when the student is ready, the master will appear." It was a reasonably popular saying in occult circles, and for Madam Bel Carmen's sake, she hoped it would be here agreeably appropriate.

On the day they set out for Cambridge, the weather was uncharacteristically warm and a light rain had begun to fall by the time they reached the house on Trowbridge Street. Though it sat on a lot once occupied by a merchant storefront in the early years of the 18th century, the current terraced townhouse had been built in a Queen Anne style more indicative of the slew of 1880s renovations still blanketing the neighborhood. A series of asymmetric forms accorded the double-hung windows and small-paned upper sashes a whimsical if juxtapositional feel.

The wrought-iron railings and decorations that framed the L-shaped stoop gave the impression of broad stemmed English Ivy which was clearly meant to offset myriad elements of Classical and Renaissance detailing mixed with Romanesque Revival styles. The appearance of texture was a mingling of weathered brickwork and dark brown wood trim along with the late addition of a series of small, copper, stars hammered into a line along the right edge of the door jamb. Even more oddly, their tarnish indicated that each star was at least a few years younger than the one that preceded it.

The remains of last autumn's leaves persisted, gluing together cracks in the brickwork and concrete of the buildings on either side of the squat, three-story, row house. Brown spikes of grass were all that covered the rectangular patch of lawn at the front of the walkway and a window box of long dead flowering kale and sedge hung precariously by a single nail in the bay window's outer frame. It was Madam Bel Carmen's excitement alone that colored the dreariness with a dash of purple to the kale and a bit of yellow to the sedge, her animation and fortitude reminding her friend that this moment was as much one of revitalization to their own endeavors as the coming spring was to such neglected gardens.

A brief glimpse of movement at the curtains of the bay window caught Alice's attention, but no sooner had it disturbed the heritage lace panels than it was gone. Alice Guthrie hesitated. She almost thought it was their reclusive host if the figure had not looked more like a very small man clutching a red hat over an unusually elongated head. But it was Madam Bel Carmen who strode confidently up the step and knocked three times quickly. For a moment, there appeared to be a fair amount of activity beyond the threshold; a kind of scurrying about and shifting of furniture.

As the lock scraped open, creaking to a click against the warped wood of the four-paneled door, the two women unconsciously schooled their expressions into ones of imminent delight at the anticipation of a warm welcome. Warmer, at least, than the sodden ambiance of lower Trowbridge Street.

When the front door swung wide, seemingly of its own accord, and Somerset Sayer greeted them in the entry hall, some several feet from the threshold as they stepped into the foyer, they soon realized she was not the eccentric provocateur they had imagined. She was elegant but unpretentious, like the type-set style a's in her letters. Her voice was muted as she offered the usual salutations, as though she were merely stating a few random thoughts out loud in a room where company had gathered but not directing her attention to anyone in particular.

She wore a dark green dressing gown tailored in the Victorian style; gathered at the waist and closed at the front with three wide, black, frog clasps. Beneath it, she appeared to be dressed in a floor-length chocolate brown slip dress with a high scoop neck and sleeves long enough to breach the cuffs of the house coat and cover her hands to the knuckles. Having gathered her long blonde hair into a loose bun, the image of a recently disgraced aristocrat came replete with a stiff chin, tense poise, and a mien of placid concern.

Somerset Sayer motioned her guests into the sitting room where the bay window looked out onto the street, but aside from the wet lighting provided by the struggling outside sun, she had provided no other lamps, candles, or hearth fire. While the daylight was more than adequate to see by, it rendered the rest of the room rather charmless and dim. It was sparsely furnished; a grey divan, three grey wing-backed chairs, and an end table near the window.

There was also little in the way of decoration save for an empty, bamboo, bird cage sitting near the fireplace, an old daguerreotype of a spectacularly large man in a waistcoat framed over the divan (a giant, Alice Guthrie speculated), and a row of laughing Buddhas (Hotei, Somerset Sayer would later correct them) arranged across a wooden shelf sitting over the room's single radiator.

From her position near the end table, Madam Bel Carmen could make out little of the rest of the house save for a small dining room adjoining them, and beyond that only glimpses of book shelves and books lining the distant walls of a room on the far side of a half-closed sliding door. As they each attempted to settle in, their host offered them hot tea, provided a stack of cloth napkins, and awaited their questions with little in the way of polite small talk.

"I have read your wonderful commentaries on Andrew Lang's *Fairy Books of Many Colors,* Dr. Sayer," Madam Bel Carmen began eagerly. "A truly comprehensive analysis that I am sorry doesn't get the attention it really ought to have. But I have always wondered, you go into such great depth on each and every one of his included fairy tales, but you never mention the very first story he includes, The Bronze Ring. There must be some reason behind it and I have been keen on asking you about it since I read it."

The silence that followed was uncomfortable to say the least before the folklorist appeared to come to some manner of decision about her guests. "What is your opinion of Sihir, Miss Evelyn?"

"Sihir?" said Madam Bel Carmen, "Well, I don't think I have an opinion. By that I mean....... I have never heard of anyone by that name."

Somerset Sayer nodded absently. "I suppose not," she replied. "I always forget that the Sura Al-Falaq isn't read in lay circles these days. It is all conjuring and casting lots and astrology what-not I suppose. Most texts take the position of forewarning against this kind of sorcery, Sihir is black sorcery after all, and all the Abrahamic books paint it as devilry one way or the other, anyhow. Should come as no surprise your authors don't treat with it, scared as they are to get that Puritan devil worshipping label pasted over their lintels again."

"Ah, yes..." Madam Bel Carmen supplied nervously. "But what does that have to do with the Bronze Ring?"

"Everything." Somerset Sayer furrowed her brow. "I would not give any sort of wish-trading curse even a whit of my time. Is that not the point of the story you refer to? No. No witch-wives and red fish or slaves and black cats, or any such lame horse and copper nonsense. I have enough to concern me here as it is than to tickle the attentions of some depraved djinn."

Alice Guthrie came to the rescue. "Yes, of course, Dr. Sayer. We should have begun with our more pressing concerns, I suppose. We have actually been wanting to talk to you about one of your most recent publications, the one you have entitled *The Truth (Without Permission) of the Way By Stumble.*"

There was a distinct sound of something hitting the floor, though no offending object appeared to take the fault. It was followed by an even more uncomfortable silence. "You've seen that book?" the folklorist queried.

"Why, certainly." Madam Bel Carmen recovered. "I have a copy of it in my own library at home, bought it at a lovely little thrift shop in Branford by way of New Haven while I was on a trip some months ago."

It was unnerving how the scholar in the far seat could simultaneously grind her fingernails into her thumb while sitting so perfectly still as not to disturb so much as a wisp of hair at her face. "What did you want to ask about it?"

Flipping open to a page in her pocket notebook, Madam Bel Carmen began hesitantly. "You say in your introduction that, and I am quoting it here: *this book is written with the hope of diminishing the once widespread notion that Waysmithing is the unnecessary and fatuous interest in the broken remnants and table scraps of a bygone, and therefore superseded, antiquity comprising once great human magicians.*

"It tells a story about the concealment of the knowledge that humanity has never once possessed the capability of wielding magic proper, as we are a mechanically-inclined species and not otherwise mystically imbued. Therefore, I seek to resurrect the understanding of Waysmithing as the practical method by which the magical world may be reconstructed and manipulated, by way of thaumaturgy or wonderworking, to best serve more human concerns.

"I undertake this endeavor in light of recent pressing issues with the state and current condition of the Way By, blockaded by the Faire Stumble since the Founding of the Waxing Crescent. As such, there is in this book no pretense to the meticulous scholarship that must document every statement and it therefore contains no long bibliography and no thousands of confirmatory or overly explanatory footnotes. It tells the truth and aims to tell it in a way that is readable and imminently instructive. The author makes no pretense to an exhaustive treatise on the techniques of Waysmithing; but to persuade readers to act upon the issues at hand."

Madam Bel Carmen laid her hand across her notes. "What do you mean by that? The Faire Stumble?"

Alice Guthrie was near sure of it that Somerset Sayer would refuse to answer the question directly. Instead the scholar regarded them steadily for some moments. She had the most curious brown eyes that seemed to gaze out from some other place within her.

Then, almost affably, she invited them to join her in the far room, which she now identified as her library (or, at least, what of it she typically required to travel with her on research excursions). As Madam Bel Carmen and her companion rose to their feet, Somerset Sayer added an aside, that the question was best answered through the consultation of expertise more discerning than her own. Again, strange, considering she was the only author of *Lostwith Notes*.

The room that housed the library was larger than the sitting room and extended well into the back gardens through a series of architectural expansions. There was an oak desk and accompanying leather chair, whose muted styles complimented the sunny comfort and quiet of the double-stacked shelves. However, the golden, summery light afforded to the room by four large twelve-paned windows did not appear in accordance with the available light outside, which was still dreary and ashen with early spring storms.

Alice Guthrie, for her part, could not help but think that they had all somehow stepped not just through a doorway off of a dining room, but into some other house entirely. The view from the windows was even more perplexing, looking out into the branches of a gigantic Coulter pine tree nearly indwelt by a neighboring magnolia bush twisting its flowering branches throughout.

From between the thick foliage, no other characteristics of the outside surroundings could be ascertained, and thus, Alice Guthrie remained able to truly entertain her sense that they had traveled somewhere else quite far from where they had begun. The room was also far from that of a simple library, for in every crack and corner there lay some manner of bizarre object, a veritable cabinet of curiosities with pages and bindings for niches.

Madam Bel Carmen would immediately identify several of the odd trinkets: a trilobite, fully articulated skeletons of a small fish and a canary, a large Egyptian canopic jar, a lady's perfume bottle from the early 1930s, and a rather disconcerting looking brown house sparrow preserved in a jar of spirits. Alice Guthrie took quicker notice of the somewhat less macabre items: a bronze Krishna statue, an icon of St. Anthony of Padua (Patron of Lost Things, she recalled), a painting of Hildegard of Bingen, and an apothecary jar marked Theobrominum.

The final marvel, and the one to which the entire room seemed organized to reveal, was a massive oil painting hanging over a set of short bookcases opposite the desk. Its gilt frame, though a little overly baroque, hardly detracted from the intricate scene of Hieronymus Bosch's *Garden of Earthly Delights*. Beyond that, the books were something else entirely. Not a single cloth covering or embossed leather binding could have been younger than a century, save for a single cabinet of clean modern commentaries and literary treatises set aside behind a heavy pane of glass; as though not to contaminate the others with their profane temporality.

Madam Bel Carmen had seen many personal collections in her years at home and abroad but none came close to the volumes upon volumes of editions in Medieval and Vulgar Latin, French, German, Sanskrit, and stacked manuscripts that could only be Old Gaelic and possibly Icelandic. And most astonishingly, not a one could be later than AD 1600. Some showed clear signs of age and wear, a few broken spines and raw corners, but most had clearly been so lovingly curated that one could hardly believe they had passed down the centuries in the hands of anything less than the most dedicated bibliophiles.

Alice Guthrie stood pensively at the nearest shelf at eye-level and read off the first title in English; *A Novel Trick of the Stage – Decapitation*. She paled at the following: *Preparing for Cremation – Or, Why You Should Always Wear a Hat Before Consigning Yourself to the Fire.*

"Do not concern yourself with those there," Somerset Sayer rested her folded hands on her knee, leaning back contentedly in the leather chair. "Death is a somewhat more complicated matter in regards to the Way By and unless you care to dig your own grave with a wrought-iron hearth shovel before you go, there isn't much you can do about it from a practical standpoint."

Madam Bel Carmen exclaimed rather suddenly, “You have copies of both the Aleppo Codex and the Gutenberg Bible!”

“You know the Aleppo Codex?” asked Somerset Sayer.

“Only through recent news stories, I dare say,” replied Madam Bel Carmen, “It was scanned onto an online research forum a few years ago and there has been quite some controversy over its authority in Biblical interpretations. It’s extraordinary that you appear to have an actual illuminated transcription here! Is it genuine?”

“In a sense, I suppose,” remarked Sayer, “I came by it rather unexpectedly but I have found it to be especially enlightening in terms of Judeo-Christian magical traditions.”

“I was not aware that Christians had magical traditions.” Alice Guthrie interjected.

Somerset Sayer scoffed. “Claiming that one has no historical continuity with magical philosophies does not mean they suddenly cease to exist. I might point out the obvious, alchemy and that awful Philosopher’s Stone, and by that I mean Sir Thomas Browne and his 1643 *Religio Medici* and not Plato’s *Timaeus*. Disreputable astrology and some other clandestine occult mischief; my, what a list the Victorians have to answer for!

“But was it not Thomas Aquinas and Roger Bacon and Paracelsus, all well steeped in the philosophies of Christ, who first raised alchemy up out of fraud and disrepute to finally bring its sensible applications to fruition? Even now, one cannot deny the Christian mysticism of those such as the Masons, the Rosicrucians, and the Gnostics. Nor can one ignore the Evangelicals and their plumb lines.” In the end, Somerset Sayer’s tone betrayed some measure of contempt for the most popular secret societies on the current cultural roster even if she never fully denied the efficacy of their methods.

As Alice Guthrie wandered from book to book, Madam Bel Carmen could not help but pace among the library’s curiosities with amazement. Without thinking, a sudden exclamation passed between the two women, “We’ll certainly find our new avenue of study in here!”

“Oh, I doubt that.” Came the reply.

Madam Bel Carmen froze in her place. The shadows of the room grew longer, as if the once high noon sun had sunk below the level of the densest pine branches. The color of the needles and magnolia buds became dim and hazy. A low fog appeared to have settled on the back garden, dousing the windows in milky white brume. Alice Guthrie, quieted by the perceptible shift in mood, reminded Madam Bel Carmen as to the reason they had come to the library to begin with.

"Yes, yes...as per our letter," trailed Madam Bel Carmen. "You said our answer might be found here then. Might you offer a book we should study or a citation perhaps?"

"I might." Somerset Sayer continued to heed them coolly. "But I fear that no amount of careful reading will get you to where you want to go. In fact, I doubt even a graduate degree's worth of syllabi would be sufficient. Direct evidence is the only possible persuasion."

Alice Guthrie and Madam Bel Carmen then noted something quite peculiar at that moment. A second chair now sat next to where Somerset Sayer had remained seated behind the desk. Next to that chair was a small, round, walnut end table, designed, by the looks of its ridged edging and drop-leaf sides, as a plant stand. Laid out upon the table was a series of objects carefully arranged in a star pattern (if one might care to draw lines between them): an ornate antique lock with two keys on a black ribbon, the feather of a large parrot, a copper coin stamped with the icon of a lantern, a white votive candle, and a silver dish of water.

But neither Alice Guthrie nor Madam Bel Carmen remembered seeing Somerset Sayer moving about the room to collect the objects, move the chair, or bring in the table. Nor could either woman recall when the objects appeared there, only that they certainly had not been there moments ago. And with its large and open layout, there could not be anyone else entering or exiting the room they had not seen.

Covering their unease as best they could manage, Alice Guthrie spoke first, "Then perhaps you might have a suggestion, Dr. Sayer? My friend and I came here today with the hope that you might be able to help us understand more about the academic study of magic, specifically of any and all things Faire, given your special expertise on the subject. Miss Evelyn and I are both of the opinion that something vital is missing from the pagan and witchcraft communities. Don't you think so?"

"Indeed, I do," said their host.

"Well, our problem then," Alice continued, "is that the study of the fairy is not taken seriously. Why, I mean, there are a great plenty of literary reviews and metaphorical analyses and so on. And I know that you as well must be rather tired of all the butterfly-winged child's birthday parties and some such banal art. I do apologize if we have somehow caused offense but our coming here was to bring about something really meaningful and conducive to new inquiries. Please, madam, what can you show us that might truly aid us in changing the way Faire is researched?"

Somerset Sayer's brow rose at a gentle angle along her forehead, her eyes twitching slightly into a slow, satisfied, blink. It was as though, in the barrage of anticipated questions she had expected from her interview with the pair, this one was the longest awaited.

She remained still in her seat and said, "Very well. There is something I can offer you, but you must send me a letter detailing your list of concerns. Be sure to hand write it, I won't tolerate any of this digital font absurdity. Send it by regular post to 125 Thatcher Shore Road in Yarmouthport. If you can provide me with some manner of plan to which I can offer my contribution in a concise manner, I will have something for you then. But for now, your answer will be best initially received if you leave my library."

Downcast but deeply optimistic at the outcome, both Alice Guthrie and Madam Bel Carmen offered their thanks and made their way to the sliding door. Upon opening it, they headed towards the front door with a mind to regroup in the car on the way back to Manchester-By-The-Sea. But considering that they were now standing in Alice Guthrie's living room on Tappan Street, and not in the folklorist's parlor, they suddenly had something entirely different to discuss.

Chapter Two

As Alice Guthrie finished the message informing her son that he should take the commuter rail and fetch the car in Cambridge at his earliest convenience, Madam Bel Carmen paced the living room with nervous delight. "Astounding, Alice, absolutely astounding! I still can't understand it! Can't believe it! I must admit that I had so many ideas as to how our meeting would end but neither of us could have predicted a turn of events such as this! Magic! And right here, in Boston! But we must calm ourselves, yes, we must, as there is now the matter of the letter to compose. And then, oh, we must find confidence elsewhere in the pagan community as well! Surely there will be other allies to secure."

"Yes, I suppose." Alice offered uncertainly.

"Well, I am not suggesting that we do not proceed with caution, naturally," said Madam Bel Carmen. "Sweeping into the room with a tale such as this one, and with no other evidence immediately forthcoming, would be a fine way to see ourselves to the psychiatrist's couch or worse. But you cannot deny that we have been party to something most wondrous and without prompting or quarrel. Surely Dr. Sayer intends to demonstrate her gifts for a wider audience but lacks only the proper venues and preparations. I dare say her treatment in academic circles hasn't been the most deferential as of late." She paused at last. "Do you think that she herself might be...one of them?"

Deferential or not (though Somerset Sayer would come to describe her reviewers more as undiplomatic rather than uncivil) the problem remained as to how the existence of Faire might be introduced to the magical communities of the Greater Boston Area in such a way as to neither invite complete derision nor endanger the uninitiated with wild conjury. As the conversation continued, Madam Bel Carmen began to fret, particularly as the gravity of their experiences weighed upon her.

She could easily discern why the folklorist had not made the true extent of her knowledge public, nor invited a close examination of her capabilities, but she also could not ignore this most critical disclosure and what it meant for the scholarship and history of witchcraft in the better part of two centuries. For the moment, she believed the scholar was set to unveil herself as something other than purely human and they must, therefore, follow her instructions to the utmost detail.

It was nearly eight in the evening by the time Alice Guthrie and Madam Bel Carmen were entirely confident in their next course of action. Seeing the requested letter as the most substantial leverage they might use in any further endeavors; they saw fit to request a modicum of time at the next meeting of the Hearthcraft Community leadership committee. Scheduled for the following Friday, their single line-item in the posted proceedings implied little more than a debriefing of a recent conversation with a notable scholar and a request for input on the contents of a follow-up letter.

At precisely three o'clock on Friday the Manchester Motherhouse bustled with activity. Word had spread among the membership of several groups of magically-inclined potterers that Somerset Sayer, the distinguished if avant-garde intellectual, had requested, from them, a proposal of study. Despite Alice Guthrie's attempts to correct the notion that this request had neither been framed as a formal appeal nor was, in any way, directed towards the community at large, men and women from all over the region trickled in with the intent to add their own invitations, ideas, and recourse to the response the committee was already drafting.

It was, after all, as espoused by Amelia Cosmos, the right and the duty of all purveyors of the mystical arts to see their own enterprise justly represented. A loud call to order did little to quiet the initial din. The main practice room, now doubling as a classroom and meeting hall for its size and ambulatory shape, was so crowded that Amelia Cosmos, still the principal leader of the proprietary group, was obliged to stand and shout for the attention of all assembled. The hodgepodge congregation was not quick to respond. Several older women knitted in a far corner, pulling and drop-spindling ostentatious colors of thread in the manner of Norns spinning the fate of the meeting at the foot of Yggdrasil

Almost serendipitously, three younger gentlemen had also recently arrived from Salem, dressed in fine woven tunics bearing Ringerike and Jellinge Style Norse knotwork trimming and Mjölnir pendants. From Wakefield and Reading came palm and tarot readers, most identifiable through their distinctly manicured nails and unconsciously fluid gestures. Gloucester had supplied no less than four Wiccans of the Alexandrian tradition, though Rockport sadly only produced one. The Revere community of Gardnerians was represented almost in full, sporting several personally annotated copies of *High Magic's Aid* and *The Magus*. The remaining patchwork of Dianic practitioners, Celtic and Druidic Revivalists, and the odd Discordant, filled in the gaps as they might. It was with some measure of satisfaction that Amelia Cosmos had managed to secure a high-back cathedral chair prior to the meeting, and she now stood upon it (red brocade cushion dipping precariously) overlooking the room with a decidedly magisterial air.

"Order now, the lot of you!" She repeated. "I'll not have this become a circus."

Alice Guthrie made her way through the commotion to the right-hand seating already occupied by Madam Bel Carmen. "Yes, it is fine to see you again too Mr. Harris, and you Mr. Ellison. How fares the gatherings of the Ásatrú these days, still working on that Vanatrú schism? And hello, of course, to you Mrs. Glass! Oh certainly, we shall explain all about what it is we came to do here today. She was lovely, without a doubt. Good afternoon, Havva, yes isn't it exciting! I fear I must be getting to my seat, one moment please, I promise!"

It took several moments for order to finally be restored, necessitating the arrival of more chairs from the basement storage closet and a series of hushings traded back and forth across the haphazard rows. Poised with an expectant posture and the grim set of a studiously serious brow, Madam Bel Carmen rearranged the notes in front of her one more time before Amelia Cosmos finally gained command of the room.

Over the course of the last few hours, Madam Bel Carmen had rehearsed and re-rehearsed a rather moving speech wherein she had intended to appeal to all the higher emotional natures of the assembled crowd. In it, she boldly set forth that Somerset Sayer would provide for them some manner of confirmation, in exchange for a letter of cooperation, that not only could mystical methods and creatures be the subject of respectable research, but that she could provide proof positive of their existence!

Unfortunately, she had hardly gotten past her opening remarks, outlining this new wonder, when so many back-channel conversations filled the room with so much distraction she was obliged to redirect the attention of the gathering to a question from the gallery. From her stately cathedral chair, Amelia Cosmos addressed her:

"Do you mean to imply, Ms. Bel Carmen, that Dr. Sayer has requested from us a consultation on the nature of Glamoury?"

"Well I..." She began before she was interrupted.

"As this would be most irregular. I was not aware that Somerset Sayer took advice from anyone, let alone such communities as she perceives to be, shall we say, amateur in these matters."

Madam Bel Carmen had no interest in allowing Amelia Cosmos to get any further in her diatribe than this.

"Relations between the scholarly communities and our own are as they are and the politics of these divisions are not the subject before us today, I am afraid." She stated. "I can assure you that Dr. Sayer is completely serious in her request for our civil engagement and thus, our task, such as it is, will be to formulate a proper response. She requests not a consultation but an outline of present concerns such that the nature of uncanny creatures can be correctly described and demonstrated to the satisfaction of logical and scientific standards.

"As is befitting a serious undertaking on the matters of Faire and the nature of the work already written on the subject, we should, in all gravity and sincerity, pledge our fidelity to the project and set about this outline of study befitting our needs and interests."

A ginger-bearded Ásatrú gentleman, whose posture belied his skepticism, spoke up then that the esteemed Madam Bel Carmen and Ms. Alice Guthrie should have seen fit to coax Dr. Sayer from her hermitage in Cambridge and bring her to the meeting presently ongoing if they thought her interests so heartfelt rather than seek to champion the cause themselves without clear confirmation from the vanguard.

One of the knitting Dianic women scoffed in turn, speaking out in response to the effect that the very chaos and discord of the present proceedings ought to be enough to discourage anyone from initial attendance and that at least Madam Bel Carmen and Ms. Guthrie were attempting anything at all given the level at which criticism was wont to fly about. An elderly lady on the left margins, with snow-capped eyebrows and an unnaturally white bouffant, voiced her assent to this but was quickly drowned out in the ensuing chatter.

There was, however, a rather prudent woman in the room, smartly dressed in a grey suit without any additional adornment. She wore no amulets or bright scarves, no esoteric prints or other indications of her personal spiritual affiliations. Her name was Ceres Warren, and while she had little schooling (formal or informal) in the modern methods of magic she had a great passion for all things creative and imaginative. Ceres saw no reason why the two women presenting on this day should not have all the encouragement and support a community such as this one might offer.

Though, she was forced to admit, even to herself, that the idea of serious scholarship in regards to the actual existence of fairies seemed far-fetched and just a little childish. But now that a known scholar was demonstrating genuine attentiveness to the topic, she feared that a dismissal from the larger society would have dreadful long-reaching consequences to any future collaborations.

"My friends," she made plain, "If Dr. Sayer is in possession of direct evidence of the existence of Faire, we must know it. Evidence we may then surmise must be utterly convincing if she is proposing only a letter of concerns in exchange for it. I, for one, am also moved by the fact that such women as these, whom I consider to be of substantial mind and sound character, have met with Dr. Sayer and remain eager to carry the case forward." She turned to Madam Bel Carmen. "Clearly Ms. Evelyn, you have come away from your encounter as a righteous convert. Will you not elaborate on how this came about?"

Madam Bel Carmen smoothed her skirt over her knees in contemplation. As much as she desired to lay bare their experiences and announce that she had seen for herself the reality of the ethereal, she still believed only scorn would follow. Ceres remained standing, patiently awaiting the response and in doing so, had managed to compel the room into attentive silence more effectively than all of Amelia Cosmos's loud demands had up until this point.

Madam Bel Carmen recognized the moment as her best chance to spell out exactly what she had wanted to from the beginning, to finally convince the entire meeting of the Manchester Motherhouse that Somerset Sayer knew something about Faire that the rest of the world, academic or otherwise, did not.

For several seconds, she repeatedly made as if to speak, drawing in a deep breath and opening her mouth, only to stop and purse her lips thoughtfully. She simply could not find the right words to adequately convey the profound nature of her experiences, seeing now how the subtlety of Somerset Sayer's execution had already foreclosed on any kind of grandiose tale of wonder and amazement.

What claims could she truly make here? That she had traveled from Cambridge, and possibly to the Cape, and back again to Manchester-By-The-Sea in the space of three rooms in a single house? That random objects had appeared out of nowhere prior to the event? She hardly sounded rational to herself when she replayed it in her memory, let alone how she might then articulate these events to those who were not present. How could she get them to understand it all in such a way that she didn't undermine the entire venture?

"Well," she offered, "She is in possession of a great library and of many rare texts that I can assure you have not been seen in as many years as they have existed."

Ceres did not find this reply especially tolerable. For that matter, neither did the rest of the attending community. Ceres turned to Alice Guthrie, who had remained somewhat somber and pensive during the exchange. "Ms. Guthrie, perhaps you can explain?"

Even less sure of what she had seen and anxious under the scrutiny of so many people at once, Alice Guthrie first managed to smile obligingly, momentarily unable to collect her thoughts. She contemplated the water glass on the table before her. The sweating condensation on its sides dripping down to soak the white tablecloth beneath was an apt metaphor for her current predicament.

She feared for a moment that she might become ill and further ruin their chances for a good outcome, so much so that she carefully grasped the water glass and took a few tentative sips as much to calm her terrible nerves as to buy a few extra scraps of time. Sensing her distress, Madam Bel Carmen surreptitiously laid a comforting hand on her friend's shoulder, squeezing gently to remind her of their continued solidarity.

Alice Guthrie resettled into a more rigid posture. "I'm afraid I can offer you nothing specific but to say that I know deeply in my heart that we are on the cusp of something extraordinary. Please forgive my rambling, but I think that you imply that Ms. Evelyn and I were shown something by Dr. Sayer that we are now concealing in order to secure your support for our own personal gain. I promise you, we are not holding hostage any such information.

"It is only that she requested some measure of assurance and of a suspension of disbelief of sorts I think, before she would reveal anything further. Though, in my understanding of our brief encounter, it is that indeed there is something to be revealed. Something that would unsettle even the most ardent skeptic and, at risk of damaging my own standing among you, I should say that I am inclined, following our meeting, to believe that Somerset Sayer is, in fact, in possession of this most marvelous thing. Whatever it may be."

A vigorous new debate erupted among the assembly. Amelia Cosmos, as it came most naturally to her, once again called for order to little avail. There was distrust on multiple sides, conspiratorial whispers of public humiliation on several more, and the distinct sense that the current proposal before the gathering had all the legitimacy of a running start. In the midst of it all, Ceres Warren had had enough.

"Oh, for the love of Pete! This is absolutely ridiculous! Listen, either Somerset Sayer has what she claims, or she does not. If she is willing to offer up this proof to us, to our investigation and to a careful review and analysis, then why should we not accept? We shall draft our letter of response and ask her to produce the promised evidence. What have any of us to lose in this? Not a thing! We will ask her to show us."

The conclusion seemed so obvious as to provoke a momentary sense of quiet shame among several of the more vocal members of the conference. Amelia Cosmos, however, remained more circumspect. While she did not doubt that an established scholar such as Somerset Sayer could indeed procure something suitably bizarre enough to amaze a crowd, she grew concerned as to the possible motives behind such a revelation.

It was not beyond imagining that a member of the academic establishment (especially one who had, in the past, regarded the rise of new religions with a degree of contempt) might hand over an artifact, text, or other wondrous item which would appear to confirm the longings and beliefs of neophytes, only to publicly reveal it as a hoax or other trick meant to humiliate those gullible enough to have put their faith in the promise of its authenticity.

If this was just another attempt to make witchcraft and Magick laughable to the outside world, she wanted no part of it. But in the end, Amelia Cosmos was also herself an optimist and the possibility of even the slightest hint of a real change in the perceptions of magical practice for the better swayed her more favorably towards Madam Bel Carmen and Alice Guthrie's aims than she might have otherwise been.

Though, it hardly mattered, as most of the community came out in favor of Ceres in that: "As a well-established and respected society, it is to be expected of us that we should consider any fair inquiry and support our members in their ambitions. If Dr. Sayer has within her means to convince us of the existence of magical techniques or of entities beyond our current understanding, we should afford her the chance to do so."

There and then it was decided that Madam Bel Carmen and Alice Guthrie should, with the aid of those particularly interested, write the letter to Somerset Sayer that she had originally requested. One of the chief concerns put forward was that any demonstration of the actual reality of Faire be repeatable under strictly-controlled conditions (to address the concerns of skeptics), the second was that any magic that might result from new knowledge be regulated so as not to allow it to be used for nefarious or antagonistic purposes.

Third on the list involved the production of the knowledge itself, and that the community greatly desired any new taxonomies or field studies of Faire-kind that Dr. Sayer might be able to provide, given word of her extensive library. Fleshing out the specific details was kept to a minimum though, so that they would not overwhelm the first letter of response with too many competing interests. Regardless, Madam Bel Carmen made note that further discussions on each point were likely necessary, and certainly welcomed, before any particular agreements would be finalized. In due time, a reasonable outline began to coalesce.

Ceres considered writing a second letter herself, to be included in the first. With so many representative perspectives in the room, she worried that the collective effort might be read disparagingly towards scholarly methodologies; piecemeal as it was with equal amounts of eager confirmation and insidious doubt. While no one at the table suggested anything especially rude or impolite, it was obvious that some found the exercise to be foolish or even pandering.

After all, from what she had surmised, Somerset Sayer had said precious little in terms of what she really intended to see come of all this and it was likely that most of what everyone understood to be at stake had been filtered through the overly enthusiastic but well-meaning demeanors of Evelyn Bel Carmen and Alice Guthrie. But she never got a chance to send her letter, as the first one was sealed, stamped, and sent off just as soon as the late afternoon call for dinner was made at half past seven.

No more was said of the matter until a week later when, during a tea social and informal discussion of the newest reprinting of the *The Golden Bough,* Somerset Sayer's reply arrived.

125 Thatcher Shore Rd.
Yarmouthport, MA

Mmes. Bel Carmen and Guthrie,

It is with some surprise that I received your letter penned on the stationary of the Hearthcraft Community Motherhouse. This is not the first time I have had the pleasure of making their acquaintance through correspondence, but I had not considered that your request for scholarly support in your endeavors belied a joint project with the Boston pagan community at large. What is more, the wide variety of considerations in your outline tells me that the society of magical practitioners in the area is just as cohesive, and dare I say collegial, as they were before.

My concern is not, however, in the involvement of dissimilar viewpoints, but in the potential consequences that what I may offer will have on the integrity of your proposal and on the partnership of worldviews not well served by what you might discover. In short, very few people find themselves amiably inclined to collude on projects that will put them in error. This is especially true because, as you have noted in my writings, I state that human beings are wholly and thoroughly incapable of magic. This does not mean that magic is unavailable to us, only that our capacities to manipulate it lie in rational, logical, and mechanical methods.

This I have proven to my own satisfaction on multiple occasions. I say this not to imply contentedness in my own achievements (as I have found little professional prestige and no recognition that is not in some way mocking as a result of my work) but to warn you that further inquiries on your part may not result in the grand re-awakening of magical abilities your proposal entails. But, you did as I requested, and sent the letter of concerns I charged you with. To my understanding, the Hearthcraft Community of Massachusetts formally meets again on Friday next. On that day, I will contact you again in regards to the proof you solicited.

Regards,
Somerset Sayer

The folklorist's letter was met with both excitement and apprehension. That it was not an outright dismissal of their sentiments was encouraging, but the implication that the scholar meant to dispute the beliefs of at least a segment of their membership made Amelia Cosmos anxious. Still, the promised evidence remained in play and for the time being, speculations as to what it might be were enough to override any significant reservations the group saw fit to voice.

On the day of the Friday meeting, the mood was cautious but anticipatory. They began the proceedings with an opening ritual, as was customary. The proper circles were drawn and ritual implements carefully arranged along proscribed directions while divine permissions were sought. Much was made of ensuring the right spiritual acceptances given the agreed upon need for an auspicious night.

The black, white, and blue candles remained lit throughout the beginning of the assembly and no one complained when extra mugwort was added to the first and last parts of the ceremony. For the most part, the gathered attendants expected that the scholar would be sending them another letter, but what she did send them was a little stranger than that.

The package came in a small, six-inch by twelve-inch wooden crate embossed with an icon of a counter-clockwise spiral and stamped with the letters SPS. The contents of the crate, revealed only after prying out four hand-forged wrought-iron nails, were a folded piece of notepaper, a single green taper candle, a box of matches with wax tips, and some fifteen pendants bearing a scallop shell, painted yellow, to which was attached a tiny arrow rendered in pewter.

It was a curious package to be sure, left on the front steps of the Motherhouse by an unseen delivery. No one recalled at any point having seen it while arriving for the meeting earlier, and it had been discovered only moments after the opening ritual by Lua, who had come in late as per the usual. Sensing that the package was anticipated, however, she brought it straight into the meeting and loudly announced her finding just after the closing chant.

With both Madam Bel Carmen and Alice Guthrie in attendance, the decision as to who should explore the package was at first a little fraught but without complaint from either it was Amelia Cosmos who lifted the folded paper from the crate and carefully uncreased it against the table edge in front of her. It was not a letter per se, but a set of instructions.

To my dear anticipants, and to all others of strong conviction,

I fear the contents of this package may find you uneasy, but I can assure you that the evidence so requested will shortly be made clear. However, for such proof as you so require, or that which could fulfill the preconditions set out in your response, I must lay before you a simple task. I admonish you here to follow my instructions most exactingly and to spare no concentration on carrying out each step in an absolutely rigorous fashion. Upon completion, what you seek shall be plain to you. Your task is thus:

For each participant, don one of the included pendants and only one. I apologize that more could not be included, but for this exercise I must limit the witness to a number of no more than fifteen.

Whomever so volunteers to lead the endeavor should carry with them the green candle and matchbox. Carry the candle always in the left hand, striking the matches with the right. At no point should the candle be lit with any other sources than those I have provided.

As a group, begin walking on Central Street, heading westerly until you reach Bridge Street. Follow it until you reach Norton's Point Road to your left.

You will find that, in short order, Norton's Point Road will fork, breaking into two equal sections making their way parallel to one another towards the shore.

Light the candle with the first match. In whatever direction the smoke drifts, take the corresponding fork. Follow the direction of the wax smoke without deviation, regardless of whatever barriers of property you might encounter. This must be performed without detour.

Upon reaching the shoreline beyond, spy closely on the horizon the first boat that you can see and light the candle again. Follow the smoke along whichever direction by shore and sea it may indicate.

In due course, you will reach a single withered tree set rather far out into the tide-line. Circle the tree thrice in a counter-clockwise motion, relighting the candle with each full turn.

Then, face the shore. Walk up and over the ridge of the grassy hill before you and consider for yourselves what you might find therein.

"What a strange assignment." Amelia Cosmos remarked absently. "Of all the things I might have expected, this certainly was the furthest from my imaginings. Does she mean to send us on some sort of goose chase?"

Madam Bel Carmen turned her face, as though she had found the contents of the letter unexpectedly disagreeable but did not want to let on as to the extent. It was not that she was unwilling to make a demonstrable effort in earning the right to remain at the founding levels of this new form of scholarship, but the proposed task felt more akin to a grammar school playground game than a worthy erudite investigation.

It was as though Somerset Sayer meant to exact some initial measure of dignity from each and every member of the Hearthcraft Community to hold in trust, lest some unwanted critique threaten her reputation further. In other words, by setting them out on some eccentric public spectacle, she meant to ensure that none of them might ever call themselves respectable ever again since she need only point out the day when the most senior members of the assembled pagan orders of the Greater Boston Consortium spent an afternoon trampling through the township brambles in search of fairies.

In her dejected state, she almost admitted it would be fair, since she was already beginning to doubt her own experiences and it would serve them right for putting faith in such nonsense. Alice Guthrie spoke haltingly. "I attest that one of the chosen group should be Ms. Ceres Warren. Her counsel has long been looked upon favorably here and she is the closest we may get to a third party in verifying our perceptions. I do not know what it is that we will be expected to see but perhaps she may offer something in the way of deciding whether or not the extraordinary has been sufficiently achieved?"

Amelia Cosmos also remained adequately perturbed. She was not especially amenable to undertaking a mystical walking tour of any sorts and even less so as the instructions indicated that they might well be treading en masse through backyard gardens, privacy fences, and out-buildings. In fact, this seemed precisely the thing meant to maximize their inevitable humiliation, except in this case to the satisfaction of a prosecuting attorney. Unexpectedly, it was Ceres Warren who cast the first deciding vote.

She would be happy to enlist in the service of scholarship and would take up one of the enclosed amulets with pride. Then surely, Alice Guthrie added, they would know the proof of the matter when they beheld it. With such a number of them in attendance, there would be no question as to the outcome, good or bad, of the whole affair.

Sensing the unrest of their respected leadership, many among the assembled began to loudly question what form this evidence was meant to take and how it was that Somerset Sayer could not be bothered to be more specific. Madam Bel Carmen did her best to calm them with quick amends and hasty excuses, but she could not please them completely, as she did not know how to explain herself fully and she was only beginning to ponder what the ultimate conclusion of this elaborate stroll was likely to be.

All bickering aside, one by one, the members of the Hearthcraft Community came to terms with the task before them and set about to put together an agreeable and representative company of practitioners to complete the chore as charged in the now potentially nefarious instructions. Naturally, Amelia Cosmos assumed the role of head-woman, taking up the candle and matches with a determined flourish. Ceres Warren, Madam Bel Carmen, and Alice Guthrie were assumed, and they were merely handed their tokens without dissenting commentary.

In addition to the first four then came Elfriede Davies of Salem (a Wiccan by trade but recently considering a shift into Dianic circles), Heath Laney and Noelle Seward of Gloucester (both Ásatrú though not of the same company), Cyrus Lowell of Ipswich (a curiously long-bearded fellow with no particular leanings), Keenan Burroughs and Gayle Esparza of Beverly (traditionally Wiccan but with more Druidic influences than most), Timothy Flores and Chris Campbell of Essex (a married couple long-experienced with sacred geometry), and finally, Nyla Cromer, Emelina Huang, and Hugh Dickinson of Boston proper (of which nothing in common could be determined).

All that remained then was the final determination as to when this endeavor should be carried out. Given the nature of the terrain near the shoreline, it was unanimously agreed that a time in the early morning the following Monday should be preferred and that a gathering place near the Manchester-By-The-Sea Town Office on Church Street, just off of Central Street, was the best suited for minimizing any initial attention their appearance might generate.

There remained some concern as to how a company of people, sporting candles and amulets as such, might be cause for unpleasant disruption at the Town Office, but seeing as only the chosen fifteen would fully shoulder the brunt of any lengthy public notice, they decided that the plan should move forward. The night before Somerset Sayer's instructions were to be carried out it began to rain rather heavily and a thick fog settled over the harbor. The sounds of passing cars and the murmur of excited voices were subdued by mud and growing indecision, though little could dampen the occasional vocal tremor of chill or nerves and the aimless pacing of several sets of impractical shoes.

Amelia Cosmos had pronounced an early morning hour not much past dawn, such that careless observers might be judiciously avoided. The appointed group took their breakfast of eggs, sausages, and pancakes at a quaint seaside diner not far from the town office, though finding their moods in an unexpected state of melancholy, each remained relatively silent as the waitress poured their coffee and kept the table well supplied with warm toast and jam.

It seemed an odd gathering, without the pleasant chat one usually associates with a group of well-dressed ladies and their gentlemen companions taking a meal at their leisure on an otherwise unremarkable weekday morning. But for the assembled concern of the Massachusetts Hearthcraft Society, the pall remained an unavoidable part of an otherwise unutterable conversation. None dared, at least not at the present juncture, to speak any doubts aloud lest they be later blamed for an unsuccessful venture, having inadvertently blighted the undertaking with expectations of bad luck.

"Fine weather then." Remarked Madam Bel Carmen sarcastically, breaking the oppressive silence.

"Yes, yes, small favors, I suppose." Cyrus Lowell offered in a playful rejoinder, sipping his coffee with slightly less nonchalance than was typical to his mannerisms.

"Perhaps the rain will have cleared the harbor-side in the very least." Gayle Esparza poked cautiously at her fried egg. "Fewer people out this way I'd think, though I brought my umbrella. No one stares overly long at anyone with too much rain and a low umbrella."

"Well, I for one am quite looking forward to our little excursion," Elfriede Davies interjected brightly. "You know, back in Salem we organize tours like this all the time. It's no bother and no matter to those out and about."

"Yes, well, Salem is a bit of a special case in that now, isn't it?" Nyla Cromer settled her teacup into its saucer with an uncomfortably offset rattle. "Half the place is a tourist trap, banking on some convenient history like it's your own personal Shoah or something, and the other half just loves to parade around in belly-dancing skirts and purple hair calling herself "witch" or "medium" just to see her parents scowl over the family dinner table. I dare say, Salem has no sense of proper practice at all!"

"Convenient history!" Elfriede flared her nostrils, straightening her posture indignantly.

"Yes indeed," Nyla replied before the inevitable counter-argument could take shape fully. "Witch museums and trolley-car tours. Honestly. There wasn't an actual witch among those poor women, accused or not, and there's hardly a witch among them now!"

"Ladies." Amelia Cosmos poised her butter knife menacingly between jam packet and toast. "That's quite enough of *that* I think. Today is a day for setting aside these old rivalries for the time being, even if just for a morning stroll. I'll not have the two of you prattling on about Burning Times the whole way down to the shore."

As the remainder of the company once again settled into a tense silence, Alice Guthrie worried at her token, rolling the pewter arrow between thumb and fore-finger as one might an unruly shirt-cuff. But as plates were cleaned and small bits of syrup mopped up with unusual precision, the outward gloom began to clear and an unwelcome light descended over the table.

Bright rainbow spots refracted through the center flower vase played like houseflies to Madam Bel Carmen's barely restrained anticipation. She wanted nothing more than to get on with it. Preventing her outburst, however, as if on cue, it was Ceres Warren who stood up and with a terse smile, immediately demanded the check. The appointed place wherein the day was to begin was the corner of School Street and Central Street, at a crosswalk just opposite the Central Street Gallery.

In an old New England town such as the one, the implications of Somerset Sayer's choice were not altogether lost on the practitioners of magics herein thrown together. The streets of such towns, though now well-manicured and edged in granite blocks for the benefit of cars and summer tourists, were once wagon lanes and cow paths in days far older than the current one. The winding roads and massive balsam poplars surrounded by sloping beach grasses looked today much as they might have looked over two centuries ago.

Since it was now also the season of dropseed and red columbine, the air about the town was one of a slower time, where tides marked the passing of hours rather than the industrial punch-clock. This was significant in that the scene set before the group was not so much one of modern distraction, but of a finely curated history not quite past.

"Shall we begin then?" Queried Emelina Huang, dressed smartly against the brisk air.

"Yes, I suppose it's best we get this done." Amelia Cosmos sniffed into her scarf, the wool still redolent with lingering hints of salt and strawberry chapstick.

Carefully, she passed the green candle and matches into the appropriate hands, took one last look about the nearly deserted streets, and set off in the appointed direction. Down past the Peele House Square and onto Bridge Street they marched, each attentive to anything anomalous they might catch, peering into hedges or eyeing passersby suspiciously as they then did in return. Nothing out of the ordinary seemed to present itself however.

Nothing down the length of Bridge Street overlooking the sea, nothing glaring at them from the boatyard, nor anything suitably watchful from the over-hanging trees on Bennett Street. In truth, given her earlier experiences, Madam Bel Carmen half-expected an incredulous shout from somewhere in the group, pointing to a glimpse of something moving in the lovegrass or some strange being gazing out at them from the saltmeadow. But they had only their determined footsteps to keep them company. That is, for all of them but Amelia Cosmos.

For a moment, there was someone. Walking ahead of them at a steadfast pace, a figure she was sure had been there only a split-second ago but who never quite manifested long enough to be sure. Patiently, she squinted into the waning mists but ended with no better sense of things than before. She thought she spied a long, Victorian-style, train-coat; of the type most often worn by a woman of rank in the last great years of Peerage. But this coat, black and without the ruched sleeves typical of its design was gathered in the back, and betrayed only a hint of the pomegranate skirt beneath it and the measured interruption in the stride of a wide-heeled boot.

Twists of white-blonde hair trailed after it and for a time, Amelia Cosmos began to believe that the revelation due unto them on this day was that of a ghost haunting the pale shores of Whittier's Cove, and not anything resembling Faire at all. She even wondered if there was a famous story, of a lady lost at sea perhaps, common to this area she had somehow forgotten. Still, she said nothing as they turned the corner onto Norton's Point Road as, thus far, no one else seemed to have noticed their ephemeral escort at all.

As they came upon the first division, a fork in the road some few hundred meters down, the assembled gathered around, as inconspicuously as they might manage, to await the first variable of the folklorist's instructions. With a nod to Madam Bel Carmen and Alice Guthrie, both of whom had remained pressed close to the forefront, Amelia Cosmos struck a match with the tip of her thumbnail and lit the candle as ordered.

Dutifully, the flame flickered to life with a few sickly hiccups, but when Amelia Cosmos removed her hand from sheltering the wick, it promptly went out. For a moment, she contemplated lighting the candle again, concerned that she had not done so with the appropriate ceremony or solemn intent that magic typically requires for proper functioning.

But before she could get much further in her thoughts, Cyrus Lowell pointed out the glimmer of ember spewing forth some rather copious paraffin smoke, all of which now formed a curious, unbroken, thread drifting through the crowd and down the left-most avenue. In this way, it managed not to touch even one of them and spiraled about between woolen hats and tousled hair as though driven by an intent of its own.

"Well would you look at that." He mused, clapping his hands together beneath a well-groomed mustache. "If that's not just a touch of the Hermetic already!"

"Let's not get ahead of ourselves." Cautioned Amelia Cosmos.

While it was a mildly peculiar occurrence, the smoke remaining so clear and constant as it moved against the wind towards the shoreline; it was not quite enough to rouse the entire company to elation as they set off again, this time down the short left-hand fork of the road towards a dead-end circle terminating at Norton's Point. They were thankful that this particular direction afforded an unobstructed path towards the sea, passing a few residential homes and reasonable yard detritus, but not corralling them, as many had feared, directly into someone's spring garden, or worse yet, lattice-top fence.

As they passed the last house on the lane, it appeared that the easiest way onto the beach from their present location was to walk out onto a small, neighborhood dock and drop down from its midpoint under a copse of trees bent low over the water. This they accomplished with little fanfare, losing only Noelle's hat in a sudden gust of wind narrowed into high-speed bursts by the elms knotted into the embankment.

Amelia Cosmos tensed against the abrupt flurry, kicking up sand as it met their gathered figures on its way to making landfall, but not for reasons of cold. Again, she saw a silhouette against the breakwater. A smooth outline against a stand of brown, jagged, rocks tumbling out into the sea from their origin point on a bluff near the upper strand. Standing in profile, this time she was certain she could make out a high, square collar, pulled up to frame a gentle brow, a sharp straight-edged nose, and a pointed chin. Perhaps she even beheld an image reminiscent of *Wanderer Above the Sea Fog*, if not for the expertly tailored angles and longer hem.

When she moved to point out the apparition however, it was already gone, and by this time Madam Bel Carmen was calling for the second match to be lit. Amelia Cosmos turned to see Alice Guthrie waving her hands gleefully out at the horizon, having spotted a ship against the *fata morgana* just beginning to form beneath the rising sun. Impatient now to rid herself of this increasingly unnerving task (of which, in her opinion, nothing overwhelmingly supernatural had yet to become apparent), Amelia Cosmos set her lips in a thin line and lit the match to relight the candle.

As it had before, the flame abruptly extinguished but the smoke once again turned, against the wind currents, to drift lazily down the point further into the cove (and as the head-woman was sure to notice, in the same direction she had once again seen the ghostly figure). Uneasy, she led the group off along the shoreline in search of the withered tree promised near the tide-line, which was actually now visible some several meters beyond the margin. Upon finding the tree, surprisingly only a short length away from where they had initially arrived on the beach, Amelia Cosmos sagged against her own zeal.

The tree, for it certainly was the tree in reference, given its garishly mummified countenance, clung to life in nearly three feet of water. For the rest of the group, however, the confirmation of the tree seemed to act as the final catalyst in igniting their sense of curious wonder. After all, had not all of Somerset Sayer's guidance proven accurate? The smoke had indeed turned in the proper directions and the described tree had indeed been where it was pledged to be.

But Amelia Cosmos was not alone in her hesitations, though she did not know that Madam Bel Carmen and at least four other members of the group still questioned the validity of their task. It was not so far-fetched to think that Dr. Sayer simply knew this area well and had mapped out a footslog with which she was already intimately familiar. Regardless of distrust though, and seeing as they had not been accosted unpleasantly at any point along this trip, they waded out altogether to light the candle and make their final circumambulations.

Alice Guthrie found this particular portion of the expedition the most fun, as did many in the rest of the community. The delight soon became infectious, and as Amelia Cosmos carefully relit the candle with each full circle, even she could not help but smile as the ragtag and bobtail company splashed merrily through the waves in an attempt to high-step the spray without ending up face-first in the surf thanks to a well-placed root. At the conclusion of the third round, they each wobbled and veered to a stop at the point between tree and shore facing inward towards a steep slope of dunegrass.

Madam Bel Carmen drew a shaky breath and offered a lopsided smile and sidelong glance to her red-faced friend. With an equally jittery wheeze, Alice Guthrie grabbed Madam Bel Carmen by the hand and hastily set off towards the hill. The sense that something awaited, something truly marvelous and mysterious, had finally taken hold and the two women forged ahead in giddy anticipation. Not to be left behind of course, each of the excited practitioners hurried after, nearly falling over one another in the rush to reach the ridgeline and finally make their covenant with the new philosophy.

Alice Guthrie broke the extent first, reaching the top of the hill with a final heave and shout over a few precarious tussocks at the summit. She thought, for a moment, that she had passed beneath an unfamiliar canopy, resembling something like chains of stacked, green, parasols set atop skinny poles burnt black. As if a great fire had scorched new colors and textures into the bark of a once grand forest, though not any such forest that might grow at the edges of the sea.

But before she could pause to contemplate this abrupt shift or even turn to affirm the presence of her companions, she stopped to behold a landscape that was suddenly airy and full of light with a great expanse of blue cloudless skies stretching across a vast and open field. Not a tree or building remained to challenge the sun. Where dappled shade gave way to a flattened plain blotched with furrows of pebble stones shining white to matt silver, she finally saw what it was she was meant to see. And there, Alice Guthrie was left speechless.

For what lay before her was the great chalk grassland expanse of the Salisbury Plain in Wiltshire, and at its center, unmistakably: Stonehenge. There was no other place it could be.

Chapter Three

To be faced with the reality of Stonehenge, as opposed to its picturesque prospects on the glossy cover of a pamphlet, is awe-inspiring even under the strangest circumstances. Especially, as was the case for the newly reassembled concern of the Hearthcraft Community of Manchester-By-The-Sea, when you were not expecting to be there on precisely that afternoon, on a day that had begun under much more mundane conditions than the present. But in short order, they found themselves in the very real midst of a monument that, due to their varied and personal bibliographies, was as much myth and legend as it was ancient history.

Unfortunately, what significance archaeology had managed to uncover in the last one-hundred and fifty years or so was largely lost on most neo-pagans in favor of the much more titillating ravings about the workings of aliens, Atlanteans, and the Lost Tribes of Israel. Which also suited most members of the public-at-large just as well, especially those whose understanding of such notions as "provenance," "microscopic petrography," and "paleo-climatology" was, in a word, limited. And not to mention those who vastly preferred a world of shadow societies and clandestine conspiracies to the routine dread of the everyday.

But if, as the Hearthcraft Community was now poised to find out, the worlds of magic and the everyday could be linked together in the spaces of a casual stroll, how might the very nature of all such existence be re-imagined! Two seemingly incommensurate perspectives now blended into one! A pity for dear Geoffrey of Monmouth and his daring Aurelius Ambrosius though, as no one seemed to have yet ascertained if the Beaker and Windmill Peoples, who had constructed the great stone monument originally, had successfully predicted Caer-Caradog or had even ever been accomplished in the practical applications of magic in the first place.

As for the great sarsen stones themselves, which could be little perturbed by the arrival of yet another group of sightseers however unexpectedly, a curious indifference had come to mark them. This was unsurprising though, given that the most impressive ring of some sixty bluestones now encircling the group of erstwhile pagans and witches had been content to ignore much the same for the better part of three millennia and a half.

It was equally odd to note, as several members did, that the Hearthcraft assembly appeared to be the only persons present, as no tourists nor other practitioners, nor their cars or distant voices, were to be found anywhere on the grounds. For a day of fine weather, such as this one clearly was, that no one else would have thought to make their way among historical trilithons or lintel capstones for a photograph or two (or even a passing spiritual experience) was patently out of the ordinary.

The great Heel Stone, resplendent in its ragged natural simplicity, also remained eerily barren. Concerning though their immediate situation might appear however, and with such a sight before them, even the studious, if quietly terrified, aplomb of Amelia Cosmos could not dissuade the excited whispers and bursts of shocked laughter. They had set out to be impressed, and indeed, they were impressed. As it was, they began to wander about awestruck.

Madam Bel Carmen tried hopelessly to shield the wide smile currently puppeteering the dimples in her cheeks. For whatever doubts she had harbored that morning in a seaside Massachusetts diner, they were utterly and rather messily destroyed now in her attempts to trace shaking fingers over each eight-meter block. It was here that she first encountered a bit of evidence concerning the nature of their travels, though she did not immediately recognize it; so consumed was Madam Bel Carmen with the enormity of their collective experiences.

But tacked to each of the main center columns, with a dab of red signet wax at the corner of each uneven margin, were a series of yellowed pages apparently torn from a poetry book dating to just around the end of the Second World War. The particular page that Madam Bel Carmen passed read *SOULS* in block capital printing, authored in smaller block printing below by one Fannie Stearns Davis. She only glanced at it however, in favor of hurrying on to the next great monolith. Somewhere in the great distance, she thought she heard cathedral bells beginning to toll the hour.

"Are we truly in England?!" Exclaimed Ceres Warren. "But how is this possible?!"

"I haven't the slightest idea, but oh, will you just look at all this!" Elfriede Davies rushed to her side. "I have long dreamt of seeing this place, Ms. Warren, and here I am, I can hardly breathe!"

Keenan Burroughs was a bit more circumspect. "This is impossible. Impossible! We can't truly be here. Not in any way. The sun is all wrong! We left Boston in the morning. Ought to be mid-afternoon in Britain by now and see that! Can't be an hour past sunrise. And the caretakers and tourists and all that nonsense! There's not a living soul here but us! It must be a trick."

"Could this be a reproduction?" Noelle Seward gathered in. "Did someone build this, maybe in a park or in their back gardens? Might we still be near Boston?"

"How could we be?!" Elfriede Davies waved about wildly. "Do you see the ocean nearby or even hear it? Where exactly did we come from? Not a gull in the sky or shore for miles!"

"It's Stonehenge."

Alice Guthrie's voice cut through the din with the gravity of absolute certainty. Amelia Cosmos straightened her jacket against a particularly chilling gust and made to challenge the woman with what little skepticism she had left to muster, but as she turned to face Ms. Guthrie her opening statements simply stopped in her throat.

Alice Guthrie stood resolute just a few feet from the remnants of an Aubrey Hole, an indentation in the ground once indicating a long-forgotten cremation pit. Clutched tightly in either hand, several small bits of paper flapped raggedly between her fingers.

"It's Stonehenge." She repeated, a tear or a touch of wind-burn at her eyes. "I apologize for not speaking up when I should have but I did not have faith. Neither of us did."

She looked to Madam Bel Carmen, who nodded and hung her head ever so slightly.

"We should have told you right off. I almost did at the meeting but, you see, we were afraid." Her voice rose against the winds, now picking up speed across the flat, unobstructed, plain. "We were afraid that what we thought we saw had been faked. That we would be made fools of. Fools to you, and even worse, fools to ourselves."

"Ms. Alice!" called out Cyrus Lowell of Ipswich. "What are you saying, Ms. Alice?"

She set her jaw against the threat of tears again. "Only that Somerset Sayer showed us exactly this. To Madam Bel Carmen and myself. And I did not believe it!" Her words caught. "Not as I should have. Because she showed us this very thing right then and there. Without prompting or asking, and I mean, how could we? We would not have known the first thing to ask, and certainly not for a miracle such as this."

Amelia Cosmos tamed her scarf against her shoulder, her brow set in a tense line low across her ample eyebrows, "What do you mean? What do you possibly mean by this?"

"Only that I have traveled in this way before. With Madam Bel Carmen. We crossed half the span of the State of Massachusetts, from Cambridge to, I daresay, the Cape coast somewhere I think, and we did not but cross a threshold between a sitting room and a dining room. And more again after that. If such a thing can be accomplished in the space of two small rooms, is it ever the wonder that so much more would be possible in crossing a street or in the distance from a restaurant to a pier! We told you that Somerset Sayer, who I can only now hold in the utmost respect, took us into her great library and showed us all the rarest and most delicate manuscripts and beautiful things. All of that is true to the moment. But upon our leaving then, an extraordinary thing." She wiped at her eyes, chewing painfully at her lower lip as one does in moments of unexpected spiritual surety. She began again. "And another most extraordinary thing in that, upon dismissal, we stepped politely out of the front door. The very same door from whence we came in. But there was no street, no walkway, nothing of the Cambridge town we came in by."

"Where were you then, Ms. Alice?" Came Hugh Dickinson's jubilant outburst from the back.

She straightened and raised her chin, as if to address him directly. "Why, my very own living room, Mr. Dickinson. Back home on Tappan Street in Manchester."

The collected gasps were drowned out by the punctual daily tide that was Amelia Cosmos. "Madam Bel Carmen! Can you confirm this?"

Madam Bel Carmen swatted her hair away from her forehead, turning to meet the wide-eyed gazes of her fellows. "I can, and I most certainly will. Ms. Alice has spoken nothing but the truth here. But you all must also understand why we couldn't explain this at the time. We would not have been believed and the cooperation of the respondent meeting was crucial, nay vital, to getting us here today."

Moments later and with the uncomfortable shuffling of more than one attentive listener, Madam Bel Carmen came to realize that her tone seemed to suggest that everything leading up to the day's events had been, in some sense, a ruse. That Madam Bel Carmen and Alice Guthrie had conspired, upon seeing the capabilities of the folklorist Somerset Sayer, to draw the rest of the Hearthcraft Community into their esoteric inner circle potentially against their wills.

Granted, had this been the case, it would have been with quintessential good intentions and with a desire to see the pagans and witches of the Boston area united under the banner of true and objective magics, but she couldn't help but notice the sting of distrust begin to nag at the expressions of those assembled. "That is not to say, I mean.... I mean that...."

As the force and substance of the wind began to gain exceptional traction, they heard a voice break from somewhere near to the long-shadowed monuments. At first, the tentative assumption was that the voice was coming from someone who must be walking the outer edge of the main sarsen circle, clockwise against the direction of the gusts. But when they all looked about to no avail and then strained their necks to hear it better, it was apparent that the wind and the voice were in fact the same thing.

Though it was not at all clear what language the wind was speaking, or even if the sounds emanating from its twists and turns through the lintels could be identifiable as words, the tone and cadence were openly discernable as that of a methodic recitation. At one point, Alice Guthrie thought she could make out a word that sounded like "*ærdæg*," an Old English word for daybreak, followed by a tumble of syllables moaned as if in a lamentation.

Unconsciously, she huddled close to Madame Bel Carmen, who also thought she might have heard what sounded like a Gaelic call to arms, "*Boghadairean ullamh!*" Archers ready. Or perhaps it was the stones themselves speaking from memories of something they too had once heard. As the grasslands continued to bend in the fierce onslaught, several members of the Hearthcraft Community grew unsettled, even frightened.

Remembering any number of fairy tales which cautioned the uninitiated against potential abduction into Faire lands far afield, the group was soon whispering childhood memories of a significant number of these stories which contained mystic disembodied voices as well as unruly natural forces (of which wind was a popular villainous choice) and the sudden and untimely disappearances of those who dared to disturb such forces.

In the ensuing banter, Chris Campbell became almost disruptively agitated. He recalled at that moment one particular tale, as his grandmother used to relate, of a woman in Ireland by the name of Bridget Cleary, a cooper's wife murdered by her husband, father, aunt, and cousins on one fateful night in the spring of 1895. After falling seriously ill, the poor woman was tortured for days under the presumption that fairies had recently made off with the real Bridget Cleary, and that the current young woman sickly abed was none other than a withered changeling replacement. Failing to scare the Fae imposter off with wounds and threats, her family promptly murdered her and buried her body less than a mile from the house.

"Twas' a real case, I'm telling you." Chris Campbell pressed. "Detailed in the exact in the Irish Crime Records Archive!"

"My god..." Elfriede Davies curled her fingers to her lips.

"Such things befall women so often, you know!" Added Cyrus Lowell. "Divine magics being so attuned to them and all."

"Well that's just nonsense." Emelina Huang snapped, nearly tearing out several buttons with a white-knuckled wrench to her coat-sleeves. "Another woman murdered by her superstitious family and nothing more. Nothing new there I assure you! What rubbish those old tales were. Just as bad as that Salem lot. Babies," she emphasized the word at length, "may be subject to unwarranted attack, but the Fae only truly steal the dead."

Nyla Cromer nodded gravely in alliance.

"Do you hear that?" Noelle Seward grabbed at the cuff of Heath Laney. "I could have sworn I heard someone saying, 'I see her, I see her now.'"

As the wind did not subside, the chosen fifteen gathered close as they peered out over collars and scarves and into the tumultuous air. It was then that the voice drew down to a singular focus, and the words it spoke heard plainly:

The Summer King holds a crown, that only he may wear.
But upon the dais high above, just a bramble thicket there.

Weighed with frost it does not stir, nor in season change its mood.
A crown of oak and thistledown, once a year renewed.

When he places it upon his head, the roots grow down into his brow.
There to draw on royal blood, and lash him to his vow.

The crown blossoms thus with Spring and leaves; with this his right to rule.
But woe to those who brave the stair, and act the worthy fool.

The loyal crown is bound by name, as the one it now enthrones,
Set upon another head, it would drain the man to bones.

Madam Bel Carmen pressed her palm to her heart. Somehow, she did not believe the voice was only speaking to them.

The figure appeared slowly at first, walking with a determined stride from stone to stone through a thick haze of new fog rolling in on the plain, never passing beneath any lintel but rounding each concentric circle as though caught in an unseen labyrinth with walls of air and chambers of dirt, ash, and grass. She made her way, for it was most certainly a woman of a stiff and stately poise, through each section, haunting the spaces between monument and hill; alighting with ghostly steps up and around each sarsen as if she weighed nothing at all.

Madam Bel Carmen stared in silent wonder as the figure, wrapped tightly in a long black coat, appeared to step up the sides of the monoliths as though it were a cliff-side and she was a mountain goat, only to reach halfway, turn in a flourishing whirl, and drop back down.

Madam Bel Carmen might almost have thought she were witnessing a kind of ancient dance, meant to propitiate the angry wind spirits now assailing them, if it were not for the practiced and irreverently methodical technique by which she moved. Though her face was not visible, her body seemed to care nothing for the motions it made, only that this was what was required of it at the present moment. Alice Guthrie observed the figure to reach out with delicate hands and touch various places along the path with spindle-like fingers.

At first she thought that she might be using each point of contact as a way to steady herself through the elaborate turns and bows that caused her to continuously move around their group, though never through them or even towards them. But the figure did not appear to need much steadying. In fact, she did not always appear to be truly there at all. Amelia Cosmos, however, immediately recognized the woman she had seen before, the ghost of Norton's Point.

When the figure finally stopped, poised between two inner trilithons joined by an oddly shaped, and slightly tilted, capstone, she placed her feet together abruptly and folded one hand at the small of her back. Stepping forward, it was clear that she now moved without any pretext or inclination towards a good impression. This was not the stride of a diva making a grand entrance but rather more like the snapping of a black satin curtain at the window, tense against the cold autumn breeze, shifting barely enough to reveal the piercing light beyond.

The woman who stopped before them wasted no time in settling the badly weathered skull of a horse on the ground at their feet, the word 'Falada' carved neatly across its forehead in ornamental script. Her long blonde hair hung loose about her shoulders, reaching nearly to her waist, but, as all assembled quickly took note, remained relatively unaffected by the wind. From time to time the woman might wave an errant strand out of her way, but otherwise suffered no inconvenience at the hands of the inclement weather.

The long, black, train-coat she wore was equally unperturbed by their circumstances and drifted benignly about her heels in loose folds. As she straightened, fixing a steady if restless gaze at the faces of her rapt audience, she ended the odd and lengthy sequence of chores merely by producing a small golden hand bell from her right pocket. Resting the bottom edge against her palm, so as not to make the slightest inadvertent noise, she addressed the group.

"Now then." She enunciated precisely. "I should think you are all rather perplexed by everything at this point."

Stunned silence followed.

"I.... Hello again.... Dr. Sayer!" Madam Bel Carmen managed to find her words with some difficulty.

After another moment, "This is Somerset Sayer?" Amelia Cosmos blurted out unceremoniously.

"Well, I should certainly hope so. For your sake right now, that is." The folklorist deadpanned, hardly turning her head to acknowledge the question.

"We got your letter!" Cyrus Lowell offered sheepishly, holding his token aloft. There were so many questions filling his mind but he was far too afraid to ask any of them right then. His obviousness therefore merely a cover for his nerves.

"Yes." Somerset Sayer breathed, hardly concealing the low grumble of sarcasm. "That much is obvious don't you think?" She gestured casually towards the nearest sarsen.

Alice Guthrie pressed forward. "Dr. Sayer.... How is it that we have come all this way? How did we get here? This is really Stonehenge isn't it?" It was the most pertinent question even if the latter part was spoken as a statement rather than a request for affirmation.

"Ah, yes, thank you Ms. Guthrie. Right to the issue at hand, hardly a time for pleasantries." She tapped the horse skull several times with her toe. "This is indeed Stonehenge, in all its.... magnificent glory, so to speak. But as you have likely surmised by now, it is not exactly the Stonehenge one would expect. That is to say, there are a number of things going on about it that are not quite right."

"There is no one else here." Hugh Dickinson offered.

"The sun should be higher." Keenan Burroughs repeated.

"Precisely. Well done." Somerset Sayer continued, "That is because, you see, while you are indeed standing in the presence of Stonehenge in the south of England, you are not yet fully...how do I put this exactly...on the right side of reality familiar. Close, I assure you, but not quite. Standing on the side of the road, if you will." Alice Guthrie took note of the folklorist's characteristic reversal of adjective and noun and wondered at the meaning of the odd diction.

"You mean, we're in another dimension?" Ceres Warren nudged Elfriede Davies ever so slightly to the left.

"Sort of." Somerset Sayer wrapped the bell in the palm of her hand and crossed her arms in front of her chest. "This, my dear assembly, is what I offered and what you asked for. This, is the Way By. Welcome."

As the attendant scholar waited patiently for some of the gravity of her words to sink in a little, she observed the practitioners of the Hearthcraft Community as they began to look about themselves once again, no doubt desperately attempting to examine their surroundings with keener eyes towards anything supernatural. She remembered that it was not that she took pleasure in their confusion and ignorance exactly, but with her knowledge of Other Worlds being what it was, she did find some amusement in the perpetual states of shock these kinds of introductions usually induced.

It had been quite a long time since she had brought anyone, much less an entire coterie, through the Near By. But as the closest and therefore most accessible route into the Way By, it seemed safe enough despite the ongoing troubles elsewhere and the deeply unsettling sense of uncanniness it tended to invoke in those unaccustomed to its particular idiosyncrasies. That, and the fact that Stonehenge, a place of deep magics in its own right, was typically avoided by most of the more dangerous Fairest on account of the noise.

She also found it a pleasant change of pace, a chance to stretch out once again in the comfortable, if chaotic, places she knew most intimately. Academic life was often isolating, and though she tended to prefer her own company to that of others, she had noticed that the latter part of the past ten years had begun to take its toll on her. Worlds were changing, and there were things that could no longer be done alone.

"Dr. Sayer?" Alice Guthrie roused the scholar from her thoughts.

"Yes, Ms. Guthrie?"

"What is the Way By?" Straight to the point as always.

In truth, Somerset Sayer had been both anticipating and dreading this very question for days. She had rehearsed countless versions of what she thought would pass for an adequate answer and liked none of them. Tried a rousing speech or two and found them condescending (well, more so than usual). Gave a purely intellectual answer and deemed it too confusing. In short, this was the entire point of this joint endeavor and she had no idea how to acceptably explain it.

"The answer to your question, Ms. Guthrie, is, I'm afraid, a very complicated one. But as you have completed the task I gave as I gave it, competently to the degree that you have all arrived at the destination I had set out for you, I shall do my best to define for you what I can." She took a breath. "The Way By is, in a phrase, somewhere in-between. It is a space that lies on the edges of our world and equally so on the edges of another world, a world that goes by many names but none so apt nor so appropriate than its native appellation. A name which I will not repeat here but which is roughly cognate with the phrase Could Have Been.

"The Way By is then the labyrinth that traverses between two such worlds, ours As It Is and theirs As It Could Have Been, which overlap at a seam joined end to end. Like a thread, to continue my metaphor, that weaves two unlike fabrics together along a very frayed and untidy border. Metaphors aside though, the Way By isn't really a place, at least, not in the classical sense. It is more like a way of moving through all places, a way to change the rules of place such that where you start and where you end up are in some manner the same thing. In other words, the Way By isn't something that exists, it's more like something that happens. Try to imagine it as though you are standing in a garden in Manchester, and at the foot of Stonehenge, but you see both of them as they are only because you are actually somewhere in the spaces that are in-between them, with a view in both directions. The problem then, of course, is in the journey, in that you might also be in one spot and suddenly not the other, or step through into the second without ever actually leaving the first. The way there and back again is never quite so straightforward. Therein is the catch, you might say. The Way By can take you anywhere you want to go, but only if you know how to get there. Or, I suppose the better way to say it would be, how not to go where you've already been."

"So, we got here by....by...." Amelia Cosmos began.

"By the Way that I prepared for you." Somerset Sayer finished quickly. "When Madam Bel Carmen and Ms. Guthrie appeared on my doorstep asking about books and esoteric papers for a grand new vision of magical inquiry, I was certain, at that moment, that nothing less than a pathway through the Way By itself would convince you. Or, at least, not to the degree that would satisfy the pursuit of evidence you laid out. There was simply nothing I might tell you initially that could take the place of the authentic experience, believe me. You would need to see it for yourselves. Theory would have to come later. But I will be honest with you. The truth is that I'm not doing this out of some charitable urge to see you astounded by the wonders of the world and I don't care much for long commentaries on everyone's opinions of such-and-such." Amelia Cosmos bristled at the sudden change in tone. "Opinions are mostly useless anyway. If it were up to me, I'd leave the lot of you right out of it all. I have been the only Waysmith to my knowledge in all the time I have been alive, the first in perhaps almost two hundred years, and the only one presently, and that has suited me just fine."

Again, Somerset Sayer tapped the horse's skull with her foot. "But things being what they are, it looks as though you might be able to be some help to the situation, such as it currently is. At least, I am hoping that you can be. If not, this is all going to be much more trouble than it's worth."

Madam Bel Carmen, having taken the time to gather her wits again following Alice Guthrie's apology through confession earlier, spoke up thusly, "Dr. Sayer, I think I can speak for those of us here that if there is anything we can do to be of service, we will put forth our most dedicated efforts."

"Oh, I'm sure you will." She nodded, staring distractedly up at the monoliths. "Though we have a bit of time at least for me to get you all up to a conversant level. The Stumble has been in place since at least the early eighteen-hundreds so thankfully I don't think it's liable to be going anywhere anytime soon."

"The what?" Amelia Cosmos turned.

"I'm afraid more detailed explanations of the problem will have to wait," Somerset Sayer clapped her hands with nervous agitation. "We've been here rather long enough I think and it's time I saw you back to your Motherhouse. No sense in having you traipsing about the Salisbury Plain any longer than necessary."

Unexpectedly, there was no protest from the group. Instead, each stood in perfectly conscientious silence awaiting instructions from the odd woman with the train-coat and skull. In the end, Somerset Sayer had to admit, she'd rarely had such a cooperative public, especially one which was otherwise so characteristically prone to criticizing everything within reach. She lifted the horse skull and tucked it into the crook of her left elbow and began to ring the small bell steadily. Suddenly, Elfriede Davies let out an astonished shout.

Shuffling through the fog came the picture-perfect forms of a Boxwood Kobold and a Welsh Coblyn. Neither more than half a meter in height, the Kobold wore a bright blue, needle-felted, jacket with gold thread embroidery covering every inch in twisting vines and raised flowers. His skin looked a brownish-green, with wide reflective eyes and a stubby, nearly invisible nose barely protruding from a fold of skin that also seemed rather close to his chin. The effect was one of a rounded head, large eyes, and a series of bloated wrinkles that passed for a nose, mouth, chin, and neck.

His crimson-colored Phrygian cap sat low on his brow and he carried with him the skull of a songbird and a fire-hardened trunnel; a nail of the kind once used in covered bridges. His arms and legs were lank and rangy, his hands hanging nearly to the ground on either side of wide, flat, feet that had a dipping, ponderous stride. The Coblyn was a fat little fellow with a long face, two short but chunky antlers growing out of the top of his head, and a fringe of grey down sprouting out of the back of his neck and across his shoulders.

His sharply pointed ears stuck out unevenly from either side of his head, the right clearly a little higher than the left and missing a portion of its tip. He wore only a small pair of leather blacksmithing pants with a pair of folded boots and carried with him also a similar looking bird skull (though his appeared to retain some of its previous owner's skin and feathers) and another trunnel wrapped in copper wire. As they passed from beneath the lintel behind Somerset Sayer, the folklorist placed the bell back in her pocket and knelt to the ground to address them.

"Hat Trick, Coat Check, I need the six pieces of sail and a handful of meadow fescue for Falada."

The Kobold, now identified as Hat Trick, cast a disparaging glance towards Elfriede Davies, who remained stricken as she stared at the two small creatures hovering about Somerset Sayer's coattails.

"Fescue no good." His guttural pronunciation sounding more akin to the gasps of a large drowning man than a being no bigger than a three-year-old child.

"Hmmmm. Fine. Sweetgrass then. But no quaking grass this time, mind you. If I have to spend one more afternoon slogging through The Fens there will be hell to pay."

Hat Trick nodded, the tip of his cap bouncing comically against the collar of his jacket, and vanished into the meadow. Coat Check simply dug around in his pants pockets before producing a mass of wadded cloth, which he wordlessly handed over before surreptitiously pulling a face at the assembled crowd.

"Dr. Sayer?" This time it was Amelia Cosmos who interjected plaintively.

"Yes, Ms. Cosmos, what is it?" Somerset Sayer had regained her feet and was now clearly involved in some manner of hand-held ritual, placing each section of sailcloth into the various orifices of the horse skull named Falada and reciting unintelligible words as she did so.

"Are.... are those...."

"Fairies? Sure."

"Fairies, yes, but.... they look like.... like..."

"Gremlins!" Hugh Dickinson exclaimed.

Somerset Sayer paused her ministrations and looked up. "What were you expecting? Butterfly wings and boobs?"

Amelia Cosmos spluttered unbecomingly. "Well no, certainly not. I think we can all say that no one has been harboring Tinkerbell fantasies here but.... I guess I just never expected to see, in the flesh no less, something like that... which...."

"Someone like them." The folklorist returned to her skull, smearing some manner of dark paste into the engraved letters making up the late horse's osteo-frontal label.

"I...I beg your pardon?"

"Someone like them." She repeated. "Regardless of whatever it is that comes out of this entire venture, Ms. Cosmos, I would highly caution you against ever referring to a member of Faekind as 'that.' Especially when they are within earshot. It's an understandable human habit given the faults of the English language but they find it terrifically offensive."

"They are your friends?" Alice Guthrie attempted to smooth the insult.

"Something like that." Somerset Sayer turned to accept several sprigs of a long-seeded grass from the newly materialized Hat Trick who, though now covered in several new mud stains, seemed especially pleased with his contribution.

"Dr. Sayer?" Nyla Cromer faltered. "Were they," she extended a single finger downward, "the voices we heard earlier then?"

Somerset Sayer paused with grass seeds halfway sprinkled into the skull's eye sockets, tilting her gaze forward. "Voices?"

"Yes," Nyla continued carefully. "Before we saw you we heard voices among the stones. I was just wondering if that was you...and the.... well..."

"What did they say?"

"The voices?"

"Obviously."

"Well, I heard something that sounded like Old English, I think. And shouting and clashing sounds like a fight? And then someone said something about a summer king, a crown of brambles?"

The look on the folklorist's face could only be described as pensive, her fingers subtly whiter against the polished bone, but her rejoinder remained blunt and betrayed nothing of the thoughts in her head. "No."

"Oh."

"Now then." Somerset Sayer loudly returned her attention to the group. "You will notice a series of pages attached to the sarsen stones of the main circle. Do, each of you, go and collect a page. There are quite a few so you shouldn't have any trouble. Simply pick one and return here."

As the community members did so, slowly at first, still awkward with shock (and with many the furtive glance backwards at both folklorist and folklore), Hat Trick tugged insistently at the hem of the Victorian coat.

"So those?" He uttered gruffly, pointing a clubbed index finger in the general direction of the company.

"Yes those, I'm afraid. Or, a few of them anyway." Somerset Sayer bent slightly to look down at the crumpled face from over the edge of Falada's protruding jawbone. "It's not ideal, I agree, but we can't wait much longer and, you must admit, the appearance of the two ladies Bel Carmen and Guthrie was quite serendipitous. Especially given their subjects of interest. For a time, I was starting to think I might have to begin attending conferences again."

The little Kobold let out an arduous sigh. "Too much problem. When She comes, they be chaff." He drew out the last three words with deep, aspirated, syllables.

Somerset Sayer nodded in reply, "When She comes, we all might be."

Hat Trick clucked his tongue and chuckled into his soiled lapel. "Summer King, then. Eh? Dead be speaking. Ashes in holes be speaking."

"Don't get me started."

The group returned, Madam Bel Carmen holding between thumb and forefinger the page she had passed earlier; *SOULS* by Fannie Stearns Davis. While she kept the growing feelings of doubt and disquiet she was now experiencing entirely to herself, she could barely conceal the cold sweat breaking out along her forehead and neck. *"O folk who scorn my stiff grey gown, My dull and foolish face, —* " the line she read upon plucking it from the stone, "*Can ye not see my Soul flash down, A singing flame through space?"* the line she now covered with her thumb. It seemed such an inspiring stanza, the words of a woman living a life invisible in a time of great injustice.

But as she approached the assembled Hearthcraft members, and watched as Somerset Sayer prepared the final items for their departure, she couldn't help but think that these words had been chosen for another purpose. *"And folk, whose earth-stained looks I hate, Why may I not divine, Your Souls, that must be passionate, Shining and swift, as mine!"* The mocked scholar was a caricature no longer, and she was beginning to think that the journey of the Hearthcraft community was likely just at its beginning.

Madam Bel Carmen felt uneasy. While many of the others had been more frightened than she when the reality of their experiences was revealed, she had seen this magic before (if briefly). That is not to say that she did not believe all of these things to be the most spectacular, the most wonderful, things she had seen in her entire life; but she sensed deeply that this was not purely meant for show. While Somerset Sayer had admitted as much, the weight of the situation was beginning to settle; she was growing tired of her own anxieties, and she wondered as to the terms of their roles in what was certainly a larger transaction.

After all, were not Fae themselves known for their carefully calculated exchanges and dangerous deal-making? And as one so intimately familiar with such dealings, would not this plan also be meant to ensure maximum gain on the part of the so-called Waysmith (whom she was still unsure whether or not she was entirely human)? What machinations were they blind to by virtue of sheer bewilderment? Whether this was meant for a greater good she would happily take part in anyway, she did not know, and that alone would have given Madam Bel Carmen pause if not for the additional problem of Fairie being, after all, not a phenomenon exactly known for its trustworthiness.

Perhaps its navigator wasn't either. If only she had detected the same inclinations in the fidgeting of Amelia Cosmos earlier she might have made an unexpected ally, but as yet, she had not. The presence of the two little Fae creatures also did not help matters and she thought the one with the black eyes especially untrustworthy when it came to the welfare of all gathered. The Coblyn rarely spoke and watched them all with a fixed and unblinking stare from beneath the lower hem of the scholar's great black coat.

In the end, Madam Bel Carmen could not shake the realization that had Somerset Sayer simply wanted to assure them of the existence of Fairie beings she would have only needed to produce her two assistants; two creatures so clearly uncanny but with whom she was so well acquainted, and not sent them to places and circumstances so far outside the limits of comprehension as this. Goblins of reasonable manners would have convinced anyone.

"Gentlemen, if you would, please." Somerset Sayer addressed the two creatures with a flick of her thumb and index finger.

Without further prompting, the two Fairies went about a set of preparations that, as the short time passed, clearly belied something of their names. Hat Trick climbed up the back of Somerset Sayer's coat and swung his feet over her shoulder so that he was sitting comfortably next to her ears, the other hand hanging on to both his bird skull and the raised seam at the top of her sleeve for balance. Once situated, he produced a small, pearl-tipped hatpin from beneath his cap and fastened it somewhere within the folklorist's hair.

Satisfied he had it where he wanted it, he then produced a second, identical, hatpin and stuck it clear through the front brim of his own hat so that the pearl end hung over his right eye and the sharp point precariously near his left ear. Coat Check fussed briefly with the buttons of the train-coat nearest to the ground before making a show of carefully picking off any stray threads, bits of grass, small splatters of mud, or other detritus that appeared to offend his senses. He adjusted her lapels just so, fixed a seam with a small clip he pulled from his pocket, and brushed off some errant leaves before finally declaring that all was well and that they were ready to proceed.

Somerset Sayer smiled benignly. "You can never be too careful about the things you bring with you. You never know what might try to hitch a ride."

Hat Trick and Coat Check held their bird skulls closely; Coat Check quietly picking a few extra splinters from his before tucking it beneath his arm. Somerset Sayer, on the other hand, then produced a matchbox from her coat, took out a match, and struck it against Coat Check's rumpled sleeve. With it, she lit the cloths protruding from Falada's eyes and waited as smoke began to billow from what was once its nose and mouth. As the smoke drifted out to swaddle the collective in thick swells of blue-grey, hiding their presence from anything or anyone who might chance by, Somerset Sayer regarded the group once again.

"Take your pages and follow me."

Chapter Four

Alice Guthrie sat at her front window as she had now every morning for several days. Hot tea, cooling untouched, sat on the small end table near the knitting chair. There was a notebook in her lap, looking very much equally untouched, a pencil freshly sharpened, three small erasers, and a heavy, leather-bound, and somewhat unwieldy looking volume of poetry all closely at hand. There was no light in the room save that which peered through the windows; a muted, greyish, light that only served to highlight the long undusted surfaces and unwashed fabrics of a comfortable, if modest, New England living room.

For anyone who knew Alice Guthrie, however, this would immediately seem odd, because she had always been a fastidious woman and took great pride in the cleanliness and artful organization of her rooms for company. Even the piano looked forlorn, sheet-music packed away and stool pushed farther underneath the keys than was necessary for mere tidiness. She watched out the window at passing cars and strolling neighbors but saw little of either of them.

Dogs barking late into the night had not disturbed her (seeing as she had not been asleep anyway) and she had set the boiling kettle aside and poured her tea at just before dawn without so much as even considering whether or not she wanted to drink it. It was at times like this that she usually preferred reading, but lines of lengthy prose simply could not keep her attention long enough before her mind was once again away on other matters. So now she kept only poetry on her sitting-room tables; a few lines here and there for distraction without the investment required by the authors of entire paragraphs.

Yet despite her subdued demeanor, there was, within Alice Guthrie, a great maelstrom of ambition, emotion, and argument. Enough, she might dare say, to impress even the driest and haughtiest of Old World pedants, and it was with the intention of bringing her thoughts to some acceptable conclusion that she now sat before her front window for the third day in a row. Madam Bel Carmen had been by to check on her, but unfortunately for the both of them, Alice Guthrie had found her capacity for conversation much dulled since their return.

Her children also came and went, ensuring that their mother was at least minding the basics of self-care and not spiraling into some manner of untenable depression (and in fact, finding it strange that, once engaged, she did not seem depressed at all despite her appearance; rather, only intensely distracted). Her daughter, Fiona, gamely attempted to draw her mother out from time to time; at one-point indicating that she had something important to discuss, but when Alice Guthrie finally shook herself momentarily clear from her thoughts and adopted her characteristically warm and responsive demeanor, nothing came of it past a few exchanges of small talk and pleasantries.

When her son mentioned to her that it was as if she were in a dream, she did not correct him. In fact, she did not yet have it within her to tell him that although she was very much aware of the material world around her, it was as though that world had indeed slowly turned into a dream, because she was now waking up to somewhere else entirely.

"Do not stray out of sight." Somerset Sayer's words echoed in her mind. "If I cannot see you, you should rest assured that someone else can. And such circumstances almost never end well for anyone."

They had set out from Stonehenge in billows of slate-blue smoke, still able to see their own hands extended before them, but barely their compatriots a few feet away or their guide with the horse and goblins. They walked for a time, it seemed, to nowhere in particular. As they walked, however, Alice Guthrie began to notice a curious light-headedness. Not the kind of light-headedness one gets as the result of too much drink.

It was more like the lightness of waking from a deep sleep, where one's senses of touch and weight have not yet returned from the distant places of dreaming. She no longer felt her knees bending or her feet touching the ground. It was more as though she were flying through each turn, floating upwards or downwards as she so desired, simply willing herself to where she wanted to go rather than taking any conscious steps in any known direction.

It did not strike her as concerning, however, that she had no idea at present as to where she was going or even how she might get there. She had a guide, after all, and didn't need to be concerned about it. Regardless, she had a deep sense of the landscape around her changing, though she could not make anything out past the continuous smoke from the horse's skull appearing to float on ahead of her. It was an unusually contented feeling, with no anxiety or fear at the strangeness that surrounded them.

As in a dream, the discomfort of the uncanny and unfamiliar fell away and it simply felt as though this was the way the world had always been. She also felt somehow that she knew this world and understood all the events that had led up to this moment, even though she hadn't the slightest idea of what was happening or how it was made to happen. Her memory of the preceding conversations at Stonehenge felt faded and inconsequential but she endeavored to keep her attention sharp and to remember what it was she was supposed to be doing.

Look for the others, that was it. But she could not see them properly in the haze, save for a few incorporeal figures moving about here and there. Soon enough, she also noticed that the grass of the Salisbury Plain had given way beneath their feet and began to turn to cobbles and fieldstones. Alice Guthrie paused then to scrub the toe of her shoe at a few of them, seeing if she could dislodge one to take with her (though she was not sure why she wanted it so suddenly), but found them bizarrely stationary. It was as if each stone had been glued to the road, or that the road might be made of a single material only meant to look like cobblestone, or whatever it was that they now made their way down.

It was then, with a start, that the smoke around her cleared and she felt her senses abruptly snap back into full consciousness. The jarring and desperate feeling of suddenly needing to catch herself from falling caused her to cry out for a second, and grab hold of Madam Bel Carmen only a few inches ahead of her. Steadied against her friend, Alice Guthrie gathered her wits about her and looked to see where it was they had so carelessly landed. She caught her breath, along with the gasps of the other members of the Hearthcraft Community, who found themselves standing in a theater, in a grand old operatic proscenium in fact, huddled amongst the clapboards and façades of a playwright's set. Somerset Sayer was nowhere in sight.

Alice Guthrie beheld the scene as best she could manage. Red velvet seats lined every square foot of the front of the house save the crescent-shaped depression of the orchestra pit just past the blackened edge of the gas-lit stage. Opera boxes, adorned in gilt flowers, stacked neatly overhead; at least three or four balconies high. A great crystal chandelier descended nearly fifteen feet from the late Art Deco medallion at the center of the vaulted ceiling; each section of lateral thrust and counter-resistance edged in gold-leaf and painted in the simulacra of a cloudless, starry, night.

As the smoke continued to clear around them, many were left with the impression of emerging into an actual night where smoke played the role of drifting clouds and the glittering of the chandelier were twinkling stars. For the moment, they also appeared to be alone in the great theater. There were clearly no other persons discernable from where they stood. No one sitting in the seats out among the empty audience, no one treading with careful steps up along the catwalks above them, and no one else accompanying them in the strained silence.

The lights in the house were down and the hall beyond dark and deserted, but the stage lights were on and several spotlights were now trained on each of them where they stood, clearly illuminating a small circle of stage and just a small space beyond. Although Alice Guthrie herself was nearly five feet and eleven inches, with hands she often thought too big to ever rest comfortably in a sewn pocket, she felt dwarfed by the grandeur of the theater, which possessed the kinds of vast spaces that can only truly inspire choked awe and reverence when they are enclosed by four walls and a distant ceiling point of reference. It was then that she turned to the set.

It was a curious set to be sure, as the stage itself was divided by it into two sections: the front half of the stage (upon which they all currently stood) where there appeared to be a series of ornate chairs facing the back curtain. All of which were set up to the right of a miniature box office containing a small Formica counter and a bizarre-looking upside down chair, and the back half of the stage, which was adorned with the building-fronts of a medieval town (Ye Olde Shoppes abounding) propped up some several feet forward of a backdrop of tall wooden trees.

Each ornate chair at the front of the stage appeared to date from any number of different times and, most likely, different stage productions, but each gave the impression of having been once reserved for nobility. There was a plush chair of crushed blue velvet and gilt framing fit for a 17th century French king; a high-backed cathedral chair carved with mischievous cherubs and symbols marking out each Station of the Cross; a monarch's butterfly chair in mahogany and teak carved with the heads of lions at the forefront of each armrest; a gothic throne emblazoned with the motif of the sun; and a beautiful lotus chair piled high with Tibetan carpets, sadly vacant of its great lama who might be resting his feet and teaching wisdom.

The box office, on the other hand, was a shabby thing, barely the size of a shoebox and almost as sturdy. It was painted red, with a rounded plastic ticket window, and tiny orange and yellow lights arranged in a progressive pattern around the edge of the two-foot marquise which was, for the moment, blank. Inside, Alice Guthrie could only make out what looked like a mechanical dentist's chair with cracked, red plastic coverings and two circular gears attached on either side of the main stand bolted to the floor beneath. The chair itself, perched on the center stand, was upside down and appeared to have some kind of harness attached to the backrest.

All in all, the little diorama looked wholly broken down and forgotten, completely out of place in the grand mise-en-scène. It was as though a child had once come to play while the real builders were constructing the set and left this little altar at the entrance of a magical world they could neither quite reach nor quite comprehend. The back half of the stage was far more spectacular. Each building front was fantastically painted with intricate details of stone and mortar with long wooden panels and supports.

The illusion of reality was unprecedented, down to each wilting window box, each boot-scuffed threshold, and a half dozen weather-worn signs. Droplets of water, as though from a late evening rain, could still be seen clinging to the doorposts and windowpanes and the smell of damp wood permeated the chill air. Over the blacksmith's stand, years of caked soot and iron filings stained a doorframe still lit by the forge embers within and the tavern, whose carved sign bore the resemblance of a green-skinned elfin creature hugging a similarly-sized pint of ale, declared in chipped, white, lettering that they had finally arrived at the Wobbly Goblin.

The windows of the tavern were also lit from within, the inconsistent flicker of light reminiscent of a dying fireplace and a few ill-tended oil lamps. Alice Guthrie thought that she could hear voices inside it and the clanking of cups and plates, but each time she paused to try and fully make it out, the sounds simply disappeared. There was also a kind of trading post, with a shield and sparrow painted in black stencil on the front door, and a woodcarver's shop, advertising a new array of musical instruments and horns. Playbills sat in neat piles near the chairs at the front of the stage, emblazoned with the title: The Prince of Denmark Proudly Presents – "The Mousetrap."

"Welcome to the Chalk Circle." Somerset Sayer strode suddenly and purposely out of stage left, with neither Falada the smoking skull, nor Hat Trick or Coat Check this time anywhere to be seen. "Don't worry, I'll have you all back home soon as promised. The Circle just happens to be the safest path at the moment and seeing as this place doesn't really get going until after dark anyway, our presence ought not to cause undue disruption."

Alice Guthrie looked up once again at the painted night ceiling and wondered quietly to herself. She had only ever been a mediocre student, once derided by her teachers for her habit of reciting facts and details without the inspiring luster of curiosity. But now her passionless diligence and dedication seemed almost insulting to the world before her.

Producing the hand bell again from her coat, Somerset Sayer once again commenced a steady and persistent ringing for nearly half a minute and then, without further ceremony, she simply sat down on the stage and waited.

When the tiny gnomish creature finally appeared, he grumbled something incoherent, rhyming about mending a shirt like bending the rug. For all intents and purposes, he was a very old, if very tiny, man, with short tufts of white hair, looking for all the world as if it had been chopped in a punitive measure by a very dull scissors, and a face nearly disfigured by deep lines and dry wrinkles.

He was compact, as gnomes go, and though his feet appeared splayed to the mid-arch and his belly round and protruding like a billiard ball, he nevertheless maintained an efficient balance and stride, as if carrying two great weights in either hand balanced across the beam of his shoulders. His striped box-office uniform, sized for a doll, was frayed at the edges, gold stripes flaked out to an antique yellow and the red offset pattern stained with caramel and lint.

To Alice Guthrie, he had all the allure of a gentleman's birthmark that had begun to sprout hairs. He cast one furtive glance at the gathered crowd, saving a somewhat more poisonous stare for the folklorist herself apart from the rest, before walking over to the seated scholar and simply holding out his hand expectantly. With a nod, Somerset Sayer reached into her hair and pulled out the pearl-tipped hatpin from behind her ear, handing it to the gnome with a delicate turn so as not to accidentally impale him on a spike almost half his size.

The gnome inspected the hatpin carefully, turning it over and over in his hands like a baton until he seemed satisfied that it was, indeed, what he wanted (Alice Guthrie thought then that all he needed was a drum major's hat to complete the ridiculous image). Throwing an obscene gesture towards the group, he then climbed upside down into the miniature chair, belted in, and stuck the pin into the gear bolt near one of the circular wheels at the base. With the lever then in place, he used it to slowly turn the entire odd contraption right-side up, indifferent to the grinding and screeching of unoiled gears. Once correctly positioned, he adjusted a round cap over equally frayed looking grey bangs, put on a cheeky if rather false-seeming smile, and held his hand out into the ticket window.

Somerset Sayer, and the coat that could produce just about anything at this point, then pulled a yellowed movie ticket from her pocket, carefully unfolding the crisping paper and placing it carefully in the gnome's hand. He checked the stub with a sneer, stamped it from the countertop at his side, and handed it back with a motion to proceed past.

From over her shoulder, she offered a wry smile to the group. "*Labyrinth. 1986.* He gives me that look every time but it always works."

It was, at this point, that Madam Bel Carmen appeared to be able to take no more. "Dr. Sayer," she quite nearly sobbed out the words. "Please, I implore you. Can you not explain any of this? Where are we again? I do not understand what is happening here."

"Memory." Somerset Sayer rejoined.

"I beg your pardon?"

"Memory." She repeated, but this time, with no hints of malice or condescension. "It doesn't work here. Not at all I'm afraid. Your confusion is because, as is the way of human thinking, you are trying to remember something. How you got here, what you have seen and heard, who you met and what they looked like, and just now, what it was you wanted to say. The Way By cannot be traversed by memory, however. It exists only now and never contiguously, just as it will again."

Alice Guthrie picked at her thumbnail and tried valiantly to phrase her question in the way that seemed most appropriate. "But if you cannot remember the way back, Dr. Sayer, however are we to get there?"

Somerset Sayer rose to her feet, brushing a few stray threads from the front of her coat. "One does not *need* to remember anything here, Ms. Guthrie. In fact, attempting to do so would only cause you more distress and, I dare say, get you good and properly lost. You see all of the things around you, do you not? All these beautiful, intricate, and engaging objects?"

Alice Guthrie nodded, casting a glance about.

"These are all the memories you will ever need here. Observe them closely, be mindful of when and where they appear, and learn to read them as you would a great mystery novel you don't know the ending to. A bit like Morelli's detective to be sure, knowing the artist only by his brushstrokes. All these little lost things that foreshadow the plot just ahead of you, if you are observant enough to notice them; they tell you where they have come from and they alone can tell you where you are going."

Noting the continued discomfiture of the assembly, the folklorist continued. "You must try to think of the Way By as a kind of story, Ms. Guthrie. A half-remembered tale from your childhood wherein you may have forgotten most of the details but you can still recount the narrative of events almost perfectly. Never the intricacies perhaps, but always the same sequence. Stories are tricky that way. They move through time and space in peculiar ways, though directing you somewhere if you care to follow their lead. In that way, to walk the Way By is to read a story."

"Is that what you are doing for us here? Reading us this story?" Amelia Cosmos braved picking up one of the playbills and waving it about.

The smile that then graced the scholar's brow was a frightening one, with a glint in her eyes that belied something far more sinister in its practice. "In a sense, my dear Ms. Cosmos. Just like you are the ones writing it."

Alice Guthrie startled from her recollections, droplets of rain loudly pelting her front windows. The power had gone out, but the low mid-day light remained sufficient to illuminate her immediate surroundings. It took her a moment to realize exactly what it was, however, that had so suddenly and violently roused her. Two children, dressed in rain slickers and too-large pairs of boots, splashed gleefully in the puddles near her front walk, shouting out something to do with sticks, bricks, and wicks as they leapt through the tea-colored run-off. As they passed her doorstep, one of the children, who appeared to be a boy of nine or so in a blue poncho, stooped to rescue a toad in the midst of being washed down the rain gutter.

With a holler, he held it aloft and sprinted down the road after his sister all the while yelling, "I found mud! I found mud!" Alice Guthrie looked on them with nostalgia. Childhood was when time had been propitious and she was certain she knew the world. She still knew all the games that children played in back gardens and on rainy streets, the kinds of games that adults had long since abandoned for the correctness of an unspoken contract. No more nonsense, isn't that how it went? But now she thought of all the times when her mother and grandmother had read to her before bedtime, all the stories that they told in the firelight of a late winter's evening.

She pondered then the fading memories of her trip through a lens tinted by the reminiscences of her early life, but she stopped short. She saw then the image of her grandmother reading her a bedtime story, slowly turning the woodcut stamped pages of the nursery rhymes between fingers that shook with age, and reciting each line in turn with a voice that had only steadied with time. And then the dreams that followed in the furrows behind her calm and soothing voice. Each night, sending her down the Way By with Wynken, Blynken, and Nod.

"The only thing that I am not quite keen on," Somerset Sayer had gone on to say, "is that, I suspect, some of you may get it into your minds to, shall I say, editorialize. You are far too certain to make errors in your writings or attempt to, let's see, translate to the best of your questionable abilities. Authors can never quite resist putting something of themselves in their writings and the public never tires of reimagining and re-canonizing them. The writings I mean, not the authors. No one is a saint here. As such, I caution you. You must endeavor to learn to read, in this case. Take care not to begin guessing at the prospect of a twist ending before you've even mastered the initial semantics."

"Twist ending?" Madam Bel Carmen shifted uncomfortably on her feet.

"Never mind." The folklorist passed her hand dismissively. "Let us, instead, attend to our return, shall we?"

"Does anyone ever accidentally come wandering through here?" Elfriede Davies stared wide-eyed up at the starlit ceiling.

"No. No, certainly not." The scholar replied immediately before a short turn of silence. "Well. Cats. Sometimes they stop paying attention and can get lost in the Way By from time to time. Not dogs though. Dogs always go around."

Sliding the grossly worn movie ticket back into the unfathomable depths of her train-coat, Somerset Sayer once again began to move about the stage. She paused from window to window, looking in on someone or something that the assembled Hearthcraft Community could only begin to imagine (oh, and imagine they did!).

Every now and again, strange sounds emanated from behind the closed doors of the set façades, but the folklorist seemed unperturbed by whatever goings-on she observed from within. Finally, she stopped beneath the weather-cracked sign of the Wobbly Goblin tavern and called out to the gnome who had remained at his post within the shoebox-office.

"Thistlehogg? I should think I will take the key to Fisherman's Home then?"

The small man beneath the marquis scoffed and began to clear the considerable phlegm from his throat. "I don't give concessions to Smithy." He snarked out.

"Naturally not." Somerset Sayer craned her neck at the window of the tavern. "But on good authority the curtain will rise promptly at eight. What will your guests think with this lot here, standing right in the midst of the opening soliloquy? I am not under the impression that so many of the Faire will take too kindly to that."

"They will think you are most impertinent."

"And you most permissive."

The gnome hissed out an epithet which, had it not been quite so guttural in the delivery, would likely have shocked at least a few members of the attendant society. The scholar merely smiled, and continued to watch the happenings about within the tavern, her arm against the window sill and her feet crossed at the ankles. Lit from this angle, Somerset Sayer appeared younger than her years; wisps of her hair brightly framing the portrait of her face in dramatic chiaroscuro.

Her high brow and angular face were a compliment to the sharp ridge of her nose and the curve of a bow-shaped mouth, even with the remains of a childhood dog-bite still visible in the crescent on her cheek. She remained poised there, her ensemble of embroidered olives, plums, and chocolate brown tucked demurely beneath a black, woolen, shroud. Alice Guthrie pondered at the reason she might always be so characteristically dressed: to endure stoically whatever indignities may be meted out upon her in a day or to deliver the eulogy at a funeral with only a moment's notice?

But she found herself charmed by the folklorist's elegance and amused by the faint theatricality of her activities. And yet, she was also unsettled by the practiced ease of her words and gestures, which seemed capable of making anyone feel like a stranger in their own home despite what should be its warm familiarity. Thistlehogg, however, unbuckled from his chair and, with another equally colorful choice of words, pushed open the back of the box office.

Clopping his way across the stage, the gnome fetched a set of keys from a cabinet near the orchestra and began flipping angrily from key to key until he grasped one such bent-to-nearly-broken one that seemed to satisfy his impatience. Key finally in hand, he then stalked back the other direction, making something of a show of taking a wide route around the outer edge of the stage that would have him clearly avoiding any contact with the waiting group. As the gnome continued to make his overly complicated ambulation across the stage towards Somerset Sayer, Madam Bel Carmen turned to the scholar.

"Where are the.... I mean, your two..."

"Gremlins?"

Madam Bel Carmen tried her best not to blush shamefully at her inability to properly label the question.

"In England still, I should think." Somerset Sayer took pity. "They'll be by of their own accord in due time. I'm afraid I had a few extra errands that needed attention."

"Oh, I see...but should they..." Madam Bel Carmen never got to finish her question as Thistlehogg began to irritably jangle the keys at the scholar's feet, twirling them menacingly on their jailer's ring. Leaning down, Somerset Sayer accepted the bent key from the gnome along with a stick of unused white chalk. To the surprise of everyone assembled (well, almost everyone assembled) she then held out the key and chalk to Amelia Cosmos.

"Rather self-explanatory from here thankfully. I would suggest you draw the door on the far wall near the tree-line. No sense in disrupting the town square with all of these comings and goings. Give the key a single turn, leave it in the lock, and I will see that it gets back to its proper place afterwards."

Not wanting to leave the memory here however, it was then that Alice Guthrie's recollections took on a speculative tangent. But even now she could not tell if what she saw take shape in her memory was merely her own later imaginings or something she had glimpsed and forgotten. Because it was in the course of the intense focus with which the assembled group had maintained on the proceedings that no one had yet noticed that Cyrus Lowell was no longer among them.

He had, in fact, wandered off several minutes beforehand and had found himself backstage, carefully dodging the many ropes and switch-plates that lined the path between the back theater wall and the main curtain backdrop. Curious as to the more practical inner workings of the uncanny place, he made his way towards a small door with the word "Props" hastily scrawled across it in black pen. The door appeared to be plywood and gave easily against his first tentative push to the knob.

"Did you hear something?" A voice from within caused him to immediately freeze.

"No. Nothing." A second voice, this one shriller and forced, as though it had not yet settled into maturity, responded.

"Is the Waysmith by?" The first voice continued.

"Oh, I should think so by now." The second commented blandly before taking a sharp, excited, breath. "Say on, yes she will then. No chance of hanging about when She comes."

A tinkle of laughter drifted through the door.

"Hanging about you say! Why, we do that every day!" The two voices then commenced a minute or so of deeply malicious laughter before falling silent."

Cyrus Lowell carefully tightened his grip on the flimsy turn-knob and held his breath as he cracked the door ever so slightly, just enough to make out the tiny, cramped room beyond but not enough to give away his presence in the dimly lit back hallway. To his surprise, he saw only a wall of marionettes, each hung on an iron hook and dangling just above a crooked shelf.

But as he swept his gaze from one end to the other he grew increasingly concerned, as he could see the entirety of the small prop closet from his particular vantage point and there was certainly no one in it, let alone the two people he had expected to find and eavesdrop upon more fully. With no movement beyond he boldly pulled out the door and peered inside.

Of the puppets, there were so many kinds! The closest to him, and therefore to the door, was a rather cartoonish marionette of a king, sporting a long, white, beard that protruded from his chin as though he had been hit in the face by a giant snowball, and a puffy handlebar mustache just beneath his bulbous, cherry-red, nose. His gold-painted crown sat lopsided on a wide and blushing bald pate and caused his head to wobble comically on top of an absurdly wide Elizabethan collar. The rest of him was clad in a blue linen jacket, knee-breeches, and a pair of soiled stockings to complement a pair of buckled shoes and a faux-fur belt.

To the king's immediate right hung the marionette of a small dark boy whose hair was carved in the fashion of a Renaissance angel, thick waves and coils brushed back from his face and neatly tapered between articulated shoulder-blades. Aside from that, he wore a white button-down shirt, neatly tucked into a pair of tweed trousers held up by miniature suspenders.

To his left were even more marionettes than Cyrus Lowell could count: a beautiful, fully-articulated, Indian elephant painted to look as though it was covered in brightly colored blankets and gold bangles; a white horse with bridle and saddle of equal accomplishment; a knight with a full-suit of hammered metal armor nearly three feet tall; an old hermit with a downcast face dressed in rags; and an ominous, headless, marionette dressed in a grey blouse and soft-pink pinafore.

Nervously, Cyrus Lowell worried his fingers at the edges of his own beard, taking a step into the prop room to better survey the collection. Dust had long settled into a feathery patina across every surface of the room and even the strings of the marionettes showed their neglect with sticky tufts of filth clinging to every strand.

Breathing a shaky sigh of possible relief, he nodded to himself that he must have been overhearing a conversation from elsewhere in the theater that had likely just echoed in the ghostly way that acoustics often do and prepared to return to the Hearthcraft assembly. He turned towards the door then, only to find the king staring curiously back at him, his head cocked as it had not been before and his bright painted eyes actually tracking his movements accordingly.

"Ha!" The marionette cried suddenly, causing Cyrus Lowell nearly to fall backwards into the far corner. Clacking its wooden teeth together in a fearsome imitation of speech it sneered at him thusly, "We are in luck! Audiences are in shockingly short supply these days!"

"Oh indeed!" Cried the angelic boy, "I have not seen anyone since the new Director came along and the Stumble grew by and by. My King! Look! I do believe the gentleman wishes to speak!"

"I......I....." Cyrus Lowell staggered through sheer terror. "I'm...I mean.... who are you?"

"Who am I?" The king blustered, beginning to swing his limbs about in a disjointed sweep. "Why, everyone knows me! I am the Summer King!"

Suddenly, the entire chorus of marionettes burst into laughter, their haunting, disembodied, voices shaking their wooden bodies enough to rattle the hooks in their moorings and cause their limbs to bounce and knock against the wall. Cyrus Lowell could only think to scream but found then that he could make no noise at all.

"Oh, I do beg your pardon," the king chuckled and made as if to wipe a tear from the side of his face. "I hope you will excuse our impertinence but might I ask you a question?" A short, strangled nod bade him continue. "Yes then, can you tell me, is there, out there upon the stage tonight, someone dressed all in black; a thin-faced woman who speaks like a twisted hedgerow?"

"You..." The panicked man swallowed hard. "You mean Somerset Sayer?"

"Yes! Yes!" The marionettes cried.

"Do you know Somerset Sayer?" Cyrus Lowell asked.

"Well, I..." The king began, waiting for the jubilation of the others to quiet down. "I have not met her in person as such, but one cannot miss the grave and noble bearing of the Smiths even if obscured by the house lights of the theater, sir. So, in that, I have seen her most certainly but yet await to make her acquaintance. Perchance I may?"

"What are you?" He could think of nothing else.

"What do we look like?" Came the accusatory tone of the old hermit in rags as his head bobbled outwards into better view. In better lighting, it was clear that the painting of his face had not been properly done, his cheeks rouged to a feverish level and his eyes nearly scrubbed off, and what had once been a bouffant of white hair was now worn down to a few sad remnants clinging by virtue of aged tallow to a bare, wooden, head. The poor man had little to recommend him but for a monastic fringe and an ether frolic.

"Puppets?" Cyrus Lowell felt his resolve to explore weakening, and he wanted now only to run from the macabre animus and find his way back to the stage where he hoped he had not frightened everyone with his absence, or worse, angered their erstwhile guide.

The king made a noise somewhere between a cough and bark. "And not much better at it than good ol' Bonaparte!" More laughter clattered out from the others.

"Napoleon?!" The knight abruptly called out from beneath his griffin visor.

The king paused and then reached down to pull up his own right foot before examining the sole of his shoe with consternation.

"No! Joseph!" He shouted back.

The angelic boy groaned and rolled his marble eyes. "Eight-hundred years and as thick as the rope they hung him with."

Cyrus Lowell could take no more, and with a faltering step he began to move towards the open doorway.

"Off already?" The king dropped his foot, swinging it aimlessly against the lower shelf. "I had hoped maybe you might stay awhile. We've got a most excellent list of readings prepared! In fact, we can do them all! Respective to Henry's Third through Eighth, that is, and even a bit of Lear if you like."

The white horse clapped its front hooves.

"Meantime, we shall express our darker purpose!" The king began to perform his lines, gesticulating with chaotic fervor. "Give me the map there. Know that we have divided, In three our kingdom: and 'tis our fast intent, To shake all cares and business from our age; Conferring them on younger strengths, while we Unburthen'd crawl toward death!"

"Bravo!" The angelic boy saluted while the metal knight simply clashed his gauntlets together approvingly. The terrified man shook uncontrollably.

"I'm, yes, thank you but I'm afraid I really must be getting back...I, well, I've been gone a bit too long now and I think they may be looking for me, and I really should be getting back, you know. We're really just on our way back home and..."

"Well that's a pity." The king readjusted his head to a more upright posture. "I really do miss the audiences. All stumbled away now though I guess."

"Ah, well then. Best of luck to you." The angelic boy untangled his arm from the mess of threads he had managed to wrap around his hand and proffered a back and forth motion which Cyrus Lowell took to mean a wave goodbye. The white horse also raised and lowered its head a few times in a subdued kind of bow and the headless girl merely raised her arm dismally to pat at her neck and point towards the door.

"Thank you, I, uh, thank you." He turned to leave, looking out across the darkened backstage stretching into the considerable distance before him. But for a moment, Cyrus Lowell paused, one last bit of curious courage prompting him to grasp the door and turn. "Are you really the Summer King? The real Summer King?" he looked at the swaying marionette king.

The king scoffed brightly. "Of course not! He's gone off to Boston. Right after you!"

Cyrus Lowell turned and ran.

Upon reaching the group still congregated at the forefront of the main stage, out of breath and still shaken, he was a bit flustered to see that his absence had not caused any alarm (mainly because it had not been detected, or so he seemed to think). Still, he quietly stepped back in line just in time to witness Amelia Cosmos scratching out a large chalk rectangle beginning at the base of a clapboard tree and then adorning it with simple shapes that would ultimately give it the basic appearance of a door.

A circle for a doorknob, a few lines to mean wooden planks, and a keyhole a bit exaggerated from what would be necessary given the actual size of the bent key. What he did not notice in the interim was that his return had not actually gone entirely unobserved, and that the discerning eyes that trained on him now belonged to a Waysmith not quite so easily deceived.

"Make sure everyone is accounted for on your return, Ms. Cosmos." Somerset Sayer spoke up from her comfortable slouch in the monarch's chair. "We wouldn't want anyone to be missed."

And so there it was that Somerset Sayer and the Hearthcraft task force of mysticism and magic had parted ways. Alice Guthrie sighed and pinched the bridge of her nose as the lamp on the table next to her came flickering back to life. Fisherman's Home, as it might be surmised, apparently referred to a section of the Boston wharf, or at least it did at that particular moment. Which is precisely where they all found themselves a short time later and after considerable bickering, sans Waysmith, drenched from head to toe by the wake of the twice daily ferry-boat.

To her knowledge, and by the intermittent reports of Madam Bel Carmen, there was still no formal consensus from the Hearthcraft Motherhouse as to the exact nature of their travels or precisely what should be done next. Many assumed that Somerset Sayer would contact them again within just an hour or two with further instructions or some workings of a plan for their participation going forward, but as the days passed and no such instruction appeared forthcoming, disgruntled and impatient mutterings held the floor more often than not.

Even an unauthorized repeat of the walk from Central Street to Norton's Point (with a few pilfered tokens) proved fruitless. The two gentlemen and one very resentful lady who attempted it had simply ended up on the back porch of one Mr. Charles Geise, much to his displeasure. But of the scholar, nothing. There was no word from Somerset Sayer and no hint of the extraordinary things she had shown to them. As had become her habit of late, Alice Guthrie began to wander from room to room, wishing that she could once again regain command of the particulars of their travels.

Here she was, a sensible woman of middle age, with a comfortable home, the cherished joys of family, stout savings owing to sound financial frugality, and she could hardly be drawn into the daily cares that she had once so firmly reckoned with in her pursuit of a good and meaningful life. Her life had simply gone adrift somewhere, perhaps right along with old Wynken, Blynken, and Nod right there in their little wooden storybook shoe.

She had something of a mind to return to the regular meetings of the Hearthcraft Community of Massachusetts, but the noise and the sight of so many people only made her more inclined to retreat to the quiet of her living room, and besides, she could not think of what it would be that she might say to them. Surely, they had experienced the very same things as she had and she could offer nothing more in terms of the movements of one utterly dissembling scholar.

A knock at the door-jamb gave her cause to turn, pulling her finally from the unenviable descent back into Wonderland.

"Mom?" It was her daughter Fiona. "Can we talk?"

Chapter Five

From his turn out onto Bath Yard, Bath Lane was six minutes. From Bath Lane to Shortheath, Tom figured he could be closing in on Hooborough Brook before the hands on his watch reached ten in the morning, beating his best time by a minute and a half. He checked his watch again, jogging along at a steady pace, oblivious to the ebb and sway of Swadlincote's National Forest passing by his every step. New plantings had finally taken hold in the old growth just beyond the crest of the surrounding hills.

But the Old World propriety of medieval Needwood and Charnwood rose higher; meeting for tea it might seem, between the western outskirts of Leicester to Burton upon Trent and stiffly agreeing, with cut-glass airs of polite disinterest, over the fine poise of English oaks and ash, and the dreadful manners of Corsican pine. As the road fell away beneath his metronymic stride, Tom eased into his breathing, unconsciously picking at the neck of his t-shirt to expose more sweat-drenched skin to the early morning air. From Shortheath Road, he turned right towards the pond-side and after a skip or two and a few stuttering hops, paused for breath on the margins, taking his first real look about since he began jogging this route almost three weeks ago.

The ancient forests of England had always unnerved him despite the fact that he had been born in East Riding of Yorkshire and had spent a significant majority of his adolescence engaged in various childish activities in and around Dalby of the North York Moors. Since childhood, however, forests had been storied places, where lurking villains lay in wait and everything ill that might befall a hapless child was sure to be sudden and unforgiving. Forests were the unconscious mind, his university professors had mused, the dark places that harbored everything that could not be faced in the conscious light of day. Why else would they figure so prominently in myth, and always with a warning never to stray? In the spaces where no one can see you, Tom had thought, the world takes its revenge.

He scanned the forest edge, taking passive interest in pitched battles between a band of sparrows and a nest of politicking wrens. They swirled overhead with irritable chatter. It was then though that a squat gnarled oak near the beginning of the tree line caught his attention. It was unremarkable, save for the curious twists and whorls of the bark covering the lee side of the trunk. Bent away from the wind, its roots spread out with knots and shoots, doubling back through tussocks of shorn grass a bit too much like decayed fingers sunk into a muddy bog. In the slanted light of morning, Tom thought for a moment that he could make out a face; brow furled, the bridge of a bent nose, and cheeks puffed and scowling against the elements. He sucked in a raw breath and checked his watch again. He was due back by no later than noon.

A movement between the leaves startled him, something shifting at the edges of his vision as he squinted into the gloom. It moved again, dappling the meager sunlight into long, unspooled threads entangled in the fallen leaves; a whip-stitched landscape of summer radiance amidst autumn's ghastly remains. He couldn't make out the form as such, but it seemed a strange kind of deer, moving with fragile steps at a tentative, hesitant, gait. The head of the beast however, did not bob or glance about as he thought a deer more characteristically should.

Rather, it seemed to sway slowly, almost ponderously, from side to side, with large limpid brown eyes set upon the rise of delicate, angular cheekbones. An ashen coat, blanched in the sun but near pearly in the shadows, flashed through the trees. Its face was long and aquiline, with a softly rounded muzzle and large, faun-like ears set too far to the side. Though he could make out no antlers, he could see a kind of shimmering in the light around its eyes and neck, where vaporous misty locks of a grey-white mane occasionally rippled into view.

He watched silently for several moments before the creature stopped, and to Tom's tense anticipation, turned and looked back at him. He saw something else then, but his mind would not accept it. The birds had fallen quiet and no longer chattered their displeasure at Tom's intrusion, sitting row on row across the branches peering down in silence. He pulled his cellphone from the pocket of his running shorts and adjusted the camera, attempting to pull at the screen's zoom feature in order to get a better look; hoping that a fast shutter might reveal a little something more about what his eyes could not quite comprehend.

But as if caught up in the wind, the creature began to list into the trees and the birds suddenly scattered in a burst of indignant chirps. Tom threw up his hands reflexively as several of the more belligerent little songbirds collided in mid-air, showering him in a sprinkle of down and dander. One such bellicose sparrow even went so far as to cuff him in the back of the head with a few well-timed wing flaps. He spluttered with disgust, flailing his arms over his head in a futile gesture of defense, but turned back to the woods just in time to see the creature begin to fade into the rushes beyond the oak grove.

Spying a small path, little more than an animal trail through the worst of the undergrowth, Tom dropped down the short roadside ditch and made his way out of the thicket and onto the fat thatch of the forest floor. The spongy mass of leaves and needles crunched and crackled beneath his feet as he swatted away flowering pods of grass seed and ornery twigs scratching bleeding welts across his shins. The trail was hard to follow, with unpredictable twists and turns through the glades of broadleaves, but the deeper he went, the brighter everything seemed to become. Leaves of ash and aspen, translucent as stained glass, shielded him from the sun arching over the canopy.

The brambles of poison oak and mistletoe gave way to sparse patches of cotton grass and bee orchids, stands of pasqueflower, pink rows of Dorset heath and primroses with bright blue spring gentians just beginning to bloom. A pair of small butterflies flounced through the air and into view, disrupting the slow drift of white dandelion seeds. For a moment, he thought that he may have stumbled onto a conservator's garden or that perhaps he was closer on towards the Social Club just a few hundred meters to the north than he thought.

But he saw no brick-and-mortar buildings in the distance, no sound of cars turning into the lot, and no sign of the visitor's center he remembered passing along Bath Lane just a short time ago. He realized then that he must have been walking through the wooded stands in pursuit of his vision for some time. He could see nothing of the vast grassy playing fields and market yards he remembered as being predominant along this particular section of the National Forest reserve.

To Tom's recollection, the woods of Shortheath Road were barely larger than a suburban block and that it wasn't until further down Hooborough Brook that anything remotely resembling the primordial weald such as he now faced might be beheld. The sour taste of bile rose in his throat. He could see some distance in every direction before his gaze was entirely obstructed by copse and timber, but he could make out nothing beyond but more woods. Suddenly exasperated with his own half-remembered childhood fears, he shook himself free and began to walk once again in the same direction as before.

The forest end would have to come into view sooner or later, he reminded himself. He stopped once to look around for the strange creature from before, but as he could see nothing but the briar, he sighed disappointedly and resolved to simply return home without further delay. As he rounded the bend, absently pulling bits of leaf and dandelion from his short, curly, hair and chastising himself for his fruitless curiosity, the toe of his running shoe slid into the oblong spaces of a tree root emerging from the ground and sent him sprawling face first into a mire of ground-cover compost.

Tom landed with a shout, one shoe still on his foot and the other remaining with the tree. He groaned against the smear of dirt across his face and chest, feeling a searing set of new abrasions opening up all the way from his forehead to his knees. Slowly, he rolled over and sat up to survey the damage: a bloody knee, scraped elbows, and a twisted ankle almost certainly. Then, a sound from the foreground alerted him. To his shock, a man, seated at the base of an unusually wide English oak, stared wide-eyed back at him. A disheveled man with oily skin thick with filth, ragged cargo pants and a stained shirt. He was barefoot and unkempt with an untidy collection of broken plastics and glass bottles discarded among the bulbous roots. Clutched in his hand, a bent spoon.

He looked as though he might have been sitting in that same place for quite a long while given that his leathery appearance and mud-slicked hair blended him quite convincingly into the wood, making him seem an integral part of the tree he hunkered down within. Only the quivering of his chapped and seeping lips gave him away.

"I, uh...sorry mate." Tom tried to laugh. "I just got a bit lost I think."

The man stared at him with a look both vacant and increasingly malevolent but said nothing. His eyes were fever-bright but pitch-stained with dilated pupils and a bloodshot bruise spreading across the left side of his cheek. He watched as Tom carefully got to his feet, patting at his shorts before leaning down to retrieve his cellphone from the leaf litter. But the man beat him to it, snatching up the phone and dropping his spoon among the detritus.

When he tried then to grab for Tom's clothing, in an ostensible search for a wallet he imagined, he staggered back, nearly tripping again on the uneven ground. Tom let out another shout, shouldering the man backwards into the winding roots of the oak, trying, with all of his off-balance might, to wrest the phone away.

"It's mine!" The disheveled man screamed out with sudden vigor, his voice hoarse and unused. "I want to go back! I want to go back! Let me back!" He continued to shriek over and over again. They tussled there, Tom with one hand grasping the man's right wrist and the other peeling back his grip, finger by finger, to retrieve the mobile. He would get it certainly; the hermit's strength was waning and his pleading had quickly devolved into pathetic moans and whimpers, repeating again and again that he only wanted to "go back."

That he needed out, that he needed only to "get more" or else he couldn't find his way. "I can get more! I need more! Give it to me!" He sobbed. "Don't make me stay here, please!" He begged Tom to let him see the way again, that he needed just one more chance.

"Let go, you crazy git!" Tom snapped, finally wrenching his phone free from the man's trembling hands. "Get a fucking grip!" But the ragged man wailed in despair, ripping a portion of his unsightly beard right out of his skin as Tom recoiled in horror, ready at that second simply to turn and run.

The man roared and leapt across the ground in a fit of possessed rage, and in moments he was on Tom again, flailing and kicking with inhuman strength. The man's teeth sunk into his forearm and the mobile once again dropped to the ground. The horror then took its due. Tom didn't feel the knife right away, only thinking that the man had punched him flat in the gut. When he saw the blood, he didn't feel the second blow at all.

The third he saw coming, the glint of the tar-encrusted blade pressed into his attacker's palm and burying itself in his neck. In an instant, in the span of just a few passing and otherwise insignificant moments, his entire world ended. He screamed then, the sounds of pure terror bursting out from every part of him. The rushing in his ears caused Tom to stagger backwards, the entire world careening over his head in the choking grip of vertigo. He clutched at his throat, unable to stem the flow of blood rushing out of places he couldn't quite feel or even quite see. His hand felt hot and slick as he squeezed instinctively but kept losing his grip in the cruor spill.

He didn't see the gleeful shrieking man roll into the leaves to claw for his phone nor did he see the white-glimmer of iridescent light that drifted out of the garden towards them. He didn't see the world around him come to life as his own drained out upon it, nor the veins of ivy in the trees go red as they supped it. He felt only the stinging rasp of the forest floor on his back as he fell and the relentless creep of dead-cold overtaking his limbs; moving up from the tips of his fingers, stilling his hands, and winding into his chest to choke and mock and steal his breath. Hot tears, regretful tears, spilled down his cheeks and he begged the sun for forgiveness. He called it God, but it was all the same right then. The world went black and silent.

Strangely, silence had a voice. It called him by name. "Wake up." It said. "Wake up now, Tom."

Had he dreamed it? Was the forest really, as he had always thought it, only in his nightmares? But silence spoke in whispers and in mangled phrases falling out all together at once.

"This is a dangerous place to sleep."

He opened his eyes.

"You should never have come here."

"So far to go, so very far to go now."

"It will drain a man to dust."

The sun shone down from directly above him, a few discarded leaves spiraling out from their great heights to alight on his face. The forest floor no longer painful and abrasive but a warm, gentle pressure at his back. With some difficulty, he sat up. A beetle tumbled out of his hair and slowly wandered off. His body felt oddly stiff and unused, as though he were awakening from a long sick-sleep, or that his hands and arms had somehow simply forgotten what it meant to move.

The monstrous, wild man was nowhere to be seen but as Tom's vision began to clear, he beheld something quite out of the ordinary. Where the scraggly man had once sat, now rested the most unearthly woman he had ever seen. She was frail in constitution and impossibly slender, a wisp of a girl in a simple linen peasant's dress. Ethereal; her face was pure white and elegant as bone china; the work of a ceramicist who had mastered the nuance of Kaendler's sculpted figurines but whose fire had failed to impart stability.

Rounded eyes of blown glass refracted the light, throwing out eddies of old silver and tarnished gold that sparkled together in empty reaches of vast and unfathomable space. Her hair was equally white, pure and unstained as fresh milk flowing over her shoulders and pooling into the tiny folds around her waist. Tom felt his voice crack in the back of his throat and a sudden bout of coughing caused him to squint and wipe frantically at his neck. Touching the tender skin there, he stopped abruptly and, shaking, looked back up to see her smiling down at him with a charitable gaze.

"It's alright." She spoke in a voice like wind chimes, both near and far away.

"I...who are you? Where's that man, that man with the knife?" He began to turn in panic.

"It's alright." She repeated. "He's gone now."

As she tilted her head to regard him fully it was then that he noticed the scar, a jagged line from the top of her forehead that almost neatly bisected her face into two even halves. It was faint, but obvious enough in the subtle wrinkling of her eyes and mouth when she spoke that it extended from the top of her head, over the midline of her nose, clefting both lips into a slightly uneven join and ended at the base of her chin. He stared back in fear.

"Who are you?" He asked.

"I am Clarisant." She replied, accenting slightly on the second syllable before clipping off the end.

"Clarisant." He repeated dumbly. "I…I don't know how I got here. I mean, there was this man and then he attacked me, but then, I don't know…I…"

"Died." She knit her brow. The expression of concern faded into an affected gesture of compassion.

He froze, the same death-cold sensation he had felt earlier gnawing now at his soul rather than at his body. He reflexively placed a hand on his chest and slowly looked down. But he saw nothing. Nothing there at all. His t-shirt was torn and ruined with dirt and grass, just as it had been in the fight but the skin beneath was utterly untouched. He saw no scratches, no rashes or scrapes, and no wounds. His eyes darted from side to side; no blood on the ground, no blood on his hands, or staining his clothes as there certainly had been before. He turned his gaze back to the woman seated on the tree trunk.

"Dead." He shuddered. "I was dead."

Though he had phrased it as a statement, she nodded imperceptibly. "Yes."

"Then…" He tried to swallow the thick mass in his throat. "How am I alive? Am I alive?"

"Yes." She stated plainly. "I have brought you back." For several seconds, he could not speak.

"How?"

"Because it is my right to do so." Her words were matter-of-fact but her face remained soft and vulnerable in the refracted light of mid-day.

"You bring people back from the dead?" He still felt out of breath, struggling to regain life again with each sob, still unsure as to whether he should be drawn to the strange woman or cautious of her.

"It is in the nature of unicorns to heal all that is wounded, and give life back to those from which it has been stolen." Her words had an uncanny cadence to them. The stress in her phrases was all wrong, rising where it should have deepened and descending where more force was expected. It sounded to him as though she were not only unfamiliar with the language but with the act of speaking itself. "I bring you back because I choose to. You live because I will it."

He stared back at her incredulously, but the hammering in his chest was enough to remind him that the events of the past hour or so were nothing anywhere near the range of normal. He took in her expression, which had not wavered at all over the course of their conversation. While she adopted a light smile from time to time or even a look of pity, it occurred to him that the rest of her face did not appear to move as it should. She did not blink at regular intervals and her eyes did not crinkle when the corners of her mouth did. Her gaze suddenly felt alien, uncomprehendingly curious and heartless in its too distant empathy.

"A unicorn?" He coughed. "You don't look like a unicorn."

"Then why did you follow me, if not because your eyes deceived you?"

The ashen creature in the woods. He was suddenly fixated by finding his phone, which he did moments later, seeing it half-buried in the surrounding detritus. The screen had been shattered and the housing was wet with dew and mold, but he held it tightly anyway.

"What did you do with the man, the lost man?" He dared not look her straight in the eyes again, peering up from under his brow.

"He should have known better... than to spill blood... here in this place." She sighed passively. "Not with such angry trees. Their ancient hatreds run deep... and they are unbending"

Tom warily got to his feet, still with only one shoe, steeling himself against the tremors in his knees and in the tension in his legs and shoulders. Clarisant held up one hand and flexed her fingers towards a stand of trees a short distance from where she sat. "Go that way." She said before turning her chin upwards to the oaks above. "Go home. Tom."

He wanted to run, desperately wanted to run and never turn back. But something in her demeanor seemed to discourage this desire and with halting, uncertain steps, he began to walk towards the trees but never with his back fully turned. It wasn't until he saw the gravel hiking trail on the far side that he finally broke; sprinting as if his life depended on it. He checked his watch. It was almost noon already.

Clarisant watched him go, listening to the reckless crashing of frightened prey through the undergrowth. In response, the roots beneath her once again began to tighten their coils, shifting and sliding up from the soil. She patted the trunk reassuringly, tasting again at the salt of panic in the air.

"Hush now. You have had enough. Whet your vengeance. But be patient."

She rose from the brambles to reveal the blood-sopped dress beneath her, soaking her thighs to trickle down through the gathered folds. Congealed drops splattered onto her feet. From where she had sat, the remains of a soiled and broken man were clutched tightly in the roots as his limp and lifeless body was slowly consumed beneath the base of the massive trunk. Threadbare clothes and yellowed nails rotted away in an instant, blood trickled out onto the ground, blotting the leaves, only to be swallowed up by searching, invading, root-veins spreading out across the loam.

The sound of his breaking bones echoed throughout the hillside, calling the carrion-seekers home. The smile that then touched her face was of a murderous kind until the hate-filled edges of a snarl suddenly ruptured it. The porcelain skin that the jogger had so notably remarked on to himself began to fracture, a spidery web of breaks and imperfections suffusing every part of her lithe form. Its crackled surface bent and distorted into a corrupt insult to beauty. At her forehead, the now unseemly scar split into a black, ichorous, wound; oozing out what remained of wasted blood and bone onto her raging breast. The gaping hole it left was unclean, with deep and unholy caverns where something marvelous had once grown.

Something that had been callously ripped from her body at its very origin and left to the cankerous ravages of putrefaction. Still, a pin-point light from within its depths belied a baleful fortune. Her eyes took on a vicious luster, clouded with crude imperfections and the glint of unspoken malice. She bared her teeth to the wind and tore the corpse-stiff dress clean from her body with a single wrench of bloodless fingers. Her body roiled beneath its pale placid skin, joints rending free in the advent of a spectacular transformation.

"I am the wind across the sea." She cried out. "I am the hart upon the rock." The forest swayed and bellowed. "I am the muse who grants the song. I sing the sun into its bower. Who can tell the age of the moon?" The ground thrashed beneath her. She pressed her hands into the sun-drenched air. "I am the birds of the sky, who could speak before words. Who can tell what was never known?" The trees split asunder, ripping their taproots free from bedrock.

"Kill the ones who water the garden." She intoned. "Pile their bones upon the road and pull their fences beneath you. Then none shall pass this Way again."

High above, the birds sang their anthems of war and the forest groaned aloud in hunger.

"A company of women and men, for all intents adrift, passing so blatantly into the Way By. And you did not think it would be noticed?"

Somerset Sayer scowled over the empty teacup in her hand, staring down at the artful arrangement of leaves floating in the dregs. The silken voice that so abruptly disturbed her was a familiar one, though one she had not had very recent acquaintance with nor one she had expected to hear as she pored over a stack of antique manuscripts. She didn't even bother to look up because the voice was clearly seated opposite of her library desk, sunk comfortably into the wing-back chair that faced the window behind her.

She stared into the cup a few moments longer and rolled the tea around the bottom as the fragments of leaves and cardamom pods took on oracular shapes. He had come along the Crooked Road, a Way By path that might occasionally reveal itself in the spaces between sites of holy reverence. A circuit once used by religious pilgrims, but long since abandoned from before the time of Charlemagne. The only ones to brave the precariousness of this particular Way now were either in possession of some unprecedented amount of leverage among the Faire or were of the most terrifying sorts themselves. She canted the teacup. He was on edge but, as always, far too polite to show it. She gingerly returned the cup to the windowsill.

"And to what do I owe the pleasure?"

"You dare ask me that?" He replied in a low voice. "Never once have I been a stranger in this house nor made my presence a disturbance. But you, who have so obfuscated your intents and traveled the Way with any such malfeasance as might suit your purposes, think to ask as to the reason why I might now take issue."

The folklorist smiled despite herself. She had always found his overly formal way of speaking to be oddly endearing. He composed his sentences with such an anachronistic flourish he might well have been born arguing the finer points of English with Marlowe himself. And yet, it suited him perfectly.

While he did not always dress the part, usually to be found in a tailored coat of rich slate-blue cotton twill and hunting boots to his knee, the Summer King was no less noble in bearing when he chose to wander the pagan fields without his crown than when he spoke as sovereign corps-état. And now, he wanted to know why a group of cluelessly uninitiated people had been seen tromping through the Way By, at Stonehenge, and passing through the Chalk Circle with none other than Somerset Sayer at the helm. It was a fair question given his station.

"Avenant. Your Grace." She dipped her head in formal, if a little feigned, reverence, sliding her most recent manuscript acquisition to the side and folding her hands politely in her lap. He looked older than he had before and she couldn't fail to notice that the white tips of his hair had bled further upwards into the sable locks he currently kept tied in a loose plait at the nape of his neck.

When she had first met him, now almost two and a half decades ago, the white ends had been little more than tinged points, barely a contrast to the vibrant auburns and chocolate browns of a young man's unmanageable coiffure. Now, the white tresses extended from the small of his back nearly to his shoulders and the peppering of minute scars all along his forehead and neck were becoming more pronounced. Still, neither his appearance nor his demeanor betrayed his prime, and even though she could picture him as she had seen him as a child, he never looked older than a man in his early thirties.

"I am sorry then, that you had to hear it this way. I had figured the gossip would take a little longer to reach you." Somerset Sayer motioned for Coat Check to fetch more tea, though he needed the moment to respectfully avert his shocked stare before scurrying off to find the tea box. But the Summer King was not so easily parlayed out of his irritation.

"And what alliances have you cultivated this time? Who, may I ask, has been so graced as to accompany the Waysmith for the first time in her living memory?"

"Not any one of *skill*, if that is what you are insinuating." She replied. "But a few, at least, of passing curiosity. Not much in the way of useful education. But necessary."

"I fail to see the wisdom in this."

Somerset Sayer restlessly tapped her fingers as more tea, sugar, and clean spoons slid over the edges of either side of her desk. He reached over and lifted his cup expectantly.

"Once again, you've talked yourself into the belief that this is some nefarious plot on my part."

"Clever plot." He rebutted, sipping at his cup. "Never nefarious."

"Well it remains to be seen if this is clever or not. Best laid plans and serendipitous luck have never been my forte, you may depend on me for that. But it started with a letter, a most unexpected letter at a most unexpected time. Which shouldn't surprise you. I was, however, sure to complete my inquiries before responding. Those to whom you are referring are simply the core constituency of the local society of magic."

He paused to regard her pensively.

"Oh no, not magicians of that sort." She waved her hand dismissively in response to the disquiet in his gaze. "If such a society of magic to which your concern implies were to actually exist here in Boston I think I would have found them out long before now. No, their potential is more that of imperfect vassals, those who might mind the land as it were while the knights march off to war. But the Way By is undisturbed here, as I am sure you noticed on your way through, so there is little need for you to be upset."

"On the contrary," he began.

Somerset Sayer tensed at his words, dragging her fingernail against the glazed roses of the china cup. Coat Check appeared with the wherewithal to offer a few pieces of toast.

He continued. "She has much to gain in such a place as this. How many poets and orators are buried in these grounds? How many unquiet dead? The most ancient and revered trees of this land feast upon cemeteries of war and grow thick and tall on leaking coffins. How many great bones might she disinter to feed the Stumble's ever-expanding greed?"

"She might do that anywhere." The scholar replied.

"Perhaps." He calmed. "But *you* are here."

The Waysmith clicked her teeth and once again appraised the reigning sovereign, collapsed as he was on her library chair. According to many medieval accounts, the Summer King was a Fairie of the purest lineage, stretching back through time all the way to Nuada Airgeatlámh and the victory of the Tuatha Dé Danann at the Battle of Trees.

It was also said that Nuada, his most esteemed ancestor, was the first to wear the Bramble Crown and take up the spear Claidheamh Soluis; Glowing Bright, and who made peace with the mystic leaders of men and dictated the first secret texts of the Way By to the druid-poets Amergin and Taliesin.

Not the first Waysmiths ever to have lived certainly, but the first after that to walk the Near By paths under treaty and without fear of Fairie reprisal. In the centuries following Nuada's time, however, men forgot their ancient agreements and wrought destruction on all imagined lands. To make matters worse, there had been only eight sovereigns since, in the line of succession to the Throne of the Summer King (a place she knew as The Gathering on the Hills but which the Fairest simply called The Sæl). And not all of them in a contiguous line. As a result, the Bramble Crown was often bare and unattended. The Throne sometimes empty.

But for all Somerset Sayer's endless analyzing, she still found the rules of age-old ascension to be frustrating; an eternally convoluted reckoning of blood and worth such that she was never sure who was supposed to occupy the role and who was not. Her favorable inclination to the current sovereign notwithstanding, of course. But in the end, the man she called Avenant, who held the Crown now, had paid dearly for an honor he did not want, even if he had taken up his duty without complaint when the time came. And so here he was. A king now in the latter half of a three-hundred-year reign. For this and other reasons, Somerset Sayer found his current caution more chilling than his usual reserve. He never came so far into her world without great purpose.

"And it is to these most fortunate circumstances that I owe the happiness of your visit?"

"Yes." He said plainly, ignoring the slight timbre of her sarcasm. "And I am afraid that my words may be the prophecy of dire warning you feared, though I wish very much that they were not. I truly wish, more than anyone, that I would not have been the one to bring fevered tidings, but ere the Way grows dim. Death has claimed a new mount and this one runs with the fury of a thousand wretched and unrealized lives."

The folklorist nodded gravely. He could only be speaking of one thing.

"But I have before me an extraordinary thing, do I not?" Somerset Sayer raised an eyebrow at her old familiar patron as he suddenly shifted topic. "A Waysmith to whom nothing could be promised and who knew nothing of the world. With a scholar's love of solitude and a Fairest's love of silence. She would sit hour after hour chattering away with books in a room full of a child's loving collections, arranging her beetles and bottle caps and river stones just so." He looked wistful though not unaware, as though he anticipated she might contradict him at any moment.

"And yet you found me useful."

He narrowed his eyes then, though he did not turn the admonition to her directly.

"I am happy it was you." He scolded. "The Way By was calling unto you long before I arrived. Even if you did not yet know it. But my nostalgia is of no consequence in this matter. I apologize for my distraction."

She shrugged and set her cup aside. "My own indomitable Virgil, here to take me once again into the belly of Hell and Creation."

"I do so hate that analogy."

She smiled. "So, tell me then. What is it that troubles you?"

The Summer King drew an arduous breath. As he wore no ornaments or jewelry, his graceful fingers instead worried at the wooden buttons of his embroidered coat. The scene at his forearm, a stately peacock facing down a tiger curled to pounce, shifted menacingly, suspended forever on the threshold of battle in the bindings of endless thread. His fine elfin features drew back to reveal the sharper hollows of his face. She had always thought him handsome, more so for his constant studiousness and the care with which he chose his words than the commanding elegance his noble ancestry had bestowed upon him. But handsome, nonetheless.

"She trades in life once again, but her reverence for it has not returned."

He spoke of an evil they both already knew.

"And to whom does she address her vengeance now?"

"To those whom the strands of the Way drift closest."

Somerset Sayer chewed at her lip. “Then there is the promise of nothing but calamity.” The folklorist observed. “She will begin as before. The quiet artists and pitchfork philosophers. The scientists who labor on in obscurity. Actors and playwrights who do the same. Writers and teachers and poet-soldiers. She’ll take them all again, each and every one in time. She will drown their thoughts as she drowns their bodies; in madness and in destruction. Trade up our Christmas Ghosts from Past, Present, and Future to Debt, Depression, and Diabetes.”

She found little humor in the joke but he chuckled in acknowledgment.

“That hardly sounds like the proper set-up of a good and decent fairy-tale.” He gently replied.

“The Unicorn Queen.” The scholar resultantly deadpanned, “is a delight for little girls. What now walks the abyssal reaches of our world is nothing of the kind. Don’t placate me with the troubles of good and evil. She is no counterpart to light. She is the cruel despair that comes in its absence. The kind that simply lets you kill yourself rather than bothering with the honor and dignity of doing it for you. This is a darkness that doesn’t make heroes, Avenant, it allows them to consume themselves and blames them for it in their own eulogy. There is no great battle to be won at the hands of a patient enemy and no great story to be told that triumphs over her with celebrations.”

“And yet she strides on in splendid procession.” He remarked. “She will not rest when the trumpets sound, as they say. She is coming and this time she comes for you.”

He sighed, unhappy with the harshness of his own tone despite the urgency of the matter. “I’m afraid our bond will have been my lapse. I sought to protect you and now I will have delivered you onto the doorstep of your enemies for the second time.”

“I know.” She stood up from her chair near the window to replace a folio onto its proper shelf. “And this is why the time for great heroes has passed.”

He turned in his seat to rest his chin on the back of his hand, elbow propped precipitously on the armrest.

"There is no one story that can speak to how this ends." She continued. "No one telling that can encompass every thread. But instead, like all the rest, I see a tale that will become part of a great compendium of stories, all in concert with one another, all speaking to the same thing in a thousand different ways. That's how people really tell their stories, isn't it? All together, down and down through time, trading them with whomever they meet until they overtake the world? In the Way By, you're never on the same path as someone else, but the fact that you're on the path at all tells you that someone else has been there, isn't that how you put it?"

The Summer King attempted an affectionate smile. "This constituency of magicians." He stated with a tone of finality. "Will they be the tellers of your tales?"

"She is immortal, but she is only one, Avenant. A story is immortal because it is many. She can wait as long as she likes, but she cannot out-wait us all. If she comes for me expecting a single combatant, she will instead find a hundred."

"Clever plot."

A great clamoring arose from the far side of the living room, just outside the library door. In the room beyond, where dusty sitting furniture still awaited the return of pleasant afternoon chatter, Coat Check scurried about the curtains over the front window. Drawing and redrawing the pale sheers, he motioned, in his characteristic fashion of holding up a circle of thumb and forefinger and two additional fingers to indicate a number, that there was someone at the door.

Another tremendous din erupted from the stoop. Somerset Sayer did not bother to look at the wing-back chair at the front of her desk because she knew that he would already be gone. It was not that he did not care to be seen by the rank and file of humanity, but more that Avenant indulged only a select few to circumvent the standard protocols that one would usually be obligated to honor before meeting and addressing the Fairest who was and is the Summer King. Replacing another set of hide-bound books back onto the library shelves she took a moment to compose her scattered thoughts. She had not at all been prepared for even one visitor today, welcomed and appreciated though he might have been, let alone another of the more mundane variety.

"The Summer King has a crown, that only he can wear." She recited absently, falling into the well-trodden rhyme that had comforted her in childhood turmoil and had always helped her to refocus. "But in the hands of other men, a bramble thicket there."

She paused and recalled the events at Stonehenge only a few days prior. "Weighed with frost at winter's break, dead and cold is he. Pale and sick with thorn and stick, woe is there to thee."

Coat Check glared over his shoulder, pounding a tiny fist against the adjoining wall. "In, yes? In, no?"

Such a crown one cannot tame, 'tis neither fair nor just. Placed upon another head, it drains the man to dust.

"Yes." She handed the little Coblyn a set of keys. "I'll meet them in Cambridge."

Locking the library door behind her, Somerset Sayer passed from the threshold of fair breezes on the shoreline and into the gloom of an unfavorably drizzly Boston afternoon. A pile of urgent letters tipped onto the floor as she accidentally scuffed the edge of the dinner table, but she brushed them aside with a careless toe and continued on towards the front room. She had not been in this house in several days, and already a creeping pattern of wear was beginning to show along the molding.

A few flecks of dried paint began to flit down into the rug. She did not know who might be beating the very framework of her door into submission at such a time but the imprecise rhythm of the strikes, followed by a kind of restless shuffling sound, told her that her callers were human. She waited for the next predictable round of thumping to subside before pulling back the latch and addressing her visitors directly.

To her surprise, upon her doorstep was none other than Ms. Alice Guthrie; soaked to the bone and in quite a disheveled state. The usually fastidious lady stood shivering but resolute, as was her preference. Her mouth was set in an anxious frown, creasing the corners of her face as much with tribulation as with the pruning of skin that comes with too-long exposure to the wet. Rain-blown strands of greying brown hair stuck to her face and tangled in her fingers whenever she brusquely attempted to wipe them aside.

Clutched in her opposite hand was the coat sleeve of a young woman Somerset Sayer did not recognize. Unlikely to be more than sixteen, perhaps closing in on seventeen, the girl looked nothing short of miserable. But to the scholar's eye, similarities in the curve of their eyes, the subtle downward turning of their noses, and a shared style of dress that could only be described as painfully New England, indicated that this was almost certainly Alice Guthrie's daughter.

The girl hung her head as her mother drew her forward, avoiding any pretense of eye-contact for as long as she could possibly manage it without inadvertently walking into a wall. The thunder advanced closer and the storm began to whip up into a greater frenzy. Taken slightly aback, the folklorist said nothing.

"Dr. Sayer." Alice Guthrie sniffed and heaved a deep and distressing breath, more from cold than from indignation. "Please. We need your help."

Chapter Six

The marmalade cat yowled at the doorway, a drawn-out wailing kind of sound hovering over the floorboards for the fifth time in less than ten minutes. But even when offered a wide-open invitation, he would never simply walk through it; not without turning thrice in a circle from the fourth stair adjacent to the landing, flicking his tail just so, and whining a high-pitched note of indignant protest. From where he sat now, some two feet from the threshold, he could carry on the fine tradition of wearing out the patch of weave centered over the ivy medallion on the oriental rug in the hallway.

He could also only barely see the young woman still bent over her piles of open textbooks, studiously ignoring him to the best of her abilities. Residue of a late-night coffee swirling at the bottom of a cup momentarily distracted her nervous fingers as she peeled back another page of drawings, reciting each named diagram in turn. What resulted was a personal mantra of gross anatomy.

"Fibula, Tibia, to Cuboid. Navicular, Cuneiform, Metatarsal, Phalange. Talus, Calcaneus in forefoot to hindfoot. Okay, now, up we go to Patella, Femur, and then, wait, Os Coxae or Os Pubis? The joint is Os Ischium?" A defeated sigh. "Crap." Another round of anxious mewling spilled from the doorway before she finally pulled her fingers out of their death-grip in her hairline and spun around in her seat to face her tormentor directly.

"What?! What is it, Nosey? For the love of God, what?!"

Noseworthy, whose name had been drawn from a number of obscure sources rather iconically appropriate to the scrawny orange feline with the wide face, cross-eyed stare, and comically large muzzle, remained unmoved. Rather, he took the opportunity then to stretch, arch, yawn, and sit back down to lick at his paws with casual disinterest. In retrospect, he would have been better off as a plainer cat. Because, in all honesty, his features bordered on the grotesque; a head twice as long as his ears were wide, a great parish pick-axe of a face with two dark eyes stuck into it sideways, and a ruff of orange-yellow fur poking out at odd angles over too-high cheekbones.

Taken together, however, it all made for a proud and confident profile; like the silhouettes of great war generals with their mutton chops and sagging jowls: secure in their competence if still rendered melancholy by memories of conflict and carnage. For his counterpart though, it was a particularly difficult time to be a medical student. Tuition had gone from bad to worse and the idea of absolute dedication so espoused by her tenured advisors, though noble in concept, was laughable in practice.

Rent and food were a zero-sum game, and it was not for the first time that evening that Elizabeth Pennybaker, staring down one thread-bare cat on a dusty rug, mused on the irony of sinking her life into furious debt for a fleeting promise of possibly digging it out again later. She turned back to her failing copy of Netter's *Atlas of Human Anatomy*, overlaying several of its severed pages onto the nearby Grant's *Atlas of Anatomy*; better to highlight some of the more esoteric relationships between artistically-posed bones.

With a dejected sigh, she half hoped that the skeletons might suddenly spring out of their pages, take up a sword and a shield or two, and just do battle with her right there in the halls of Old Squat, the last and loneliest student apartment house on the row. Her rallying cry to arms would rouse her sleeping house-mates who would rush to her side, vanquishing the restless dead with mystic spells conjured by the anemic first-floor post-doctoral fellow in English, potions and elixirs lobbed by the chemistry graduates from the stairwell of their third floor flat, and unerring precision strikes levied by the physics lab research assistant and his perpetual motion pendulums across the hall. And then, delirious celebration and drink would follow with a proud song of victory from their very own doctoral candidate of musicology, a fourth-floor virtuoso of the French Horn.

When her musings failed to materialize however, she continued to stare down at Noseworthy, Old Squat's resident mascot, still patiently grooming on the rug. "And a fine familiar you will make, eh?"

To his credit, Noseworthy paused in his ministrations to look up, flick his tail again, and cock his head in feigned interest.

"Maybe not." She slumped, pinching at her shoulder and neck. "Should have gone with the black cat then, huh? No soul of magic for the ginger houseguest."

Dropping her elbows back onto the makeshift desk, Elizabeth casually spit out a few strands of unwashed auburn-black hair before shoving the pile of books aside and unceremoniously flattening her forehead onto the wood. A sharp pain twitched up her leg. Something had landed on her foot.

She slid her face from the desk and looked downward to see one of a number of small books, binding cracked open midway with pages draped across her toes. Barely larger than a thick packet of playing cards, she lifted the offending volume from the floor and turned the embossed cover into the lamplight. *Lostwith Notes: The Truth (Without Permission) of the Way By Stumble,* by Somerset Sayer.

It was no doubt another one of her aunt's thrift-store finds, gifted to her most ostentatiously following her last birthday. She had forgotten about it completely, along with quite a few other odds and ends still in their original wrappings. Curious, and not more than a little beyond the capability of reviewing anymore Latin labels suspended as they might be in the formaldehyde of early British academia for the evening, Elizabeth turned the book over in her hands, pushing her thumb between the pages that only momentarily before had been crumpled-up on top of her bruised foot.

"Angels and demons, blood and redemption; these are the metaphors of only one such religion." She read aloud absently. "*But such things no more govern the world outside than notions of pure good and evil govern this one. There is not some hidden truth to be gained by faiths and rituals alone, because they are wrong about it all, each in their own ways. They have failed to grasp, truly, the complexity of our current situation and cleave to grand universals where there are none. The point of the matter is this: there is no one coming to save us. And if that shatters your beliefs in a God Almighty, then I am pleased to say that neither you nor I have lost much in the bargain."*

Brow furrowed in concerned amusement, she skipped ahead: *"To the Western mind, the greatest frustration of existence is the ability to imagine entire new worlds coupled with the inability to create them. God is, then, the one who can create the worlds He imagines, and we, of course, supplicate Him in the ineffectual hopes that He will do the same for us. Therefore, the power and by that token, the genius, of the sacred texts is in placing the burden of interpretation upon the readers themselves, and through the assumption of mystery, place the task of relating such texts to present events upon the one determined to believe. By supplanting will for exegesis, it is where our trouble began."*

"Huh." She chuckled. "Well if that doesn't just beat all, eh Nosey?" Distracted by a loose fringe twist, the cat did not reply. Elizabeth began to flip through the pages idly.

"I wonder who writes this kind of stuff?" She said, to no one in particular. "It's like reading Dickens at a Christmas party. One hell of a pretentious performance even if you're pretty sure there's a message in it somewhere. You know, the kind that comes to you sometime after the mulled wine kicks in."

Noseworthy craned his neck, looking up towards the far window with a curious bob or two of his head. For a moment, Elizabeth thought that she could make out a soft tapping sound on the lower panes, four swift tics and a long scrape, before the neighbor's dog whipped into a sudden frenzy of yips and barks. She could hear him straining at the backyard gate, scrabbling his paws in the dirt trench beneath the latch with a deep whooping howl. Every now and again, the noise was punctuated by a short snuffle and a wheeze. She rose to investigate, but by then the tapping had stopped and shortly following, so had the dog.

"Just Benny barking at the trees, Nosey." She sighed, pulling her chair back from the desk and eyeing her cup with trepidation. "Come on. Let's go downstairs. I need more coffee for this."

Picking up both cup and book, she rolled on the balls of her feet and stretched out her lower back in an over dramatic fashion, shooing her furry companion out of the doorway with the loud clap of a block of pages abruptly snapped shut in her hand. From the landing, he looked back over his shoulder at the young woman as she followed, twitching his tail and scowling. She huffed low and critically as she approached, reaching down to soothe his ruffled back with a few conciliatory strokes.

"Oh, quit now." She admonished. "The French Horn is worse."

As she descended the angled staircase slowly, so as not to lose bare-footed traction on the polished wood, she took a moment to examine the book again. It had a cloth covering in a light olive green, gold-embossed lettering in an early American-colonial hand, and visible stitching along the binding, Elizabeth wondered for a moment if the volume that she held had been hand-made: it looked so rough-hewn and informally stamped. Dangling the mug from its handle hooked over her thumb, she opened it at random to another page and rounded the second flight, Nosey just a few steps ahead as he trundled down in advance.

"A child carrying a wooden box is running through a field full of fireflies," She read to the retreating bottoms of Nosey's padding feet. *"And in a burst of sudden inspiration she catches a single firefly, a single spark, in the box. But when she opens the box again later, she finds that the firefly is gone and all that is left are the traces of where it once was."*

She crossed the entryway, through the archway in the living room, and turned left into the kitchen without bothering to glance up once.

"In our books and stories, we catch our single spark. Our boxes, these texts, capturing a piece of light, illuminating for the moment, our own position in a dark expanse. But later, when we open them again, we find that the spark has gone and only traces of where it once had been remain. Too often, we go searching, like children, to find more of these empty boxes. Strewn in a field of fireflies. But we ignore them flitting all around us, still seeking the one that left."

She dropped her arms with a heart-heavy splutter, setting the book down onto the linoleum countertop near the sink.

"God that's sad." Nosey meowed resolutely in response, taking a few habitual turns around his empty food dish. "I guess our old friend Somerset here doesn't think too highly of the light of inspiration and the indomitable human spirit." Theatrically over-stressing the first syllable of each word to make clear her sarcasm. "Though I really have to say, when it comes to piles of musty medical books, she's not too far off the mark. Hnnnn. Maybe she was pre-med once too."

She left the book there, on the counter, turned to the *Analogy of Fireflies* as she set about to brew a new pot of very black coffee, bending and twisting her neck and shoulders to work out the kinks that had settled in over the past several hours. Saddened that this little late-night foray into the kitchen wasn't likely to net him an extra midnight snack, Noseworthy took one last lap around the water bowl before scampering across the tiled floor and leaping up gracefully onto the counter. From there, he sauntered over to the *Lostwith Notes* and sat down, dangling his tail into the sink and catching a few stray water droplets from the faucet.

A passing breeze through the open kitchen window tousled his fur and caught up in the slightly skewed pages, turning the *Analogy of Fireflies* backwards through a section that was bolded as *Arguing with Imaginary Women*, to *The Maimed Hand,* and finally coming to rest at a place where the binding had been worn into a permanent crease, *Beauty and the Abyss. "I had to write it all down somewhere..."* it began, *"It might as well be here."*

From very early that morning, a thick haze had slowly settled in every town up and down the eastern seaboard. Characteristically gloomy and overcast in that ominously coastal fashion and whenever the drizzles of fine mist rolled out during the late afternoons, Amherst, Massachusetts became a drowned, sopping, and wretched thing. Through curtains of grey-green and white, the streets closed in all around, with the flattened façade of old red-brick structures and antebellum brownstones hanging like a series of gigantic paintings on the walls of a gallery blurrily out of view.

On occasion, when the wind decided to dash in over the Quabbin Reservoir, a few splatters of rain might accent the mood with a splash straight to the forehead. Nightfall hadn't improved matters much, and even now the first volleys of a windstorm brewing up the coast rattled Old Squat to its colonial bones. The house groaned, unsteady for lack of care and proper nourishment. And as if to argue the point further, Benny once again took up a fresh round of pacing in the back gardens across the walkway.

Still waiting on the coffee to dribble itself into a standstill, Elizabeth shivered and curled her fingers into her sweater with an irritated sniff. Huddled into the knit of her collar, she spied the open kitchen window and rolled her eyes with a frustrated growl; clearly the absent-minded work of one of her roommates, perpetually oblivious as they were to the frigid nighttime temperatures and the necessity of saving on the heating bills in a house warmed only by century-old hot-water radiators. The clock above the window struck 3am with tinny chimes and the clatter of a tiny hammer on a broken hinge. She made to reach for the sash, casting an impatient glance to the coffee pot, but was startled backwards when Noseworthy stood suddenly and bawled out sharply, eyes narrow in warning.

"Nosey!" She scolded, shocked breathless, as the orange cat balanced precariously at the very edge of the counter before leaping onto the rolling kitchen island, and then turning around again to stare worriedly back at her.

“You shifty booger, you scared me!” She mocked with a playful swat in his general direction. But Noseworthy, though not typically an anxious sort of cat, would not even acknowledge the gesture. He remained alert and fixated, paws flexing and unflexing against the well-chopped wood block. The tense posture and raised haunches seemed so very unlike him, with his spindly legs half askew and tall ears wound-up straight to attention. Elizabeth followed his gaze right through her chest and wheeled about to see what had him so agitated, shifting his front paws back and forth as though he was in a precursor to a vigorous pounce.

Through the darkness came two birds, bounding through the cross-drafts with exceptional ease. Without pretense, Sparrow and Wren alighted on the windowsill. Sparrow, to his name, was the common sort of *Passer domesticus,* with a brown head, a grey body, and a black swipe across his pinched, flea-ticked face. Wren, only an ounce smaller by comparison, was more reminiscent of a vintage Robin Redbreast; an orange stain spreading unevenly over his chest and belly.

However, his needle-sharp, upturned beak and equally vertical pert tail feathers flicking in the wind announced his passerine heritage. In contrast, though, he had retained the dumpy, rounded, body, so well suited to the dark crevices of his preferred prey, but it seemed thinner than it ought to be. They hopped and flitted about for a few brief seconds, eyeing girl and cat suspiciously with the familiar cocked head and sideways glare of miniscule songbirds.

“Oh.” Elizabeth let out a long, relieved, breath. “That’s what this is all about then. Nosey wants to chase the birds. I should have figured.”

Sparrow warbled something out tunelessly, more like a chittering that was all phrase and no harmony but still recognizably bird-like in cadence and tone. Wren responded, though much more melodiously than his counterpart, and fluttered down out of the window and onto the open book. Elizabeth watched curiously, and Noseworthy with great agitation, as the tiny bird skittered about on the pages, appearing to read the words printed there out loud by turning his head from side to side, peering down closely, and enunciating each chirp with a final trill.

The scene was all so strange that, for a moment, Elizabeth began to wonder if she was simply dreaming the entire thing; face-down and drooling on an anatomy book, asleep at her desk upstairs. Wren continued his little caper, springing from page to page and twittering out a series of notes as if to dictate his own review of the material. When he fluttered his wings enough to turn a page, Elizabeth dared to take a single step closer. A knot in the pit of her stomach telling her that something was abruptly not right in the world.

The first item to catch her attention appeared to be a wire wrapped around the leg of the Sparrow still perched on the windowsill. Two ends twisted together trailed behind him and she thought she could make out a tag of some sort at its end. It was rectangular, with a hole neatly punched at the top, and made of yellowed card stock which trembled in the wind but did not fold or curl. Whenever it angled upwards, she could make out handwriting in flowing but badly faded pen-strokes; a Linnaean name, a place; London, and a date; ending with 1909.

"A specimen tag?" She offered incredulously. It was enough to warrant Wren's sudden attention, and he turned to face her, his tiny clawed toes gripping a dog-eared page-corner.

Elizabeth took in a shaky breath, careful not to inadvertently look away from what she still could not entirely believe she was seeing. The Wren...had no eyes. In fact, now that she was a bit closer, it appeared that Sparrow didn't either. Where little black beads and diminutive lashes ought to have been, there were white puffs of cotton stuffing rolled into place for shape and substance. Where there should have been smooth downy feathers clean from ruff to breast, she could make out the stitches of an untalented taxidermist. Feathers, which had previously seemed so regular, were ragged from mothballs and one-hundred and seven years forgotten in a museum drawer. She gasped. These were dead birds.

The heat of dawning horror began to creep into her neck, and Elizabeth took a single involuntary step back. For a second she thought to reach out towards the book but couldn't make sense of her thoughts long enough to decide on any specific response. From his position on the kitchen block, Noseworthy sprang into action. It was some four feet between him, the book, and the bird but he made the jump with two acrobatic turns of his tail and landed, claws out, with a crash straight into the sink.

An unholy scream burst out of the Wren as he was knocked upside-down into a stand of wooden spoons, but he recovered quickly, rolling over and standing upright with feet splayed and wings arched over his back. Noseworthy glared at the intruder over the rim of the sink, yellow eyes squinting into a feline sneer. He then delicately placed his front paws, each in careful turn, onto the side of the book's cover before pulling himself up onto the counter in one fluid, stalking, movement.

Stunned beyond capacity for words, Elizabeth stumbled, nearly tripping and knocking herself cold as she grabbed onto the kitchen island for support. She watched as the sly ginger cat slunk low to the counter, his gaze locked onto a little bird determined to hold his ground and stare him down. Her eyes darted up to Sparrow still peering out onto the scene from the windowsill and what she saw next she could not, even into her later days, adequately describe. From beneath stiff wings she observed two fleshy arms emerge and when the Sparrow's head tilted back, a face from underneath the black and white bars on its throat.

The skin of the partially revealed little creature was white and flaking, like birch paper, but pressed over knotted limbs the width of a twig. When it contorted its face, with its too-wide milky-white eyes, in some gesture of speech, it emitted a harsh and atonal sound as a simulacrum of birdsong. When the sinister creature moved, the miserable bird moved in concert; not in the manner of a puppet and a puppeteer, but as though the bird had made its way into the clutches of some obscene avian necromancer reanimating mummified flesh to whatever bizarre errand might be conjured up at the time. A tortile, sinuous imp of a creature wearing the preserved carcass of a bird and commandeering it as a vehicle of flight as though it were a live one.

There were also no additional feet, other than the legs and toes of the bird, that she could make out, and in her somewhat dissociated state, Elizabeth briefly wondered if the creature had them tucked up inside the belly of the bird; riding around in its body like a tiny corpse bomber plane. From the feathers obscuring his sides, she then watched with sickening dread as Sparrow produced what looked like a sword of sorts. It was a broad flat thing, not more than two or three inches in length, with an ignoble twist in the blade and a tarry coating that dripped from the end. The translucent eyes of the imp tremored slightly and fixed on the cat stalking past the window below all the while a smile of prickly, hair-like, teeth began to spread over its lips.

Shaken from her frozen reverie, Elizabeth screamed at the creature, grabbed her half-full cup of boiling-hot coffee and flung it straight at the windowsill.

"Nosey! Look out!"

Sparrow had but seconds to duck as the clay mug sailed cleanly out the window, dousing the sink and frame with a rain of steaming Sumatran. In the momentary confusion, Elizabeth lurched forward and grabbed both Noseworthy and the book; though more precisely, she had grabbed ahold of Noseworthy who had reflexively grabbed ahold of the book in a failed attempt to not be pulled from the counter. And with both arms wrapped protectively around the now frustrated and yowling cat she raced into the living room intent on reaching the stairs (though to what end had not yet occurred to her).

The two homunculi were not far behind as they shot out of the doorway on borrowed wings, brandishing their tiny sabers and tittering an angry battle cry. Unfortunately, before she could reach much further than the living-room sofa, Sparrow struck, smacking full force into Elizabeth's face and slashing at her eyes with a quick riposte while she was blinded by the bird's flailing feet and flapping wings.

Succeeding only in cutting her cheek, Elizabeth dropped the squirming Noseworthy to swing wildly at her attackers. Wren dove in next, sinking his blade into her shoulder but for all his well-aimed precision, it ended when a solid hit from the book in the young woman's hand sent him careening through the air and into the end-table lampshade. Spying his chance at last, Noseworthy scampered forward, deftly avoiding his mistress's trampling feet as she continued to swat madly at Sparrow who whirled overhead, and flung himself onto the couch and then onto the end-table to finally do battle with the grotesque and squawking little bird-flesh hobgoblin.

Elizabeth continued her fruitless defense. Several more wounds opening up on her forehead, across her chin, and into her hands as she tried in vain to repel the Sparrow's relentless attacks. Against the deadly spike in his hands, she had only *Lostwith Notes* as a shield and already the book's cloth covering was showing the injuries of close combat. Bits of thread and paste-board, along with downy feathers and dander, began to swirl around the room as Elizabeth tried desperately to gather both her wits and a workable strategy.

But in the late-night dreariness, complicated by the dim light still filtering out of the kitchen, she could barely see the two birds as they sped up, down, and around in every conceivable direction. A thrown pillow missed its mark by a long shot and she immediately regretted not picking up a knife or pan from the kitchen when she had the chance. Another barrage of blows and she felt the bridge of her nose crack as blood began to spill down her face.

Coughing and gagging, she flailed her arms around her head and momentarily felt her elbow connect with something, but in an instant, it was gone. She glanced around, ducking her head below the book in her right hand with her left covering her nose. Still unable to see where the attacks were coming from, she made a sudden break for the kitchen, wiping a handful of blood on the doorjamb as she passed.

"There's a pan on the stove. Pan on the stove, come on!" She stuttered through the pain, inwardly screaming at herself to act and to act fast. "Just have to get to where I can see them. Just have to see where they're coming from! Gah, where am I going?! Which way...no, back...Back way..."

She heard the screech behind her as she skidded to a stop, her nails scrabbling along the countertops for purchase; heard the flapping wings descending from above, and then, she reeled and everything around her fell deathly silent.

Silence had always been an eerie thing for her.

Like a blank canvas, it has the potential to be anything one might imagine it to be. Not a masterpiece in and of itself, it defies interpretation; ready to be filled up with all the ascetic desires of the listener. But this silence was not the normal absence of sound, rather, it was more like an overabundance of noise, everything deafeningly loud and all mixed together so that no particular strain could be discerned nor any direction wherein it might have come from fixed.

It throbbed with a life of its own, reverberating in her core as though it too were a living thing come to possess her and order her about. Elizabeth pulled her hand from her face and squeezed her eyes shut against the incomprehensible din of echoes retreating into the distance. She was dizzy and nauseated and tried to wipe as much of the blood from her face as she could, some still trickling into her eyes from the gashes stinging her forehead. She clutched at her stomach to stave off a fresh wave of vertigo and tried to get her bearings.

She steadied, but not before an unexpected calm descended over her and she was able to finally breathe deeply again. Something like the shimmering tone of a bell settling over a room for meditation accompanied by nothing but her own heartbeat and her own breath harsh in her throat. She opened her eyes. The one thing she knew immediately was that she was certainly no longer in the kitchen. In fact, she did not recognize this place at all.

A fine dust hung in the air, with a few flecks of white dandelion and bits of feathers floating down out of filtered moonlight. She stood at the end of a hall, a lengthy expanse of doors behind her and a single door before her. What little light might illuminate her surroundings came peeking through a skylight overhead, looking up onto a passing half-moon so choked with clouds that not a single star would join it.

She felt as though she might be in some subterranean warren or a monastery, where an entire unseen world lay hidden under the cover of the obsolete. But how it came to be that it would exist just a few steps off of her kitchen, she hadn't a clue. The door itself was dust-caked and old, with the kind of latch and ribbing that might betray it for a three-masted ship's door if not for the building packed in all around it. On the wall, nearest to the drop-handle, a bloody handprint, but for the rest of the décor, a most vile shade of apricot. The birds were gone and no winged noises implied their presence elsewhere. She looked all around again and again. No Nosey. No one else at all.

She glanced down at her own hand, still smeared in blood, and on impulse raised her fingers to compare it to the print. They seemed a match, but not for the fact that the print on the doorjamb had clearly been there for some time. It was hardly even raised or cracked; rather a simple brown stain soaked into the wood. She pulled her hand away and made for one more scrub at her face to clear her vision fully.

She wondered, at first, if she hadn't somehow entered some old cathedral, like the one she remembered from a visit to Strasbourg years ago. But the tympanum above this door did not house a collection of famous saints as one might expect from a church. Instead, it appeared to be a carving of foliage with a small horse, a wolf, and a woodsman kneeling with an ax.

The remnants of hand-painted lettering, some still in beeswax resin colors and the rest just smoothed impressions where paint had worn away, remained on the upper central portion of the door. She raised a finger to trace it out: Dry Storeroom 1.

Without context or further direction, forward seemed the only viable option and, thankfully, the handle gave easily. But she did not enter right away. Instead, Elizabeth opted for the cautious approach and simply pushed the door open far enough to hear the clang of the inner latch on the opposite wall. She swallowed once and lowered her head beneath the lintel.

Having spent the better part of her undergraduate years picking her way through various comparative medical collections, Elizabeth Pennybaker had no trouble what-so-ever in identifying a museum storage room, piled high with out-of-date exhibits necessarily kept out of sight and other detritus the history of scientific exploration might rather forget. She thought back to her medical texts, some of which were still piled on her desk (and a few equally and just as painfully dated), and wondered if, in some way, she was wandering through her books.

She wondered if she hadn't been right the first time and that she was still dreaming, with diagrams of leg bones and dissected veins and arteries stuck to her cheek while she snored indelicately. With a sudden thought, she looked down and around the floor near to where she had first arrived, and to her confused delight, found *Lostwith Notes* lying in a heap at her feet. Picking it up, torn and tattered from her earlier experiences, she tapped the dust from its ruined cover and tucked it securely in the crook of her elbow. It somehow felt necessary to have it along, though she could not explain why.

Mindful of where she stepped, Elizabeth crouched low to clear the door and took in the oddities of Dry Storeroom 1. What occurred to her first was in regards to the overall nature of the displays she saw, shoved haphazardly as they were into every corner. These were the Victorian kind of museum arrangements; the ones that were organized systematically by taxonomy or specimens laid out in ranks like evidence presented at a trial, completely unadorned save for their neat, hand-written labels.

These were the kinds of exhibits that existed when museums only had one manner of story to tell. Animals and plants posed with an eye towards dramatic themes or minerals laid out in a pageant of colors, types, and histories. Stacks of drawers with row upon row of beetles and butterflies, a bit chipped and ragged, or trilobites and ammonites separated out into strata as an homage to the rocks they came from. And then there were the birds, two hundred or more, in a massive glass case wheeled against the far wall, partially covered with a painter's drop-cloth. They told the story of the collector. They bore the rot of the collected.

Thoughtfully, Elizabeth ran her hand over the bird case, smearing away some of the accumulated dust as a chill ran through her. Several specimens were clearly missing, the outlines of their preserved bodies pressed into the foam backing. She turned around, both aghast and in awe, of a shelf of snakes in formalin jars. In the decades since their deaths, they had lost their brilliant colors and now hovered like ghosts suspended in their preserving spirits. Behind them a second row of jars filled with turtles and academically pickled eggs.

Near to the floor was a block of carved human heads meant to show the defining characteristics of races, labeled Caucasoid, Mongoloid, and Negroid: a sad reminder of encroaching scientific racism hidden beneath the partial remains of a stuffed zebra head. In the time long before she had fully settled on medical school, she remembered showing her mother an old textbook description of the supposed traits of the different types of Man. Having emigrated from India as a child, she had wanted to ask her mother if any one such type appealed to her or where she thought her daughter might fit into the labels, given that Elizabeth's father was of Irish descent.

Elizabeth then frowned, remembering the look of sorrow on her mother's face. Padma Pennybaker was a proud, educated, woman whose family had made great sacrifices to ensure her every opportunity since the deaths of her own grandparents, Elizabeth's great-grandparents, and several of her grandfather's sisters following the violence of Partition. All that they had brought with them were two icons passed down through generations: a great Ganesh who sat in the garden, and a secret Kali who only ever made appearances at funerals.

And here now was her own young child, innocently holding out the colonialist's menagerie and pointing to a caricature of herself in a book printed more than a hundred years before she was born, and asking if it was her. With a looming sadness, Elizabeth continued to take in the shambles of Dry Storeroom 1. It now seemed less like a forgotten museum storage room and more like some terrible recess in her own mind; a dark corner of bad memories made manifest that she would much rather have permanently forgotten.

It made more sense that way; with clear categories of knowledge and learning and ordering ineptly pushed away from any connections that someone might make between them, packed away out of sight because they could not be divorced completely from the stories they told. It was obvious to her then that the ichthyosaur skeleton hung on the wall above the door was the accusative remains of all of her favorite childhood goldfish that kept dying when she forgot to feed them.

The books of crossed out notes became all the stupid and hurtful things she had uttered out of ignorance or carelessness recorded for posterity. The drawers were the bug collection she brought to her 1st grade show and tell. Painstakingly collected over an entire summer, it was smashed to pieces on the playground by a boy who tauntingly informed her that kitchen cockroaches didn't count. She assumed such words were in reference to herself though, since she had never seen a cockroach, much less collected one.

The birds and the dried flowers pressed in books made of paper-pulp were the memories of a far-away homeland she had never visited, but which seemed so near in the stories her mother and cousins would wistfully tell her. Even the snakes seemed appropriate. Her father had been terrified of them, and had warned her endlessly that she was made doubly unfortunate when it came to the dangers of serpents, supernatural ill-omens as they were in both India and in Ireland.

Unwelcome memories continued to appear out of nothing, only to sink back down so that others might take their place. Elizabeth became more convinced than ever that this was all a horrible nightmare and that she would be quite happy to leave this place just as soon as she could figure out how to wake herself up. It was then that it occurred to her that there was something out of place, something that didn't quite fit in the right way. A strange feeling, really, considering that nothing up to this point had truly been familiar.

It was a scroll, from what she could see of it, rolled up and wedged between a Wright's Ocean Floor Globe and a tea tin on the shelf above the bottled snakes. It wouldn't necessarily have caught her attention if not for the bright-red resin and isinglass wax that had been dolloped across its top seam and the bloody thumbprints still imprinted on the bottom coils. She approached it slowly, still clutching *Lostwith Notes* under her left arm, and reached up to pry the object loose. As she did so, Elizabeth realized that it wasn't a scroll at all, but a piece of thick burlap rolled up over something thin and rounded which drew across the wooden plank with a scrape that sounded like ceramic.

It was also much longer than she had at first anticipated. Only the bottom few inches had been visible from beneath the globe stand. The rest of it, some nearly two and half feet in total, having been slid lengthwise into a hole in the wall, tipped at last from its redoubt until it fell to the floor with an explosive clash. The sound, like daggers of white-golden light through her vision, staggered her. What really should have been no more than a clatter of cloth-object on stone tiles grew into a jarring blow, ringing out and shaking everything in the room clear of its moorings. But then it unseated her mind as well.

A long hallway again stretched out in her vision.

The door at the end, slightly ajar.

A voice crying out, sickness overwhelming the cry until it was consumed to a whisper.

Her name, from spittled lips and then a dying breath.

"Agh, stop that!" Elizabeth heaved over at the waist. "Just stop it!"

She finally broke, "Stop it, stop all of it, stop it! Where am I? What is this supposed to be? A..a...nightmare?! Hell?!" Pressing her palms over her ears she screamed long, loud, and endlessly until she was forced to breathe again or pass out. And then she turned back to the doorway and screamed again. "Is there anyone there?!" Another breath sucked into her lungs, "I said, is anyone there?!"

Nothing and no one answered. She sobbed and stamped her foot, choking again on the leftover blood and bile still caught in her throat. "WHAT DO YOU WANT?!"

She wiped her cheek with *Lostwith Notes* and grit her teeth as she balled up her fists and tried desperately to pull herself together. Bad memories continued to seep into her skin and she felt more tired now than she had ever remembered feeling in her life. Loss. Desperation. Exclusion. Unbelonging.

The air was growing heavier and each time she took a step or examined an object it felt like more of an effort. It hurt to think, it was exhausting to face the memories that arose without warning, and she could not help but feel drained, picked apart, and hopelessly battered. She felt pushed up against the rocks, trapped and confused. Nothing in the past hour or so had made any sense, everything was changing around her at dizzying speeds without reason, and she wanted nothing more right then than to crawl away from it in defeat.

She didn't know what had actually become of her, she didn't even know if Noseworthy, that stupid and brave little cat, was alright or not. If something had happened to Old Squat, or if this is what it felt like to take permanent leave of one's senses. Surrender crept into her body. A winter-like chill, a dampening stilling cold that started in her hands and stole steadily upwards into her arms and chest. Her knees buckled and Elizabeth sat down hard onto the floor, her feet sliding out into the dust.

She could hear the beetles starting to stir on their stick-pins; tiny rasping legs reaching out to pull them free of the mounting board before they tottered their way unsteadily over the lip of the drawer; still impaled like spindle tops through their desiccated bodies. She knew then somehow that they would soon come for her in droves, eating her away until her own skeleton might grace this room as one more forgotten exhibit. The mummified birds began to awaken as well, stiffly kicking out their brittle feet to tap on the enclosing glass. The snakes uncoiled in their jars and pressed their malformed heads to the corks sealing them in.

Elizabeth thought that she just might let them come and do with her whatever it was they intended. It occurred to her that it didn't seem like such a bad end, to die here among all the things so astutely safeguarding her memories. It was a sad place certainly, but it felt homely. After all, it was alright to weep and mourn in a room where no one would be there to see you. A safe space where all her failings might be laid bare, and then cataloged, and eternally revisited. She marveled, in fact, at the degree to which this unfamiliar chamber seemed to suit her so precisely; with all the curated, preserved moments neatly set out for review.

While she certainly had no concrete memory of any such place as Dry Storeroom 1, it felt like somewhere she had visited often; not really located in one identifiable place and not really in any other, just somewhere in-between. A good place for someone like her, she mused. Melancholy pressed on into despair and began to form its first apparitions in the ashen filth settling into her hair, her skin, and her wounds. Suddenly, she thought she saw light glinting off of smooth black skin. Black as pitch with an oiled sheen. Red eyes flickering to life in the depths. From somewhere deep in her psyche, another thought took shape. It was an arrogant thought; ungenerous, ungrateful, and rude. It revolted inside of her.

She didn't want to be here. It was time to leave.

Her foot grazed the cloth-bound bundle still lying on the floor. Brushing a large approaching scarab beetle out of the way of her hand, she reached out and pulled a few frayed threads in order to yank the burlap free. It did not give. Pursing her lips, she tangled her thumb and forefinger into the leading corner and whipped her arm up with a flourish, unrolling and unraveling the package with a tear of burlap and paste. What tumbled out did not ease her confusion.

What lay there on the floor, pivoting slightly back and forth over the uneven ground, a single silver white spire the length and breadth of a fencing dagger. A spiral sort of horn, if she was to be precise; a flawless braided twist of fibrous cast-off that, under normal circumstances, would be a very dull prize. But this was no ordinary natural thing, and though traces of white hairs and skin still held fast to its shattered base, even now stray bits of light could occasionally be seen through its strands. From beneath a sinewy husk, a glowing core shone from within.

It was a fine thing for Elizabeth to stare down at its intricately unblemished beauty and she even took notice that she was wont to smile at its subtle twists and spirals and to want to trace her fingers through each winding quirk and plume. As its light broke through the murkiness, she smelled the warmth of sunshine, and heard the hush of wind in a field of golden wheat, rolling and undulating in a summer storm. She heard a whisper from somewhere far away, in a poetic cadence of voice not unlike her mother's.

"Where would I go, should I see a road? What places are there to be? What is there, if anywhere, that is not otherwise me?"

"What?" She blinked, and looked about the room uncomprehendingly. Her thoughts were chaotic. Who was speaking?

"Where will I be if I am not here?" It echoed disembodied all around her. "And if I am not here, where will I be? Were it not for thee?"

The beetles made haste and skittered away from it, the birds recoiled from their tapping, and the serpents burbled back down into their waters. The horn came to rest in the spaces between slate tiles, pulsing in time to a fluttered heartbeat wracked with suffering. Elizabeth suddenly straightened and pushed herself onto her knees, the words bursting out of her very center, shouted out as through her life depended on it.

"Mama? Where...?!"

Where, indeed? Elizabeth Pennybaker careened wildly as the pan on the stove tilted to the right, knocked off balance when she blundered into it, and a puddle of coffee, still dripping out of the percolator, had now grown to the size of a dinner plate. A second, equally-sized, pool was now also forming on the floor. The window was still open, looking out onto the front lawn. Benny barked in the distance.

She swallowed once for good measure and finally came to a stop, cautiously taking in the scene around her. It was late. The kitchen was quiet, but largely in the same state she had left it. All was well. Just a little spilled.

Wide-eyed, Elizabeth Pennybaker did not move for several minutes.

Slowly, she finally laid the *Lostwith Notes* onto the kitchen island; blood, damage, and dirt leaving it nearly unrecognizable.

"Nosey?" She called out, still too uncertain in the reality of her surroundings to chance much more than a strained whisper. "Here kitty, where are you?"

With all the pomp and circumstance of a triumphant colonel, the marmalade cat with ginger tufts appeared in the kitchen doorway. With rounded cheeks and whiskers held high he minced and paraded around the room with a loud perfunctory purr before trotting gleefully over to where she stood. And with a chest puffed with well-earned pride, he spat the combined bodies of Wren directly at her feet.

Chapter Seven

As the tray wobbled nervously in front of her, Elizabeth carefully pulled back the dry, brittle, bird husk to reveal the once living thing within. She loosened it by cutting away the stitches at the breast and steeled herself for what she might see. She had not slept in the hours since the pitched kitchen battle nor had she done much to patch the seeping wounds in her face and shoulder beyond Collier's antiseptic and a few spare bits of tape. The memories of her ethereal journey, though still quite raw and amorphous in her mind, were, for the moment, set aside in favor of the physical reality before her.

It had already taken her quite some time to gather herself together, dust off, and lay the creature out onto a suitably portable surface, but she had always found that a solid, meaningful, task with clear goals in mind never ceased to set her to rights in times of stress. Something to be done was always better, to her reckoning, than something to be contemplated. Noseworthy had also remained resolute; making repeated laps through the cleared spaces on her desk and occasionally pausing to watch her flick away bits of feather as she worked well into the first hints of dawn.

Bent over her makeshift cooling-pan dissection tray, with an array of instruments cobbled together from the basement utility drawer and an old clay-sculpting kit, she felt something like the revered (if eccentric) surgeon of Philadelphian fame, Thomas Dent Mütter. But rather than staring into the face of Madame Dimanche, reproduced in wax, complete with long, brown, horn extending from forehead to chin, she faced a distinctly different kind of oddity. Here, and not as in Mütter's titular museum of medical curiosities, was the sort of thing that defied rational explanation; not because it wasn't a natural creation but because it did not present itself ordinarily. To her right, *Lostwith Notes* lay open to an equally disquieting page: *Dolorous Nature and What To Do About It*.

She raised a long needle and probed around thoroughly enough to pry the imp from its avian medium. Shaking one arm, and then the other, free from their gnarled grip on the bird, the withered body landed with a soft pang onto the metal. It was an all-together unpleasant sight, to say the least. His head and eyes were deformed, his face awry, twisted into a rictus that could levy the curse of all curses; the whole creature was barely larger or more robust than a sugar spoon. More head than body, dangling spindle limbs capped with fingers and toes half the length of its torso. Its lower lip appeared inverted, and the chin drawn down almost in full contact with the sternum along with several small punctures from triumphant teeth. She glanced over to the book.

"*To remedy evil,*" the first paragraph began. "*The Waysmith should at once endeavor to treat all manner of things, great and small, with all due deference and yet, retain the spirit that her credulity and conscience is owed to no one. She must feel, as deeply as she might gain awareness of the beating of her own heart, that when called to combat she might be fully armed in each respect of the contests presented. To this I advise a (chest) plate to glance the blows of suffering, a strong and confident (arm) in warfare, and a discerning (eye) to impossible riddles. Each shall be called upon in turn.*"

Somewhat further down, she had begun to find the chapter a bit more helpful: "*There are few, if any, strange happenings which are consequent of accident or coincidence. Short of a cosmological event, wherein the explanation for the disaster can be reckoned by astronomical and physical laws, nothing that proceeds from the liminal boundaries of the Way By is truly subject to the antagonizing powers of Nature which have thus so overmatched us. We therefore must be vigilant in our inquiries and mindful of inimical bias when resuming intimate acquaintance to the creatures of Faire and their like. For they have a tendency to hide themselves within the preconceived notions such as we already hold regarding their appearance and to deceive all but the most intuitive with disguises crafted from the finest prejudices.*"

Elizabeth stuck the edge of the razor into the whitish skin at the creature's pulseless throat and drew down to reveal the anatomy within. The segmented structure of the spine, though somewhat more obvious from the back, was revealed by pushing softer bits upwards. In totality, the skeleton of the upper torso mimicked a scolopendromorphic shape, with a centipede-like stacking of cylindrical vertebrae and ribs that curled forward like chitinous legs.

Below that, a papery pelvis in the manner of moth-wings and two swallow-tail legs with tiny long-bones and pendulous feet. The overall color of its insides was a pale lavender; a bluish heart nestled between pink lungs (she could only assume they were lungs), a brown and peach thimble of stomach then perhaps, but nothing below that but what looked like a bubble of water and drops of pearly soap.

The skin bled ash and soot, wafting up from the sagging body as dust-motes in the early morning sunlight. She pulled up a section of chest muscle, or at least some of the grey strands that served as such, and clipped it free with the blunt end of a fingernail scissors. Noseworthy paced around again and sneezed his objection to being so-long deprived of his prize.

It had three true ribs, a wide jugular notch, and clavicles fanned out into four distinct points. Then there were nearly six floating ribs (the legs of the centipede, as she later described it) and an ascending neck that bore the clear indications of the cause of death: a fanged bite straight to the hyoid region which had severed the internal veins. She looked up from her task to Noseworthy.

"Nice work, fuzz-face. Never seen you so much as look at a mouse disapprovingly from across the room and here you are, saving me from...from.... well, whatever this thing is."

She glared down at the tray.

"And what is this supposed to be anyway?! I'd think I was dissecting someone's idea of a gross art project if it hadn't been stabbing me in the face a few hours ago. No sign of the other one though, I'm guessing...." She trailed off with a note of concern.

She picked up the remnant of the bird carcass and turned it over in her palm. It had been completely hollowed out, save for the necessary support bones in its head, back, feet, and wings. Beneath the wings were two tiny holes punched out for the arms and a hood made out of the throat folds just below the beak. On the inside of the body cavity near the tail, there were two small skin rolls for placing knees or feet and a snippet of thread or sinew looped from the end of one wing bone, which poked out at the scapula, to the other. It seemed to have gone slack in the interim. Curiously, she reached in and pulled on it.

The wings of the wretched little bird shrugged and bobbed in time with each tug of her finger. The feet stretched out with toes extended. In some macabre sense, the Wren made as if to land but its movements were jerky and uncoordinated, and it wasn't long before the string ceased to do much at all except to mercilessly twitch the poor creature in unsightly ways. She tried moving other parts of the bird, but found them too stiff to manipulate without threat of continued damage to the already crumbling specimen. She set it back down onto the tray and returned to the imp.

Examining what looked like soapy droplets splattered across the innards, she cautiously swept up a speck or two onto the end of her finger and held it up into the brighter window light. It smelled vaguely of citrus and another substance like moldy leather or wet autumn leaves. Musty, but with a foundation of fresh soil or memories of campfire smoke. She rubbed it between thumb and forefinger to get a sense of the thicker texture; not like blood particularly but similar in the ways that it separated out into several different component parts.

To her surprise, her hand began to shake as the droplet dried into a film on her skin and with sudden alarm she quickly jumped up from her seat to grab the edge of the curtain and wipe it clean; leaving a translucent smear through the fabric. Thankfully, the effect appeared to be minimal and her hand and her nerves steadied in short order. She grit her teeth through a relieved breath.

"That was dumb." She stated out loud, mostly for Noseworthy's edification. "Okay, no more playing around with things we don't exactly understand."

Shooing the ginger cat from his perch at the corner of the desk she gathered up the fairy remains, placing them delicately into a zip-top plastic bag she had been thoughtful enough to pack with tissues beforehand. The bird went in first, wrapped in a paper towel, followed by the body of the imp wound up in plastic wrap. In an irritable after-thought, she even picked up a pen and scribbled "Who Knows" on the white label square at the top of the bag. She then rolled up the entire package and wedged it, along with what had survived of *Lostwith Notes*, into a large cigar box she had previously been using for pencils and lip balm. Noseworthy huffed in protest.

"Sorry Nosey." She called over her shoulder as she dug through the books on her bed for her cellphone. "But I can't let you keep the end of science as we know it, or my sanity, as a chew toy." A sad mewled response was her immediate answer.

"Yes, yes, you were very brave." She reached out to scratch the spot between his ears. "I have to figure this out now though, okay?"

An ardent follower of the adage that a belief in the infallibility of opinion was anathema to scientific inquiry, she found her phone hidden under a pillow and quickly dialed the only possible number she could think of for a second opinion.

"Hi! Aunt Evelyn? Please tell me you're free for lunch today?"

In the ensuing conversation, Elizabeth had made plain her desire for their meeting to take place in relative privacy. For this reason, and because Madam Bel Carmen had remained in the vicinity of the Boston area for several weeks now, they were able to meet half-way, at the Café Etteilla; a cozy if somewhat remote neighborhood diner with a series of enclosed breakfast nooks always readily available for clandestine purposes.

Elizabeth had said nothing of the real motives behind her sudden desire to meet other than that she was under the impression that her aunt, versed as she was in certain esoteric disciplines, might offer her some much-needed advice regarding an unexpected problem she was having at school. Figuring that "a problem" and "at school" were just truthful enough for the present moment. To her profound relief, her aunt was delighted to hear from her and was available at once. So, Elizabeth packed the cigar box securely in the front seat of her car before setting out immediately, that she might arrive at her destination at a proper time.

As the signposts passed and the early commuter traffic thinned, she was grateful for the calming hum of the hour-long drive; glancing down at her directions from time to time to remind herself of the correct highway exit near to Worcester. As she mulled her situation over further, she silently cursed herself for not having taken the time to get to know her estranged aunt a little better back when Elizabeth had been a small girl aspiring to greater (if implausible) adventures and the whirlwind of life was a little less chaotic.

Madam Bel Carmen, then Evelyn Chanton-Pennybaker, had been married to Elizabeth's father's brother Eirnin, the eldest of the three Pennybaker boys. Upon his passing from an undiagnosed heart condition only a few years later, her family had not maintained much in the way of contact with the newly widowed occultist woman whom many of them blamed, directly or indirectly, for the death of her husband. Irish-Catholic by inclination, the Pennybaker men nonetheless had a long history of marrying women far outside such traditions; Elizabeth's own mother, Padma Balakrishna, being one of the most recent of them and Evelyn Chanton another.

Following Eirnin's passing, Elizabeth didn't know much of what had become of her aunt short of the few letters and cards she always received on important occasions, chiding her to focus on education and character-building experiences above anything else. She also saw her at the occasional family gathering and spent some time with her as a school-aged child, but as she had been very young at the time of her uncle's death, they had drifted apart by the time Elizabeth was in her mid-teens.

According to her mother, when asked by the always inquisitive young Elizabeth, why her aunt's name had changed so much in the ensuing months and years, she received only the explanation that "Bel" was in some reference to her standing in paganic religious circles; derived from an old Mesopotamian word for "master" or some such thing, and that Carmen was a Latin back-translation of the Haitian-Creole "chanton," meaning "song."

By no means meant as any sort of rejection of her transatlantic African heritage, Evelyn Chanton-Pennybaker had chosen to change it at the same time as she had formally and legally dropped her married name. Opting then to reinvent herself entirely without, as she had put it, "the burdens of names that others might presume to choose for her." As for the "Madam" she could only speculate and once told her daughter that, given the complexities of Madam Bel Carmen's character, that she had likely adopted the moniker under the antediluvian rules of polite etiquette that stated that it should be used whenever a lady's name was not otherwise known.

As this was routinely the case for one Evelyn Chanton-Pennybaker turned Bel Carmen, Madam had merely come to supplant the common confusion. But in Elizabeth's case, a simple "auntie" would do. Humming quietly to herself, Elizabeth finally turned off the main roads and found the Café Etteilla with thankfully relative ease. It was located amongst a series of New England furniture shops and antique stores on a rubbly lane between the towns of Sturbridge and Auburn, just a few minutes off of the Massachusetts Turnpike.

She immediately liked it for the two tall, shady, oaks overhanging the porch-like entrance and for the sparse foot-traffic of bargain-hunters trolling the sales of dinner chairs and Revolutionary War-style knickknacks. It had the kind of indifferent neighborly atmosphere she preferred to pubs or restaurant bars, whose hospitality was mostly proverbial and alcoholic.

Whereas the family-owned diners of more rural Massachusetts had retained certain charms, set up as they were in old estate houses or historical inns; attractive primarily for their former associations than for their conspicuously off-kilter construction. It was precisely the kind of atmosphere she had always imagined her eccentric aunt to be the most perfectly at-home in – perusing the dusty detritus of history with all the other people who found it as endlessly fascinating as she did.

Her strongest memories of her aunt had always involved the picture of her, swathed in brightly colored scarves and flowing skirts, holding aloft some broken trinket or another as she went on at length about its history, uses, and reasons for becoming obsolete. Evelyn Bel Carmen had enjoyed, when she could, taking her young niece on walking tours of various rubbish sales throughout the small towns dotting the country-side and regaling her with all manner of stories about enslaved witches, hearth women, secret practitioners of local wisdom, and the often strange and exciting objects they used to accomplish their crafts under the ever-watchful eye of the Protestant ministers.

Now more than ever, Elizabeth wished for those days again so that she might pinch herself into greater attention. She had retained so little of what she had been told and was constantly surprised with the feeling of how much she must have missed in that time. On entering the café, she was, however, even more surprised to find said aunt already waiting for her; steaming cup of fresh café au lait raised level with her head as she questioned the cook not far behind the ticket counter, toiling at his stove, on the state of the eggs he was scrambling.

"Aunt Evelyn!" She called out cheerfully.

The woman turned, "My dear, dear, Bitty-beth!" She responded, brightening the mood instantly with the use of an old childhood nickname. "My goodness girl, it's been ages." She stopped then, taken aback, catching full view of her.

"My God!" She exclaimed. "Look at you! Elizabeth Pennybaker, what on Earth happened to your face?"

Elizabeth, cigar box clutched tightly in hand, obliged the matronly inspection with an ironic twirl-around and a curtsy before sidling up to the counter.

"It's alright, Aunt Evelyn, really. I promise I'll explain. I'm just so glad you came. I just...well.... I guess I just really needed to talk to you and..."

Madam Bel Carmen set down her cup with a note of reprimand.

"Nonsense. And there won't be another word about it. If something's troubling you, and I most certainly can see that there is, then by graces we'll have it out. There's no sense in apologizing for asking for something already happily given. My goodness, what a mess. Now then, let's find ourselves a table. There's a quiet little alcove just there at the back, behind that divider wall. I think that ought to do nicely."

In short order, they collected their drinks, placed their orders, and retired to the small space beyond: a square table in natural cedar and two straight-backed chairs conveniently nestled beneath a window.

"Now." Madam Bel Carmen began, gently touching her finger-tips to the bandages at her niece's nose. "What sort of trouble is all this?"

"Aunt Evelyn," Elizabeth began hesitantly. "Do you remember that old book you sent me for my birthday a few months ago? The one called *Lostwith Notes*?"

Madam Bel Carmen knit her brow and nodded, rolling her hand in a gesture meant to encourage her niece to continue.

"Where did it come from? Do you remember?"

"Yes? Of course, naturally so." She swallowed the hot coffee with some difficulty before continuing. "It was one of two copies I chanced across while visiting a rare book shop in Branford near New Haven. There had been a recent dismantling of an estate belonging to a very old woman by the name of Armistead-Carter, I think, who had left a rather extensive library of what-nots. Her children sold the bulk of it off and I was simply lucky to have arrived at the shop on the day they were setting it all out. But my heavens, darling, what does all this have to do with that?"

Elizabeth took a breath and prayed for sanity, staring down into the swirls of coffee with only the mildest hope of divination. "I need to tell you a story, Auntie. And it's a really incredible story and all I'm asking is for you to hear me out. And, if I'm being honest with myself, I'm not even all that convinced yet that telling anyone is really a good idea but...right now...I'm not sure what else to do. No one else would believe any of what I'm going to tell you. Not even sure I believe everything I'm going to tell you. So, before you say anything, just remember that if we have to, we can just forget about the whole thing and hopefully pretend I'm not crazy."

Madam Bel Carmen nodded, concern beginning to strain the deep folds of apprehension above her eyes.

Elizabeth slowly set the cigar box on the table before her. Taking care to upend the lid where her aunt could not easily see its contents, she produced the sorry remains of *Lostwith Notes*. Most of its pages were bent or warped, leaving the impression of having been soaked through to the center. Torn beyond recognition if not for the barely legible embossed title, its front cover was nearly split in half, with bits of binding hanging by loose threads. The blood-stiffened cloth not unlike the coats worn by Victorian surgeons as a badge of honor in the days before antisepsis. Madam Bel Carmen's worries only grew deeper.

"Last night," Elizabeth began, "I was working on my anatomy lessons. And, well, everything was very normal. It was late, probably well after midnight. Nosey, our cat, was being a pain as usual. And I happened across this book that you had given me. Just sitting there on my desk."

Elizabeth blanched slightly, still unsure as to how exactly she might convey the following events. "I just, I'm sorry Aunt Evelyn, I really have no idea how to say this without it sounding completely mental."

Madam Bel Carmen reached across to grasp her niece tightly by the wrist. "However it comes out, it comes out. I'm inclined to believe more than you might think these days."

She nodded. "I went down to the kitchen to make some more coffee and I was just, casually reading I suppose. Those parts about truth and fireflies and whatever it was about not seeing things as they really were and I get downstairs." Here she began to fidget absently with the book again.

"And as I'm waiting on the coffee these two birds just...fly in through the window. Little birds, you know, like a couple of sparrows. No big deal, right? Could happen anytime. But. Aunt Evelyn...they.... weren't birds. They weren't birds at all."

"How do you mean?"

"They were something else. Like goblins. Or fairies."

Madam Bel Carmen froze, her jaw beginning to tremble despite her efforts to remain steadfast and unreadable.

Elizabeth, interpreting her aunt's uneasiness as something else entirely, rushed on. "They were awful. These little creatures of some kind with tiny arms sticking out the sides and horrible faces inside the body of a bird; riding around in it like a...like a.... I don't even know how to describe it. I thought I was hallucinating, you know? Just having a complete break with reality right then and there. And then they attacked me." She held her palm in front of the delicate wrapping over her nose. "They did this. And to the book too. Though, to be fair, I suppose, that was probably because I was trying to hit them with it. Aunt Evelyn, I know this sounds crazy and believe me, I wouldn't be telling you all this if I didn't think I could back it up somehow, but there's more."

"More?"

"Yes," Elizabeth glanced around, wary of any who might be overhearing or an unexpected waitress come to refill the coffee. She dropped her voice conspiratorially. "I was trying to fight them off, I really was. We were all over the place. The kitchen, the living room, the entry way even, but it was so hard to see and I think I just made a run for it. I ran back into the kitchen and I was looking around for a pot or a butcher knife; you know, anything that I might be able to use. They just kept coming and diving and, I mean, it was insane. Fighting off demon birds and then there was Nosey and he's yowling and shrieking and...."

"Elizabeth." Madam Bel Carmen placed one hand gently on the top of *Lostwith Notes* and the other on her niece's arm. "Slow down. It's alright, I promise."

Elizabeth tried to relax her shaking. "But then, something happened. I.... I wasn't in the kitchen anymore. I was in the kitchen and then I wasn't. Everything was just...gone. I was in.... I'm not even sure. Somewhere. Somewhere else."

Madam Bel Carmen nodded, hairs all along the back of her neck beginning to rise. "Can you describe it? This somewhere else?"

For a moment, Elizabeth was forced into silent contemplation. Everything was tumbling out without adequate preamble and she couldn't help but wonder if her aunt truly believed her or was simply humoring a clearly distraught girl in the midst of a stress-induced psychotic break. Tears threatening to spring forward at the memory of the place she had seen, she wanted to finish the story, and in the same breath her utter humiliation, with some degree of dignity.

"It was a room, like a storage room. In a museum, I think." She tilted her head backwards and sniffled, feeling the droplets forming in the corners of her eyes. "But everything was sort of grey and hazy. Certainly not anything I remember being just off the kitchen, right? But there wasn't anyone else there. Just this room, and it was filled with all these run-down specimens of things. Really old things. You know, like animals in formalin jars and mounted bug collections and stacks of old pressed plants. There was this dinosaur model hung on the wall; it looked like a prehistoric dolphin, and then these cases full of dried birds. And you want to know what's even worse about it? I can still feel it, but I'm having some trouble remembering it now. It's like I can picture it all so clearly when I'm not focusing on anything but when I really try and concentrate on something, it starts to fade away."

"Like trying to remember a dream?"

"Yes! Like trying to remember a dream. But, Oh Aunt Evelyn, I swear to you I wasn't dreaming. I mean, I thought I was for a while even, but it wasn't a dream. This place was real. I know it was real!"

Madam Bel Carmen again paused to squeeze her niece's hand reassuringly. "I know." She said with a strange sort of intensity. "I know, Elizabeth. Go on."

"And I remember thinking that it didn't seem weird at all that I was there. It was like this place was just a regular place I had always been wandering around in and these were just my things like they had always been my things. It felt like I was completely normal in having jars full of snakes and a bunch of old globes and some butterflies bigger than my head. And then I started thinking about all these other moments at the same time. Thinking back to when I was really little and I sat on my bed and cried for hours because my goldfish had died. And when it finally got so bad my mom went out and bought me another one, that one died too because I would never feed it. Or this time when this boy in elementary school broke my show-and-tell project. All these stupid little things from when I was a kid."

Without prompting, she continued. "But then it started to get worse. I could hear my mom crying. Like she did when Grandma Bibi died and she couldn't afford to go back to India for the funeral. Like when she got sick. Then it was a while later, and my dad was there, picking me up and telling me everything was going to be alright even though I already knew he was just trying to hide all the pain he was in. I felt that moment right before I saw my dog Joey get hit by a car. You know that feeling when you can see what is about to happen but there's not a thing you can do about it? But a part of you already knows that something precious in your life is being taken away? It's this fear that just tears into you and then it stays there, holding on and holding on inside of you until you can't even remember what it was you were supposed to be afraid of. So instead, you're just angry. It was like every memory that was like that all flooding in at once. All these horrible things, Aunt Evelyn. Why was I thinking about all these horrible things?"

The waitress bustled in, laden with syrup and breakfast plates and an amiable chirp. Madam Bel Carmen and Elizabeth Pennybaker accepted their meals with strained smiles.

"If I was to hazard a better comparison," Elizabeth poked at her eggs. "I'd say I was in one of those Barnum funhouses, but not the ones that are supposed to make you laugh. This was more like the ones that are made to show you all the worst things about yourself with screwed-up mirrors and clowns in cages. And I was just...... stuck there. All I wanted was a little more coffee and maybe a few hours' sleep but instead I'm crashing through the house, beaten up by a couple of monster bird-goblins and then I'm tossed out into some kind of...of.... Purgatory! It doesn't make any sense! I was NOT hallucinating! But I was there! Last night this all just happened, I swear! Real as you and I are sitting here now."

Madam Bel Carmen resolutely took a bite of pancake. She chewed slowly, carefully, and with great decorum.

"How did you escape?" She finally asked.

Elizabeth visibly deflated. "I'm not sure. I'm really not. All I can remember is the overwhelming sadness of it all. But not sad like I wanted to cry sad. Just a weight, a feeling like I didn't want to get up again because my body was just too heavy and I had been carrying it for too long. But also that there really wasn't a point in putting it down because then someone else might try to pick it up again; and who would want that? It's like I was being weaned off of everything happy and comforting and good so that someone could finally set me aside without me making a fuss. And it all felt okay. I wasn't angry about it, I wasn't scared about it. It was just....okay."

"Well something certainly must have happened." Madam Bel Carmen straightened reprovingly.

"Maybe? I don't know." Elizabeth finally chanced a mouthful of sausage. "But you're right, I did get out. Right back into the kitchen like nothing had ever happened. Except for the most obvious thing..."

Before she could continue Madam Bel Carmen interjected. "I know where you were, Elizabeth."

Elizabeth accidentally lost the shreds of hashbrown through the tines of her fork. "I'm sorry?"

"I know where it was you went. I've been there too."

"Aunt Evelyn, you couldn't possibly have been..."

She was interrupted a second time by Madam Bel Carmen's finger tapping fervently on the cover of *Lostwith Notes*. Her polished nail scratching across the only two completely unmarred words still left: Way By.

"It was here. Elizabeth, you were here."

Elizabeth was nonplussed.

"Aunt Evelyn. I've read this book. Cover to cover since early this morning. The author is some kind of philosophical crank. Obsessed with fantasy and imagination like it's going out of style. She's talking about some kind of abstract life of the mind or something. I mean, she has whole chapters about how science and religion and history are all trapped inside this...this...narrative. This story, or whatever navel-gazing head-space she's trying to get at, is supposed to be some kind of fiction that we're all telling ourselves. Or, I guess, more specifically, it's some kind of story that we're all just hell-bent to *keep on* telling ourselves. Because..." She struggled for the words. "Because if we don't, everything stops, we all die, humanity descends into chaos, I didn't really get it."

Madam Bel Carmen was silent for a long time.

"But." Elizabeth idly pushed her fork across her plate before setting it aside. "I can't completely ignore that something happened and that maybe...maybe there is something to it that I'm not quite getting."

Madam Bel Carmen looked up, and for the first time that morning saw the protected vulnerability in her niece's ragged demeanor.

"I know it wasn't a dream. I'm not making it up. I didn't have a nervous breakdown. Because if I did, then I guess I can take comfort in knowing that the rest of the world is going down with me." Elizabeth pushed the cigar box across the table and then placed her hands in her lap, waiting.

With some hesitation, Madam Bel Carmen pushed her plate to the side and positioned the flimsy balsa wood box in front of her. At first, all she could see was a mound of tissue and plastic, with only a slight brownish discoloration in the mix to indicate that there might be anything else within. She also detected a curious smell which she identified as lemony but more like the type of fragrance used to scent leather polish than the actual fruit. Beyond the first layer of packing she encountered a small roll and, with exaggerated fastidiousness, lifted the mass onto the table. Elizabeth stared on solemnly; unsure whether to expect a sudden expletive or a jolt of revulsion to follow the anxious unveiling.

Madam Bel Carmen continued to free the bundle, pulling out each section in turn, until she inhaled suddenly and dropped the thing, wrappings and all, back into the box.

"Elizabeth!" She barely managed to contain the volume of her exclamation. "Elizabeth, by all that is holy, what is that?!"

"It was Noseworthy's doing." She spread her fingers innocently. "After I found myself back in the kitchen, bleeding like crazy and thinking I was about to throw up, he just comes trotting out from the living room with all that, and the bird, in his mouth."

Madam Bel Carmen cautiously peered back down into the box, picking at the assortment of ties and swaddling until she could once again view the body of the imp unobstructed.

"The bird is in the bag at the bottom." Elizabeth added. "It's mummified, like the specimens I was telling you about, but completely scraped out. Empty. This thing was inside it, like I said. Using it like some kind of flight suit. Creepy, disgusting flight suit..." She trailed off.

"And the other one?" Madam Bel Carmen tapped the table for her attention. "Did you not say that there were two?"

Elizabeth nodded. "Yes, but I don't know what happened to the other one. I'm guessing it must have flown away back out the window. I mean, it was still open, so there's no reason to think it didn't. And Nosey hasn't coughed up anything else since."

The enrapt occultist continued to examine the creature laid out now in such a paradoxically funereal manner. Using a napkin to lift matchstick limbs and to gently peel back the outer layer of skin to see her niece's careful evisceration of the upper torso, Madam Bel Carmen noted that the sunlight currently streaming through the window was having an odd effect on the miniscule corpse. The eyes, which were lidless and nocturnal, were beginning to color; from milky-white to a pale orange-red and the translucent skin, which only a moment ago had been a clear map of blue-purple veins, was turning brown and brittle. The veins blackened into root-like scribblings on parchment coverings.

Madam Bel Carmen snapped the cigar box shut.

"My dear." She announced to a startled Elizabeth. "There is really only one course of action for us to take next."

"There is?"

"Indeed." She pushed the box back across the table and into Elizabeth's unsure hands. "I must take you to Somerset Sayer right away. Well, right away as I can get into contact with her that is. She can explain this, I am certain of it."

"Somerset Sayer? This author?" She gestured incredulously to *Lostwith Notes*.

"Dr. Sayer is a folklorist of the highest caliber and an expert in these matters, I assure you. You were not listening to me, I think, when I told you that I knew where it was that you had gone. I know, because, Elizabeth, I too have seen it. This place out of nowhere, where the irrational is rational and the ordinary becomes extraordinary. Where the whole and the reasonable fragment and your mind threatens to leave you bereft, with nothing to hold fast."

Her vehemence cowed Elizabeth into conscientious attention.

"Now let me tell you a story. I have seen a place." She leaned forward, pressing into the table with jittery fingers. "A place that exists without explanation or logic or soundness of sense, where the creatures from fairy tales carry on as natural as you and I are sitting here talking now. I would even daresay call it another world, but I know that it isn't. Elizabeth, this place is real and what is more, it is not even some other alternative dimension, but a part of the world we live in and have always lived in. We can't see it, I don't know why, but it has always been there. The Way By. That is its name."

Elizabeth worked her jaw, thinking she should speak, but then thought better of it as her aunt continued.

"But what I don't understand most of all is how you were able to go into that place and then return, all on your own as you say. I have been led to understand that this is not usually possible. Nor why now of all times since you've never mentioned such a thing before? Much too much a coincidence for my liking. But I have had the esteemed privilege of knowing Somerset Sayer, you see, I have met her in person here on the coast not too long ago. When I first came down this way, I had intended to meet with her about an academic idea of mine, but in just a few short weeks I have had revealed to me so much more. She has this power too. This uncanny, remarkable, no preternatural, ability to walk into and out of this place at will. She speaks of it, in so many ways, like you just did. Like it is a place more familiar to her than even her own hometown could ever possibly be and this place, well, I would say that it seems to know her back. The creatures there, they are no stranger to her than, say, a flock of starlings might be to us. In the book, here in the introduction, do you see it? She has a name for this ability. She calls it Waysmithing."

Elizabeth took a moment to look down at the dilapidated *Lostwith Notes* with a new, if still deeply mired in coping mechanisms, perspective.

"The Way By." She repeated absently. "But...but this is allegory, right? This is all just...a concoction. A parable...a...a..."

"A fairy tale?" Madam Bel Carmen reached across the table and pulled the box lid open.

Elizabeth wasn't sure at that moment if she should laugh, throw the box to the ground and stomp on it until it was no more than splinters, or cry.

"Bitty-beth." Her voice quieted with compassion. "Something extraordinary has happened. I'm so sorry it came to you like this, I mean, I know that if my own initiation had been so terrible, I might not be sitting here, going on and on with such enthusiasm about my experiences. I might be telling you to run and hide and never look back and to never speak of such perverse things ever again. Or that the writer of this book was a charlatan and better off thrown in a swamp for her spreading such reprehensible lies. Or worse, that we're off to see a shrink, hopefully highly recommended. Such an awful ordeal. But you've seen it with your own eyes, and not only that, these... bird-creatures... attacked you out of nowhere, meaning to cause much more than just a few slashes, I think. If you hadn't somehow blundered into this memory room and then back again, who knows what would have happened to you!"

"Dry storeroom number one."

"What was that?"

"That's what was painted on the door." Elizabeth continued to stare ahead unseeing. "I just remembered it. And there was something else too." She cocked her head to the side. "There was something I found, hidden in a wall."

Madam Bel Carmen mutely pushed the cigar box closed again as she again reached out for her niece's hand. "What was it?"

"A sword, I think. But, no, maybe not. A horn? It was wrapped up in some old linens, like cheesecloth, but I think I remember seeing a bright light inside of it." She met her aunt's uneasy stare. "Aunt Evelyn, I think that's how I got out."

"What do you mean?"

"Ugh, it's still so hard to think about it. But as you were talking about 'perverse things' I got this image. I remember finding a horn, or an antler maybe but long and straight, or something like that had been stuck into the mortar between bricks in the wall. It was sitting under something else too but, now I can't think of what it was. But when I saw it, I grabbed onto it, and when I grabbed onto it.... something changed. Something about the room was different. Arg, I don't know, it keeps fading away. But after that, I was home again."

She began to scratch the table in a repetitive motion. "Is it weird that I keep thinking about a lamp? Like a lamp moving underneath the cracks through a floorboard?"

"Well, that settles it then." Madam Bel Carmen leaned out of the alcove and loudly called for the check. "We're going to Dr. Sayer right away. You're going to tell her everything that you've told me here and we'll be taking that eyesore with us."

"Auntie, I really don't think..."

"Enough. There is simply too much at stake. We don't know what happened to you exactly, we don't know why you were attacked in such an uncalled-for way, and we don't know if or when it will happen again. I know, I know, you're just like your mother. All rational explanations and cold, hard, facts. Well, I should say that the cold, hard, facts are right there in your balsa-box and I happen to know just the person we need to set this all to rights again. Isn't that what we are supposed to do after all? Get a consult? Or are you saying that you'd rather chance another incident like this one and pray that your housecat will save you?"

"Hey now." Elizabeth attempted to rally her humor. "Nosey was a brave and valiant protector."

Madam Bel Carmen smiled. "Of course, he was. But there's no guarantee that the next thing that comes through your window, or out from under your bed, will be so easily undone."

She sighed. "Okay. You're right I suppose."

"But," Madam Bel Carmen raised a pointed finger, "I should think that such a bright up-and-coming medical student of your talents would have done a more thorough job and tended to her wounds better than this."

Elizabeth chuckled wryly. "Well, I was a little distracted."

"Yes, well, I can only imagine. I know it's a trip, but why don't you follow me into Manchester? We'll take the freeway around Boston metro. Shouldn't take us more than an hour and a half. Stay with me for the weekend, at least. I'm keeping an apartment there right now and it will give you a chance to clean yourself up and get a handle on things. I'm pretty sure I have some extra clothes that will fit you and if not, a little short-order shopping is gladly done, and I'll see if I can get a message through. A dear friend of mine, Ms. Guthrie, ought to have some idea as to the whereabouts of our evasive folklorist."

If there was one thing Elizabeth knew about the women in her family, it was that when their minds were finally made up, there was little point in disagreeing. But it wouldn't have mattered to her all that much regardless; she was exhausted, confused, and grateful for the faith her aunt had placed in her and for the promise of an advocate. If nothing else came of her experiences, she was coming to appreciate that at least, on a level she could not express. Barring that, it would be a weekend sojourn back into the mystifying wonders of her aunt's eccentric life.

Something her mother had always been keen on limiting. She distressed her thumbnail against the corner of the cigar box. No matter how foggy and distant the memories of the previous night were becoming, the contents of the box could be neither forgotten nor ignored. As was her nature, if she hadn't called her aunt when she did, she might have simply chalked it all up to too many late nights and too much caffeine. The storeroom was already so distant in her mind as to invite easy dismissal. But the box remained. The imagined had, indeed, become the real.

"Alright. Let's go."

Chapter Eight

"I wasn't going to tell you, but..."

For this particular conversation, Fiona had chosen the far end of the sofa across from the armchair her mother typically preferred, figuring she could attempt to anticipate her reactions more quickly. Alice remained among her papers, scattered across the end table and floor as per usual, but maintained the better part of a strained posture. She had immediately taken note of Fiona's unbrushed hair and the characteristic way that the ends of her brown locks stuck together when neglected for longer than a day or two. She had also not failed to notice the darting gaze and avoidant diction that could only mean that whatever it was that her daughter meant to tell her, it wasn't good.

Fiona kept her hands hidden. It was an unconscious affectation, but she had a habit of emphasizing greater points when she spoke with a series of full-body gesticulations and for now she wanted nothing more than to take up as little space in the room as possible. If she had been capable of disappearing altogether, even better. But seeing as this was not the case, she opted instead to turn inwards on herself, drawing in her stomach and pressing her chest downwards onto her knees. She dug her thumbnail into her cuticles and steeled herself. There was just no good time for this. There was no good time for anything anymore.

"I need to tell you something, but I'm afraid that you're going to, you know, get how you get." Fiona toyed with a bit of dried pasta stuck to the side of the couch cushion. "Like, stop listening to me after the first part and I really, really, need you to hear the whole thing, Mom. Okay?"

Alice Guthrie scowled. She had already mentally prepared herself to take the first impact of an on-coming crash but was, by no means, prepared for the brutality of traded blows.

"Of course." She responded automatically. "Fiona, what's going on?"

Fiona took a deep breath and curled her toes against the upholstery, unable to meet her mother's eyes as she forced out the words she had been desperately evading for days.

"I'm pregnant."

The words took several moments to settle in their throats. For the first, they had erupted with the acid taste of vomit and now drifted back down her gullet to churn out her stomach. For the second, they had dropped as a weight onto her tongue and then slowly trickled down to choke out her larynx. When no more words were then forthcoming, Alice made the first attempt to speak but found that she could not force a single sound past the ruins of an imagined future slowly falling in around her. Falling in around Fiona. She buckled beneath the crushing realization.

Alice Guthrie had never been an overly formal sort of person. She did not ascribe to needlessly complicated rules of etiquette or meaningless points of order simply for the sake of avoiding unpleasantness. She was forward but kind, attuned to the occasional necessities of social ritual such as the demands of friendship might require. She always nodded along in conversation to demonstrate her interest (pretended or genuine) and sat with the correct bearings of polite engagement; feet crossed at the ankles, straight-backed, with hands folded in her lap. But now, such things failed her with a noticeable slump to her shoulders. As she stared unblinking, the stricken gleam of tears washed the color out of her eyes. Fiona waited, still folded in on herself and contemplating the weave of the throw.

"Fi." Her mother started, unable to find suitable footing. "Fi, I...I don't know what to say I..."

Fiona rushed ahead. "It's okay, Mom, it really is. I mean, I've already been thinking about it, you know, and I don't want to keep it so..."

"But you don't even have a boyfriend!" Alice Guthrie interjected. The sudden exclamation derailed her and Fiona was forced to regroup, but a few scrambled seconds later she still could not regain her ground.

"I..." Her daughter began. "I...um...." The first wave of tears erupted, leaving Fiona unable to finish the practiced part of her speech.

Despite her initial shock, Alice Guthrie was not outraged. She leapt up from her seat and crashed down at her daughter's side, hauling the girl into a crushing embrace, nearly holding her aloft over her knees. For all the endless ruminating she had done in preparation for this conversation, the girl's meticulous plans were immediately drowned in anxious sobs. There had been too many sleepless nights and too many failed attempts at undoing the new reality which had finally overwhelmed her, reducing her to despair, and introducing her to the first inklings of an urgent solution.

"I don't!" Fiona managed through her mother's sleeve. "It was-there was-I mean, it was just this one time and I didn't even want to but he said I'd be okay..."

Alice froze, her grip on Fiona's arms becoming worryingly tight. "Who said you'd be okay?!"

"Mom please, I can't." She took a drowning breath, "I didn't mean for any of this, I'm so so sorry, I didn't know what to do. Please don't hate me."

"Fiona Guthrie!" Alice pulled the shaking girl up to face her. "I would never ever hate you. Not for this, not for anything else. But I need you to tell me exactly what happened."

Unfortunately, even this could only be a momentary distraction to the pressing issue at hand, but if Alice Guthrie was certain of one thing, her daughter was in trouble and right now this required a level of grit, thoughtful consideration, and proper organized concern.

"I kind of went on a date. Nobody you know I don't think, just this guy from school. It was so stupid. It wasn't even a date really. Just hanging out."

Alice refrained from intervening in the growing self-loathing her daughter was so trenchant in demonstrating. She feared and suspected the worst but needed to have the entire truth out before she made any unforgivable mistakes in her response.

"Anyway, I didn't want to but he just wouldn't stop! I thought maybe if I didn't say anything he'd get bored or something, but I was so stupid!" There it was again. "I should've told him off but it's like it wasn't even really happening. I should've just said no and punched him. I don't know what I was thinking! I just wanted it to be over so I could go home. Mom, I'm so sorry, this is all my fault!"

"Fiona, are you telling me.... are you telling me you were raped?"

"I...I don't know. Yes. I guess. Well, but no, I...I just didn't want to."

"But you said no? You said no to what he was doing?"

"No. I don't know. I didn't really say anything. I don't remember saying anything, just told him I didn't like it. I didn't want him to but then, I don't know. I said I wasn't into that and he just said okay. I didn't...I mean...I don't know."

The truth for which Fiona Guthrie struggled was an ever-present, if elusive, one. Her mother had already drawn her own conclusions about the half-articulated intimations of assault; one where the young woman had said neither yes nor no and had, therefore, been presumed an adequate participant. A vaguely resistant prop. An obstacle to overcome. It was this that Fiona could not reconcile.

Alice Guthrie watched as her daughter continued to try and explain the ambiguities, to organize thoughts that defied chronology or category. She twisted herself into knots trying to work it out as she stopped, started, and then restarted her sequence of events over and over again. She had rejected his advances but not his conversation, and in doing so she had failed to notice that his invitation was actually an assumption.

She had thought to be polite, to not overreact, to play everything off with adolescent aplomb. For this her lack of anger had been held up as agreement. Only a scream revokes permission, she seemed to say. Her face fell. Alice knew the problems with this particular story all too well. She also knew how it ended: the absence of defiance was surely the confidence of consent. But broken, fractured; the words of tales like this one never drained from the wounds they sliced into the soul. They only festered further.

"Then I got sick and I started thinking like, oh crap, what if I caught something because of it. I thought, how am I going to explain getting some kind of awful STD? But okay, you know, just walk down to the clinic and get some pills for it and it would all be fine." Fiona paused, glancing out the window for lack of anything better to help retain her focus. As the scenes of aftermath continued to tumble out, Fiona was reframing her narrative as one where she herself played a more integral role and as a result, her confidence began to return. In the part of a bit player in the scenes of another's life, her voice hadn't been anything more than a post-script. Now, she was ready to present her plan. "But it wasn't that. I just didn't want to believe it and I thought maybe if I just ignored the whole thing it would just go away. God, that sounds dumb."

"Fi, it's okay. You were scared. Oh honey, why didn't you say something? You know I would have been right there to help you! Why didn't you trust me?"

"No! Mom, it's not that! I do trust you, I've always trusted you, it's just that I...I just couldn't imagine telling you. I mean, I know that probably seems really ridiculous right now, but I really couldn't even picture us having this conversation or what I would say or what you would say. I thought you'd be so disappointed in me, Mom. I mean, stupid teenager does stupid thing. How was I going to tell you? I couldn't even believe it was actually happening to me. I kind of still can't. I thought if I just took care of it, no one would have to know and things could just be normal again. And that's the thing, I can take care of it. I've got a plan. That's why I wanted to talk to you now."

"Take care of it? Fiona, what are you talking about?"

Fiona pushed herself up from the couch and began pacing the room idly; partly out of anxiety and partly out of a need to physically re-engage with the world.

"I want an abortion." She blurted out. "I decided right away basically. So, I tried to, I guess, tried to get one. But at the clinic they said I couldn't. I had to have permission. So, I went to another place after that where I thought maybe they wouldn't ask but I chickened out. I just wanted to get it done but I was so scared and I thought they were going to call you and then the whole thing would fall apart and everyone was going to know."

Alice was reeling. Despite Fiona's no-nonsense demeanor and every attempt she was making to appear as though she was completely in control and had made her decisions impartially, her mother knew false composure. Fiona's world had been irrevocably cracked. Terror had long taken hold of her daughter's mind, eating away rationality at a calm and steady pace, and this plan, whatever it might be, was a desperate race against time and memory for a sense of mastery over events that refused to stay in the past. But in the moment, Alice couldn't make sense of much more than her sadness, her rage, and her fears of injustice.

"I've got it figured out. You see, I went to this crisis center and I can get it taken care of there. I've already talked to one of the doctors they have and we've got it worked out and so I...I just need your help, Mom." Fiona returned to the couch and grasped her mother's hand eagerly. "I just need a couple of things and I can get it done. My original birth certificate, I know it's around here somewhere, some gold or jewelry or something I can pay with because they don't do regular credit card-like stuff because of government tracking I guess, and a signed letter, that's all, and then I can fix it."

Alice Guthrie paused.

"What? Fiona, that doesn't make any sense. What do they want?"

"There's this doctor who can do a reversal. The nurse at the crisis center told me all about it. They'll do a pregnancy reversal and it'll be like nothing ever happened!"

"Fiona." Alice was circumspect but her suspicions grew poisonous. "There is no such thing as a 'pregnancy reversal,' sweetheart. This isn't something you can just undo. That's not how it works."

"No, no, it is! Look, I guess it's something maybe new but he explained the whole thing. They can do something to your body and it, like, reverses the process. Just absorbs back in and it's like you were never pregnant and there's no needles or surgery or anything. And also, this way there's no, you know, blood and stuff having to come out of you. But I think it's kind of under the table, maybe. I don't think it's illegal or anything but they were talking like it only works for some people you know? The doctor there said it would work for me!"

The dawning sense of horror Alice Guthrie felt was eclipsed only by the bile acids in her throat. "Fiona. Listen to me. This is a scam, okay? I don't know where you went or what kind of doctor this person claimed to be but someone is lying to you. I'm sorry, sweetheart, but whoever these people are, they are preying on a vulnerable and scared young girl who has just experienced something terrible and traumatic happening to her. No one should be asking you for money or jewelry. There is no such thing as what you are talking about. Maybe for rabbits I think, but not for people."

She steadied herself and continued. "Fiona, we'll go to a real doctor, alright? We'll find a real clinic if that's what you want but, oh, baby, this isn't the way to do this. I'm so sorry honey, but we have to come up with a different plan. You and me, yes? We'll make sure that everything is okay first and then, together, we'll talk about this some more and we'll figure out what to do. We're going to come up with something better. We both just need some more time to think."

Fiona wilted.

"But you're not to go back to that place, understand? We don't need such...charlatans... at a time like this."

In some ways, her mother's understanding and bravery in the face of heartbreak was worse than if she had simply sat through the entire revelation in stony silence. So much of what Fiona was feeling at this point was poised to be reactionary and the weight of empathy was almost too much for her to bear. She sniffled and nodded. Part of her had always suspected that the crisis clinic had been too good to be true, but their promises had just been too hopeful to let go of.

Clean, white-washed walls; children's story books on the tables in the waiting room; a decisive lack of actual medical equipment anywhere; and nurses who looked and spoke more like Sunday school teachers than healers. She had found the place rather by accident one afternoon after getting lost on her way to the downtown Women's Clinic, on the intersection near Francis Street. She had either taken the wrong bus or, as she later surmised, had gotten turned around in the bustle of metro rush hour.

The streets of Boston had the layout of old field roads and where one turn might lead directly to the harbor, a similar one might take you straight up Beacon Hill and into the cramped alleyways of the old colonial slave quarters. From Beacon Hill it was possible to look out over the Boston Common and to see far enough above the office buildings to get a view to Long Wharf, but once a person had entered the tangle of sidewalks, commuters, flying facades, paper begging bowls, and painted shop windows at ground level, it took a special kind of navigator to rightly walk the city.

As with so many places, the best paths through Boston were most often the paths that were only known and never marked. For several anxious minutes, Fiona had been thoroughly lost. But how lucky, she had thought, to find exactly the kind of place she wanted to find after nearly an hour wandering through winding streets and growing more and more panicked as she tried and failed repeatedly to find her way.

The doctor had said that he wasn't one; calling himself a chirurgeon instead. Fiona had laughed at the word, asking him several times how again it was pronounced. With a hard "k" and a long "i" he had said smiling, followed by an "oor-gee-on" he formed by extending his neck and pulling the corners of his mouth backwards and down. Thinking this meant some kind of holistic practitioner or other alternative medicine specialist, Fiona had met with him for nearly an hour in the offices overlooking the fountain. She remembered his odd intensity and the confident way he spoke.

"Now remember," he had said. "Bring everything on the list, it's important that you not miss a thing. There are only three items, so it shouldn't be too troublesome I don't think. See here, your birth certificate, a letter of permission which must be signed, and a little something to pay our costs is all we ask. I know the letter has you worried but don't get too upset and don't try to overthink it. Your grandmother maybe? An aunt? All it has to say is that you are permitted to be here in our clinic and to visit us, that's all. However you want to say it. And when you come back, we'll get it all done just like that. Just a few minutes and it will be over. Nothing to worry about. Don't you think? What do you say? Yes?"

Alice smoothed down a few errant strands of her daughter's hair, still concerned at its unusual straw-like texture.

"Fi? Can you tell me anything else about what happened? About this boy at school?"

Fiona Guthrie shrugged. "Not really. I mean, I still see him around sometimes but I don't talk to him."

"Did you tell anyone at school about what happened?"

"No." Fiona bit back a flash of violent rage. "What's the point? Not like anyone can do anything about it anyway. Everybody likes him, even the teachers."

Alice thought to protest but she decided not to. She didn't need to ask her daughter what she meant by that. If she pressed, she might be able to convince Fiona to speak out about it, to cause some stir and consequence, but with so much already hanging between them she filed that hope away for another day.

"Well," She sighed, "why don't we talk about it more tomorrow then? I think our first order of business right now might be a little dinner. Then, oh I don't know, maybe we can try to rally ourselves. See if our heads clear by morning, what do you think?"

It was an aggravating feeling: Alice Guthrie wanted to demand more, pick apart every possible detail, ask questions, and worry out every feasible scenario and possibility. But more than that, she wanted Fiona to regain some of her strength and to see the driven young woman re-emerge triumphant. At least, triumphant enough to see her way forward from here. Alice wasn't sure what decision she yet preferred or what path she might attempt to convince Fiona to take, but for the moment, she tried not to think about it. Tonight, the only thing that mattered was hurt and fear and the one who possessed its full measure. Even the Fae in her mind had finally fallen away.

Falling was a way to sleep, as spirits understood it. An endless descent into nothingness that mimicked the memory of drifting off into slumber, even if it never brought the dreams they craved. That day, however, the ghost of a young woman was dreaming of an endless railroad. It started with the image of a magical toy train set steaming out from underneath a Christmas tree and ended when the real engine shattered her bones in a bright instant.

Even in the furthest depths of the Way By, Mary Elizabeth Toft could still feel the gaping wounds waving their tattered edges in the puddles on the side of the tracks. Could feel the vibrations even if she could no longer hear them. All from a machine whose bars and ties had cut through her world uninvited, changed the very nature of the possible, and then left her broken in its aftermath.

She stirred, but did not awaken. At times, when she briefly did, she would wander through the places that had grown up in the once ruined path of progress. One such place had taken the form of an old theater with strange plays that she came to watch almost every night. The denizens reveled in the passengers that daily arrived there, all with the benefits of a fast and timely train schedule, because it meant that the audience boxes were always full. Whether they disembarked on foot or were carried only in visions, the Chalk Circle welcomed everyone. Everyone except her, of course. Her, they called by a different name.

Withersmith.

Once it had been Waysmith. Once it had been with reverence. Now she haunted their clapboard town with dread. The curtains fluttered, the marionettes quivered into silence, and all those outside locked their doors and blew out the lights when phantom steps sounded down the hallways. But then another troupe had arrived. A different company of travelers. Garish and loud, they had drawn her attention almost immediately, and she couldn't help but ponder endlessly on each of them.

Though one had seemed even more familiar to her than the others, and it was this woman to whom she turned her thoughts now. She had been a staid, skeptical, sort of woman who struggled to balance whole-hearted belief with protective agnosticism. A woman that Mary Elizabeth Toft had thought much like her own mother, especially when this woman had commented on her sense of faithlessness to others in attendance.

Faithlessness was something that the former Waysmith had known well, and she had thought then that this steadfast lady could make for a fine game. Sport, if nothing else, for the crows circling overhead. Though now, what was more, she was drawn to the pain that had been reverberating across the Way By every time she murmured her name and this intrigued her.

She did not know why or where it was coming from, but uncertainty was a balm to the spiteful, and the Withersmith could feel the tear bleeding through to the dark and colorless place she now inhabited. Something was calling to the ragged spirit with the promise of further loss. But when she tried to taste it, the soil seemed to rouse alongside her. It too craved blood and ashes.

The nightmare took shape around her slowly. But the Way By was nothing if not precise and it built her malevolence piece by detailed piece, drawing inspiration from her memories and her words just as much as it made use of the whisperings of the world all around. It started with contempt, and formed a sneering face. Then vengeance to make its fingers and a grudge each for its palms. Arrogance for the body to give it a certain poise all the while saving enough enmity to create stalking legs and gnarled feet. The Fae thing turned to her.

This was a Faire of the worst sort; one that hungered for suffering and only ever bargained in bad faith. But armed with teeth of malice and nails of umbrage, everything it spoke made bindings out of regret and bitterness. It breathed both truth and lies equally, but made use of all of it for the same traitorous end. It would cut out every part of a person it craved, consume them, and leave the remains to shamble on hopelessly.

The Withersmith then gave a name to it. A girl's distant voice wavered and called it Chirurgeon.

"Fetch me death." The ghost murmured as she began, once again, to fall. "Bring me agony. Find what weeps and let me dine on the fruits of torment. Go back, again and again, until it is done."

A maw glinted in the light of an empty tunnel and lured the spirits back into sleep once more.

That night, Fiona stared up at the ceiling. Insomnia had made her sleep fitful and light, and the nightmares had become so jumbled and incoherent that each hour only further blurred the lines between asleep and awake. For this reason, sometimes the ceiling was white and blank, with shadows cast by the dim light in the hall outside her door, and other times it was a canvas of twisting figures on an illuminated landscape of imagined pits and chasms.

She and her mother had said little to one another over the last few hours. Each time Alice had attempted to broach the events of the past two months, Fiona had shut her down with another forkful of food or with an emphatic shake of her head. She didn't want to talk about him. She didn't want to remember he existed at all. With tentative fingers, she poked at her stomach and then at her ribs, trying to visualize a variety of futures. In one, she followed the expected script and gave birth to a baby girl.

Her mother was at her side but there was only confusion and isolation after that. In another, the baby was sickened and malformed. She cursed at herself repeatedly for even allowing the image to come forward, though it did anyway, and she bit her hand every time she felt relief at the thought of losing it. She briefly thought of miscarriage but discarded it as unlikely wishful thinking just as quickly.

In the ideas that followed, she promised the baby for adoption but was blocked at every turn by a boy she despised and a lovely family of devoted strangers. She then entertained a fantasy of being sent away to another school in another town where no one knew her and no one cared. Anything was better than having to face two-hundred days in the crucible or normalcy. School. Doctors. Sadness.

Hiding. Fear. Pain. She imagined hating herself. She imagined hating her child. She imagined hating life. She thought of dying; both herself and the baby tragically lost in complications. She went back to the first scenario and re-thought about raising the baby alone. She tried it a third time but imagined her own mother as herself. None of her thoughts seemed right. She didn't want any of them or the worlds they created. She wanted it all gone.

Fiona rolled over and punched a depression into the center of her pillow. The light from the hall had slowly faded to a tired, still, blue, which could only mean that her mother had finally turned off her reading light and fallen asleep. It was well past midnight. Reflexively, Fiona reached down beneath the pile of clothes next to her bed and pulled out a brown teddy bear. Brown Bear (not a toddler's most imaginative name) had been her favorite growing up and was one of the few things from her early childhood that had survived the latest teenage purge.

Just him and his faithful companion, a stuffed sheep by the name of Lambie Pie. Brown Bear had been a first birthday gift from Nana. Nana, who had always understood the importance of using water in the toy tea set and of not skipping pages when she re-read the same bedtime stories. A choking sob caught her again. Fiona squeezed her eyes shut and begged the darkness to bring her grandmother back. She would have the answers for all this.

"Poor, frightened, little mouse. So alone. I know why it is you lay awake at night. Don't be afraid. I only wanted to help."

Her breath stopped. Eyes wide, Fiona scanned the room without moving from underneath the blankets. The window was closed, the door slightly open to the hall. Her clothes were undisturbed. A writing desk piled precariously with schoolwork remained untouched. In the darkness, everything was tinted a monochromatic blue-grey but she could make out nothing that might have been the source of the voice. Brown Bear shifted her in arms. And it had been a voice, she was sure of it. Something was speaking to her from behind the door.

"Brought along by kin and blood, though little did they know.
That though the doctor stitched and stitched, she had fallen far too low.

He tried his best, she wasn't saved, and off he went to pray.
But look she did down at her breast and then fainted dead away."

Fiona couldn't scream. She tried, but it came out almost like a breathless whine muffled by the covers draped over the top of her head. From the chair near the corner, she saw a lanky pair of trousers unfold itself onto the floor; saw them fill and produce Oxford shoes at the cuffs. She saw a white, button-down shirt tuck in and a white coat wrap around it all.

She thought she could make out something like a stethoscope dangling from its neck but at its rounded chest-piece was something more akin to a pair of clacking bones than a bell and diaphragm. The figure flowed from around the hinges of her bedroom door. Wild black hair crowned a slanted man, with pinched glasses on his nose and a smile that reflected white off the lenses. He had too many teeth and more fingers than he ought. She gasped in terrible recognition. The Chirurgeon drew up to his full height and glowered down at her before placing one knotted finger to his lips.

"Hush hush, all is well, all is well." His strange sing-song failing to fully fill the room. "Do not be afraid my dear, dear, Fiona. When you left, you seemed so frightened I thought I should come on a house call and check in on you."

There was a monster in her room. And now she knew it.

Fiona shook with uncontrollable fright, her sweat-soaked palms nearly tearing Brown Bear's ears. She could hear and feel nothing but the raucous pounding of her own heart. It thudded against her left side before skipping a beat and then making up for it with a painful double pulse that forced her to suppress an involuntary cough. She pulled the bear up to her chin and attempted to slide away from the looming figure, partially still unwilling to believe that she wasn't just having another nightmare.

"Wha...what do you want?" She whispered.

The meager man swayed slightly in the shadows. The angled glint from his round glasses obscured his eyes but, for a moment, though he approached with some determination, he seemed to pause at the sight of the bear clutched to the girl's bloodless face. As if spooked, he made to reach for it but snapped his hand back before crossing the outer boundary of the bed posts. He snarled back to a position near the chair.

"Now now, little one. No need for that. I've just come to help you, remember?"

"You're the doctor. From the clinic. What are you doing here?"

"I am the Chirurgeon, you remember me? You remember my name." Gone was the calm and soothing manner, gone was the gentle physician's tone. This creature came clad in withered grey skin and had a voice akin to a cold wind through a copse of dead and dying trees. His joints creaked like wood and his movements were sharp and uncoordinated, puppet-like, with strings tied around his neck. There was something like moss filaments on his clothes and his mouth emitted the pungent graveborn smell of petrichor and mold. "I come to help you with your troubles. Don't you still want help? I can make your problems all go away, child. Nothing for you to fear. We had a Bargain, I've just come to make our trade."

Fiona kicked her feet free of the restricting bedsheet. "I...I...NO! I want you to go away!"

"Oh no, not yet." He growled out, dragging jagged nails across the footboard. He rose up above her, blocking out the light from the hallway. "You and I have a Bargain waiting accord, little girl!"

She had to be dreaming. Fiona Guthrie begged all the saints she could think of to be dreaming.

Without warning, the corner blanket dropped to the floor. Fiona yelped and the Chirurgeon startled as Brown Bear leapt free her arms, landing with preternatural grace and balance at the edge of the bed. His re-stitched mouth pulled into a tight frown, his button eyes shimmering, Brown Bear raised a threadbare paw in accusation, pointing at the man with wordless recrimination. Loathing and righteous anger practically dripped from the damp seams at the sides of his head.

He flattened his round ears back. From his other paw, he produced a tiny, wooden sword. No more than two small dried-out planks nailed together to form an uneven cross, Brown Bear raised the weapon valiantly over Fiona, daring the Fae to test him. The teddy then beat his chest once with an open hand and gripped the flimsy crossguard in both paws. Fiona was rendered completely and utterly senseless. She stared in wonder and shock as her little bear, her childhood plaything and nightly companion, burst into action. She could feel his minikin weight where two plush legs sunk into the quilt and still see the smoothed impressions where her fingers had wet his cotton fur. But nothing felt remotely real.

The Chirurgeon swung first, attempting to shred the little bear with extended claws. But Brown Bear held his ground, fending off each attack with a twirl of his toy sword, never letting the man near enough to the bed to reach Fiona outright. With each touch of the weapon, the Fae recoiled, weaving around the bear as though avoiding a swinging torch. Brown Bear bounced and rolled across the blankets as a warrior over uneven ground. Each time the creature leveled a blow at him, it was parried back with masterful strokes: on guard, shoulder, counter, riposte!

The enraged Fae darted forward, yanking at the blankets and sending Brown Bear sprawling over the girl's knees. But he was not prone for long, kicking up and launching himself onto the far bedpost at Fiona's feet. The Chirurgeon swatted wildly and Brown Bear landed a solid strike onto the back of the creature's hand. Fiona was sure that the howl that erupted from the flailing monstrosity would awaken her mother. But it didn't. The light in the hallway remained dim. She wasn't coming.

The Chirurgeon balked, grasping his injured hand. "We have a Bargain, you and I." He hissed back at the girl. Brown Bear readied his sword again, pointing with renewed purpose back to the door. It was clear he meant for him to leave at once.

The fight had lasted mere seconds and yet an eternity passed between them all. The nightmare Fae breathed in the darkness and exhaled smoke.

"This will not be the end of it, you know that." It was clear he was addressing the bear this time. Brown Bear inclined his head but did not speak.

"A Bargain is a Bargain and there is nothing you can do about that. I come for what is mine."

Brown Bear turned cautiously from side to side before walking over, in an odd tottering gait borne on stuffed legs, to the bedside table. From the pile of change next to Fiona's house keys he lifted up a single penny and flung it across the room, where it hit the man squarely in the shoulder before clinking and rolling out onto the floor.

The Chirurgeon did not seem appeased and kicked the offending coin away under the bed.

"So be it." He whispered menacingly. "I will come again at a better time."

Fiona stared as the lithe figure melted away. What little particles of him remaining as he disintegrated into the speckled haze of her vision were carried away by the draft through her floorboards; the same one that occasionally wobbled her door back and forth against the frame and made the sound that had become his voice. She turned to Brown Bear, still standing straight and vigilant near her hip, watching with shifting button-eyes at the place where the Chirurgeon had stood. He turned when she reached out a hand to tentatively touch his back.

She blinked, still disbelievingly, as the ruffled bear placed his wooden sword on the nightstand before ambling back across the bed and stopping to look up at her. Brown Bear had no expression save the downturned Y of black thread beneath his nose and the wide set of the two black coat-buttons sewn onto the lighter circle of fabric that made up his face. But the simple makeup of his character could not hide his familiar affection.

When Fiona then reached out her arms, he climbed quietly onto her chest and wrapped his tiny paws as far around her as he could manage. Fiona smiled but still shaking, she closed the embrace and hugged him back, squeezing as hard as she could and burying her face in the worn plush of his head. For several moments, she did nothing but pour out all her fear and all of her sadness into Brown Bear, kissing his nose and tugging at his mitten fists. She stayed like that for hours and lost track of time.

When she awakened, she was lying on her side in a silent room. She looked down to see that Brown Bear was where she had left him, tucked up beneath her arm. She lifted him up and turned the teddy over in her hands cautiously. He was just a bear, but she smiled despite herself. He had kept the nightmares away again.

The clock on her shelf read three in the morning. Her room seemed flat and blank in the darkness, with only a dust mote drifting past here and there to indicate that there was still some depth and vitality in the world. There was nothing to indicate that anything out of the ordinary at all had happened, save perhaps a lost penny that went unnoticed in the cracks in the floor beneath her bed. Outside, tiptoes of rain scurried across the gable roof. Fiona gathered up her blanket, picked up her bear, and for the first time in almost a decade, walked down the hall to her mother's room. She had to tell her about these dreams.

Three AM and the letter was only half finished. Somerset Sayer chewed on a sigh, dipped the pen again, and continued. Coat Check dozed at her feet, still dressed in the outlandish livery he insisted on wearing every time she called on him to deliver messages to Court. The tawny shield tabard was belted midway over a red woolen shirt with a pair of olive and brown checkered leggings for good lasting effect. In the language of heraldry, the tabard's forefront was a white field parted per pale and per fir twig fess. Meaning that it was separated into four equal quarters using intricate leaf-shaped lines.

It then bore a red Welsh dragon passant, or walking with a raised foot, tinted in line with official *gules* to match the shirt. It was a coat of arms Somerset Sayer was quite familiar with, having been in use by members of a family who bore the same surname as she many generations back. Whether or not it represented any actual continuity with her lineage was not something the folklorist was particularly aware of. However, seeing as she had never had much in the way of attachment to her family history, actual or imagined, the fact that Coat Check had gone to such trouble a few years ago to dig up the images online and have them emblazoned on a thrift-store tunic was met with a mixture of amusement and exasperation.

He claimed that arriving in Court dressed in his usual felt and sackcloth was simply insulting to everyone around, therefore, some manner of uniform was required, and what better one than something to represent the Waysmith's household? Granted, his definition of "household" was rather a loose one and included Hat Trick, a set of unidentified family photographs from the late 19th century, a goldfish, two houseplants, and a smattering of cousins who occasionally checked in to see if the scholar was still alive.

On the other hand, she noted that Coat Check also never bothered with shoes while acting as her de facto herald, which, under most circumstances would be considered unbecoming of an aristocratic servire. Instead, he always delivered his messages and packages completely barefoot and with some amount of dirt caked under his nails. Better, he said when asked about it, if he was not immediately heard. Or, in some cases, never heard at all. The dirt was just an occupational hazard. She glanced down at the set of hairy toes stuck out from underneath her chair, twitching each time the little goblin snored. She returned to the letter.

By way of Harker, Herbalist, and Hunter
To the Court of *Triath nan Eilean, A Shoilse,*
His Most Faithful Majesty, The Summer King
On this day, *An Mháirt,* the first in the time of *Earrach*
Oyez, Oyez, Oyez

Avenant,

You give me credit for discernment beyond my ability. I declare to you now that I never suspected the alacrity with which the effects of the Way By Stumble would be felt in the material world. Indeed, it is with growing consternation that I note the rising incidents of reported "paranormal" experiences that indicate the extent of the Way By's seep into the Mundane. As such, I fully expect to see even greater incidents of malfeasance on the part of the Fairest Under Courts in the coming days.

What remains to be seen is how their appearance will be explained and reconciled by a world that no longer has a living memory of them. When I began my acquaintance with the practitioners of the Hearthcraft Community of Massachusetts, just a short while ago, I had, in truth, anticipated a fair amount of time between initiation of some of their more astute members and the moment in which I would be called upon to reveal the truer nature of my intentions. I can see now that this will not be the case. I fear I may be throwing them to the wolves.

As you mentioned during our last meeting, I have taken to heart your concerns about the so-called entanglements-of-the-unwitting, but I can assure you that few will remain truly ignorant and oblivious should the worst come to pass. There will only be greater discord among the people and communities of our world. Rumor-mongering and distrust will proliferate. Conspiracy theories and crackpots will sway millions. Fiction will replace knowledge.

People will take comfort in the obscurity of the truth and the Way By will oblige them. In turn, it will become cancerous; a new malignancy in the hearts and minds of the impassioned and the observant. You know, as well as I do, how potent are the stories we tell ourselves.

I also know that this letter will be met with some disquiet. I am prone to flowered prolixity and pretentious phrases. I prefer meaningless flourishes and impressions of elegance that are more likely to be read by others as lacking in erudition or as evidence of intellectual vanity. But if a letter is a mirror, as is any other social observance, then let this be held up as a reflection of my dedication and character more so than if I had sent a missive badly spelled and with mismatched paper and envelope.

One ritual is really no different than any other in this respect. There is also no such thing as heraldry in America (despite my associate's insistence on his rights to a long-forgotten icon from a distant land and time), so if I am to announce myself, I am afraid that I must do so with the suitability and propriety of literary conversation. Think of this as my letter of introduction, not in the sense that I am unknown among the Kingdom but in the sense that I am almost never in proper attendance among the rank and majority.

This brings me to the objective. I scorn to act in any manner that may reproach myself to you, nor do I wish to continue to hold clandestine proceedings unbecoming of a scholar. I take now the liberty of announcing my intentions to appear at Court and humbly request your permission to stand before the Summer Crown. In my company, I shall select a number of others to attend as well. The purpose of this venture is not altogether unknown to you, I should think. It is not unlike the days of old, when valiant knights were assembled to undertake a great quest or who were charged with a noble task.

When heroes of legend were chosen to brave the horrors of war for the glory of all. This shall be our conclave, and we ask the boons of the Ever-Growing and Ever-Blooming as we set out to vanquish our foe. The time has come, beloved. Though I wish it were not the case, I can see no other recourse. The Way By Stumble must fall, but we have not the named sword nor the mystic bow to bring it down and our heroes of old are ignorant of all but the most basic appearances of the uncanny and the mythical. It is time to make ready, and I cannot prepare them alone.

My request may come to you through the utmost formal channels, but an intimate letter has no end. When you leave the house of your family, there are no special proclamations of farewell, only the presumption that upon your return all will be as it was before you left. As such, I cannot simply bid you sincerity and a fond good-bye because there is so much more to say that I have not dared. Alas, I must clearly take my leave regardless. I shall await your response by the hand of my occasional herald. Take your time. I am sure he will enjoy a day or two in the halls of the farthest reaches.

Believe me,
Somerset Sayer
Waysmith by Sovereign Peer, Keys Addorsed

Chapter Nine

Somerset Sayer stared worriedly. Alice Guthrie, now seated at her kitchen table, sobbed demurely into the sleeve of her olive sweater while continuing to strangle each unbroken stream of words through a slow trickle of tears.

Two solemn faces, one downcast and discomfited and the second laconic and out of breath, had appeared on her doorstep not forty minutes prior. Next to the juniper bushes, they each bore resemblance to garden statues; all stiff coats and dourly bent shoulders. The heady perfume of altar candles and olibanum was all that was missing from the reverence of the pair in addition to any kind of due deference for the door that swung wide before them; which, to be fair, was hardly of cathedral quality.

Alice Guthrie had spoken first. All Somerset Sayer could recall of the ensuing conversation had been something to the effect of a need for immediate counsel and upon ushering mother and daughter into the front sitting room of the house on Trowbridge Street, Alice Guthrie had demanded that the two elder women take an immediate sojourn into the kitchen. Fiona, content to remain inconversable, sat in the window box seat. Somerset Sayer cast a glance back at her with some confused consternation and was met with obstinate silence and a steadfast glare.

It was clear that Fiona meant to defy her but for what reason, she was at a loss. She had never met the girl before and wasn't about to hazard a guess as to why Alice Guthrie had brought her along. Then, and only because she was beholden to her own constant inner monologue, she wondered as to why the girl might be putting up such a resistance to something that was as of yet unspecified? Who had her mother led her to believe the strange woman in the Cambridge rowhouse was?

"Dr. Sayer, please, I must speak with you. Alone, if we may, a moment."

"I, uh, of course. This way."

Leaving Fiona to her own devices, for whatever purpose that might serve, Somerset Sayer maneuvered Alice Guthrie through the gauntlet of carefully misplaced objects that made up most of the habitable areas of the house until she was well situated at the table and otherwise out of the way of accidental harm.

She considered some manner of small talk along the lines of asking her what might bring her to visit so unexpectedly, but on observing Alice Guthrie's notably bedraggled demeanor and flustered speech, she opted to simply wait until the woman was ready to give her reasons in her own words. Alice Guthrie stared ahead in silence as the owner of the house set about to offer her the various contents of the pantry.

"What do you say of the bruises on her arms?" Came the first of many non-sequiturs. The elder woman trembled but offered no other context to her inquiries.

"Nothing?" the folklorist replied, a shrug to round out her unease. "I guess I did not notice she was injured. An accident?"

"I did not even think to ask." Alice Guthrie sunk into the dining chair. "I must have assumed the same but I did not even think to ask. That is how distracted I have been. So much so I didn't even notice anything more than in passing. Unacceptable, I tell you. But no more! I've come to see to this."

"Ms. Guthrie," Somerset Sayer implemented a conciliatory tone. "Surely a few random bruises are nothing to be alarmed about. She's an active girl, I'm guessing. Not something you should be guilty of overlooking in the present moment." Then, taking a mental stab at what might possibly be troubling the woman, "I have no doubt that, given some time to reflect on your recent experiences, you'll be back to your old attentive self as usual. This is.... expected. Considering."

Alice Guthrie was again silent for several minutes.

"They're from sailing." She stated plainly, though she did not look up. "From a practice demonstration at school."

"Well then." Somerset Sayer said by way of feigned brightness. "Then what is this all about?"

"I should have asked. I was supposed to have asked. And now..."

"Ms. Guthrie, really, I'm sure everything is going to be fine and besides..." She did not get to finish the thought.

"She's pregnant." Alice Guthrie exclaimed. "My daughter told me that she is pregnant."

Certainly, Somerset Sayer had been expecting something out of the ordinary when mother, with unyielding daughter in tow, had appeared on her front stoop, but even the folklorist had to admit, this definitely hadn't been the first thing on her list of potentials. In truth, but more as a matter of routine, she had been expecting something of a far less ordinary nature.

Perhaps something that had unexpectedly followed her home after their last adventure or a troubling dream that warranted explanation. Unfortunately, while she then could better understand Alice Guthrie's sudden distress, she was now even more at a loss for proper responses. The machinations of the Fae and Fae-like she could deal with, but she was hopelessly at a disadvantage for things such as these.

"Then might I suggest a doctor of a different sort?" The folklorist rejoined with a calm, task-like, demeanor.

"No, no, you don't understand," Alice Guthrie continued. "She wants to terminate." She then breathed out the last word, "Immediately." A fresh string of personal reprimands and expletives erupted from the normally resolute woman in a fit of coughing.

Somerset Sayer paused only briefly before reiterating, "Again, I think there are medical professionals far more suited to this conversation, Ms. Guthrie, than I am."

Alice Guthrie dug her nails into the tabletop. She had debated at length with herself about whether or not arriving here-to-for unannounced at the doorstep of the reclusive folklorist was truly the correct decision but conflicted as she was under the circumstances and in light of what her daughter had revealed to her last night under the presumption of a nightmare, the decision seemed obvious. Furthermore, some part of her believed that she might, if nothing else, receive better comfort and camaraderie from one privy to the root of the problem even if her actual intended request had yet to be fully articulated. She balked at the thought that she would be turned away.

"My duty, Dr. Sayer," her emotional state causing her to enunciate the last syllables in a lower tone, "is to my daughter, no matter what I might feel otherwise."

"I take it to mean you are.... should I say, opposed to her decision?"

"No, actually."

The folklorist paused. That was not the answer she had expected. Alice Guthrie continued resolutely. "She was.... assaulted. It was some weeks ago now though and she didn't tell me. A date or something like it, she said. He forced her and..." She picked at the loose ends of a threaded cuff, "She didn't say no. Or, at least, she doesn't think she did. I'm not sure. She said she had decided to forget the whole thing and when I didn't notice the bruises..." Here she trailed off.

"Good God, the police then..."

"No!" The abrupt forcefulness of her tone startled Somerset Sayer from her suggestion. "No, I won't do that. I mean, she won't do that." Her lip twitched in distorted rage. "It won't matter anyway. You know what happens. Next to useless or worse. She'll be dragged through the mud for nothing. Not a thing! And this boy," She shook with remorseless vengeance, "he abused her. Bruised her. My baby, Dr. Sayer. My baby! And not a thing will be done!"

Somerset Sayer sighed and absently threw up her hands. She wished she could offer something more reassuring.

"No. It is not the way things should be but the way things are that forces our hand." Alice Guthrie continued, "I will not leave this to...bureaucracy. Not to them, you know? To pats on the back and condescending nods and referrals to a good therapist. Asking me how many lives I want to ruin. Well, all of them I say! No, these sorts of things are for us to decide, Dr. Sayer. No one asks our permission to do what they will, so no permission will be asked in return."

"Ms. Guthrie," Somerset Sayer adjusted the seat across from her, trying for another brief glance into her living room where Fiona Guthrie remained curled up underneath a blanket in the window box, fingers gently extended from beneath the corner to play in the sun. "I am sorry, I truly am, for what has happened to your daughter. She's a lovely girl and she didn't deserve this by any means, of course. But I'm not sure what it is you think I can do for you. Go to the police and have this boy answer for his crimes. Take her to a doctor, to whatever end she decides. There just isn't any way I can help you with this."

In that moment, the tone of the exchange abruptly shifted. What had been a distraught mother advocating on behalf of a child was now a jaguar, stalking silently through the underbrush on unsuspecting prey.

"Oh, I think you can."

A pall descended and Alice Guthrie leaned forward, rocking precariously.

"I'm often thought of as a fool, Dr. Sayer. Maybe it's how I look. I'm matronly, I know that. Maybe it's that I am an optimist mostly and I always want to think the best of a situation if I can. I also know that I am out of the loop on a great number of other things that just don't make much sense to me but seem to make sense to everyone else. But I am not a fool. Never think me the fool."

The folklorist raised a piqued eyebrow. The maundering consultation continued and Somerset Sayer struggled to guess at the primary point.

"I know how these stories go. And sure, they're not all true, I understand perfectly well all that. Embellishment here and there and exaggeration to frighten the witless. But I am also not witless. There are too many such stories for there not to be truth to it. Not after all you have shown us." Somerset Sayer noted here that Alice Guthrie seemed more to be having a conversation with herself than anyone else, speaking to some specter off in the distance that only she could see.

"I don't think I follow your meaning."

Her eyes moved to meet those of the scholar, who winced imperceptibly in response. The set of Alice Guthrie's jaw spoke more than her words. Her eyes narrowed to half-curved slits, her cheeks red and puffy with warning.

"The Fae," She enunciated with painful deliberation, "steal children. Don't they?"

Somerset Sayer was dumbfounded. Had she heard this right? Alice Guthrie gave no quarter.

"I should say nothing of Tam Lin? Roggenmuhme, yes? Ogbanje or the stones of Mên-an-Tol? Or shall I remind you of *The Secret Commonwealth of Elves, Fauns, and Fairies?* Taken right from the childbed, be it mothers or infants. Murdering the unwanted or making off with the unborn for petty grievances. Enslavement if not death? It is all there and I'll not hear you make excuses otherwise. I'll make my tithe to Hell if that's what it takes to protect my girl, Dr. Sayer. It's happened. It has happened to Fiona. They've come to barter a trade and I'll not stand for one second more of such creatures clawing at her throat!"

"Ms. Guthrie..."

"Oh, I see. You mean to refuse to help us? What of you, then? Were you a Changeling? Is that how you can do all this?!"

"Ms. Guthrie, that is quite enough!" The folklorist snapped in return, slapping her hand loudly onto the wood grain. "You're upset, I understand. But there will be none of that."

Alice Guthrie visibly diminished, her voice dropping to a whisper, "I...I am sorry. I didn't mean to accuse you of anything, I just.... protect her from them, Dr. Sayer. Can you...please.... can you protect her? Can't it just be undone, that's the word right, undone? Spare us this? Stop these attacks?"

"Ms. Guthrie. For the last time, will you please attempt to make some sense! You are rambling! What on Earth are you talking about?"

Alice Guthrie cast her mind back to only hours before. Her daughter, damp with sweat and tears, crawling into her bed, whispering meekly of the monsters hiding in her closet. Of Fiona, snuggling close in a way that she had not done since she was small, waking from a child's nightmares about grasping hands in the lake water and large-toothed furniture. And then listening to her mumble about the man in the white coat come to punish her and to steal her life away.

The Chirurgeon, an incubus that had been haunting her for days, rising up out of the shadows because she had promised something of herself to the darkness in exchange for a return to normality. She had then dreamed that her teddy had come to her rescue and said that it was a sweet way to imagine innocence lost. How she lamented all the conflicting emotions she couldn't seem to make sense of. How she was convinced of his illusory nature no matter how real he was becoming.

How she mused about whether or not the slanted man was her mind's way of portraying the terrible forces in her life, or the doctors that wouldn't help her, or the boy who had meted out her misery. How she was ever more certain that she needed to take back control of her life before she lost her mind entirely. "Just a bad dream, Mama." She had blearily assured. "It's all just a bad dream." But Alice Guthrie now knew better. She made this clear to Somerset Sayer.

The folklorist chanced a third peek into the living room. Fiona Guthrie had said virtually nothing upon her arrival and even though she was certain the girl could overhear them easily enough, did not attempt to emerge from her cotton-swathed cocoon. The scholar wracked her mind for words of solace; a talent she had never been particularly well-known for. Surely, the violation could not go unanswered. She understood this. Surely, Fiona had every right to her resolve and her mother to her conflicts.

Surely, this wound could be stitched and balmed and in time, heal to faded, bunching scars. But the very mention of the Chirurgeon changed the nature of the problem entirely. Chirurgeon was a name Somerset Sayer knew and she had serious warnings to anyone who might think to cede hard decisions, wrenching as they may be, to other powers. At last, she now understood completely why Alice Guthrie had turned to her before anyone else. Alice and Fiona Guthrie had been visited by one of Those Who Trade In Children.

After a thoughtful, unflinching, taciturnity, she responded. "Did she agree?"

"Agree? To the creature you mean?"

"Yes, to the creature. Be very honest with me Ms. Guthrie, did she agree? Did she make a Bargain to give an unborn to the Fae?"

Alice wracked her brain for additional details. "No." She finally offered. "Not at any point in this has Fiona said yes."

"Ms. Guthrie, I've made it quite clear by now that humans cannot perform magic." Here Somerset Sayer stopped to once again choose her words carefully. "...And.... hopefully I don't need to impress upon you the utter peril of making a deal with any manner of Fae-kind. Particularly those who actually are Changelings. Or with those who might...be inclined to make off with unwanted pain, if you can stomach their price. If Fiona, at any point, agreed to the terms of the Bargain offered to her by the Chirurgeon, she is and will remain in extreme danger."

Alice Guthrie scowled at her hands. "Can you stop this creature? Banish it?"

"Whether I can or not, I am afraid it may not matter. Anyone who wishes to encounter a Fae on transactional terms rarely has difficulty doing so and I worry more that, because Fiona has made this kind of final decision regarding her condition, it will only attract others in the absence of this one. Ms. Guthrie, I cannot stress to you enough the profound folly of ever attempting to make a deal or make terms of exchange with the Fae for any reason. This is their forte and they carry it out with virtuosity."

"Dr. Sayer." Alice Guthrie stated by way of prelude. "They are preying on my child. This thing, whatever it's called. She had absolutely no idea what she was doing or what she was dealing with. She still doesn't. Now, I am a practical woman. Of course, I have sometimes imagined my daughter would one day have children of her own though I have generally considered myself always on the side of a woman's choices but we are beyond that now. Whether I agree with my daughter's decision or not, whether I take her to get the procedure she wants or not, there is something else at work. Something that threatens her in ways I can't understand. But you can." She paused for breath. "Fiona has made her needs clear. And I will admit that I have struggled with this. Oh, mightily, you have no idea. I've asked myself over and over again if I would press her into seeing things through to the end. If I would ask her to let me adopt it so that she could still have her life as well. I've wondered if I would even be able to take her to the proper clinic and have a proper abortion done. But that's done with. It's all done with. I don't know if I had anything to do with this, or if you do."

Here she stared hard at the woman across the table. "If my experiences in the places you've taken me precipitated this or just enabled it, I don't know. But I won't let them hurt her. I won't let them take her or anything from her. I don't care how, but I am going to stop this thing from coming after Fiona. I just need you to tell me what to do."

Somerset Sayer reached out and rested her hands on the fingers of the afflicted woman.

"Alice." She said finally. "The Bargain is a difficult thing to get out of. Whether she has agreed to explicit terms or not or even partially, the agreement comes with immediate consequences. A Geas would be the least of it; a curse whose indignities cannot be taken in stride. Death and wasting are more likely if she has made any kind of exchange at all, and if you get in the way of it, it will only get worse. And I mean for the both of you. The price of a Bargain is always unthinkable and you won't see it coming until it is too late."

A faint scrabbling alerted the scholar to a figure near the opposite doorway. With barely a blink or a tilt to her head to give away the change in her attention she watched as a short, somewhat hairy, bipedal form peered out at her from the back room. Through the characteristic flour-sack belly and red Phrygian cap poised over a frown that bespoke the consternation of one of her most trusted companions, she could see the wild gestures Hat Trick was evoking in an attempt to motion her away from the kitchen. He seemed to know already where all this was going and had something to add.

“There is… something I might suggest.” Somerset Sayer proposed hesitantly to the ruddy upturned countenance of the other woman. “It’s not a guarantee, mind you. It might not work. But if it does, it could be the…safer substitute to reneging on the deal.”

“Yes?”

There was nothing in Somerset Sayer’s considerable emotional make-up that spurred her to make the loathe suggestion but rather that she knew, with Alice Guthrie’s most recent exposure to the Way By, that such a deal as Fiona may have struck in a moment of desperation may not be possible to avoid. Particularly as the few Fae that they had encountered would have spread the word far and wide of the new human travelers to the Chalk Circle by now, and she had no doubt that more than a few curious denizens of the hidden world would be wandering through to see for themselves.

Even now, the Way By was coming alive in their midst, drawn to the whispered prayers and secret longings sneaking in all about them. She moved a candle aside and placed a bit of salt beneath it to momentarily fence it back.

“There are some old magics still left. Vestiges, really. A few hidden secrets the Way By occasionally cares to divulge, but I can’t promise you everything will work out the way you want it to. And I’ll want to talk to Fiona first, no matter what, and especially before she decides to rogue away in search of some other even less amiable Fae to be taken in by.”

“What can you tell me?” Alice Guthrie was again all poise and concentration.

“Not much at the moment. At least, not until I have had time to prepare. But this is old magic, deep magic, unkind and unconcerned magic, that we’re talking about here. Buried far under the land and fossilized in stone. Quite literally sometimes, actually.”

Alice noted a small blister at the back of her hand and eyed the candle cautiously. "But if no humans can do magic, wouldn't it mean involving the Fae anyway?"

"No. Not exactly." Came the reply. "A long time ago, Waysmiths used to refer to ritual magic as Hedging. But that was mainly just to distinguish it from sortilege and rune magics. The more intellectually inclined called it Variscan Fexix, or just Varis, in polite company. It takes its name from the Latin of Variscan orogeny; the building of mountains by the tectonic forces of Earth's movement that once constructed, and then tore apart, prehistoric supercontinents. But don't let that confuse you, this isn't high school earth science. The forces that move the world have no sympathy for human troubles."

"No, no, of course not." Alice Guthrie nodded, placated somewhat by Somerset Sayer's conspiratorial concern. "What does it do?"

"Hopefully," the other answered, "what you want it to, but without the typical side-effects of working pacts. In the old, old days, Hearth Women used to work Varis magics for all manner of troubles; calling it divine feminine, Earth Mothering, womb and blood and birth, and all that. Fertility, or against it. Sex, menstruation, children, household protections, fertile fields, you name it. Varis connected the body with the land and there were once whole communities of Hedge practitioners who knew its incantations. Not so much now but there's a chance, and I really mean that, just a chance, that I might be able to dredge up some bit to help you. It's possible that some of the old Varis Terrene writings can...." She fumbled for the right explanation, "Undo the undoable. And if it can, the Fae will be left with nothing to work with. Literally nothing to hang their terms on and no way to enforce the Bargain because you cannot deal against a non-entity."

"If you think it can work." Alice Guthrie gasped enthusiastically. "What must we do?"

"First," Somerset Sayer sighed heavily, "I will need to figure out if such work is even feasible in this case. And I'll need a bit of time to do that. Secondly, I will have to prepare the proper rites. Varis is a...tricky kind of thing, not exactly subject to will-work, but it has been known to adhere to certain sets of rules. Bend the immediate environment to those rules and it may play out in the way you intend it to."

"And if it doesn't?"

“If it doesn’t, we’ll have an entirely new set of problems on our hands. Up to and including, I dare say, the potential for various types of natural disasters. Thankfully, those kinds of events are blissfully rare but you should be aware that this comes with a measure of uncertainty.” Something creaked the baseboards in a room beyond the kitchen. Somerset Sayer rose from the table. “Will you excuse me a moment?”

Alice Guthrie nodded and fidgeted as the folklorist swept from the room through a side door towards the study. The same study wherein it had all begun.

Hat Trick sat sullenly at the edge of the desk. Having been party to a large portion of the previous discussion from his position underneath the kitchen cupboards (as he was bound by fealty to always be aware of what went on in the Waysmith’s house), he dreaded the inevitable task that came next. The threshold of the study doorway gave in with the subtle shifts of the Waysmith’s manipulations and he watched in silence as she passed beneath the stag-horn lintel and began to pull a series of selected volumes from the top shelf of the library. This particular combination of books did not bode well in his mind and he thought to express his concerns right away.

“No good.” He chuffed. “No good this.”

Somerset Sayer paused, dropping an armload onto the seat of a nearby chair.

“I know what you’re thinking.” She said without turning. “But if we don’t try something, it’s a pretty short hop, skip, and a jump to a Geas or worse, a Tynged. The Way By has been unruly enough as it is lately and I have no doubt that if there is a way to get into even more trouble under a Bargain, Alice Guthrie will find it. Or it will find her, and I’m not prepared at this point to start managing other people’s Fairie problems again. If nothing else, the Varis might at least bring her some calm and direction. It tends to do that even if it doesn’t work out entirely as intended. What Chicanery hides, Mother Earth provides, right?”

Hat Trick furled his nostrils at the old pun but he knew she was right. Only moments before their guests' arrival he had shooed a small Erlkingling out from the fireplace ash-traps and back through the narrow cat-door the Waysmith had installed years ago for just this sort of problem. Herla-creatures of the Way By were persistent as blow flies when it came to the scents of suffering, always sniffing around for something pink and fleshy to snatch away and chew on for a time. As such, the creature's starved complexion and unwillingness to part with its newly secured perch had finally necessitated the use of a hand broom to dislodge the screeching rodent-twig from where it had become caught up.

With vexed murmurs of exasperation, the folklorist finally ended her search by flopping down into the desk chair and throwing her feet square into the center of a pile of papers near the blotter.

"Bide the Dead, Feed the Stumble, Hat Trick." She sighed. "I don't see any other way around it. If Alice Guthrie and her daughter get caught up in negotiating a pact, *this kind* of pact, there'll be even more problems waiting on the other side of it. And until the Way is clear we have no choice but to invoke the Varis if we want to be certain to avoid the worst of them."

"Bide the Dead, Feed the Stumble." He nodded in return.

She looked over the squat little Kobold for a time longer. His normally bright, whitish, eyes looked askance and his small mouth was drawn to a flat line beneath a fold of skin with his red felt hat lop-sided across a balding pate. She understood his concern, even if she didn't quite share his fretfulness, but she simply couldn't risk derailing her plans even with something as shattering as a young woman's violation and a mother's panic. There was only one way to help Alice and Fiona now.

"Hat Trick. Fetch me the Appendant."

Anticipating just this, Hat Trick didn't bother to make a show of his distaste. Instead, he slid from the edge of the desk to land heavily on the short stool pulled up alongside it and padded reluctantly to the far corner of the study where an unadorned and unobtrusive trunk sat beneath a layer of dust. The locking mechanism was a familiar one to him, one that could only be properly undone by Fae-kind or one quite intimately acquainted with them.

He long suspected the trunk itself might actually have been a gift from the Summer King, but the Waysmith had never revealed the answer to that question one way or the other. The gears and latches were too intricate, too well assembled from fine silver, to be anything but the work of the Kingdom and so Hat Trick took his time and care to unfasten each in the proper order. The last thing he needed today was to end up trapped in a false-bottom chest somewhere off the coast of the Cape of Good Hope without an X to mark the spot.

All in all, however, the Appendant was something he would rather have avoided. It made him uncomfortable even knowing where it was and lifting it from its woven bag was enough to redden the ends of his fingers and set his knuckles to throbbing. In all other respects, the Appendant was an unusual though not an astonishing-looking thing. A silver chain of square links encircled a palm-sized black stone attached on either end by threads of knotted filigree, but that which did not, in any way, pierce the stone itself.

The black shale nodule at its apex was more unusual still in that it was perfectly smooth, having been worn so by eons of sands and currents in a sacred river; with a single, deeply-etched spiral-shell formation of golden pyrites prominent in its center. He was wiser, however, than to ever refer to it as an ammonite fossil as most others might or as *Genus Perisphinctes*, the Latin label of a scientist. He knew it by a different name. Some called them snake stones, some called them black chrysanthemums, and others called them chakras.

But regardless of what they were called, many such objects were described throughout the ancient world as manifestations of the very essence of divinity itself in material form; the spiraling rotation of the cosmos made real and revered since the birth of human civilization. Or long before it. This one had been named Kundali and bore great powers of discipline against any spirit who might seek to enter its purview without proper permissions.

Even for Hat Trick, who had sworn loyalty to this house under the regency of the Summer King, it occasionally pained him as a warning. In the end, the sacred stones of the Himalayas concealed a great many secrets and this one had been born of the Womb of the Mountain; a secret place high in the Tibetan plateau where ancient oceans now lay entombed within the tallest peaks. It had then eroded into a black river and thus traveling from deep time across unfathomable space, it found its way into the hands of a weary traveler of a very different sort.

It was the most dangerous possession the Waysmith had retained from her time abroad under the Regent's care and she never intended to part with it, not for all the bargaining in the world. Hat Trick crossed the distance to Somerset Sayer quickly, dropping the Appendant into the palm of her outstretched hand before climbing back up onto the desk to retrieve a pouch of his own small affects. Without prompting, he was already planning the shortest route to the other implements the Waysmith would need.

"What to do?" He asked, gesturing vaguely to the amulet. Fossils were known in many religions as objects of enigmatic power, despite their paleontological origins, and Hat Trick was well aware that many a chthonic entity could take up residence within them at various times depending on the actions of the ritualist.

Somerset Sayer smiled and wrapped the chain of the silver mala securely around her wrist, rolling the stone in her hand comfortably.

"What the mad bricoleur does best." She replied with a contemplative expression. "As the spiral suspends all time and space, so too will it suspend Fiona's grief until such a moment as she chooses its expression. The Womb of the Mountain will receive what she cannot bear and contain it until someone might have need of it. And in return, its vast stretches of time will heal all mortal things, mending the body as it mends the land, by wearing away all traces of catastrophe with the infinite march of ages."

"No. No no. Kundali not obey." He pointed emphatically. "Varis not follow. Too much danger for this."

"Oh, don't worry. I have no intention of attempting to force anyone to do anything they don't want to." The folklorist reassured him. "But I rather suspect I can affect the change I want with a little careful ritual handling regardless. Sort of like digging a canal to change the direction of a river. I can't possibly make the water change direction or command it to where I want it to go but I can certainly offer it an inviting alternative."

Hat Trick nodded. "Like Alice."

"Yes, like Alice."

Hat Trick summoned up his courage and pulled the strap of his pouch over his head. The Waysmith had set her mind to something, so he wasn't about to bother trying to talk her out of it.

"Get Coat." He announced finally, before once again leaping back to the floor and jogging off in the direction of the kitchen. Somerset Sayer had no worries. He would not be seen.

"Yes." Somerset Sayer said to no one in particular. "Time to go."

Clarisant sat balanced precariously on the fallen log, her toes and a few remaining leaves dipped just past the surface of the algal water. She was nude, save for an oddly placed section of tree bark tied to the inside of her left forearm. A stray water beetle skimmed off as she wet the ends of her hair, pulling brittle strands from her snowy mane and watching them dodder away on the wind.

Idly, her hands traced the deep bruises splashed across her body and arms before delicately scratching at the dried gashes over her ribs. Purple spread out across her legs all the way up to the juncture of her thighs, with pooled blue pores and a margin that had gone a jaundiced yellow. She sat openly and unashamed of them, baring the evidence of her violation to any who dared to look at her. But of course, there was no one.

No one passed this way anymore. She pressed at the crusted mass that marred her left breast and tapped absently at a portion of missing sternum. Then there were the blood-seeped breaks at her neck, which she could not see, but which still bore the indentations of teeth. She then looked down at the worst of it that decorated her torso; a garish slash that began at her collarbone, limning downward all the way to her slightly rounded lower belly.

The wounds had all had been there so long now, she almost didn't remember how she had gotten them in the first place. She remembered well enough the blade, however; a dull flash against the sky. She placed a reverent touch to the hollow at her forehead. Some things never healed. She washed the thickening scabs again, dripping sun-warmed droplets over and over each one until they ran as pinkish rivulets back into the lagoon. In the golden light of afternoon, she read the markings again and did not resist as her thoughts once more pulled her back into another time.

The language of her youth was old and rarely spoken now, from a time when the words of her homeland had been very different from what they had become. There were great stories then and great storytellers who recounted them. In secret firelight, their voices would change into a lilting meter, with a cadence rough hewn and prickly. These ancient people feared the bogs and will-o-wisps and left her their dead in peat moss graves. Strangled and cut, the sacrificed and the murdered awaited her eagerly and she gave them respite, marveling at their interrupted perfection.

At night, she would call the Danse Macabre and summon their bodies from the depths. They would come to her in joy, celebrating, even as their skins turned to leather and the water dissolved their bones. From time to time, the nomad women would come to watch, silencing their dogs and urging their horses back, and passing on tales to their daughters of the Lady of the Lights who appeared as the white hart, and whom they called unicorn.

She pulled at the dead, cracking skin at her cheek. It came away in fragments to match the shattered fractures spreading across every inch of her face and cast it into the pond. From the driftwood near her foot, she gathered up a handful of moss and mixed it with crushed Gunnera, a thumb-pad of salt, and a dried sprig of Cardamine plucked at the starting of the first cuckoo's call. This she began to push into the yawning gouge in her forehead, sliding damp fingers against the remnants of bone and horn that she felt there in a consoling gesture.

The herbs soothed the distracting pain and calmed her ruined mind's eye enough to sharpen its vision into the past. She thought of iron and the feeling of rending flesh. The sounds of boots squelching in the muck. The sneer of a man with his hands blistered by tilled soil and tamed beasts. She watched as the piecemeal memories played out for her once more.

"...she was asking for it then...." Someone was speaking through the haze of her memory.

"Asking for what?" Clarisant remembered her reply. "Asked? Where, pray tell, was my request? I did not know that I could be so eloquent unknowingly. Was it in the fevered blush of my cheeks overworked in the noon-day sun? Maybe my clothes then? Threadbare linens and split shoes or fine silks and garlands, I do not hear them speaking when so donned, but clearly in your mind he must have heard them calling to him bright as day? Since when has cloth and ornament been so graced with the gift of speech?"

"...it is what he thought that..."

Was this a town somewhere? Had she come upon a hearth? She knew she had wandered for some time, out of the forests and dales, because she could no longer hear the wind and trees.

"What care have I for his thoughts? What is done is all the meaning I require."

"...But he is a good man, my lady. A father now, a husband. Kind to us in word and deed, and gentle in caring disposition. Surely, he makes up now for all the injustices he once inflicted upon the world?..."

"You think these things apart from one another?" She had said into the fire. "That all men's deeds are but a ledger? Dripping with red, then sopped clean with the white of guilty virtue? They are not." She closed her eyes to block out the sun.

"I tell you they are not."

"Another's life of charity hath repaid me nothing," Her words still echoed on the edges of fragile lips, "and as it is a debt owed to me that has gone too long in arrears. I shall now exact interest for that which was taken from me in recompense for his imagined entitlements. No, my sisters. I come now to collect on this Bargain." Did they think she was a witch in the swamp? A ghost? The *Bean Sidhe* who presages death by screaming into the storm? Was she not?

Ah, there he was. Blustering through the plank door and growling against the wind where it followed him in. It must have been to his wife to whom previously she spoke.

"My Lord, what was it you asked of me then?" She had risen from the hearth and turned to his frightened face, "A kiss, was it not? For a lady does not demure, you said, and a kiss is valued for such a small price of dignity. Oh, my darling, I suppose you are right. Here then. Come, claim your kiss." The memory faded and returned to the mire.

She had left that house an empty one and burned its beams into muck.

Sparrow lit down to the stump but remained at a respectful distance for several moments before lightly bounding onto her knee and emitting a series of crestfallen sounds. Lifting him up onto her hand, level with her gaze, Clarisant reached up to pet the back of the little bird with a gentle smile.

"What is this?" She acknowledged, tilting up the tiny beak to get a better look at the sour face beneath. The folds of her brow pressed in at the sight of the oval gape.

Sparrow began a litany of melancholy warbles, punctuating each phrase with jabbing motions of his tiny arms. He pulled at her fingers and gnawed theatrically at her thumbnail.

"I see, I see." She soothed. "But who was to know that such a cat could even be found nowadays."

The imp turned his face and peered up at his beloved mistress, his eyes dismal with mourning. More chittering ensued. Here, she grew concerned.

"Are you certain that is what you saw?"

Sparrow nodded emphatically, the bird head nearly coming undone from the ties around his elfin ears. He leapt back to her knee and then to the downed tree to wrench up a splinter of desiccated wood. Brandishing it as a kind of stylus, he began to scratch frantic designs into the softly decayed wood, seeming to explain his concerns by waving and patting at the lines.

He sketched out a crude map. In one section, he began to narrate a battle, one which had taken place between himself, his companion Wren, and a woman who had kept vigil where none should have been awake. They had only come to steal a few odds and trinkets, just like the rest of the flock. Sneaking in as was their habit through neglected doors or windows left wide.

But they had not seen her, he chirruped out, they had seen no one through the window at all! He then wailed over Wren's bravery and angrily cursed the nimble cat whose name he hadn't recognized. He then began to tell of a harrowing circumstance. Pursued though she might have been, the woman he described had not succumbed to mortal fear. Rather, she walked strangely and the Way had risen to follow her.

Clarisant darkened with Sparrow's frustrations. Her voice, in a timbre of distant thunder, roused the creature to faithfulness once again.

"Tell me again of the maiden with the book."

Sparrow stuck out his chin and pulled a handful of feathers from his crown. He tossed them out to the water to watch as they drifted and then began to form the shapes and crosses of divination. They moved in whorls, the breeze pushing their rotation into a clockwise stirring motion. The mangled creature then began his telling anew, twittering of an unseen threshold that had carried the woman beyond him and back again, a doorway that had not permitted him passage and, despite his worthier Fae nature, had barred his entry. What was beyond it, he had not been allowed to glimpse as the Way carried her off in rolling labyrinthian turns. No matter what he offered, it would not give.

"So" Clarisant began, looking out onto the glassy pond where the shadows of the treeline stained the water black. "Another has found her Way."

Sparrow reached up and laid his hands on the rise of her hip. He wished vengeance but he wished it even more at the hands of his Queen.

"Then it is only a matter of time before the other finds her and the Waysmith reveals her path. But this is no tragedy, my friend. It only means that there is nothing more that can conceal her from me now."

She rose gracefully to her feet as white hair flowed out around her and concealed her nakedness once again. With the fleet-footed leap of a doe, Clarisant raised Sparrow up onto her open palm and crossed the distance from branch to shore with little effort. She then regarded him coolly.

"We know what it is that must be done now, do we not?" She inquired with a mischievous glint. The little imp shrieked and bobbed in anticipation. "Go now, little one. Set out the call to the Hecatomb. Fly out across the marshes and send word throughout the Fell and the Upland. Call my haunts and devourers of travelers to me. Let the Stumble rise and feed on ash and plague. Let them come, join now the trees and brambles, and mourn with me."

Chapter Ten

"Fiona, do you understand what this is going to do?"

"I think so? Mom said it will, I guess.... end it all?"

"That's a rather fatalistic way of putting it..." Somerset Sayer continued to flip through a series of spell pages. "I would probably say nullify or revoke, but Rivers That Flow Backwards can be a little tricky to get right regardless of how you want it to work. Either way, I'm going to be doing and saying a lot of strange things and I don't want you to be alarmed alright?"

Fiona scowled, confusion and strained incredulity writ across her face, but nodded.

"Do either of you have a watch?"

"Yes." Alice Guthrie replied. "Why?"

"Put it outside on the porch, would you?"

Without question, Alice did as she was told, surveying the front room space intently as the shadows of an unseen figure flitted across the floor and up and over tilted bookshelves; covering mirrors, stopping clocks, and hiding everyone's shoes beneath a basket near the fireplace. Where over-sized gilt frames leaned too far out from the wall, they were pulled back and their wires tightened behind painted portrait throats. It was uncanny how she could catch the movement out of the corner of her eye but never quite get an actual look at whomever it was once she had turned in the proper direction. All that remained was the evidence of passing and never a face or a foot rightly in view.

"Despite the fact that the entirety of this ritual looks somewhat like self-indulgent posturing, I think that you will find these proceedings interesting Ms. Guthrie." Somerset Sayer paused to scrub excess ink off of her hand. "Ms. Guthrie the elder that is."

"Why is that?" Alice turned and locked the outer door before taking a seat on the living room couch.

"Because, from what I can see, it contains all the overly dramatic theatrical trappings of Victorian occultism that tends to appeal to the skeptical. Substantiality of mental processes, symbols as the key to insight; I mean, Birch would be giggling all the way to Madame Blavatsky's parlor window with some of this nonsense."

"But it will work?" Fiona peeked over the edges of the large tome currently weighing down the curiously ebullient folklorist.

"Work? Oh yes, yes. It'll work. It just reads a bit... melodramatically, for my taste. And that's saying something."

"*How* does it work?" Alice Guthrie attempted to interject into the scholar's freneticism.

"Some terrible poetry." Came the response. "Celtic, I think."

"I mean, what should *we* be doing, Dr. Sayer?"

"Oh. Nothing at the moment. Hat Trick! If you would please."

Though Alice Guthrie had seen Hat Trick once before, shrouded by the morning mists of Stonehenge in what could only have been a meeting that took place eons ago, she was not prepared for the stupor she would experience at his reappearance. As the Kobold toddled out from the kitchen, laden with an armload of odd-lot bric-a-brac, she observed that he had traded his blue felt jacket for a red linen overshirt and gugel hood. His skin was the same mossy brown as she recalled from earlier but the wide reflective eyes that had once seemed so characteristically nocturnal were now shaded enough to reveal a light-blue iris ring and a pinpoint pupil squinting against the midday light.

He sniffled as he tottered past, and as the little Fae began to unload his burden onto the living room rug, Alice Guthrie continued to note that he was becoming seemingly less and less supernatural the longer she examined him. His arms and legs remained lanky, his hands still hanging nearly to the ground, and he had the same bobbing walk on his too-wide feet; but by the time Fiona had taken notice of another individual in the room, his nose was more prominent on his face, his chin protruded from beneath his bottom lip, and a few locks of sandy brown hair stuck out from the sides of his hood. For all intents and purposes, he appeared almost passable for human. A disproportionately short one perhaps, but human.

"My assistant in such matters." Somerset Sayer responded to Fiona's startled gasp. "Hat Trick."

"Hat Trick?" She turned, dubious.

"Yes." The folklorist looked up from the unbalanced tome. "He's... uh...it's a nickname."

Hat Trick raised an eyebrow but continued unpacking.

"Hat Trick." Fiona repeated. "How did you get a nickname like Hat Trick?" She turned again to the busy little man at the table.

Hat Trick looked up, glowering but bright-eyed and excitable. With a nod, but without much in the way of words, he held out a raised finger in order to give himself a moment to mentally prepare. He then climbed up onto the table, facing Fiona and the scholar, and held out both of his hands before him with a magisterial flourish meant to demonstrate that he had nothing up his sleeves. He first pulled down the cuff of his right arm, followed by the cuff of his left, before twirling his fingers cartoonishly in the air around his head.

Despite herself, Fiona began to laugh and crossed her arms with mock suspicion as Hat Trick continued waving his arms in the air and flexing up and down on his ankles. All he seemed to be lacking was the appropriate circus music and the spectacle of a diminutive stand-up act would be complete. And then, with a sudden joyful bounce and a shout, which sounded something like *Ta-Da* but more guttural, he reached beneath his hood and pulled out a small, and awfully ragged, bouquet of pink flowers.

This he then naturally handed to the delighted Fiona who obliged him with a grateful clap.

"Oh, you do magic tricks! Thank you!" She accepted the bent Potentilla stems with a playful bow.

"Exceptionally handy when you need something specific for a concoction or when you run out of the necessary herbs." Somerset Sayer touched her tongue before turning the page. "Or sometimes just a decent cup of tea."

Alice Guthrie shifted slightly away from the transformed goblin. "You mean, he can conjure up whatever he wants like that?"

Hat Tricked sighed. While he was generally accustomed to being spoken of or about, even by name, while standing in the room, he was not more than two feet from the elder Guthrie when she indicated him.

"Come out what you like." He rasped lowly, sending an involuntary jolt through the seated Alice. "Nice flowers for lady. Pick your favorites. Hat Trick no rabbits, though."

"Oh, come on mom, relax." Fiona held the delicate blossoms beneath her nose. "It's just stage magic. A little abracadabra and a little misdirection, you know?"

Alice looked up at her daughter with an unreadable glare. Even now, Fiona had still not ascertained the depth of the truth at hand but Alice remained conflicted. She was not entirely sure she wanted her to.

"Good thing it wasn't Coat Check." The scholar muttered. "One deck of cards and we'd be here all day."

Hat Trick smiled, a weird squinting expression, and returned to his bundle. Somerset Sayer dropped the book to her waist and groaned.

"Please tell me that isn't what I think it is."

"Lotus wand!" He beamed, holding up each item in turn. "Rose lamen! Cup! Dagger and Pentacle!"

"Hat Trick, for the love of Puck, I told you no more with the Ceremonial Magic. I'm not drawing any diagrams, no consecration of instruments, and, ugh, no Golden Dawn!"

"This being true for the ordinary Universe..." He struggled to adopt the cut-glass enunciation one might imagine when reciting the premise to a mid-19th century mystical text. "We must include illusions, which are after all..."

"And no quoting Mathers in this house!"

After another round of infectious giggling, Somerset Sayer was finally able to make peace in her house of cats by drawing attention to the specifics of the ritual at hand. But not before Hat Trick had found great satisfaction in amusing Fiona, which had the effect of lightening the mood of Alice Guthrie, which had the circular problem of encouraging more out of Hat Trick until the folklorist was sure that no magic was going to be possible at all that day.

"Alright, Alright." The folklorist commented absently. "Best to get on with things before Hat Trick finds his way to a curtain and a dove pan."

Alice Guthrie agreed. "Indeed. Is there anywhere specifically we should sit?"

"There is fine." Somerset Sayer inclined her gaze to the couch. "Now, there are two things of vital importance here in the next hour or so. Firstly, I need you both to promise that you will do exactly as I tell you, without hesitation, and without stopping to question me. You can ask me all the questions you want when it's done, but for right now I need your assurance that you will carry out the tasks I give you without fail."

Alice looked at Fiona and Fiona to her mother. "Okay. Yes."

"Excellent. Secondly, I hope I don't need to reiterate that what we're about to undertake is not an easy thing. It may not work. It may work but with additional unforeseen results. It may work entirely as expected and you will still need to deal with whatever consequences or issues that might arise given the.... uh... circumstances. Do you understand me? Varis can only address the immediate problem. It can't make you feel any particular way about it."

Fiona fidgeted with the browning petals in her lap. Agitated, she stared at her lap and picked a bud from the thickest stem to crush between her fingers. Unexpectedly, Somerset Sayer reached out and took the girl's hand.

"Fiona, what I am trying to say is that whatever you choose to do with the anger and the hurt and the pain is up to you. They belong to you. They're yours. Nothing, and no one, can take them away from you until you choose to release them. And only then when you are ready. I know that this doesn't exactly seem like a good thing right now, but it is. I'm going to do everything I can to heal the wound, or the physical expression of it anyway. It's going to be up to you to find the rest of the remedy for yourself after that."

The girl did not respond outwardly, but Somerset Sayer felt the tight squeeze to her hand that let her know it was time to begin. The folklorist carefully placed the book at the edge of the coffee table, knelt down in front of the couch, and produced the black spiral pendant from her shirt pocket.

"Fiona, I want you to imagine yourself. Your younger self, like when you were a little girl. Maybe around six or so. I want you to imagine her sitting here in front of you where I am and I want you to tell her a story about the woman she will become. About her future self."

"So, me?"

"No, her future self isn't you."

"I don't understand."

"Your future self, Fiona, is someone even you aren't yet. Someone who is yet to come. Closer in time for you maybe but not you. I know how bizarre all this is going to sound but I want you to think of the movement of your life like it's a river. Rivers, you see, are shaped by the landscape around them and their flow and their direction is all about the rocks and trees and deep, deep, stones beneath. And when you think about it, this in turn influences all kinds of other things like how people travel and get food and build their homes. This is how we are going to tell the story of your life, okay? Because once we do that, we can understand how a river can change. How a river can flow backwards."

"Rivers can't flow backwards."

"Actually, they can, in a long-term sense. Many rivers haven't always flowed in the same direction as they do now. Sometimes they change when new mountains form or when canyons are cut. Sometimes small rivers come together and create one great river, and sometimes people change the land around them and this makes them move. But I'm not here to give you a geology lesson, Fiona, my point here is that this is about a kind of metaphor. A metaphor I need you to understand intrinsically if this is going to work. And I need you to start by telling me a story."

"I'm still not sure I get it."

"Okay." The scholar paused. "Well, think of it like this. You are going to imagine being you when you are older; thinking back on this moment now. About who you are now. What do you think that older you would want to tell you now? There? Does that work?"

"Yeah, I think so. But you'll think it's stupid."

Somerset Sayer let go of the sigh she'd be holding in for far too long. "No, I won't. Listen Fiona, when I left academia, I left behind a certain kind of thinking. Peer review, you see, is a lot like art critique. It's a war between the artist and the critic where they use the canvas as a kind of back-and-forth battleground, or I suppose in this analogy, the story. But eventually, what comes out of it all is something that merges those two voices; the artist's or the author's intent and the critic's judgment of it. We need to tell a different kind of story. We need to change what certain things mean from your perspective, from their very essence, from the inside out. I'm not here to judge your story. I'm not here to tell you what you really mean by something or to tell you how others understand what you say. I'm here to help you tell it in such a way that the world you inhabit changes. I'm not your adversary. We're partners in this. okay?"

"Promise you won't laugh?"

"Consider it my part of the bargain."

Somerset Sayer and Alice Guthrie exchanged a knowing look.

"Okay. Um. What kind of story should I tell, uh, her?"

"Look at the things around you." The folklorist motioned to the room, the shelves, and the pile of miscellany still crowding the table. "Use them to inspire you. Incorporate them into a story about what you think your life is going to be like, let's say, fifteen years from now. Imagine yourself at thirty-something and talk to me about what kind of person you think exists at that time. It doesn't have to be elaborate or Shakespearean or anything like that. Just, help the little girl that you see understand what it is she will look forward to. About who will be thinking back about her one day."

Fiona felt her hands begin to sweat and she used it as a momentary excuse to rub the jagged ends of Hat Trick's wilting bouquet against her palms. She imagined broad gashes opening up in her hands, where it was not sweat that dripped onto the cut ends but blood. She imagined the base of the stems taking hold and the roots growing out into her skin. She imagined those roots burrowing deep and stitching the wounds together as the flowers became reinvigorated, opening up their faces towards her as the pain faded away. She held the flowers closer and hoped that they could keep her from falling apart.

"Fine. Well. The woman we will become dresses in fun clothes." Fiona began. It felt contrived; artificial. Hesitant, she looked at her mother and then to the scholar, each who only nodded and waited for her to continue. "Bright colors all the time. It's like..." She paused and looked around the room. Settling her eyes quickly on a scarf hanging near the door. "It's like that time you played dress up when you were really little and took all those old, ugly, coats from your grandma's closet. Just because you thought they looked so cool and grownup. And you could wear all the make-up you wanted because nobody cared because you were just a little kid. But now, every day is like that and it's all okay because everyone in town knows you as this crazy artist type. Crazy artist types are like that. You make sculptures sometimes. These really huge sculptures out of metal and clay and things you find on the sea shore."

As Fiona began to haltingly weave the threads of her story, Somerset Sayer shifted into the altered state of dual consciousness that served her best during moments such as these. She breathed deep, letting the sound of the girl's voice pull her mind into a calm and meditative stance. As she did so, her eyes became unfocused and the world around her began to shift into the curious mishmash of the Near By. It was a kind of mosaic that never held still for very long. Objects winked in and out while strange creatures passed by on their way to other adventures.

Passing thoughts and ideas manifested in unexpected ways while daydreams played out one overtop the other. It was a whimsical space but one touched on all sides by dread and a looming sense of danger. The things that passed through peoples' minds were not always cheerful and kind and the Way By was unbiased when it came to the things inside the darkest niches of the human soul. None need have worried however. The house on Trowbridge Street was carefully curated and there was little present in the ethereal spaces of the Waysmith's living room that she did not have near complete control over.

The folklorist glanced about to gain her bearings. Lacewings floated in on the warm sun to tend to the houseplants with a bevy of tiny tinsnips. A threadbare gnome wandered by as he cut and bound the lichens growing on the Uzbek rug and where the head of a headless cow sat balanced in an armchair, three cadaverous mice were working tirelessly to paint its portrait on an easel made of brass. A half-chewed dog's toy composed ballads for its dear departed companion on the strings of the parlor piano but not before the bust of Barrett-Browning had sufficiently finished off its cigar.

A quiet had descended in the interim, however. There were no mirrors or clocks to disturb the ambiance. No shoes to indicate a direction. No spying eyes to observe them. With practiced ease, the folklorist pushed past the initial chaos into a more analytic view, searching for the hidden structures in the nonsense before her.

"She lives in a house surrounded by trees." Fiona continued; her eyes twisted shut as she fumbled through her words. "An orchard. She picks apples every fall with her friends."

Fiona's story began to take shape in her mind, in the minds of those who listened to her, and the Near By responded. Somerset Sayer watched as the first blank sheets of paper were pushed in on the wind. Followed quickly by reams of unlined loose leaf. Piles upon piles of white squares caught in a hurricane that could only be seen and not felt. She noted several sheets smeared in ink and graphite, some with sections of scribbled writing erased or re-written. They came tumbling out of the fireplace, through the cracks in the walls, out of the fixtures in the ceiling, and down the stairs in the hallway. A few were crumpled up or torn into pieces, but almost all remained blank.

"You're doing fine, Fiona, keep going." The folklorist stood to direct the deluge.

This was not the first time the folklorist had experienced the Way By in this fashion. In fact, during her own younger years, she had often encountered the dream-like realms appearing to her like the pages of an adolescent diary. It was also not uncommon for many people to imagine their raw potential in this way, as the unmarked papers in a sketchbook or in a journal. She had long figured that the popularity of scrapbooking and photo albums as a method of recording one's life experiences probably had something to do with it, so the relative ubiquity of these kinds of formations didn't surprise her. Truthfully, Somerset Sayer had actually hoped that Fiona would be so predictable in this endeavor. It made picking up the pieces that much easier in the end.

Opening windows to alter the flow of air and pushing back dams where they formed in the thresholds of the house, the scholar began pulling up pages one by one and laying them out beneath the items on the table. Which, to the eyes of Alice Guthrie, of course, looked as though the scholar was aimlessly wandering about the living room, gathering up lint from the floor and lintels, and smearing it onto the polished wood surface. She remained in concentration, however, encouraging her daughter with meaningless affirmations and light touches to her knee.

The first page the folklorist freed from the heap looked as though it might have once contained lines of copied text, but the spaces between words appeared as though they were now being used for musical notation. Quarter notes obscured the loops of the cursive lettering and a quick smattering of sixteenths created a strike-out line across the rest. The second page, however, gave her pause. On it were the indentations of something that had been drawn over with ink. Blotter smudges made it nearly impossible to discern what but Somerset Sayer could make out the impressions of fingernails and the half-finished doodle of a torso bound in the leather straps of a Chirurgeon's scaffold.

"Oh, Fiona." She whispered inwardly. "I am so, so, sorry. I see it. The Fae who steal children indeed."

"She's a botanist." Fiona finally announced. "She does research in the summers and, as a hobby, she sells flowers on the side of the road. And there's a man that lives a few houses down. He walks by with his dog every day and buys something from her."

There appeared to be little rhyme or reason to the pages that Somerset Sayer continued to choose from the growing piles except to say that each one bore a series of faint, disconnected, outlines. Almost as though they had been used as tracing paper laid over a much larger and darker image that the scribbler could not quite make out.

And as Fiona began to gain confidence in her story, going on to describe romance over coffee dates and the field guides she would write, the scholar set about to rearrange the selected pages and objects in much the same manner as tarot cards; using the wand, cup, dagger, pentacle, and rose to mark the suit corners of each sheet in the customary spaces.

Once she had the pattern to her liking, she carefully raised the fossil pendant and held it over the table so that the spiral of the ammonite faced downwards and the entire stone was free to sway or twist in whatever direction it liked. Chewing nervously at the inside of her cheek, she then raised the Victorian spell book and carefully balanced it at her hip so that she could both read the text highlighted within and keep an unbroken gaze on the starry black stone.

"Beneath coin she stands shivering, and wasted skin away;" The Waysmith was now full into her focus and held the Appendant over the pentacle sheet. She could not, however, prevent the annoyed wince that passed through her as she recited the histrionic prose. "This past is left to quivering, and forgotten to decay."

She moved the stone to the drawing beneath the wand. "Dreams of light now flowering, and darkness too obsessed; Frustrated Death stands glowering, by a spirit's hand caressed."

To the eyes of Alice Guthrie, and to Fiona who had paused her story while trying to come up with the next part, a curious thing began to happen. Small droplets of water were now condensing at the edge of the stone dangling from the silver chain. As the folklorist continued her recitation, they fell, in unnatural timing, onto the coffee table arrangement. As they did so, the stray bits of fluff and lint that she had gathered up from the living room rug were pulled inwards by the growing puddle and coalesced into what looked like vague, misty, shapes. Neither mother nor daughter, however, could quite make sense of them. To Somerset Sayer, however, there was a somewhat different event taking place. The water from the stone was falling onto the papers she had set out and, as she had hoped it would, began to dilute the inks and wash the markings clean.

"'Neath the rough rose's thorn, a cover, to the heart which guards its wonder;" The stone flicked droplets onto a paper, smearing the lines before they faded out completely. "With a bloom doomed to hover, o'er mud and slime thereunder."

She then reached the cup. "Come now to intertwine, these threads yet uncombined." At that, even Hat Trick had to stifle a groan. "Show to failing eyes sublime, how it is these things align."

Finally, she passed the flowing stone over the paper beneath the dagger. The drops came faster and heavier, resulting in a meandering stream dribbling off the edge and down onto the rug. "Blood flows fast when from the kill, floods now slow and drain downhill; Surrender now your very core, and once awash ye fight no more."

Only Hat Trick could see the changes that came into the world next.

Somerset Sayer remained fixed on the stone turning slowly on its chain and picked her prose very carefully, the emotion in her voice barely betrayed with a tear that slid down to the corner of her mouth.

"The mountain is adorned in all the colors of spring. Flowers bloom on the leeward side and any crag that faces the sun is never grey but yellow, pink, blue, and white. It stands the highest of all the peaks on the great glacial massif and can be seen from every direction. All the world speaks of the mountain with reverence, in awe of the vast spaces that she fills. The village at her feet thinks of her as their own and names their walking paths and hidden lakes in her honor. The clouds are moved by her great heights and sculpt marvelous shapes in the sky. Travelers use them to discern the mood of the weather and to determine when the time of safe passage has come."

Hat Trick moved closer in anticipation as the folklorist continued without breath, in a voice only the Way By could hear.

"In shadow grows a forest where fragile and beautiful things live. They find great abundance here and are never left wanting. The birds sing each morning and announce the coming of first light. Great elk stamp through the underbrush chased by packs of joyous wolves who will never reach them. As both elk and wolf know, each morning the chase begins and each evening it is abandoned, but they look forward to the next race just on the horizon. Then the frogs take up the chorus from the birds when the light grows dim. The snow never comes here and the leaves never fall. Something unknown flashes in the distance and carries death and disease away on scampering feet. This is the story everyone tells. The river must flow around her. This is the story that everyone knows. The river has not yet worn her away. The peak rises still too quickly from deep in the bedrock. The Earth raises her up. There is no story... but this one."

Fiona shuddered and abruptly stopped her narration. Unseen by all in attendance, the spiral of the stone made a quarter turn, the center suddenly disappearing into the smooth and rounded nodule. Faceless now and hidden, it had consumed the part of Fiona's story laid out by the Waysmith and had thus rendered it powerless. The pages lay blank, though only Somerset Sayer could take note of that detail, and as the water first slowed and then vanished, the dark stains of what once was written sunk back into the imagined world, leaving it with nothing but a gossamer sheen.

The folklorist stayed motionless as Hat Trick leapt forward, producing a box of matches from beneath his hood. To the shock of both Alice Guthrie and her daughter, he pulled a handful from the cardboard cover, struck them, and immediately set the entire coffee table alight. Fiona jumped back involuntarily as the objects and water were consumed with preposterous vigor. For all the bright crackling, Somerset Sayer may just as well have doused the table in gasoline than clear waters wrung from a stone.

To her credit, Alice Guthrie managed to catch the shout that nearly escaped her lips and instead, let out a long, confounded breath as she leaned away from the draughts of heat. Somerset Sayer slowly allowed her shoulders to relax. Holding the Appendant over the flames until they died down and extinguished of their own accord, Alice Guthrie could not help but comment that the table had been left shockingly unharmed though covered in a layer of fine grey ashes.

"Alright, now." The scholar spoke up, a little more loudly than she needed to. "Fiona. I want you to carefully place your hands onto the table and cover them with the ashes."

Checking first to see that the table was not, in fact, burning hot; she did so, looking up to the Waysmith with cautious curiosity.

"With your right hand, touch the ammonite stone." She waited until she had done it. "And with your left, I want you to use the ashes and draw one line across your eyes, one line across your mouth, and one line across your chest."

Fiona complied.

"Now, repeat after me."

And she did.

"If footsteps falter, crawl, or crumble; what is done is done to humble. A final choice, lingered, last; what is now is now and not the past."

With that, Somerset Sayer tossed the book onto the couch, straightened her spine to release the tension, and dropped the pendant into a small, cloth pouch in her hand. She could feel the heat emanating off of the usually cool surface and she hoped that there would be enough time to return it to its chest before she would end up having to explain why the pouch was crisped and burning. An issue she would have to deal with continuously until the latent potential suspended inside of it had calmed. She chanced a satisfied smile.

"Is that it?" Fiona furled her brow, looking now with some disgust at the dirt smeared over her hands, face, and clothes.

The scholar let out a snort. Rather undignified but genuine. "Is that it?" She repeated.

"I mean," the girl corrected, "Is it...done? I mean, gone?"

"Yes. It seems to have worked."

"How will I know?"

"You mean aside from the obvious, given time?"

"I...uh..."

"Fiona." Somerset Sayer motioned for her attention. "Look."

The confused girl took a moment to follow the scholar's gaze towards her lap, where Hat Trick's Potentilla bouquet still sat, but now alive, bright, and bursting with new blooms and shining green leaves just beginning to unfurl.

Madam Bel Carmen wasted no time in throwing together a bag of clothing, various occult accoutrements, and a few toiletries. As she did so, she also set about to loudly chide her niece into hurrying along with her choices of attire.

"Now, my darling." She called from the bedroom. "Be sure to think of something practical. We might be doing some walking and I haven't a clue what the weather is going to be like. Where we're going, that is."

"Where *are* we going?" Elizabeth stared into the guest bedroom closet with growing concern. Suffice to say that her and her aunt's taste in general fashion, while both characteristic to the personality of each, were not remotely related.

"That's...hard to say." Her aunt replied from the end of the hall.

"You mean you don't know where we're going but we're going there anyway?"

"You'll see when we get there. You still have the box with you, yes? You didn't lose it?"

"No, Aunt Evelyn. I didn't lose it. Not the kind of thing you really forget about."

Madam Bel Carmen huffed and pulled a second bag from underneath a pile of shoes. She felt the intrinsic need to prepare Elizabeth for what she might encounter once they met with the enigmatic folklorist but she hardly knew where to begin. To wit, she was also unsure just exactly how much she should reveal at a time such as this. She couldn't completely explain the terrifying creature in the balsawood box but nor could she offer nothing as to its possible origins.

"Well alright, dear." She shouldered her two bags and trotted down the hall to the door of Elizabeth's temporary room. "See what you can cobble together there and I'll be right back. I just need to make a quick phone call."

"Sure." Elizabeth nodded, not bothering to turn from the unusually daunting task at hand.

Taking care to be well outside of earshot in the downstairs kitchen, Madam Bel Carmen pulled her phone from her purse and made quick work to bring up the familiar contact, silently praying that the honorable and good Alice Guthrie would not be otherwise engaged.

It rang for an interminable amount of time before a tentative voice finally came on the line.

"Yes, hello?"

"Oh, thank the gods, Ms. Alice, I am so happy to have caught you."

"Oh, oh, yes, Ms. Evelyn. I...well...things have just been a little complicated lately and I'm sorry I haven't gotten the chance to get back to you."

"Not a worry, not a worry at all. I do need to ask you a question though if you have a moment?"

"I suppose. But only a moment, my daughter and I have... a few things to do."

"Of course. Yes, I was just needing the contact information for Dr. Sayer if you still had it. Something has, well, I'm not sure how else to describe it, but something has come up that I think you should be present to see. But I will need to consult with Dr. Sayer first and foremost, and not to put too fine a point on it, as soon as possible as well."

"Oh. Well. I should ask her then to speak to you. I am here with her now, actually."

"You are? Right now? Ms. Alice, is everything alright?"

"Yes. At least, I think so. Oh, Ms. Evelyn, so much has happened I don't even know how to explain it all. But I am here with Dr. Sayer in Cambridge. She's helping me see through a spot of trouble. Should I see if she can speak with you?"

"By all means. Thank you, dear."

A bit of commotion erupted on the far end of the line and as Madam Bel Carmen listened, she thought she could make out a few voices all pressed together over the static of the poor connection. One seemed to find the entire thing amusing, though why an unexpected phone call might be funny escaped Madam Bel Carmen. Another encouraged the contact while yet a third could only be described as mildly exasperated at this particular turn of events. Finally, a familiar voice took the phone.

"Hello, Ms. Bel Carmen. What can I do for you?"

"Dr. Sayer, I am just delighted to have caught you. Really, it is just pure karma on my part here."

"Not the term I would use but alright."

"Anyway, I need to see you just as soon as you have a moment. I know, I know, you are not especially partial to company and probably not at a time when you are already socially engaged, I can hear, but this is urgent. It...well...it has to do with fairies."

Somerset Sayer sighed.

"When doesn't it?" She deadpanned.

"I...have no idea. I..."

"What's the problem, Ms. Bel Carmen?"

"Well. I have one."

"I beg your pardon?"

"I have one. Here. In a box. A dead one."

A long silence followed.

"I'm sorry. Did you just say you had a dead fairy in a box?"

"Yes, that's exactly what I said. And I need you to have a look at it. Just as soon as you can, please."

"Okay. One more time on that one. You have a dead fairy. In a box. And you can see it?"

"Yes, that's what I told you. Well, to be completely transparent here, I didn't put it there. My niece did, you see. She says that it attacked her last night. More than one even, but this one was killed by the cat after a rather serious scuffle. It cut her up something terrible. So, she put it in a box and came to see me, knowing, as you know, that I have a particular penchant for this kind of thing, and of course, I immediately thought of you. Why wouldn't I? And I wanted to get ahold of you right away and..."

"Madam Bel Carmen."

"Oh. Uh. Yes?"

"Let me get this straight. Your niece got into a fight with what she believes to be a fairy. It injured her but in the course of this fight, her cat killed it. She then put it in a box and came to see you and now you want me to..."

"Not *believes,* Dr. Sayer. We are certain of it. It is most definitely some kind of imp or devil or some creature. Horrible, ugly, desiccated little thing. Just awful. I took a look at it with my own eyes and I can assure you that this is no case of mistaken identity just because of what we've all been through."

"Huh. Well. Shit."

"Can you help us? We'll bring it over just as soon as you have a minute. I'm really very concerned about this, Dr. Sayer. I mean, do you think that something might have followed any one of us back? Could these things attack us again? Why would they go after my darling Elizabeth? She couldn't possibly have had anything to do with anything involving our work with the Hearthcraft people."

"No. I really don't think that's it."

"What should we do?"

"Where are you now?"

"At my house in Manchester. Elizabeth just drove back from Amherst."

"Alright. Then I think you should get back in your car. Preferably with the box. And drive to Cambridge. Seeing as Ms. Guthrie is already here, I'll put a kettle on."

"Yes, Oh, wonderful, thank you so much, Dr. Sayer. We will be there just as soon as we can. We'll drive straight through and we should be there in about an hour I should think."

"Fine. Oh, and Ms. Bel Carmen?"

"Yes, Dr. Sayer?"

"Don't take the route through Methuen, keep your windows rolled up at all times, and don't pay any toll, or anything else, using a copper coin. Do you understand me?"

"Yes, of course I understand. But, why?"

"Trust me."

Chapter Eleven

In the hands of a better storyteller, Clarisant was certain that the lilac wood might still shimmer with the leaves of great beech trees and the denizens of the forest might still be protected in an expanse of underground warrens, in bushes, in nests and caves, in mounds of earth, and in treetops. The snows would never come and the leaves would never wither or brown. Rather, it should always remain at the very height of spring and bursting with life on the cusp of full flourish, because that is where all of thc tales would start and end and leave it. But back then, her skin still smelled of oak and mistletoe and had not yet turned from the colors of sea foam to that of the virgin apple blossoms which would never bear fruit; soft as windblown dandelions.

She did not look like Pliny had once described her; she was neither fearsome nor possessed of a deep, bellowing voice. She was not much like a horse, nor a deer, and did not have the feet of an elephant. And her horn had not been black, but straw and alabaster, with tangles like vines and dry grasses to a point sharper than Damascus steel. She was an elfin thing, prankish and lithe. In earlier days, it would amuse her to no end to change her form at will, as the Way By permitted, and to scamper about as any number of mischievous creatures of legend.

She would follow the huntsmen as a hart, sporting with their long-striding steeds and warning their gamc away along the path. She would sing the songs of birds and watch children in their gardens laugh at her mimicry. Shc would tease the farmers at work in their fields and jest with them by dashing through the rows as a fox and hare and by hiding their plows in the thicket. She had shone so unbearably bright then. But the day came, not long after, when the Way By had first given her the form of a woman.

Now the snow was falling in endless thick flakes. The trees were barren, and though there was nothing but ragged branches to block the view to the horizon, the deep places of the wood were murky and obscured by gloom. It was cold and the wet chill prickled the skin. Clarisant watched as the path before her fell away and blended into the distance. The verdant colors mixed with mud to wash out the last of the light into sinking grey pools and indiscernible fog. The canvas of the Near By dripped clean in wooden knots and streaks and left its livelier paints to soak back into the ground. The painters were all gone now, of course, and their brushes lay in piles of discarded kindling.

She was used to being alone and the path was a familiar one. Upturned furrows marked the bends and turns like scars, she thought absently, which are so much better at telling the future than they are at revealing history. The landscape swelled and murmured as she passed, where old injuries anticipated the oncoming storm. She walked on to where the crows ended, to a twisted cemetery gate barely visible above a low wall of stacked tombstones. More out of macabre habit than curiosity, she counted the bones half-buried in the berm. Still some twenty men and not a single one beyond the threshold. She smiled. She even remembered some of their names.

The Way By grew restless and fixed its form into that of an agitated swamp. The air became heavier and the crows paused in their incessant chatter to observe her approach. When tree roots tightened at her footsteps and the sky began to bend towards her, Clarisant stopped and addressed the unseen ramparts.

"I do not break bread." She called into the silence. "I do not give milk. I do not stitch."

A kind of breath was loosed into the wind. The gates made no attempt to keep her nor the wall to deter her, and she walked on towards a pyre on the highest hill.

The Way By Stumble had stood since the reign of Evil Merodach, a half a millennium before the common era. But never before had it appeared as it did now, nor had it gouged so deeply in the soul of the world. Beyond the rusting, impotent gates at the wall were a dozen great funeral pyres on a dozen hills high enough to blot out the sun.

At its center, an ancient ash tree a hundred feet high, stripped of its leaves, and a trunk smoldering eternally from within. The orange-red glow visible throughout the hardwood crevices remained her beacon as she took in the great mound and cast her eyes about the cremation grounds.

Here, they had burned witches. Here they had burned everything that might turn the Way By against their rule: rebellious slaves and heretics, the captives of war, the marginal and those called impure, holy women who had abandoned their cloisters, faithless wives and useless widows, unsettlers and travelers, renunciates and deserters, martyrs, and children given over to sacrifice. And here is where she now brought the rules of her own nature and lay the murdered at the feet of a sacred forest in ruins. But even now, the ground was not so easily corrupted. Nature never received tasks with more suspicion than those that were meant to bind the creative and the dead.

This was largely because the dead, firstly, had no need of reconciliation between their former lives and life that did not now include them. The Fairest, conversely, were typically offended by the participation of allies they did not profess to need, even if they already knew that such companions were already fused with them. This meant that the dead often had to be compelled to act in favor of the summoner, while the Fae were generally discouraged from doing so. And Clarisant needed both if her aims were to be achieved. Both, who must be lashed to the course of the Way By Stumble and brought to heel. As a result, there was nothing Clarisant might say that would save any of her actions from the unfortunate reputation of their kind. She would be hated no matter what she did, and this she took in stride.

Many a thoughtful mind did perceive, however, that the order that she had brought forth into the Stumble was of a kind preferred by neither the quick nor the dead – but rather that which placed them into very different relations with one another. That is to say that nothing among the supernatural was unnatural, except perhaps for her. She stretched and once more counted the seven trees in attendance. Rising above the endless field of bones was Yggdrasil, but the wells of Urðarbrunnr and Mímisbrunnr were nothing but parched mouths gaping in the sky. Neither did the spring of Hvergelmir flow out any longer and all its rivers had long since run dry.

On the hills surrounding them, the tree Mímameiðr sat upon the pyre of the deserters next to the remains of the Hoddmímis holt, the woods meant to give shelter from the apocalypse. To her right rose Læraðr, the tree of betrayal and the pyre of the heretics. To her left, Ağaç Ana, where the White Mother once sat. To this tree went the pyre of holy women, martyrs, and children. And then on to Iroko, where the pyre of the mad still roared loudly and beyond that, Ashvattha, a bodhi tree whose infinite roots spread out to touch all human action in the world and under which the Buddha had once gained his enlightenment.

And finally, there was Kalpavriksha, the tree of wishes, where the pyre of lost daughters blistered the soil. The great forest of trees that made up the Stumble were all those trees sprung from the seeds of the world's lore. Far too many had once held a memory and far too many more had adorned the breastplates and amulets of lesser men. They moaned and cracked beneath the weight of centuries of burning, the bones of the dead and forgotten piled in their roots, flames still flickering in yawning mouths and empty eye sockets. But even then, it was not only a hellscape. There was simply no word for a dirge that has consumed a thousand years.

Clarisant stepped through the pyre of witches on bare ashen feet. She surveyed the dead impassively, looking here and there for the tell-tale signs of the one she sought. And then she saw her, and delighted. She was precisely where she had last left her. The bones of Mary Elizabeth Toft were jumbled into a reckless pile beneath the furthest low-hanging branch, where the splinters of her crushed ribs would not become lost in the clutter beneath. Beneath her curled finger bones was a second depression marked out in the charcoal, but empty. The perfect place she had already set aside for another.

"Transgressor!" She shouted. "Interloper!"

"I am here."

"Come to me." The unicorn commanded.

Mary Toft appeared as the Way By allowed, in the gossamer shades typical of ghosts while forming her hands, face, and all other expressive motions out of the ashes swept up in the breeze. She could, however, maintain the red colors of her coat through the glowing embers of wood and bone yet available to her. Her hair she made from fallen leaves, though they disintegrated into powder at the slightest tilt. Beyond her, several more shadows rose out of the dust but saw fit to keep their distance and to betray nothing of their names or faces.

"Am I to suffer you again now?" The shape of Mary asked. "I was having a dream. A beautiful, puzzling dream."

"And what did you dream?" Clarisant responded, knowing through experience that ghosts, rudely awakened, often tended to focus on miscellaneous things.

"There was a great gothic archway in a dark hall. The stones were grey and white, like marble, and they glittered just a little. There was moonlight in a black sky overhead. There were rooms and rooms which I saw, filled with wonders. Ancient beasts and magnificent creatures of the deep. Birds who still sang even though they were long dead and decayed. Maps that did not show the way to any physical place; some that might bring you to another kind of world entirely. And figures in paintings that might speak to you, if only you knew what questions to ask them or strange old catalogs, filled with diagrams of animals not known to any forest of the Continents."

"You have imagined a place of your youth." She retorted.

"I know of no such place." The ghost rejoined. "And seeing as I did not intend to dream it, there is no memory from which it might have come."

"Perhaps a book then. Since you are all so fond of them."

Mary Toft reflected on the parts of the dream she had not said. About the black-haired girl that she had observed in the room at the end of the hall, nor about the wrappings she had seen stopping a gap in the shelving near a globe bearing an upside-down ocean. She did not mention a cat prowling along the baseboards or the fact that, in her dream, she had warned him of the birds and told him that he must always jump for their tails. She also said nothing of the darker creature that had awakened before her and who had wandered over the threshold of the Chalk Circle seeking the home of an even younger girl for his own ends.

"You did not come here for my dreams." She turned back to regard her executioner.

"I did not, that is true. Rather, I have come to collect upon you."

"I owe you nothing."

"It is not by your Bargain but mine. Bind the dead, feed the Stumble, Mary Toft, and I will have what I am due."

"What you intend to ask is beyond me. I do not see as once I did."

"For too long you and your ilk escaped me." Clarisant rejoined. "But now it's time at last for me to put an end to the exile Waysmith and see to it that all of you finally serve as was always intended. The Way By may not be yours to wield any longer, but you know its intimacies as truly as any spritely kin. You will find her, bring her, and any with whom she may have shown the Way."

"She is protected. Hidden. Even you cannot defy the Summer King." The ghost spat back.

"That is why you will go, my lovely." Clarisant reached forward to idly stroke the vaporous locks of hair. "Some of us may come and go in the telling but in the end, no one escapes a fiction. Fairy tales and ghost stories, these are not but ordinary life and a human is nothing if not ordinary. Shape what is before her. Change the Way. She will find the path that has been set out quickly enough. Go, the Stumble binds you."

The ghost of Mary Elizabeth Toft looked upon the Unicorn Queen with both dread and defiance.

"When she comes, perhaps it is you who will share our fires."

Clarisant smiled then and inclined her head. "That is not the fate to which I was invited."

At that, the unicorn in human guise raised her hand to pull at the dust-mote threads of the red coat. Out of them, she then wove something that looked akin to a cloak and mask but whose features were indistinct. It was with this ephemeral garment that she demonstrated how the spirit might make herself invisible and how she might, despite the fact that few living people could normally perceive her, also make herself known at vital moments. Unsurprisingly, the ghost of Mary Toft did not offer anything in the way of thanks for the objects but instead, donned them with silent acquiescence, allowed herself a brief glance to the others in attendance, and discorporated.

As the figure of the withered spirit faded into nothing, Clarisant returned to the great pyre. With a tentative touch, she began to trace the knots and grooves of the crumbling ash, stepping around it again and again in contemplation.

"I've heard your stories." She said aloud to the hovering spirits. "Every one." A choke of loathing made her breathless. "They are all the same. Heroes who overcome, who make their lives meaningful again. Villains who oppose them and die by their own hubris, or are overcome. It is every one of your nursery rhymes. Legends. Origins. Tales of the first lands of Men and Gods. Which, in the end, are really nothing more than a reflection of what the storytellers imagine themselves to be. But it's always about you. Isn't it?" Her hand passed an open niche but she did not recoil from the fire and heat emanating from within. "Always the same. All these fables and novels and plays on a stage, always about the one thing that you can taste, and hear, and smell but can never see. Can never quite understand. I see your people reaching out, into the Way By, using their magic words to remake it in their own image." A mountain of bodies shifted beneath her. "They conquer everything with their wants and their desires and their longing."

She stopped beneath a great expanse of boughs and breathed the painful air. "For how long have I brought them to this place? How long have they burned? I've brought all your authors and your playwrights. I've torn artists from this world in screams and despair. I've shown them the knife and the tainted cup and watched them drink it each and every time. They kill themselves rather than face the next inspiration. I've been burning books from the time you began to print them and your poets from the time before that. I am the Muse that writes their songs and I have eaten them all from within." Her hand slid into the inferno raging inside.

When it again emerged clutching a thick clump of ash and cinder, the tuft was still glowing hot. "For centuries I allowed you to burn, and still you remain. But now, I must thank you because you have given me this; the soot and slag of your own stubborn demise. Purified. And I will salt the world with it and banish mortals from the Way By forever."

The spirits gathered further and closed in around her, but Clarisant felt no fear. The Stumble would not release them and no matter how long they wailed through their anger and despair, it would feel like little more than the flurry of mayflies to her and would die back just as quickly.

"As for our beloved King," she began to no one but herself. "The world tires of him. I tire of him. And soon enough, she will tire of him too."

Clarisant gathered the ashes out of the great tree and from the surrounding corpses. She then placed them in a roll of linen bound around her waist. It charred the fabric but did not burn through. Once satisfied that she had all that she might be able to carry, the unicorn set out again from the witches' pyre and back onto the road that would lead her to the woods. She passed the gates and the wall of tombs and returned to the gap from which no part of the pyres could be seen.

From the woods she followed the game trails into the ruins of Ruddigore Castle and then to the Torquilstone before turning onto the sunken brickway near the head of a mountain called the Beast with Horns. Once there, she had only to find the edge of the Great Fens, the bog where dwelled the skeletal Ankou with their creaking carts, to follow it straight through onto the grounds of Stonehenge proper. But as soon as she could recognize the unmistakable sarsen stones in the distance she turned again; this time towards the high ridge of tussock grass flowing out to sea.

With keen observation, she noted that this path had recently been crossed and with some degree of notable skill. Several trails of fading footprints marked a line from the ridge and out into a treacherous marsh of mosses and predatory flowers. But before them, from what she could make out, had gone a horse. The crescents of hooved toes cut the way through the quagmire with purpose and none of the footprints seemed to deviate from the chosen direction. Her eyes narrowed; there was no finer guide through the dangers of the Morass than the bellwether horse Falada. And where the spectral Falada walked, that wretched woman was sure to follow.

But Clarisant also followed. She hardly needed the path, however, as she knew precisely where it led. Beyond the turns that marked the beginning of the fields of men was a waypoint, a rest stop for those, Fae or human or otherwise, that made a habit of traversing the spaces between the Way By and the conscious world. The denizens of this place called it the Chalk Circle, though she had once known it as the gateway to the meadows of Asphodel; the place where human souls were allowed to pass through the Way By and into the Beyond. It lay on the island of Hy-Brasil, off the coast of Ireland, but it could not be glimpsed any more than once in seven years when the sea mists cleared. Today, this was her destination and she took her time arriving.

Clarisant paused at the entrance to the Theater-City. It was always different for each person who visited it. Buildings would be moved around, cardboard forests rearranged, and all manner of other props strewn about as might be necessary for whatever it was that the traveler would be seeking. For her though, the buildings had gone silent and there was no light to be seen from within their windows. The stage was clean and quiet. The costumes hung up and the props packed away in their chests, but she knew better than to think the place deserted. The Waysmith had passed this way not long before and there would be no one here who would wish to speak of it to one such as her.

Moreover, they would have been warned of her possible coming and would know that there could be little gained in trying to convince her of their honor and respectability. But this did not concern her. Clarisant had not come for either information or succor. Rather, this had long been planned and anticipated; all that remained now was keeping to the script. The rest would come to pass as foreshadowed. She plucked a program from the pedestal near the stairs, dropped it open to a page, and called out to the hidden townsfolk.

"The Summer King who wears a crown, that only he may wear." She chanted mockingly. "Sits on a throne high above, with tangles in his hair." Nothing and silence, hung with dust.

"Weighed with sloth he does not stir, nor in season change his clothes. A crown of facile foolishness, with mud caked to his nose."

A clatter from beyond the curtain told her that the puppetry was now awake. The concerned whispers were quickly hushed away but she could still discern the words of rebellion. Stage directions were mumbled and the actors took their places. The fringe at the bottom of the velvet curtain flicked back and forth with scuttling feet before once again going still. With a wry smile she drifted closer, to the clapboard tavern near a painted foam well. Again, she called out, loudly and into the darkness.

"The crown placed back upon my head, its roots will singe and brown." She snapped her jaw on the final cadence and ground her teeth for added emphasis. "There will be no more royal blood, when I burn his kingdom down." She tossed her program into the well with a wet slap.

"The crown will crumble and decease, and with it the right of rule. So woe to you who bend the knee, and say that I am cruel."

She felt the vibrations move through her feet that signaled the coming resistance. She stood wide and readied, framed in the dim circle of an overhead light. Her sing-song tone became threatening.

"Your loyalty was bound with shame, like the one you still enthroned! Set upon a lower head, none rules the one disowned."

The Chalk Circle burst forth in a mad rush of shouts and cries to battle. The Puppet King in his purple cloak was the first to clamor forth with a small gnomish man in a striped vest close at his side, yanking his upper strings wildly as he tried to keep pace. Behind him followed a jumble of marionettes, running and vaulting towards her. The tavern façade was knocked clean over as two elderly women in rags and costume jewelry leapt over the roof, brandishing swords made of pasteboard and tin. The first took a valiant swing at the Unicorn Queen but found that she was easily brushed aside. The second landed a more solid blow and Clarisant snarled back with a wound to her thigh.

"Onward, Luna dear!" She cried. "I've got her now!"

"Then shall I be next?" The first woman yelled over the din and swung again.

Clarisant dodged the blow and dipped sideways as a rather menacing looking bird marionette dove at her feet. Viciously, she snatched up the puppet and crushed it before throwing its battered remnants to the floor. More weapons flew through the air but achieved only glancing blows.

As it was, the Unicorn Queen was not unarmored, though no Fae alive could have predicted how invulnerable she had recently become: Clarisant's crackled skin had distorted to form long, hatched marks in the shape of Ogham runes, spelling out the protective magic of the The Seven Trees Who Feed Upon Blood, and their blades could not breach the powerful protections that the Stumble had etched into her scars. They then bled into view as ancient words on her face and arms. The more her wounds seeped, the darker the Ogham became, the harder she was to harm.

The second wave rocked the port door far to the left of the curtain. As sections of the stagecraft walls began to separate, all manner of Fairest rushed forth in a hastily coordinated attack. But for all their planning and anticipation, the unicorn's response was more prepared than any of them had initially conjectured. Even the goblins and fiends seemed surprised at the ferocity of the defensive. The first wave consisted of swarms of small Fae and puppets, tooth fairies and pixies armed with thorn spikes and iron nails.

Leading them was a small band of Boxwood kobolds and two Welsh Coblyns, kin to Hat Trick and Coat Check, each dressed in brightly colored, needle-felted, jackets and Phrygian caps. But even before they had fully engaged their enemy, the second wave tumbled through the east wall with a howl. Consisting of organized troupes of orcish Hags, a few sorcerous Ljósálfar, and the human-like Changelings, they made beelines for Clarisant, smashing through props and terrain and cracking clapboards like glass.

It was chaos. Plumes of dust and debris filtered down through the cracks in the ceiling above as an outright war was waged in the confines of the theater platform. For Clarisant, the walls were literally closing in on her as groups of Fae fighters began rolling them forward as phalanx shields. Spears and arrows winged past her head, swords and sticks pierced her chest and back, and entire mobs of fairy kin charged forward and retreated in concert as they attempted to bring her down from her feet. The unicorn shrieked in rage. She couldn't shake the feeling that this wasn't just a frightened response to an encroaching foe, but that she was unexpectedly facing a long anticipated and fortified resistance.

Blinded by the sudden barrage, she reached into the melee with deadly fingers and broke a kobold in half. A handful of sprites met the same fate, their delicate wings twirling down to the ground as shattered whirligigs. To an orc axe-master, she danced nimbly clear of a mighty side-swipe before ripping his gullet out and forcibly feeding it to a Hag. Two more armored trolls approached as she did so, clearly well practiced in avoiding her initial strikes and unmoved by her atrocities.

But the first was not prepared when she sank her teeth into his cheek deep enough to tear his jaw free of his head. The second leveled his sword and succeeded in driving the end into her hip but could not retreat in time to avoid a blow to his breastplate, rending the metal and sending it into his heart. The blood fueled her further and soon there was no distinction between her own injuries and theirs in the writing on her body.

"The alicorn wound!" One of the old Changeling women yelled. "Dawn! You have to go for the wound!"

Clarisant braced to meet the woman head-on as her imagined sword swung wildly for her face. She slipped from the blows, each with an ever increasingly powerful thrust but the woman could not land them. When the last swung too wide, the unicorn retaliated and sent the Changeling's body to the floor with her face torn free and skull cracked in thirds. The massacre was relentless but soon too many fighters found themselves reluctant to close the distance. Their shock became palpable as none could have fathomed that she could be so strong, that she was somehow capable of tearing flesh like paper, and the murderous unicorn only seemed to grow angrier with each engagement.

"Miscreants and traitors!" She snarled. "Impostors!"

"Dawn!" She heard the scream over the shouts and grunts of her immediate attackers. As the second woman crashed through the middle lines, Clarisant took the moment of distraction to spy a rope tangled in the walkways overhead. It had come loose from its moorings near the spotlights and had caught the edge of a metal slat that would easily reach to the stage. An elf in fine leathers closed on her with a short, curved blade.

He too died quickly when her hand reached first his chest followed by his neck. The blade she claimed as he fell and with it, she immediately slit the throat of an oncoming Bodach. As it too fell, she stepped back to throw the Tatar saber squarely into the bottom of the walkway above, dislodging the rope, which unfurled and dropped to the stage with a clunk.

"Bring her down! We have to bring her down NOW! Fight!" Someone cried out in desperate terror.

Three more fairies met their gruesome end before Clarisant managed to hoist herself high enough to free her movements from the pinning wave. Using a passing orc's helmet for leverage on her heel she then leapt and pulled upwards until she reached an approaching Foawr, a giant readying massive stones to crush her. But he was not fast enough to avoid her in the air and he went down among his comrades less a tongue and several teeth. As she landed central to his considerable bulk, she turned to a young Sidhe and made swift work of breaking her neck, hauling her meager body onto the giant, and then plucking out her left eye.

With a hiss, she palmed the bloody trophy before turning it outwards and slamming it whole into the yawning gash in her own forehead. Screams erupted from the crowd as smaller creatures scrambled away and hid in the niches. Several more fighters took an involuntary step back, now regarding the Unicorn Queen with two pale blue eyes of her own and one green one rotating violently in the center of her brow. This, again, was magic they feared.

"Enough!" She bellowed. "One more of you and I will see that your dead join the Stumble and breathe nothing but contempt and disgrace for all the time that is yet to come. With one eye I may see the truth, with two eyes I can find the Way, and with three so shall I change the turning of the world to suit me."

The crowd shifted and looked to each other for courage as their leaders tried to rally the numbers. Several of the more grievously wounded shied away but among them, a gnome stepped forward. He was grizzled with exhaustion, with a bright jacket ripped across the shoulders, but resolute. Defiant.

"Thistlehogg." Clarisant nearly spat the name.

With stained sprigs of white hair and a nose twisted into wreckage, the gnomish man in a box office suit stood between the Chalk Circle and her.

"You cannot pass this way." He said. "You may kill more of us, we may not be able to escape you, but the doors are barricaded. Even you will not be able to unlock them. The Circle is closed!"

"I see." She smiled.

Here she noted that the crowd was smaller than before; no doubt that messengers and scouts had already been dispatched and the more peaceful denizens smuggled to safety in the furthest reaches of the Way By. What stood before her now were the martyrs and warriors ready and willing to fight to the last for the chance of the others to escape her. She imagined that some battered Faire was already breathlessly sprinting to the Court of the Summer King, waving and sobbing their message of terror to the guards and begging audience at the base of the Cabium Throne. And then she saw just such a messenger, through the hazy reflections of her stolen third eye. He was indeed breathless and bloody, fast moving on foot, through a dark and drizzling avenue she did not immediately recognize.

At each moment when the little Brownie stopped to catch his breath, he would whisper something to the stray dogs and rats. They would stop and sniff and then point the way forward and off he would be running again. The Unicorn Queen had no mercy though, and with a trill reverberating down through her acquired Far Sight she called to the birds. Almost immediately the sparrows and wrens, armed with needlepoints and miniature pikes, descended upon the gasping creature and she let the images of his demise fade from her view with the sounds of his screams.

What she did not see however, was a tiny Faun stealing his way down a garden path to a door nestled in the roots of a rosebush. She did not hear him knock thrice or race down the stairs to a conclave of under-dwellers. She did not see him fall into the arms of a Coblyn in a red woolen shirt and a tabard with a red Welsh dragon. Rather, satisfied with the first death, she had already returned her senses to the present.

"Now you see it, Unicorn." Thistlehogg scoffed, having mistaken her momentary trance for a blight of rage. "There are too many ways in and out. The Chalk Circle is the door to all doors, that which holds everything within itself and keeps inside that which is invoked."

"Oh, my sweet, sweet, earth-dweller." Clarisant spoke gently and drew herself up to an imposing height. "Still you do not know to whom you speak. I am not Re'em nor Al-mi'raj, I am not Shadhavar, I am not Qilin. My name is not Jewel nor Elidor nor Amalthea. I am the Liminal, the Lady In-between, Governess of the Threshold. My name is not uttered by virgins nor is it recorded in holy books of men. There are no offspring who bear my essence nor ancestors whose memories I keep. I am Regina Immortalis, Unus Cornus Imperium. What I create, I destroy. What creates me, consumes the world."

Thistlehogg nodded gravely but he knew that his borrowed time would not last much longer. However, poised as she may be to slaughter the lot of them, she was at an impasse. The doors and ports were blocked and there was no way out of the summoning circle; the runes were destroyed and the passages of salt and sage collapsed behind them. The safety of his kith and kin held him steadfast as he uttered a quiet prayer for the vigilance of the Waysmith. He might not be partial to her methods or her kind, but he understood her promise.

"Helots and liegemen, I implore you." Clarisant raised her head and addressed the readied conscripts. "You are brave, of that I have no doubt. You will raise your swords until the very last moment, of that I am most confident. You will live on in the stories and songs of your children and your companions, that is also true. But I am afraid that your ending is not of your choosing. Your stories will become mine and I will spread the tales of your tragic deaths with impunity. I will watch the terror take hold; the shock, the sickened panic, will wipe away all reverence for your sacrifice. Do not fear it though. Your destruction will not have been in vain, because if not for you, none shall pass this way again."

Her hand, supple and sure, emerged from the linen pouch at her waist. In her fingers, they discerned a grey and listless powder. It smelled of sulfur and boiling flesh, with flecks of bleached white bone and red glowing embers embedded throughout. Many exchanged confused and concerned looks. Did she mean to attack them with fireplace ash or demoralize them with the remains of their own long dead? What ghoulish magic had she in store for them now?

Clarisant gazed down impassively as the restless troupe. She could feel the uncertainty already rising within them, the desire to lash out at her once more, to fight and die in heroic glory that would ignite the spark of defiance within every Faefolk, fata, kin, and creature from the Near By to the distant spires of Dinas Emrys and the Court of the Summer King. So great that even the immortals of Kunlun Mountain and Takama-ga-hara far, far, to the East would be called down to fight. But this, she would deny them utterly. And in so doing, deny the world its unity.

Thistlehogg watched as the Unicorn Queen simply opened her fingers, letting the ashen mixture sift and flow down onto the body of the giant upon whom she still stood and from there, in a river of silver sand, onto the floor below. As it touched the giant and then the stage, the stalwart gnome could not believe what he was seeing. First the giant began to crumble, as though his body had dried in the sun for an age or more. The embers ignited into his bones and began to burn the long, wooden, planks as they too disintegrated. And then, it began to spread. Several of the larger soldiers jumped back as the ground beneath them gave way. A whirlwind of embers burst up from the growing sinkhole and for those caught in the first gusts of ash, they shrieked their surprise as flesh melted and turned to dust.

A young sprite screamed as her comrades were consumed en-masse in its wake and then, the entirety of the Chalk Circle began to fall apart. They tried to run, but as had been the plan all along, there was nowhere to go. The church was burning and they were locked inside. In an instant, the ashen shadow was everywhere, devouring everything it touched, burning Fae and theater alike into nothing in an instant. Within seconds, there would be no trace left of the tavern or blacksmith or chairs for expected audiences. Nothing but a wasteland of asphyxiated space in a hollow void where once an entire realm had stood.

The curtain fell into a pile of stained lint and blew away. The terrified marionettes saw their strings eaten through with rot until they too tumbled down into gilings. Many of the Hags and orcs met their ends with grim solemnity, ravaged from the inside out, while others fell trembling to their deaths, erased by the ruthless glide of indifferent annihilation.

Thistlehogg crouched near a gaslight at the edge of the stage. He saw clearly then, his final moment approaching, and did everything he could think of to meet it with decorum: imagine a calming scene, sing a favorite song, think of a favorite poem or a rollicking good story. Sourly, the only thing he seemed to be able to remember at the moment was a sad Gailey's song. Something that might have been drunkenly sung in a pub hall on a rainy day. He cursed the idiotically grasping nature of his mind's choice, but the laughable strains and verses were already playing over and over on his tongue. It would seem that he would not even allow himself to die in grace.

A chattering wail shook the flagstones.

A stifled gasp churned through the remnants of the company.

The ashes ate the walls and the barricades and all the doors and clapboard trees.

The paint peeled and fell, shards of metalwork and glass hopped away with the churning pulse of destruction.

The last of the valorous fell to the floor.

Despairing, the gnome crawled forward to break the impact of a falling nixie whose hands were already eaten to stubs, catching the wounded fairy in his arms. A deep gash was quickly forming across her chest. From the tip of her collar bone on the right side, all the way down to her hip, the blood swelled into the fabric of her borrowed dress before spreading out on his arms.

"No!" She cried, reaching out to the widening sky as a wilderness appeared beyond crumbling walls.

"Hush now." He chided. "It is almost over." But the tears that dripped down her cheeks, he realized, were falling from his eyes.

Clarisant leaned down to him as he sat staring while the Stumble consumed the Chalk Circle, burning it into nothingness – wiping it away as if it had never been drawn.

"How?" He stuttered.

"Watch carefully, Thistlehogg, for I am cleansing my house of trespassers. And washing away the stains of the betrayers who have suffered the wretched to live. The stench of humanity will soon air out. The Way By is purified today."

"You..." He choked. "Why? Why would you do this to us? To our home?"

She returned a vicious sneer. "Do you think you're special? No. You are *just* the first. Avenant will watch his entire kingdom burn before the end."

The ash could not be stopped and it leapt quickly from the dying nixie to the gnome. A second insult opened up Thistlehogg's left leg. Biting back his pain, he barely noticed the third wound beginning to trace its way from his ear down his neck, snaking backwards towards his now exposed shoulder blade. Doing his best to stanch the wounds, he tried to offer what little comfort he had as new cuts and slices began appearing everywhere out of nothing on the frail body held tightly in his lap. But at last the lady grew calm, almost serene as he watched the oblivion reach into her heart.

"It's alright." She smiled through mourning eyes. "It's alright, I'm ready. It's going to be fine.... I...."

Through his sorrow, the last thing Thistlehogg would see was a unicorn, bright and vital, vanishing into the new horizon.

Chapter Twelve

Somerset Sayer and Elizabeth Pennybaker observed one another from across the kitchen table. Between them, the scuffed remains of King Louis the XIII on a rearing white horse glowered up from the lid of a cigar box only slightly more worse for wear than the corpse draped inside of it.

"So, you put a fairy in a snuff box."

"It's dead."

"I can see that."

The very thing which had necessitated their rather rushed introductions sat at the center of a distressingly concerned round table. Alice Guthrie was seated to the left of Madam Bel Carmen who hovered near her niece at the far end. Continuing around was Fiona Guthrie, recently recovered from her perplexing ordeal and attentive to the tension thick in the late afternoon air. To her left, Hat Trick peeked just above the rim of the walnut table ledge, remaining as unobtrusive as a glamoured Kobold might.

"Do you know what it is, then?" Elizabeth eyed the infamous folklorist with only the slightest level of suspended disbelief.

"It's a Para-Sprite." The Waysmith answered. "One of a rather large flock of such creatures who inhabit the carcasses of birds for all kinds of nefarious reasons. They tend to favor road kill though, so I am a bit surprised that this one seems to have stolen a taxidermy specimen and converted it into an apparatus of some sort. But I think that the more pertinent question here isn't really what it is, but how you happen to have it."

"I told you." Elizabeth Pennybaker maintained her air of incredulity. "They came in through the window. There were two of them and they just started attacking me. I thought they were regular birds at first. Obviously." She gestured towards the box. "I had to fight them off, well okay, I guess it's only fair to say *we* fought them off. My cat, I mean. He's the one who actually killed it."

“Makes sense.” Somerset Sayer gently lifted the stiff form from the box and began to turn it over gently in her hands.

“Makes sense?!” The student scoffed. “Oh please, do explain. What about any of this makes sense?”

The folklorist was impassive and continued to carefully examine the small imp closely.

“This place that you say you saw; can you tell me about it?”

“Not really, no.” She sighed. “I mean, sort of, but just bits and pieces. I was thinking about it the whole way here but now it’s mostly faded away. I remember some images, well more like ideas than images, and a feeling. Not much else.”

Somerset Sayer nodded. “That’s typical in the first weeks. Learning to retain the memories is sometimes the hardest lesson. Which is why it’s always first.”

“Lesson, what lesson? What are you talking about?”

The Waysmith laid the imp down onto the table.

“The unfortunate reality is that I don’t think that there is really any way to do this simply, so I won’t bother. What you saw is called the Way By, the placeless space, where the world we know and the world as we are in the process of making it are fused. A kind of…imagined world.” She paused to search for better words. “Maybe think of it as a dreamworld, if that helps. Though, that’s not exactly the best description. If it is anything, the Way By is the fire that burns inside the forge of Creation, spoken into being at the beginning of all things. Undisciplined, it will consume you and everything around you. Temper it, and it builds the world. But it is the fact that you saw it at all that concerns me the most. That these Para-Sprites then attempted to kill you outright, means that we have a much more serious situation on our hands. And since I cannot doubt that a sprite was, in fact, the cause of your troubles, I can conclude only one thing.”

“That is?”

“That you are a Waysmith. And for that, Ms. Pennybaker, I am so very sorry for you.”

Elizabeth scowled at the woman across from her. “Uh, thanks. But, not to sound ungrateful or anything, is that the best you can do? I mean, I’ve read your book, you know. The *Lostwith Notes*? It makes about as much sense as you just did. What is a Waysmith? What is the Way By? Look, my aunt brought me here because she said you could help, or at least explain what’s going on.” She motioned towards the cigar box, now imp-less. “So, just explain it then.”

Madam Bel Carmen and Alice Guthrie exchanged concerned glances.

"Do you like unicorns, Elizabeth?" The folklorist queried flatly, picking at the imp in the manner of a rather gruesome scab.

"I'm sorry, unicorns?" She very nearly stood up and walked out right then.

"Yes."

"Sure, I guess. Unicorns are cool." She deadpanned.

"When I was a kid," Somerset Sayer began, "I was obsessed with unicorns. I had everything. The pink glitter posters, the little plastic horses, stickers all over my folders at school. I had read every fairy tale book I could find, as long as it had unicorns in it. I read and re-read the stories all about how they would come to visit little girls and grant wishes and all that, and I dreamed of the day that a unicorn would come and visit me. I was sure it was going to happen eventually. One of the few benefits of being eight, really. Funny thing about that though. One day, one did. And it was the worst day of my life."

The table remained silent, wide-eyed.

"My mother loved fantastical stories. But even more so, I think, she loved that I loved them. She'd read them to me when I was little. When I was twelve, I built a fort in my closet. It was a pretty slap-dash kind of thing, papering the walls with some family pictures taped over movie posters and my own drawings. I even did these little cut-out collages from pictures I would copy from magazines in the library. Typical tween girl celebrity crushes, favorite TV shows, and all that. After a short while, I found myself spending a lot of time in my closet. I would go there to read or draw or sometimes just to daydream. I would imagine going on all these wild adventures or invent new monsters that my toys could fight."

Elizabeth Pennybaker began to squirm. The story seemed so ordinary in its content but something in the telling was making her uneasy. There was an insidiousness to the folklorist's tone. Somerset Sayer looked off into the distance.

"But mostly I would go into the closet to hide. My parents, you see, were especially talented at finding things to scream at each other about and their favorite topic was about how much my father drank every night. God, it's almost boring isn't it? A six pack of beer and a bottle and a half of port wine were the usual precursors to a solid hour of yelling and throwing the dishware. After that it was about who he was cheating with this month followed by something about money and whatever else. You can't really make out specific words when one person is sobbing and the other one is hoarse. But as long as I had the closet, I could tune it all out. I would stare intently at this picture I had of a road in a sunlit English wood and imagine what it would feel like to be walking down it. I would start with the sound of the gravel beneath my shoes. Then I would feel the sunlight on my face as I passed underneath the branches. There would be birds singing high above me and the smell of flowers would blow in on the breeze. Nothing but the peace and quiet and solitude of nature. Eventually, I got so good at the visualization, I wouldn't hear anything at all going on downstairs. I didn't even hear the first time he punched her."

Alice Guthrie frowned into her clenched fingers while Madam Bel Carmen stiffened into an indignantly regal pose. Elizabeth Pennybaker remained still, now somewhat unnerved that she could distinctly see the picture of the English wood described by the folklorist, almost as clearly as if it were hanging on the kitchen fridge behind her. She could hear the birds, smell the wisteria and lilacs, and now faintly detect the distant sounds of choking screams. It caused a shudder to pass through her, though she remained puzzled. She'd known this woman for only a few minutes and here she was relating a tale of deeply personal heartbreak. Somerset Sayer continued however, still gazing off into the distance.

"My father came home very late one night and it was pretty obvious that there was going to be a fight from the moment he started yelling about the state of my mother's nightgown. I don't remember what it was about specifically but it doesn't really matter. When I started hearing glasses breaking, I crawled out of bed and went into my closet. But for some reason, on that particular night, none of my strategies for tuning them out were working. I stared at the picture, I wrapped myself up in blankets, I shined my little flashlight around to read some of the poems I had pasted up, I even pretended to whistle some of the bird songs that I had composed in my head. Nothing helped. All I could hear was shouting. He was swearing and she was crying and everything around them just kept on shattering and falling apart. Sounded like the whole house was coming down. So, I did the first thing that came to my twelve-year-old mind and grabbed some of my markers so that I could draw a unicorn on the picture. A unicorn, right? Something pure and wonderful and strong to come and save me. And as I did, I concentrated even harder on the gravel and on the sunlight in the leaves, and I decided right then that I would one day go to this place. I mean, it was a real picture after all, so the road and the trees and everything must certainly be real. This peaceful place existed somewhere. So, I was going to go there."

"And you did." Elizabeth Pennybaker interjected, holding her lip between her teeth to hide the slight trembling that had begun there. "You did?"

"I did." Somerset Sayer nodded. "Just like that, the road was there and I was on it. Instead of closet walls there were trees and leaves. My little flashlight was really a broken sunbeam coming through the canopy. The pebbles on the road crunched just like I thought they should and everything smelled like summer. And I walked on as though I had been there a thousand times. It didn't strike me as strange or confusing at all. Just a gentle dream from a sleeping child in the corner with the plaster mildew and the cockroaches."

"This is what you meant, in the book." Elizabeth Pennybaker gestured to her pocket. "Finding your Way?"

"It was a start." Somerset Sayer responded. "But I wasn't alone."

"At first I thought it was just a trick of the light. There was something up ahead of me on the road but I couldn't quite see what it was. It looked like a person but only vaguely, like it couldn't figure out exactly what shape it was supposed to take. I remember thinking that it was almost like my marker lines were appearing and disappearing in the spaces between the sunbeams. I was a little ashamed even. If I had been better at drawing, maybe the creature wouldn't have to struggle so much to be seen. But then, there she was, a unicorn plain as day. She was walking towards me on the road, just out of the tree line." She paused again before continuing.

"There were birds of all kinds flying around us. Just this ridiculous menagerie of songbirds and swallows and I think even a parrot or two. But I wasn't really paying attention to all that, of course. I just stood there staring as she came up to me. This magical, beautiful, gentle thing; here for me at last."

After too long an ensuing silence, Alice Guthrie prompted. "She took you away then?"

"Hmm? Oh no, not at all." Somerset Sayer was finally roused from her reverie. "She asked me where I was going. I don't remember exactly what I said. Something pithy, like, "away," or something similar. Then she asked me why and I told her. I said that they were fighting again, that everyone hurt and everything was broken. I said that they were my parents but they didn't want me. That all they did was scream. It seems weird now when I think back on it. Standing there in the middle of a country road in the woods, explaining to a unicorn that whenever my father drank too much, he wrecked the house and left my mother bruised and sitting silently in a chair by the window. But she was gentle. Calm. I trusted her. Children aren't terribly sophisticated when it comes to these kinds of things."

Fiona Guthrie raised her hand. "What did she do?"

Somerset Sayer smiled. "She took me home."

The girl looked bewildered. "You mean, there really *was* a unicorn in your closet?"

"No. We came back in through the front door actually. We didn't go back the way I came, back down the road like I expected. Instead, she led me through a path that wound around a few large trees before she showed me an old door that someone had leaned up against a trunk. It was a pretty sorry looking thing but when I turned the knob, it took us into the front hall of my house. I was awestruck at the time, naturally, but it's a pretty common method of travel in the Way By, as I am sure you're catching on to."

Elizabeth Pennybaker added matter-of-factly. "It was a doorway in the kitchen. I mean, last night."

"Thresholds." The Waysmith corrected. "But we'll get to that. Anyway, so there I was. Back home, standing next to the shoe mat, and listening to my father pacing and crying in the kitchen. I thought that was odd. He was always the one yelling but instead he was just mumbling and sort of wandering back and forth. Everything felt off. Our house was loud, not quiet. But then I saw the unicorn next to me. She startled me, though. Not because she was standing there but because she had...changed. There was this tall, pale, woman draped in cords and rags walking down the hall towards the kitchen. She also seemed gleeful, but in a malicious kind of way.

"I hid behind the couch but I'll be honest with you, it took me years to really remember that night. The police said that my father murdered my mother with a kitchen knife after she got mad at him for driving home drunk. The final verdict was that he killed himself afterwards. I'm pretty sure the investigators simply came to that decision because the only other person they found in the house was me, unconscious, behind the living room sectional. They found him seated at the kitchen table, eyes wide open, jaw slack, with the knife all the way through his neck."

"Jesus." Elizabeth Pennybaker exclaimed.

"I'm sorry." Somerset Sayer addressed the table. "I shouldn't be so graphic, it's impolite. But, it might surprise you to learn that, it wasn't all bad in the end. There was someone else in the house that day as well. He was sitting behind the couch with me."

Alice Guthrie chanced at a look at her daughter, who sat horrified and unmoving. The younger Waysmith also remained perturbed, but wasn't yet showing the extent of her frustrations outwardly. Somerset Sayer rested a few moments before responding to the tension.

"Perhaps I will wait to say more about him then, but suffice to say, my introduction into the Way By was nearly as abrupt and disorienting as your own. What saved me was a great teacher, one who not only took pity on myself and my situation but one who has remained unfailingly kind and patient when he had every right not to. He is the reason, if I am being honest, that I am undertaking this entire endeavor at all; that I am gathering the lot of you together for what may be the end of us all."

"The end of us?" Madam Bel Carmen interjected. "Dr. Sayer, I assure you that I am here only because I know that you can support my niece and hopefully teach her something of what you know, and this." 'This' being a polished nail pointed at the forgotten imp. "I don't believe I've agreed to anything else."

"I'm afraid that you have, Madam Bel Carmen." The folklorist retorted matter-of-factly. "If not by design than by unfortunate circumstance."

The elder woman scowled openly and glowered at the Waysmith speaking.

"Listen, I've given you the story that will be of greatest use to you in the coming days." Somerset Sayer sighed. "There's more, of course, but at the moment I need something from all of you. If it hasn't become clear by now, it will soon enough, and that is that there's trouble. We're all in trouble. The Way By is in trouble. Under normal circumstances I would have happily remained here in obscurity, writing books no one will ever read and making arguments no one cares to listen to. And on the side, I don't know, maybe passing the time with a few paintings that'll one day be sold for a dollar at my funeral estate sale. I'm not exactly the world's most pleasant company and I generally don't make a habit of inflicting my lack of social graces on anyone if I don't have to, but I've been left without much of a choice. I need your help. I need you to help me stop her."

Elizabeth Pennybaker didn't have to ask who "her" was, but Madam Bel Carmen did.

"Stop her?" Her tone flat and unyielding.

"She is called Clarisant." The Waysmith continued. "From the moment we met the world hasn't been right and now it grows worse by the day. You see, you need to understand this. Every time we build something, every time we remake the world around us to suit our needs, our wants, or our viewpoints, the Way By changes. Sometimes in small ways, sometimes in profound ways. This is why we feel so differently in different places; how places evoke certain memories or how they might be conducive to creativity. Or suppressive of it. It's why we are driven to change things around us in order to change ourselves. We name things. We rearrange our décor. We claim space or give it up. We make sets for plays, galleries for art, cabinets for our curiosities, books for our experiences, or paths through the wilderness. We seek out the places and objects that speak to us. *This is the Way By*. And everything we do reflects back to us what we put into it. All humans do this and have done this, but somewhere in there, people began to change things for the worse. They began to steal from the Way By the things that were never meant to leave it and feed into its fractures the things it was never meant to swallow. When this went unchecked, inevitably, someone came along and cut a hole so deep into the fabric of imagination that what crawled out of it has been devouring us in return ever since. And that thing has cut down every Waysmith she's ever encountered. By the grace of the Summer King alone, a man I met only by chance while sitting behind a floral couch on the worst day of my life, do I remain beyond her reach but only just."

Elizabeth Pennybaker took up the thread. "So, a Waysmith is what then? A person who sees the Way By? Like, sees it for what it actually is?"

"Avenant once called the Waysmiths 'Those Who Drift Through the Land as Fallen Leaves.' I tend to think of us as little pieces of paper that you can tear off and drop like breadcrumbs. That way, when someone gets lost in life, they have a chance of finding their way back by picking up the scattered bits of what you've left behind for them. Artists and writers and historians can all tell you how this goes."

"You're not making sense again." Elizabeth Pennybaker frowned with implied accusation.

"People often talk about how they are trapped in their bodies." Somerset Sayer raised a passing glare and returned it, "But that's really just a problem of perspective. They're not trapped in their bodies; they emanate from them. The mind emerges from the brain, the person emerges from their body, the Way By emerges from the world. A Waysmith perceives these emanations beyond their physical realities and in so perceiving them, can change them. And this is why you will have to learn, as I did, how to tell the right kind of stories. The rules. The conventions. All the things that people love and return to. Because only then can you change the story and only then will things be different. That is the charge and the curse of being who and what we are, Elizabeth."

The Waysmith stood up from the table. "Right now, there is a wound and it has torn through this world and the Other for as long as anyone can remember. Almost fitting that we gave it a name as childish as the Stumble, for every hour, more of both worlds fall into it. As its reach extends further and further, it corrupts our insight and twists our desires. At the vanguard of our worst impulses is a creature who should have been the best in us. Clarisant, a Muse of the Bright Revelation, a Mother of Inspiration, the Genius of Insight, and the Exalted Catalyst seeks nothing now but complete and utter destruction. She is coming and she will consume you, and me, and all of us. Since the alicorn..."

Here she pointed to her own forehead, "...was taken, she has become nothing but Agony and Anguish and, soon enough, she will consume everything in her path. Call her Hate or call her Harrowing, it doesn't matter. A piece of the past that just keeps coming back and coming back and coming back until it's the only story you're capable of telling anymore. And the worst of it is, I simply do not have the time to make you understand all of this in the way that I would wish to. Everything you are going to see and hear from this point onwards will make even less sense than what came before it. I'm going to show you things that have no business existing and little, if any, relationship to logic. I'm going to take you to places that occupy times and spaces that don't conform to reason and I am going to ask you to do things that will seem like they violate every fiber of your being. Much of it you will eventually forget. But you are going to remember this moment for the rest of your lives. You are going to remember it because this is the moment that you sat at a table, surrounded by people who were once strangers to you, and were told you were hunting a unicorn. That the Great Hunt had begun."

Alice Guthrie raised her brow in shock. "Dr. Sayer, well, I...I mean, are you saying that we're all going back? Like at Stonehenge that time in the field? To the little village?"

Somerset Sayer placed her palms onto the table and smiled. "My dear Alice Guthrie, we're going so much further than that. For the rest of your considerable days, you will have every opportunity to discredit the teller but never the tale. I'm taking you all with me, back to the beginning, where together, we might just have the strength to stop the destruction before it's too late. Hope springs eternal, as they say. Ms. Pennybaker? I will need your eyes and your doubt. I will need you to face every demon that comes at you with wit and strategy, and if I should fall you will have to find the way back for yourself and the others. No one else can. Mrs. and Ms. Guthrie respectively? I will need your steadfastness, your courage, and your innocence. The two of you will see things in ways that the rest of us cannot. And Madam Bel Carmen? I will need your knowledge and your wisdom most of all. If anything, the mourning that Clarisant inflicts upon the world will fall upon you more heavily than anyone else. But the burdens you have borne in this life have given you strength to carry a weight far greater than those around you. And of you all, beyond this, I will need your wonder. Your curiosity, willingness for amazement, and joy at feeling reverence makes you the perfect hunting party. That is why I intend to have you named Flidais Venatica, Huntresses of the King! *Ut hoc Nomen semper agis. May you carry the Name henceforth and always.*"

Fiona Guthrie broke into the widest smile her mother had yet laid eyes on and leapt to her feet with a near-involuntary shout.

"Hell yeah! Let's do it!"

For what reason came the sudden joy though, Alice Guthrie was unsure. But one look at her daughter told her that Fiona Guthrie had already come to understand the folklorist in a way that she had not.

"Precisely." Somerset Sayer straightened, turned, and retrieved a darkly-colored long bow from the umbrella stand near the coatrack. The sleek, black walnut stock shimmered unnaturally in the light and the two spiral ends that held the string seemed to tighten of their own accord as her fingers wrapped around its center. She then reached above the upper shelf to retrieve a quiver of arrows that, strangely, no one had noticed sitting there before. She continued.

"We're always told that once we become adults, we need an adult's understanding of things. So, why should wonder be any different?"

It was an odd saying that she clipped to the truth as though it would somehow illuminate the proceedings any further. Unfortunately, it was also generally lost on the assembled group. Hat Trick, on the other hand, was already in a rush to prepare and stealthily reached across the table to gather coins wedged in the wood slats and then the salt and candle. These things he scurried away into a series of small pouches attached to his waist before trundling off, unseen, towards the library rooms once again.

Elizabeth Pennybaker pushed back from her seat and glanced down once more at the slowly decaying imp. "I guess that's for the unicorn then?" She motioned to the bow and red-fletched arrows now slung across the folklorist's back and adjusted with a belt around her quickly donned wool train-coat. The Waysmith looked up with a matter-of-fact tone.

"No. It's for the birds."

Chapter Thirteen

These creatures, whose bodies were the landscape, were little more than enormous phantoms moving across a far horizon, too massive to be fully comprehended. One colossus, whose head made up the forested cape of a great continent, might have been mistaken for the entire southeastern coast of Brazil. Each smooth but lumbering step it took disrupting the waterfalls on its face just enough to reveal an eye embedded in a great chasm, in the craggy depths of a seaside cave.

Another looked to be a skeleton-king, the size of a mountain, sitting astride a mossy beast greater than Leviathan, the points of his crown dragging through the clouds and disrupting the stars. A third may even have been a chimera, paddling in aimless circles through an upside down sky. The world here inside the Way By was far too many sizes too big for anything less than abject terror and amazement.

The gathering of women stared in awe; all save for the one who had brought them to this precipice through a cobblestone path beneath the pine in the back garden. But over the wall and through the geraniums had not led them to a quaint lawn as one might have noticed through the windows. Rather, the stone stairs leading through the bushes had quickly fallen away into a rocky outcropping and the sounds of wind through the great pine on Trowbridge Street turned out to be the crashing of the surf on a seaside cliff. In the distance, an island appeared out of the morning fog.

It had a strange shape, like a great whale testing the surface of the water with only the tip of its snout exposed. The rocks along the shore had the same shapes as barnacles and where only the tops of trees could be seen poking through the haze, they formed a thistle-like wreath around the center. As the wind swept the last of the mists away, it was, indeed, a great forest of evergreen trees before them with a single one rising up above the rest. A giant sequoia perhaps, taller than a castle tower. And at its base a fortress in fallen leaves; a kingdom built on tangled branches and upturned roots, suspended in the air and traversed only by the wind.

Somerset Sayer had said that they were going to the halls of the Summer King, that they would be walking the Way By until they reached the hallowed ground of a place she called Lilylit, which resided outside the boundaries of consciousness within poetic phrases like the Kingdom By The Sea. What she had meant by any of that was unknown to everyone but Hat Trick, whose only response was to hop about in glee. So, the assembly had no choice but to trust her. After all, as Madam Bel Carmen had said, one cannot argue with a fairy tale. They are true both by necessity and by virtue of their form.

Elizabeth Pennybaker drew a trembling hand down her face as she tried to take it all in. She turned and looked back over her shoulder, almost hoping to see the house they had just left and finding nothing but a great grassy plain. She turned around again to the vast expanse before her and stared into the distance. A mountain range rose to its feet and began the slow process of trundling into the sea.

Its head was similar to that of a stag, with ears made of drifting snowcaps and great oaks like antlers shimmering with a thousand tiny branches waving in the sun. The sky above them moved through an eon of time in a split second; churning through the births of a hundred stars before each streaked away in a flash. In an uncharacteristic show of compassion, Somerset Sayer laid a calming hand on her shoulder before striding past the group of them to the edge of the rocks.

"We'll walk from here." She announced.

Alice Guthrie very nearly went to correct her, in that they had been walking the entire time, but a large June beetle with the face of a very old man bumping along the ground was enough to make her quite literally lose her words.

"The path through the rocks will take us to the bridge." The Waysmith continued. "From there, we enter through the main gates which lead onto the courtyard. After that, we pass into the domain of the Summer King. I'd caution you to watch your steps but, given the circumstances, I think that might be a bit too much to ask. If nothing else then, remember this: there are three rules to surviving in the Way By. First, never, ever wander off on your own. If you do not understand how the constructs of dreaming work, you will get lost and you will not be able to find your way back. Things around you will appear to change suddenly and without logic or reason, which means that the way you came is probably not going to be the way out. Second, never, and I mean *never*, make an agreement or promise an exchange with a denizen of this world. The creatures of the Way By are tricky, manipulative, and incredibly dangerous. They will not take pity on you because you are well-meaning or inexperienced. There is no forgiveness for honest mistakes here, only consequences. And lastly, ritual and ceremony have tremendous power in places like this. Small gestures or words might seem meaningless to you, but I guarantee it that they won't be meaningless to someone else. For that reason, speak plainly when you must speak at all and don't be careless with your thoughts or actions. Mean what you say and don't equivocate. If you don't know what to do, ask me. I'll try and get us all through this with as little disaster as possible."

She stopped then and turned to address Elizabeth Pennybaker directly. "And if *you* get lost in the woods, ask the trees."

The younger woman was taken slightly aback at the sudden intensity. "What? Why are you telling *me* this?"

"Elizabeth. Ask the trees."

Madam Bel Carmen peered out over the edge of the cliff to get a view of the path wending its way down to the sea. She was startled to see what appeared to be people wandering about on the rocks below; or at least, people in the sense that their silhouettes had two arms, two legs, and a head on top.

"You say," she began. "That we are to see a king? The king of what?"

"His name is Avenant." The Waysmith followed her gaze to the figures along the path, but said nothing of them for a moment. "But you are probably better off just calling him Your Grace, as is customary here. He is the Lord of the Faire and the rightful Sovereign of the Way By, King of the Summer Court by right of arms. Ard Rí also works."

Fiona tore her eyes from the horizon to pose her question. "Ar-dree?"

"The title of the Summer King as spoken in the ancient tongue." Somerset Sayer explained. "Triath nan Eilean is also sometimes used but for our purposes it is probably just easier for you to remember Ard Rí." She turned back to the cliffside and the small crag in the rocks that indicated the beginning of their path to the island. "As for the creatures you see pacing around down there, try not to be too jumpy when we pass them. They won't do us any harm but they can be a little...frightening, on first encounter."

"What are they?" Alice Guthrie joined Madam Bel Carmen at the precipice.

"Lamp Heads." The Waysmith rejoined. The two women looked up at her with consternation. The folklorist only shrugged in response. "You'll see."

Fiona Guthrie took a slow, deep breath in the warm summer air. "A fairy king." She chuckled. "Does that mean he has, like, Knights of the Round Table or something, too?"

Somerset Sayer huffed lightly before motioning Elizabeth Pennybaker to join her at the front of the group. "Not exactly. Though, it's possible we may see the king's guard when we get to court." Before the inevitable questions could commence, she continued on. "They're called the Octadic. The guardians of the crown, I mean. There are eight of them, obviously. Edeltraut, Estaret, Mede, Aranaugh, Arafin, Hafath, Archer, Elief and Ergobet."

"That's nine." Said Elizabeth Pennybaker.

"What?"

"That's nine." She repeated.

"No, it isn't."

"Yes, it is. You just listed nine names."

Somerset Sayer raised an eyebrow with mild concern. "Yes." She replied matter-of-factly. "Like I told you. There are eight of them."

With that, the Waysmith turned on her heels, pulled the longbow from over her shoulders, and began to pick her way carefully down the rocky path.

Elizabeth Pennybaker stared at her receding form for a moment before turning to Alice Guthrie and Madam Bel Carmen, both of whom were still leaning over the ledge and eyeing the treacherous distance. "I don't get it. That...that was nine. Right?"

Alice Guthrie smiled. As she began to make her way past the younger woman, she also paused to rest a hand on her shoulder. "I find," She started, "that the fewer questions I ask, the more things actually make sense. So, in this case, it's probably better if you just... go along with it for now." And off she went.

In short order, she was joined by the others who now formed a line as they each struggled with maintaining their footing on the path down to the shore. Madam Bel Carmen, on the other hand, was not in the least bit surprised to see the Waysmith, and not far to her right, Hat Trick, nimbly stepping and springing from rock to rock as they made their way down, rather as though they were both playing the world's most dangerous game of hopscotch. From time to time, Somerset Sayer would stop, check the progress of the rest of the company, look up into the sky with longbow in hand, and then continue on wordlessly. But the creatures that the women had noticed from far above did not make their appearance until they had all nearly reached the bottom.

Suddenly, Fiona Guthrie screamed and slid precariously forward on a patch of loose gravel but before she could go headlong down the slope, Hat Trick leapt from his perch on a nearby boulder and successfully pushed her back onto her feet. Reflexively, the girl grabbed onto his head, which was still somewhere mid-waist to her, and flailed her feet before regaining purchase on a grassy tussock and mumbling a few embarrassed words of thanks. Elizabeth Pennybaker moved forward to steady her, but when she looked up from where they had stopped, she nearly gasped aloud. A wedge-like shadow had overtaken them unawares.

Towering over them was a man made of sticks, broken boards, and driftwood: two, lengthy, branch legs and a quarterstaff for a torso, split at the top into several spindly root-like arms, and a head made from a massive ship's lantern nailed into the dockwood at its neck. The brass oil lamp inside was lit and from behind the protective bars cross-hatched over three of its sides, Elizabeth could make out a face reflected in the glass. She stared in unblinking terror as it leaned forward over the rocks, its wooden frame groaning and popping as it did so.

"Don't panic." Came the even tone of the Waysmith from behind her. "It's one of the Lamp Heads. It won't hurt you."

For several seconds, the only noises Elizabeth Pennybaker could offer in response were incoherent. As the ten-foot creature continued to study her, however, she found her voice in a low whisper.

"What. Is. That?"

"The ghost of a ship wrecked in the shoals." Somerset Sayer replied."They're not hostile."

"That's...a...a dead sailor?" She gulped.

"No. A ship." The folklorist sighed. "You really do need to pay better attention to these things. Perished sailors don't generally end up here, save a few very, very, prominent exceptions. The Lamp Heads are the remains of ghost ships who have finally run aground or who have begun to disintegrate on the ocean floor after, who knows, a few centuries or more. When they wash up on the beach, they just kind of wander about for a while. Sometimes they pull the drowning out of the shallows, if they can reach them. But otherwise they tend to wait for people to come up along the coast and then lead them down to the water's edge."

"And..." Elizabeth swallowed and took a few steps back from the slowly tilting lantern face. "And then what do they do with them?"

"Nothing." Somerset Sayer shrugged. "No one's really sure why they do it or what they might want. They just do. Anyway, let's go. We need to make the gates before nightfall. Even I don't want to be caught out in the forests of Lilylit after dark."

For several moments, the gathered women remained frozen in their respective places, watching in wonderment as the tall, wooden creature finally seemed to lose interest in their activities and began to stalk away, gently swinging its head back and forth as it combed across the sands of the beach. Fiona Guthrie turned to look at her mother as the others fell back into procession.

"This," her voice was breathless and her eyes beginning to tear. "Is the most incredible thing I've ever seen."

Coat Check stood anxiously outside of an ivy gate. Really more a kind of netting strung between two bent willow trees; the ropy stems of hedera and Irish climbers then looped around and back and upwards and over until they formed the shape of a filigree gate nearly as high as the canopy above them.

With no trellis or wall behind it to anchor them however, it was a little unclear as to how they managed to keep their delicate curls and intricate knots, suspended as they were against the backdrop of a low afternoon sun. A few stray lilacs had also managed to take root though, and now adorned the barrier with long lances of white and purple flowers. He had been waiting nearly two hours, and picked clean three mossy depressions in the ground, when he finally heard voices coming towards him from further up the way.

"Did you see that?!" Came the first, bellowing out through the trees. "That had to be forty yards! Maybe fifty!"

"I didn't even see them!" Came the second.

"It wasn't that far, but I appreciate the compliment." Followed the third, to which Coat Check finally relaxed. He easily knew the voice of his mistress apart from all others.

Five figures appeared in the glade, striding confidently forward. At their head, the familiar flourish of a black Victorian train-coat, a whip of blonde hair, and two great grey shrikes impaled on the end of an arrow. Coat Check hurried to greet them but not before he and Hat Trick exchanged their habitual nod.

"Long wait!" He exclaimed as Somerset Sayer handed the arrow and birds off to him to be disposed of outside of the Kingdom's boundaries.

"My apologies." The Waysmith replied. "We had to take a longer way around. The Saplings are out in force today and I didn't want to accidentally lose someone to a creeping cherry."

Coat Check nodded absentmindedly.

"Did you deliver my letter?" Somerset Sayer queried.

"Oh most, most, yes." He rasped in his usual fashion. "Heralds make good and court is now waiting. All are expected and none to answer. The Summer King shall call the Hunt! Much impatience. Much, much fear."

"Good. Then we should not keep him waiting any longer. Lead on."

Elizabeth Pennybaker canted her head as the small fairy creature in the lane tugged on his ragged tunic, emblazoned with a dragon, before setting off towards the ivy wall with an air of pride.

"Herald?" She turned to the Waysmith. "You actually have a literal herald?"

"Hn. And not just any herald. Let's go."

There had never been a grander experience in the lives of the women therein. The castle of Foras Feasa in the island kingdom of Lilylit was simply magnificent, if one could even have called it truly a castle. A willowy path, lit by incandescent winter cherries, swept up high into the boughs of the trees where wide branches formed the length of hallways, and leaves and flowers the tapestries on the walls. The spires were the tops of ancient pines, with banners of butterflies and wood moths caught in an updraft.

Where stained-glass windows looked out onto the expanses below, a second look revealed only cobwebs speckled with dew refracting the midday light. It was as though the structures that made up the ramparts and arches were only there if you were looking for them, seeking out patterns that made sense in the chaos of Nature rather than any intentional act of building on the part of the Fae who lived there. It was a castle suspended in air, both present and not, tangible and ineffable. And in a moment, it felt as if it could simply disintegrate; having never been there at all.

The path then took them into a rolling fall of wisteria and onto a platform inlaid with a mosaic of forgotten things grown into the wood. Coins, shells, toys, buttons, broken dolls, and refuse made up the image of a unicorn rearing on a mountaintop, facing a maelstrom of moss and lichens. As the storm grew darker in the recesses, shadows and tree-dappled sun made up the ominous clouds swirling together at their feet. As the wind shook the trees overhead, the equine figure appeared to move and twist in anguished anticipation of a battle too long in coming. It was a rather frightening thing all told, with a sense of menace and urgency that was difficult to parse.

But from the mosaic and out into the Great Hall, called the Sæl, the wonders were grander still. A massive terrace of roots and stone brought Waysmith and company into the presence of the Summer Court at last, though it did not escape any of them that the room was devoid of any actual people. It seemed that, for now, they were alone in the garden. Alice Guthrie was the first to notice the dais and throne at its center though, cut into the cross-section of a tree too impossibly large to be real. The dais alone had so many rings that it must have come from a tree that was recording the passage of time since before mankind had even stood up.

But it was not dead, and the loamy edges of the bark on the furthest outer ring were still green and growing, adding new boundaries to an ever-expanding Hall and new canvas to the story playing itself out in the mosaic. The central heartwood in the middle of the stump rose up above all the rest into a column more than twenty feet high and at least half as much across. Within its bends and burls, a throne emerged and upon it was a man who could not be described as anything other than the High King, Sovereign of the Way By.

Somerset Sayer immediately took a knee and tapped the floor loudly with the tip of her longbow when the others did not immediately follow suit. Each, in turn, then hastily paid their respects in the manner that best suited them but not before both Madam Bel Carmen and Elizabeth Pennybaker had taken the time to appraise him thoroughly. He was not what one expected in an elvish king.

He did not wear much in the way of ornaments or extravagant fabrics, opting instead for a simple kaftan coat in solid blue and an embroidered sash that bound his midsection with an emblem made of brass and teak. The emblem itself was also simple; a vaguely geometric design reminiscent of three wheeled spirals, the triskele, overlaid with an icon of the Crann Bethadh, the Tree of Life. His long dark hair was also left loose and drifting into soft waves around his face and shoulders, which only made the bleeding out of its snowy white ends more pronounced against the richer colors of his clothing.

"Hail Avenant," Somerset proclaimed in an uncharacteristically grandiose tone. "An Rí Samhraidh of the House and Line of Nuada macBalor, who was called Finn Fáil, known now as Neachtain: The One Who is Washed Clean. Ard Rí de Là-arn-a-Mhàireach. He who is Maine Mórgor: One Who Undertakes Great Duty. Tiarna an Dál nAraidi: Lord of the Lands and Peoples of the North."

Avenant gracefully rose to his feet and stepped down in acknowledgement of the fealty offered below. He then smiled. To Elizabeth Pennybaker, he seemed handsome but distant; with pleasantly angular features, characteristically pointed ears, a strange patterning of deep scars across his forehead, and a penchant for leaning slightly to his left. To Madam Bel Carmen, he was otherworldly; an empyrean and ethereal being who embodied the great Names upon which he had been bestowed.

An Rí Samhraidh, the Summer King. *Ard Rí de Là-arn-a-Mhàireach.* The High King of the Morrow. To Fiona though, his smile seemed almost rakish and even a little dashing. But to Alice Guthrie, his eyes flashed with the spark of subjugation and revealed him to be deeply inhuman.

"Hello, Somerset." Avenant addressed their leader with a surprisingly familiar and affectionate tone. As he did so, it became suddenly apparent that they were not alone in the Great Hall. On either side of the throne, four silhouettes came into view: an Archer, a Cavalier, a Ranger, and a Knight on the left, followed by a Crusader, a Huntsman, a Druid, and a Scribe on the right. The Octadic did not move far enough forward for the women to see them all plainly but when it became obvious to Elizabeth Pennybaker that the Scribe was possessed of two separate faces arranged on a single head, she then knew what Somerset Sayer had meant by nine names in eight members of the Guard. Everything here tasted of riddles.

The folklorist raised her head in response and smiled at him wanly. "Hello, Your Grace."

"My greetings to your Company. Welcome to Lilylit. I'm sure you all have a great many questions at this point."

"Are you really an elf?" Fiona Guthrie breathlessly blurted out from her position next to her mother, who startled as a result. Somerset Sayer looked at her askance but decided not to chastise her for it. Her ebullience was actually becoming a bit infectious.

The High King also seemed to take it in stride. "I suppose you could call me that." He replied gently, with a voice low and genial. "We are normally referred to as the Aos Sí, or, I think, just as the sídhe. But if 'elf' is easier for you, I do not object."

As Fiona shyly nodded and then returned her embarrassed gaze back to the floor, Elizabeth Pennybaker took the opportunity to be heard.

"Questions, yes, and I'm sure we'll want to get to all that when we can, but Dr. Sayer has brought us here for a specific reason, I understand. Perhaps now is a good time to lay it all out?"

Avenant regarded the younger Waysmith with a measure of interest. She was tall and vigilant, with a late-autumn complexion and a roll of mismanaged black hair in the process of escaping the braided bun it was not at all interested in staying a part of. His golden eyes then belied some unvoiced memory of experiences long past, but he did not let her see his disquiet at the fact that he could perceive how the Way By came to her. How it bent at her passing; how it anticipated her anger and rose to answer.

"Yes." He replied. "I think that is wise."

"May we approach?" Somerset Sayer tilted her head sideways to indicate the assembled group.

Avenant sighed and brought his hand up to stay the Guard on either side of him as he returned to the throne and sat down again. "You may."

With a measure of gentle coaxing and direction, the folklorist managed to get each member of the company seated on the inner edge of the dais, not more than a few feet from where the Summer King now overlooked them. The Octadic remained still and watchful as well, hovering just beyond clear vision.

"It is my understanding," Avenant began, "that you have each visited the Chalk Circle prior to this?"

"We have." Alice Guthrie replied. "A wonderful but shocking place, if I may say so."

He nodded. "Then it will pain you to know that it is no longer."

"What?!" Came the Waysmith's sharp retort.

The Summer King met her stunned glare and dipped his head sadly. "Word has come from the Near By and I am afraid it is terrible news. Clarisant set upon it in such a manner as no one could have predicted. She had, as far as we can tell, some kind of eldritch magic at her command; an ash that consumed everything it touched as wildfire might consume a dry wood. Those who stood against her have fallen. Those who dared to remain were rendered unto dust. Those who escaped came here and are under the protection of the Crown."

Somerset Sayer fell hard against the lowest step of the Heartwood and swallowed the sob that threatened her. She had known and loved the habitants of the Chalk Circle since her very earliest days in the Way By and, though it was occasionally a frustrating and macabre place, it had almost been like a second home to her.

"She destroyed the Chalk Circle. Which means that there are no more barriers to stop her. Where is she now?"

"It is hard to say." Avenant leaned forward slightly; the only indication of the gesture of solace he actually wanted to offer. "She passed beyond the borders of our sight immediately after. Since that time, the Dead have been boldly making headway into the nearest reaches of the material world. If it were not for the Lamps on our shores, I have no doubt we would already be in conflict with them."

Alice Guthrie placed her hand on her daughter's wrist but addressed the Summer King. "What do you mean, the Dead?"

"The enemy you have all been called upon here to face is one I hardly have the words to properly describe to you." Avenant began by way of settling into the sweep of the throne and resting his hands on the gnarled burls on either side. "She is Clarisant, by those who know of her, and the Unicorn Queen by those who dare not speak her name, lest they attract her attention. I have also heard her called Aon-Adharcach Banrigh but that is not a title that I think she has answered to in a very long time. But regardless of what the world may or may not know her as, she is the antithesis of everything that you hold dear and if nothing is done to challenge her, your world will likely see the death of wonderment for the very last time. And our world may very well cease to exist entirely."

"Unicorn?" Elizabeth Pennybaker raised her hand questioningly. "But why would a unicorn do something like this? I thought they were supposed to be.... you know..."

"The speakers of love and light?" He supplied.

"Yes, I mean...Dr. Sayer told us a little about her but...why? Why is she doing all of this?"

Avenant closed his eyes and took in a deep, almost pained, breath. "Because we didn't save her."

Madam Bel Carmen produced the next logical step. "Who didn't save her? From what?"

"Anyone." He answered. "Clarisant could once have been called the best of us. The pinnacle that all virtuous and resolute lords and maidens aspired to. She was the Wild, the Unbending, the empress of the woodland and the virgin goddess who held absolute dominion over all that was bright and good in the Near By. When she traversed dreams, inspiration followed and she mused for some of the greatest artistry and intelligence seen in the ages of living memory. But when men grew greedy, they began to take more than what they were due. One might say, they simply began to eat her alive. She was taken down, torn apart, and devoured by that which became what you now call industry; by people who could never be satisfied no matter how much they gorged. It should have been the end of her, just as it has been the end of most of us. But instead of fading into the twilight, something much more sinister took shape. Took her shape."

Fiona swallowed and glanced nervously at the Octadic forms shifting in the murk beyond. "What happened to her?"

"Each wound she suffered no longer healed, each insult she bore was no longer obscured by time or tenderness. She faced the world a battered and abused creature, but not cowed by any of it as they may have wanted. Her injuries became armor against those who would seek to control her. Those who claimed authority over her only found themselves at a loss for words when she rebelled against them, charging them with the crimes committed against her. And then the worst of it befell us all. Few know the entire tale but we know that a man possessed of great skill in navigating and map-making found the barrow that served as her sanctuary, lured her from it with promises of deliverance and restoration, and then cut the alicorn from her as one would slit the throat of a deer in the hunt. In so many ways, it was all the same. The betrayal was unforgivable. He, and all his family, were the first to die in the fires that came afterwards."

"Ever since that time," Somerset Sayer continued in his stead, "She has turned what was once mastery over life into absolute power over the Dead. She kills indiscriminately; always feeding more bodies and souls into a morass that has slowly begun to overtake the Way By and everything and everyone in it. This Hecatomb is a thing we hardly speak of for fear of the word alone dragging us down into hopelessness, preferring to call it the Stumble. It's a cancer, is what it is. A malignancy of death and despair that is growing stronger every day. And as it does, the world around it, the Way By and the world we know, change."

Elizabeth Pennybaker winced imperceptibly at the phrasing but rubbed her chin absently. "I know this is going to sound weird but I think I understand what you're saying. In a sort of general sense, anyway. It's like that cliché, right? Hurt people hurt people? The more destruction she causes, the more people she kills or maims, the more pain that goes out into the world. The more pain that goes out into the world, the more it responds with even worse pain. And around and around we go until we get...well, to now. I mean, that's basically what happened to you in a nutshell, isn't it Dr. Sayer?"

The folklorist nodded thoughtfully. "It was by the grace of Avenant alone that I wasn't next in her orchestration of carnage. It had long been her intent at the time; to kill every Waysmith she could find and thus prevent any one of us from calling the Rite of the Hunt or even just working the Way By against her. She almost succeeded and she has every design to succeed in the future."

"The Hunt," Madam Bel Carmen spoke up. "Yes, you mentioned that. Is...is that how we stop her?"

"I'm afraid it is." The Waysmith answered. "And that's why I brought you all here. Centuries ago the royal houses of the Seelie instituted a ritual called the Great Hunt, which could only be called once in a generation. Every year, on the eve of the Spring Equinox, the councils of the Summer Court would meet to determine if the Rite was necessary. If not, the turning of the seasons would commence as normal and a new age would be ushered in. If it was indicated, they would then speak the binding words of calling and strike their Bargain with the Court of the Sun. It was at this time, and only this time, that a Tuatha Dé Danann, a True Fae, could be defeated."

"Great Hunt." Alice Guthrie pondered. "You mean like fairy tale hunts? Like the...uh...Hunt of Odin? Um, King Arthur? It's usually some kind of mythical creature being hunted by...elves? Or the dead? Right?"

"Well, since you like fairy tales so much, let me tell you another one." Somerset Sayer announced with a smile. "Before the Age of Men, Nature was ruled by the Fae. Of the Fae, there were two important divisions. For our purposes right now, I'll use the Old English terms, though many people around the world have different names for them. Anyway, there were the Seelie, the lawful houses of light and the Unseelie, the chaotic houses of the dark. But it was mankind who misunderstood this division as being between the True Fae and the Earthbound Fae, as...as... between truly supernatural beings and those who were born of mortal flesh. This is not the reality of things such as they are here in the Way By. Rather, the True Fae are called Aos Sí. Beings of pure nature and harbingers of magic who passed into this world from The Other Place eons before the memories of men began; ancient creatures born of the divine dreaming of the world. The Aos Sí on Earth, specifically those who had direct dealings with humanity, were called the Tuatha Dé Danann and those lineages, those heroes and legends of the old world, were collectively known as The Court of the Sun. The Court of the Sun then, essentially, were the ones who taught magic to the human travelers they met over the years and who then ruled supreme over the natural domains of creation. Follow me so far?"

"Not really." Fiona replied. "But keep going."

Somerset Sayer cocked her head and gave the girl an incredulous look. "Alright. Over time, the Aos Sí, who the Waysmiths now call the Dreaming Fae, began to intermingle with Nature and with the peoples of the ancient world. From these unions were born the bloodlines of the Aois-dàna, the Earthbound or Waking Fae. It was the Aois-dàna who eventually split into the Seelie and Unseelie Courts; the twin rulerships of Spring-Summer and Autumn-Winter. In other words, my Hat Trick and Coat Check are Aois-dàna; and there are many different kinds of them, each according to their own unique kin. While Avenant, as you know by now, is Aos Sí; much as all members of the highest courts in the Way By are. Now, I'll spare you the long, long, histories of rulership in the Way By, and who ends up ruling where and why, but suffice to say that all of the assorted Fae eventually separated out into various kith and kingdoms and dominions and eventually incorporated all manner of Fae-peoples, changelings, etcetera in courts and bloodlines and what have you. But..."

She raised a finger to ensure she had the others' undivided attention. "This is where our story comes in. The harmony between the Court of the Sun, the Seelie Summer Court, and Mankind was always fraught and uneasy. To maintain any kind of long-lasting unity and cooperation between Fae-kinds and the ultimate balance of Nature and humans, there had to be a method of justice that could be brought against the most powerful members of the Fae world in the event that things went.... badly. In essence, the Way By would not be able to function if one side held too much destructive power over another. So, the Court of the Sun offered up a solution. Once an Age, the Summer Court could name a Hunter, usually a second or third Prince or Princess or close to it but specifically someone not Heir Apparent to a throne and, in many later years, this included Waysmiths drawn from the ranks of the initiated. It was then the task of the Hunter and their closest kin, a Company of the Hunt, to pursue, capture, and subdue the named quarry. It was the only time humans were ever given boons enough within the Way By to ever kill a True Fae. It is the only Rite that makes this kind of battle possible."

Madam Bel Carmen furrowed her brow in response to Somerset Sayer's rather professorial telling. She still didn't understand what this all meant but she did understand that they were being set against a foe with the capacity and the desire, not just to kill the lot of them in short order, but to drag the world itself into the depths of sorrow. Sorrow that may be well deserved in some ways, but would be nothing less than a blight against the notion of hope itself.

"But even at the height of its time," the Waysmith continued, "the Great Hunts were so terrifying that they scarred the memories of people for generations. Seeing a Wild Hunt often heralded great catastrophes, like wars or plagues. Many also began to see them as harbingers of death. I have encountered tales that those who even so much as heard the horn or the baying of the hounds would fall dead in an instant or that the riders would harvest up the souls of the sleeping to participate in the chase and then not return them in the morning. During the battles and treaties of mythic times, all manner of men betrayed or attacked suspected Fae for no other reason than that they feared the return of the Hunts; despite how necessary they were."

"So," Elizabeth Pennybaker summed it up for them. "We're here to join together and be tasked with a Hunt. Specifically, hunting a unicorn. Because if we don't, she will continue cutting a swath of death and dismemberment through the world, through both worlds, until...until what exactly?"

"Until there's nothing left but ash." Somerset Sayer concluded.

The younger Waysmith let out a long, slow, breath. "This is nuts."

The others stared back at her silently, with little to add but both acknowledgement and reprimand. She shrugged. "Okay, then. Yeah. How does this happen?"

"Well," Somerset Sayer sat up, slightly more enthusiastically. "As you might imagine, there's only one person in all of the Kingdoms of the Way By and trods of the Near By and paths of the Deep Way that has the power to formally call a Hunt and to imbue it, by weight of Geas, to be undertaken."

Each of the assembled women turned, and collectively they regarded the Summer King as he deftly rose to his feet and bid them all to do the same. With a bit of a scramble they managed to once again form into a cohesive group, with the folklorist at their center facing the dais and resplendent king. It was clear that he had already been prepared for what was meant to take place this particular afternoon but he seemed reticent all the same.

Avenant turned slightly to address the Octadic behind him. "Bring up the Bramble Crown." He commanded. As he returned to the company, he smiled lightly and bowed his head. "This is the only time I will ever ask this directly. Kneel."

The Way By was at last a boon to them. No matter how abrupt or discordant the world was, everything seemed to make its own sense. There was no confusion or intransigence because each of them could make of the event what she might will of it, just as one might make sense of a vision. In Fiona Guthrie's view, she had been at last whisked away to a fantastic realm beyond imagining; where she had been chosen out of all others for a chance at greatness.

To Madam Bel Carmen's eye, however, she was being offered the very secrets she had always been convinced were just out of her reach. Taken away by selfish forces for their own gains. Secrets that would change the essence of her sorrows and break the bonds of suffering she knew too intimately. Finally, she could refuse the torment and turn away the miseries that life insisted on handing her. For Alice Guthrie, a handsome, elegant king was about to impart upon her the freedom she'd only guessed at.

Giving up his power and decision for hers, such that no one would ever again question her right to stand in this place. Elizabeth Pennybaker, on the other hand, had absolutely no idea what to do with any of it and thought the entire experience absurd. But for all of them it took a singular form; a grand ceremony of naming and welcoming attended by all manner of things great, small, and unknowable.

For the two friends of the Hearthcraft Practitioners Community of Massachusetts, a whimsical teenager, a disgruntled folklorist, and an erstwhile medical student who had only recently been party to dispatching an imp with her cat, they quickly and unexpectedly found that taking a knee before the Summer King of Foras Feasa was the very acceptance of a new kind of being. As they listened to the Sovereign's pronouncements, they came to understand that they would no longer be divided by titles or age, by generation or experience.

They would be no longer practitioners and scholars, or students and teachers. They were the Flidais Venatica, the Huntresses of the King; tasked now to go forward and to, if necessary, give their lives in service to the Hunt. In service to a world drowning in disillusionment and doing everything it could to forget that any of them had even existed at all. In service to destroying the one that should have been its beating heart. On a slab of black stone, the Bramble Crown was brought up from the furthest reaches of the Great Hall; out of a tangle of ivy and blackberries and nightshade tearing into shreds on its razor-sharp tines.

It was a surprisingly menacing thing; a warp and weave of icy thorns and briers threaded together into a circlet with a garland of nettles and gorse as its jeweled points. Frost breathed from its center and the two Octadic who carried the stone on either side were often forced to shift their grip about it to avoid having their hands frozen to the slate. To the horror of most of those in attendance, they watched as Avenant appeared to steel himself for a moment as the Knight and the Cavalier knelt down before him and raised up the stone and crown as if in supplication.

Gently, he reached down and lifted the Bramble Crown from its setting, ice and mist forming immediately over his hands and stiffening the rims of his sleeves. Strangely, he did not seem overly affected by the cold, but by something else that stirred in his soul just as soon as he touched the crisp tines.

"Are you certain of this?" He looked to Somerset Sayer one final time. "Once the Call is made, there is no going back. It cannot be unmade."

The Waysmith nodded with a measure of confidence none of the rest of them felt. "I'm certain. This is the only way. You know it's the only way. If there were any other, I would already be on it."

With a low murmur and a sigh, the Summer King raised the Crown that only he could wear. Placing it onto his head, he immediately dropped his hands and cried out. Fiona Guthrie gasped as she watched several root-like sprigs erupt from the base of the crown and begin growing, with alarming speed, directly into the elf king's head. It split the scars along his brow and burrowed beneath his hair until small trickles of blood began to seep from the cuts and drip down onto his shoulders and collar.

But it didn't end there, and Avenant twisted, though he somehow remained standing, as an ominous crackling sound could be heard emanating from the coronet. More roots sank into his skull, pulling the crown flush to his head and causing the rest of it to swell and pulse with blood. No doubt, his blood. The company startled back and prepared to reach out to him but finally the last of it began to subside, and as the Summer King regained his bearings and raised his head, the brambles and frost vanished beneath a full bloom of oak leaves, hibiscus, yarrow, sea holly, and snapdragons.

Gone was the sinister thornbush that had been revealed to them, and in its place, a crown of sublime glory wrought in nature's exquisite designs. As he then looked down at them, even his eyes had changed. No more were there the soft golden-brown regards of a gentle and patient man, but in their place the windswept grey-blue of the Way By Sovereign. It also became clear to them why Avenant was not especially given to wearing much jewelry or other accouterments.

As he stood before them, regal and imposing with a mantle of strength that seemed almost beyond him, curls of ivy began to appear through the seams of his coat; wrapping around him until they had formed a royal robe of indescribable beauty. Lavenders and sky-blues, sea-green and white, with all the colors of the sunrise in every conceivable blossom and vine from his shoulders to his feet. As he drew himself up, he shamed the very gems of the Earth; whose comparative immortality gave them the only advantage. Wherever he stepped, mosses with tiny white flowers followed him.

Somerset Sayer was the only one of them to turn her face downward. She didn't want him to catch the look of sadness that she could not conceal as the auburn hues faded further from his hair, raising the empty white locks nearly an inch higher than before. In their brief exchange beforehand, they had said nothing, and everything, about the cost of her request and the life he would give up to make this pact.

With solemnity, the Summer King spoke the Geas, the binding words of the Hunt, into being. He stated the Challenge succinctly, using a simple customary rhyme, letting the Way By intertwine with it and give it substance.

"A key is hidden, find it.
A wound is bleeding, bind it.
Hope was lost, return it."

Somerset Sayer set her jaw and listened as the deep, moth-eaten, magics of the Way By rose up to meet the words and to weigh them against the memories of the trees that grew imposing and strong all around them. As the Geas was made real, the very trees circling the court bent and swayed with fervor, in response to the power of the Bramble Crown, as they recited the challenge they were to meet in riddles that sprout and grow.

Oak raised its voice first: "A memory is all that is needed, for the story cries out in joy when the storyteller returns again to her own words."

Followed by Birch and Willow in time: "But before it can be revealed, the Wound shall be laid bare. If it is not, no force may heal it, and you must leave then with this burden of failure in payment of the pain that came before."

Then Ash, to add its own distinction: "And into exile each of you will go, never to return."

And Elm, entwined with Mistletoe: "But should the memory confess what has brought it to be, raise then that which gives life anew and bring it to the place that She shall name, where a guardian stands before a jumbled corpse, consumed by trees. Fell the guardian, and return what was taken."

Finally, Holly, hidden in the mire: "Do this, and the Way shall be reborn, in the bower beneath the sun."

"Fellows." The Summer King addressed all assembled. "On this day, the Aequinoctium, the right ascension of spring is illuminated by the procession of the sun. But this equinox is not like any other we have seen in more than a millennium. Today, we do what can be done on no other day but this one. Today, we call the Great Hunt. As our ancestors once did in ages past, the Fae born of Waking and the Fae born of Dreaming will again meet each other on the Field of the Wild. It is our charge to claim one of the Dreaming, an Aos Sì, and bring her unto us. In so doing, we also honor the old treaties and pay the price by giving of our own. This pursuit on the thresholds between sleep and awake will then herald the new Spring. New life will come to our world once again, such as we have not seen in an age." He paused, considering the route of his words carefully. "But our quarry is swift and clever. She will not be overtaken easily. We must therefore use all that we have at our disposal: our cunning must be brought to bear on the riddles presented, our strength on the battles to come, and our wit on the strategies of our prey."

An eager hum arose from the company of guardians and huntresses alike. The Octadic remained intent until the King passed his hand over his eyes and into the embedded roots of dozens of differently named trees at his forehead.

"Tá an fiach orainn." Spoke the Summer King. "Let the Hunt of the Unicorn begin."

Chapter Fourteen

"I think Fiona has a crush on you." Somerset Sayer stated, announcing her presence to the King.

Avenant smiled, but as he was still turned away from her, the folklorist could not see it. "That's very sweet of her."

"You say that now." She chuckled, approaching the dais with characteristic indifference. "But the minds of girls can run amok with such things. Especially here."

Avenant did not turn to regard her but rather remained passively observant as half of his Octadic continued the ritual-like motions necessary to soothe the Bramble Crown into frost-bitten rest once again.

"I suppose. But I do seem to recall another young girl, rather some time ago, who arose out of a similar situation and was, shall I say, none too worse for the experience."

Somerset Sayer rolled her eyes in response but felt no actual reprimand coming. "I didn't have a crush on you."

Avenant tilted his head over his shoulder benignly. "Yes, you did."

The folklorist sniffed indignantly but then sighed with a measure of consternation when her eyes drifted over the still-fresh wounds etched along his forehead. And beneath them, layer upon layer of twisting, scattered lines, writing out their secret history of trials and ascension in an erratic script. Even without the power of voiced utterances that would allow them to actually speak, she understood what they meant. At least they were no longer actively bleeding, but the ragged cuts stood out prominently against his otherwise unblemished skin and fair features. When Avenant once again redirected his attention, she came up alongside him with familiar ease.

"Where will you take them?" He queried.

"Well, the imp essentially proves two things." She replied. Thankfully, Avenant was quite accustomed to the Waysmith's circuitous responses and did not remark on the apparent non sequitur of her answer. "The first is that Clarisant knows about Elizabeth. She knows there is another Waysmith and that puts her in an extraordinary amount of danger. Secondly, it means that Clarisant wants something from her. Whether by design or by accident, no one encounters Para-Sprites unless they're seriously looking for something."

"And intent on finding it."

Somerset Sayer nodded impassively. "Yes. Which pretty much means the beginning of our path is already laid out for us. I have to know where Elizabeth Pennybaker went on the night she was attacked."

"How do you imagine you'll discover this, then?"

"Oh, easy." The Waysmith chuffed, observing as both Hafath and Arafin began to struggle with a few wayward vines in their attempts to quiet the Bramble Crown. "I'll ask the cat."

Avenant laughed; a low, deep, sound that Somerset Sayer had always found unusually comforting. "I am not surprised. You've always had the better affinity for the creatures. So, I suppose you'll be off then."

"Just as soon as we have a new daybreak. I promised Alice Guthrie and Madam Bel Carmen some time to explore the grounds before we left. It's their first time this far into the Way By, after all. The blooming fountains really are spectacular this time of year and I can't fault them for a little distraction."

"Distraction?" He looked askance at her. "I remember a time when you might have spoken of Lilylit as a wondrous place. Perhaps even majestic." He was, of course, referring to the massive blossoms that served as the castle's main garden fountains, fed by the waters of a thousand spouts drifting through the sky on an apparatus of planetary rings tracking the path of the moon.

"Please. I've never been given to hyperbole." But she smiled anyway.

"Perhaps not. At least not where the Kingdoms have been concerned."

The hint of sorrow in his voice gave form to her otherwise shapeless emotions and Somerset Sayer turned to him, touching his sleeve and feeling the last few summer leaves threading through the seams dying away beneath her fingers.

"Ave, I know this isn't what you wanted. I know that the last place you wanted to see this go was into a Great Hunt; something the Summer Crown has not declared in an age or more. And for good reason, I know. But we've already waited too long. The Waysmiths have been all but annihilated and the Stumble grows further and deadlier by the hour. She has already consumed entire worlds in her rage and now even the Near By is falling to her destruction. Dreams are crushed before they even form and homes that once warmed with joy are haunted by loss and emptiness. Wherever she goes, there will be a melancholy; the kind of sadness that breathes your thoughts as air and gulps down your soul as it drowns. And when it finally stops all that is left is the cavernous hole where it was sitting when it ate itself to death. You know what she will do."

"I know." He brought his hand to hers where it lay on his arm. "Only oblivion follows now. I wish I could go with you, though. Such power and privilege and yet, I can do so little with it some days it seems. If I could, I would clean it all away and hang the stars back up where you left them."

With a sigh, the folklorist drew nearer to the King. Under the wary glances of the Octadic, she came to rest her head against his shoulder, surreptitiously playing with the whitened ends of his hair with the fingers curling into the back of his coat.

"You already did. A long time ago. For a scared little girl hiding behind a couch when the world ended."

The Bramble Crown at last drifted into peacefulness; the chill of an early frost crystallizing over the gnarled knots and twigs, drying a few errant snowberries with a killing draft of winter wind and alighting the first flakes of snow into the air around them. As they drifted down from the boughs high overhead, they came to rest on every surface and twinkled like Christmas lights.

Silence fell across the throne of Foras Feasa but Somerset Sayer stayed awhile longer to revel in the stillness and the quiet, to feel the warmth of a gentle man who was still standing watch against the fears of a thousand night-frightened children, and to remind herself to memorize the moment so that she might recall it in a time of need, such as one might with the most significant phrase in a much longer story. This was because, in just a brief moment, she would need to leave and find the younger Waysmith. There was so much to tell her.

Fiona Guthrie gazed dumbstruck off of a balcony overlooking the whole of Lilylit. There were marvelous gardens and fantastical artworks to be certain, but she had only just become aware of the greater picture of where she stood. This castle, which she had initially thought looked much like a fort children might build in the backyard woods, was itself growing out of the rings of a felled tree. Which was to say that each concentric circled enclosure of walls, baileys, and courtyards were actually the growth rings of the tree upon which they sat.

As she also recalled that the throne of the Summer King looked similar, the young woman concluded that the fortress of Foras Feasa must have been tended into being out of the ruins of something before it, rather than cut, nailed, and built. Everything else that carpeted its floors and walls then suddenly made so much more sense to her. The Fae made the world as they wished it to be by patiently directing the forces of nature in the way they wanted them to go. Even if the end result was chaotic and unpredictable, it assumed the form of whatever structure they had laid out beneath it. Somerset Sayer had also said something to that effect, she thought, back at the house on Trowbridge Street.

It was then that Fiona Guthrie again took notice of a strange detail. Despite the grand majesty of Lilylit, it was all empty. There was no one here and there hadn't been anyone new to her but the Summer King and his retinue since they arrived. She had seen no courtiers nor townsfolk nor anyone serving or ministering to anything or anyone anywhere. She saw now that she stood at the center of a grand cathedral in a beautiful capital city but no one appeared to live in it. In fact, it was so deserted that she was suddenly worried. This had to be intentional.

Were the people of the court purposely avoiding her and the others? Was it because she was somewhere she didn't belong? After everything that had transpired in just the last few days, Fiona Guthrie honestly still didn't know what to do with herself or what her role was supposed to be. In the growing hollowness, she felt even more like an after-thought; only along for the ride because she happened to be there when the suggestion was offered.

The thought struck a nerve. Most of her life she had felt like everyone's last choice but in such a benignly innocuous way that her pain was never evident. She was usually on the fringe of every group of friends but not because they didn't like her, but because they had failed to notice she was there. And she was never invited to meet anywhere unless she was the one who proposed it. Even then, the conversation quickly forgot her.

Perhaps the other kids at school merely saw her as good filler for their personal followings or, more likely, simply thought her plain and uninteresting. When a boy had at last come along, pretending to see the bright spark she held within, was it no wonder then that she'd fallen for it? To finally just be seen was worth anything. Which turned out to have cost everything.

Fiona Guthrie sighed and returned to the inner hall. She felt so conflicted; to be standing in such an unbelievable place while all she could feel was loneliness and estrangement. It wasn't at all what she should be feeling, what she wanted to be feeling, and she remained so consumed with her thoughts that she did not notice the space around her begin to change in response. Unwittingly, she passed right by the portrait of a gentlewoman, sword in hand, decisively beheading the man below her as her maidservant looked on.

As she meandered by, the woman seemed to turn and reach out, showing her the slain man's face as if to indicate something she had missed. Another painting turned in its frame; a Baroque woman dumping a Roman soldier head first into a well. The man, upside down and helpless as she stood over him resolutely, seemed to at first beg forgiveness and then to fall away in rage as the central figure looked up to regard the girl on the other side of the canvas. But then her face contorted, out of an expression of determination, to one of warning as she seemed to gesture again and again towards the mouth of the well at her side.

The sconces in the walls flickered low but still Fiona did not see them. The walkway was bathed in ominous shadows, but she did not notice. Nor did she hear her mother calling from somewhere behind her. Alice Guthrie, as it turned out, had been looking for her daughter for the better part of an hour and just as she was on the brink of returning to the Waysmith for guidance, she too happened across a pair of portraits in a hall that moved of their own accord. The elder Guthrie stopped the moment a woman in the furthest image beckoned her.

When she approached, she beheld the gruesome scene of a bloody man and two women absconding with his head. She glanced down at the name plate. Judith Slaying Holofernes, it read, followed by the name Gentileschi. She glanced back up as Judith, so named, motioned her on; pointing worriedly into the creeping darkness and raising her sword intently. The second portrait, named Timoclea Killing Her Rapist, knocked several times against the wall. Timoclea, also so named, then reiterated the gesture and seemed to mouth the words, 'help her.' A cold dread gripped Alice Guthrie's heart and she set off quickly, but to where, she did not know.

Fiona Guthrie finally came to a stop but did so only because, to her consternation, the hallway simply ended. It didn't turn, as she remembered it did coming up here, or branch off into stairwells and galleries. It just ended in a flat, blank wall with a single, massive, painting hung like a window. In it, an older man with white hair in a dapper black suit held a fainting woman as she bent backwards, all to the strange amazement of a gathered group of, she squinted, similarly dressed young men sitting in a hospital ward. Fiona scowled and checked the title card: Dr. Charcot Demonstrates a Case of Hysteria was written in cursive ink and tucked into the frame.

But why the Summer King would have such a work of art in such a primordial place as this confused her. In fact, as she began to look about herself and take in the details of the hallway, she at last started to wonder why the paintings she passed looked like they did. Renaissance and Baroque, Rubenesque with voluptuous nude women, and all, she gasped, were staring back at her. She stumbled.

With a choked scream, Fiona Guthrie felt something reach out to her from the black obscurity. Whether it was the Charcot figure in the painting before her or something else taking form through it, she couldn't tell, but she could see the coalescing of a creature as it stepped out of the wall, the portrait, the fainting woman, and the writing. The Way By all but groaned with the weight of arrogance and malice, and Fiona scrambled back as the one thing she had hoped to never see again in her life announced its presence.

"Fiona, my love." It sang in a high, pinched voice. "Fiona, my dear, there you are. I was looking for you for so long."

The Chirurgeon looked different than he had before. He breathed wafts of pestilent smoke and wore a broken mask over his mouth but he was still spindly in make-up, almost puppet-like in movement. Wads of wet hair clung to his head where gashes exposed a bleached and browning skull. His nose extended, as a wide hook, through the mask such that he appeared as a kind of plague doctor cobbled together from litter and abominable things. But he did not close on her immediately. The creature struggled somewhat to gain balance; almost as if it were injured. It floundered, as a wounded bird, to assemble itself on the rug, spitting pitch as it went. Fiona then spied the reason for his hunched position. Sticking out from between a loose fold at his ribs was a short, wooden sword and a bit of brown fluff at its handle.

"Teddy?" She mumbled.

"No." He hissed in reply; raising his head with a churlish, grating, sound. "No teddies anymore. No more hiding under the bed now, my little darling. No more sweet sleep..."

Fiona Guthrie got to her feet, or maybe she was helped by unseen hands reaching out from painted landscapes, but once she was upright again, she rallied. The monster glowered down at her, still smug with a self-assured sway. It was clearly more at home here; becoming sanguine and fearless though still badly damaged.

"I know what you are." She answered.

"Do you now?"

"You're Fae. An evil one. You sneak into houses and steal things. Steal people."

The Chirurgeon feigned offense. "I stole nothing! Nothing at all. How could you even say such a thing? I only came for what was promised. What you Bargained for."

"There's no Bargain with you." Fiona said. "I don't have what you want and it's not yours to take if I did. There's nothing here! I don't want anything from you!"

But the Fae were perceptive and the Chirurgeon took a step forward as the Way By continued to thrash itself into a labyrinth; blocking her every which way. "Perhaps not." He countered. "But there's no way out once you've chosen. And if I leave, everyone leaves. I take them all with me and leave you here all by yourself with nothing. With no one. I only asked for a small thing, didn't I? One small thing to change our fates, and then I would give you the world."

"Give me...one small thing..." She frowned at his words. They echoed down through a memory she had chosen to ignore; a memory of similar words spoken by a far more mortal voice hovering over her in an equally unfamiliar place. Cajoling her. Deceiving her with promises and then offering only betrayal and then pain. That had been what she couldn't understand. How her soul could be divided up into pieces and given away.

Or lost, bit by bit in the Bargains she made with everyone who met her. But that's who she had been to them; someone to take from. Time and attention, or care, or respect. And then her body. And then her very sense of self. Stripped away so that she would be truly, and utterly, alone. They never gave back, even when she desperately needed them to. They never kept up their side of the Bargains. Fiona Guthrie began to think that no one ever would. That was until she remembered something else: a story she had only just recently told a strange folklorist about a person she was yet to become. That story now suddenly seemed to take hold of her.

"No."

"What?"

"No." She said again. "There isn't anything *you* can give me. That's what the story was about and that's why Dr. Sayer wanted me to tell it like that, isn't it? That's what she wanted me to know?"

At this the Chirurgeon seemed taken aback. But Fiona Guthrie pressed on. "I...I think I get it. The woman I told myself about, she exists. I mean, she's not here but she exists already doesn't she? I can't possibly be alone because they're all here. The little girl I was talking to, the woman I told her about, me, all the lives I imagined differently." Her voice dropped to a threatening hush. "They exist. They look back at me. And you can't take them!"

Pitch boiled on the carpet but more and more figures began to appear in the canvases that surrounded them. "That's what you really want. You're trying to take them away!"

The creature lunged. There was danger in speaking the true terms of a Bargain, not the least of which was its dissolution. But something in the way the gallery shifted had warned Fiona beforehand and she backpedaled immediately, avoiding the Chirurgeon's first attack. He reached out for her again, trying to snag skin or clothing with deadly claws, but the frightened girl dodged away, nearly colliding with the wall and the corner of a gilt frame.

When the creature suddenly recoiled from her, Fiona Guthrie was not sure why. The Unseelie Fae emitted a faint scream, clutching angrily at a wound that had opened up on his arm. Even in the low light, she could see that it was in the shape of a small hand with five tiny fingers dug into the flesh deep enough to tear it. She looked around quickly but saw no ally and nothing to explain where the blow could have come from.

"So." The Chirurgeon growled. "You think they're going to save you now, do you?"

She looked around again and still saw no one.

"You think," the creature was closing on her again; head bowed menacingly. "that they're going to come for you. For you? You think they care enough to fight for you? Maybe that they will die for you? That the past will rally now at the present to rescue the future? No one is coming for you, girl! Accept death now and give me my due!"

She didn't understand him. Fiona Guthrie didn't know what he was talking about but she did falter and jab her elbow into a painting as she tried to press back against the furthest wall. And she thought, just for a moment, that something in the composition moved and turned the hanging towards the enraged and oncoming horror. All she could see were whirling shadows and the gallery hall dissolving into an empty, endless, void like a black maw yawning wide on the horizon.

She saw fire inside of it and mounds of ash whipped up by the wind into cyclones that lashed the agonized remnants of dead trees and scattered bones. It demanded her surrender and beckoned her closer with a relentless pull; not strong but inevitable. She was certain then that she would simply fall into it and be swallowed up. The labyrinth tipped and she had no purchase, the hallway was sinking and pitching downwards, and there was nothing she could do. She closed her eyes and sobbed. It was coming.

"FIONA!"

A hand seized her arm and stopped her fall, yanking her hard back into the gallery.

"MOM?!"

She could have screamed, cried, thrown up, or everything all at once. None other than Alice Guthrie had both hands wrapped around her daughter's wrist and shoulder as she hauled her bodily upwards with a tremendous heave.

"Don't let go, Fiona!" She bellowed down into the war-torn depths. "Don't you dare let go!"

To Fiona Guthrie's utter disbelief, she looked up to see her mother dangling over a precipice, her fingers bloodless with the effort of gripping onto her. Behind her, however, was another person, and another person after that, in a continuous line down the corridor. They appeared to reach out of every work of art; women and men, children and animals, kings, queens, peasants, performers, whores, and pirates anchored in ropes. A morass of hands holding onto one another and to Fiona and Alice Guthrie.

With a wail, the girl began to fight to grab onto them; so many hands reaching out she could never have imagined would be there, she just had to get to them. The darkness, however, had not receded and the Chirurgeon stepped easily along the wildly sloping floor. His shattered toenails and thick claws making for an easy grasp on the fibrous ground. He was reaching for her too and his hands could still cut pieces away.

"Fiona, come on!" Alice Guthrie yelled. "Come on, baby. Climb up! We've got you!"

Another voice she'd never heard before joined in. "Climb up, Fi! I will catch you!"

It was a woman with long, dark, wavy hair pinned up over a golden gown holding aloft a blade stained a clotted red.

"Yes!" A third voice, from a woman in a classic bodice and balzo hat. "Come to me! Trust me! Trust Timoclea!"

And yet, Fiona Guthrie could not take her eyes off of the blade in the hands of the woman dragging her mother back by the heels. She seemed so triumphant, so sure of victory. Even though the maw was only gaping wider, the Chirurgeon getting ever closer; no matter how hard they all held on the abyss was no further away than it had been a moment ago. A strange calm descended over her and Fiona turned her face down to where the wicked Fae had come upon her feet. He scrabbled at her legs, forcibly pushing her thighs apart, as he rose up. Sharp white teeth glittered in the flailing furnace-light as he smiled through her submission.

"Fiona! Please! You have to..."

His whispers still filled her ears, washing out the distant pleas and the reaching hands. "Yes, my little lovely. You're mine. That was our Bargain. Isn't it so much easier this way? You'll never have to be afraid again. Just let go and I will..."

A gurgle cut off the rest of whatever it was that the Chirurgeon had meant to say. Spittle drained from his twitching mouth and useless tongue. He tried again, staring down into the impassive face of a young woman who serenely watched him strangle on the blood that welled up from his throat. He couldn't form words or get his jaw to work properly; all he had left to respond with was a wide-eyed stare; stunned beyond recognition. The astonished Fae then shuddered and tried to press into her but his hands had gone numb and his body was turning slack. He then tried to cling to his captive, but was met with a foot set solidly against his torso.

Alice Guthrie continued to tow her daughter upwards; whether Fiona would help her to do it or not. She couldn't reach the creature bearing down on them, or she might have snatched Judith's blade for herself and hacked the terrifying thing into kindling for the inferno that raged just beyond. She didn't need to ask who the demon was because she remembered. The nightmare that had kept Fiona awake all those nights was pursuing her even here, in the halls of the Summer King. But it was so much worse to come face to face with it than it was to imagine it. A contorted, spineless fiend slashing at them, beating them down, and tearing the girl apart. She begged for Fiona to hold on, to keep fighting no matter how desperate things got.

"I'll hang on, no matter what! I'll get you out, baby! Don't you give in! We're almost there!"

But when her daughter suddenly relaxed in her hold, Alice Guthrie almost cried out, thinking that the worst had come to pass and that the darkness had finally snatched the life of her child right out of her arms. Frantic, she pulled and pulled harder, calling out to the hands for everything they had left. She screamed at them to wrest her daughter free. Though, sobbing, she expected to see only death returned.

What she didn't expect to see when she looked back down was Fiona Guthrie looking up at her with a relieved smile and the Chirurgeon limply falling away into the ashen plain, clutching a gushing wound at his chest. She also couldn't quite grapple with the pit below them that seemed to offer a ready entrance into Hell itself as it accepted the plummeting creature and then just began to fade away into nothingness, returning its light to the sconces in the hallway. She never would make sense of the portraits that calmly turned back to their poses or the sculptures that metamorphosed from Renaissance to Medieval to Ancient. Nor did she quite understand what she was seeing when her daughter nodded and raised a tiny, wooden sword in her hand, stained a fresh and gleaming red.

"Okay, Mom." She said. "Now you can pull me up."

"The creation of a raindrop." Somerset Sayer was explaining, hands waving in the air near one particular mosaic of mythological figures in the Sæl. "Has five stages. A shape that appears rounded on your skin. Then a shadow. Then a reflected shadow opposing that. These shadows blend and become white reflective light on the surface of the drop. At last, a dark line, devoid of all light, forms around it but it's the smallest, most miniscule, part of the story. "

Elizabeth Pennybaker folded her arms and sighed. They had been conversing for some time but had gotten precisely nowhere. "I know you're trying to help but I really don't see how any of that is useful. What does Waysmithing have to do with raindrops?"

"Stories are told in the way that best suits them, Elizabeth. When the manner changes, so does the meaning."

"Yeah, okay, sure. But...I guess..."

"What?"

"Is this supposed to be some kind of a metaphor?"

"You think I mean raindrops literally?"

She sighed. "No, it's just that, when you talk about reading or understanding the Way By, it always comes across like you're reciting a poem you think I already know. Like I'm somehow just supposed to take it up from where you left off and repeat the rest. Thing is, I have no idea what you're talking about."

Somerset Sayer crossed her arms. "I suppose that's fair. This is how I was taught Waysmithing but perhaps it isn't how you'll learn it. Though I should think that the intricate entextualization of multiple intersecting lines of comprehension and interwoven inquiry would already be familiar to a medical scientist such as yourself."

Elizabeth Pennybaker returned the most exasperated look. "See? This. This is the problem. You talk like you write. And, dear gods. Don't you have, like, a hobby or something? Anything? Or are you always like this?"

The folklorist straightened and pursed her lips thoughtfully for a moment. It wasn't that she didn't know that she was habitually pedantic, but more that she constantly worried that she would miss something in the simplification. Abbreviation was as much outside of her nature as general warmth was, but that didn't mean she couldn't at least try to make a pass at ordinary friendliness. So, she said the first thing that came to mind.

"Well, I like oddly-scented dish soaps."

"Dish...soaps?" If her state of mind had not already become unsalvageable, Elizabeth Pennybaker was certain that this exchange would do it.

"I can also make my own quill ink and write in three separate Medieval calligraphy styles but I never lead with that."

"Instead, you tell people you enjoy dish soap?"

"Oddly-scented dish soap."

"Why?!" There was a part of Elizabeth that, here, considered just going back to the stilted bookishness.

"Because it makes me seem less interesting. Even though it's true, actually."

"Wait. You want people to think you're...boring? Why would you do that?"

"Do you know what people do when they think you're interesting, Elizabeth?"

"Sure. They like you."

"No. They criticize you. They look for ways to break you down. They find the smallest flaw and pick at it until something dirty flakes off."

"So, you...keep people away, by telling them you love dish soap?"

"Basil Radish is the best, by the way. Followed closely by Peony. I mean, I never really bought into the language of flowers all that much but it seems useful when it comes to cleaning the china."

A burst and a clamor from the far side of the dais upon which the two Waysmiths stood abruptly demanded their attention. Then, as Madam Bel Carmen and Alice and Fiona Guthrie rushed up the rolling stairs, Somerset Sayer heard one of them shout.

"Dr. Sayer! Help!"

The folklorist eyed the panting trio with concern. All three of them were a mess; clothes askew, out of breath, and spattered in something that looked like flecks of dried black paint. Though Madam Bel Carmen seemed to only have suffered the same fate because she had hugged, or possibly carried, one of the other two. Before anyone could respond, however, Alice Guthrie unburdened their collective panic.

"It was him, Dr. Sayer! The Fae I was telling you about. We saw the Chirurgeon in the gallery, and he almost killed Fiona!"

Almost completely unruffled, the Waysmith turned and looked at the girl in question, who, perhaps even more surprisingly, was significantly less worse for wear than the others. Which, for the presumed target of such an attack, was unusual. In fact, she seemed rather happy and regarded the elder woman in turn with a charming smile.

"I see." Somerset Sayer replied. "Where is he now?"

Alice Guthrie gulped in another mouthful of air. "Gone!" She coughed. "Down into a hole of some kind. All fire and a horrible roaring sound. It just opened up right there in the middle of the floor. Or, I think it did. It was so hard to tell which way was up. Then it was gone and so was he!"

With a slow, deliberate nod, the Waysmith carefully worked out the implications of their account before answering shortly. "Then he's gone."

"Are you certain?" Madam Bel Carmen, who had only just heard the entirety of the story herself a minute ago, interrupted.

"Oh, quite certain. But I am afraid that it means we must be as well. If the Chirurgeon was bold enough to make a bid for possession here in Foras Feasa, then it means the worst for our plan. Clarisant is close at hand and she will not rest until we're overrun."

Then, in a benevolently knowing gesture, Somerset Sayer took Fiona's hands in her own. "Are you alright?"

"Yeah." She nodded. "I'll be fine."

"Any pain or lingering disorientation?"

"No. I don't think so?"

"Good." She stated and turned back. "Elizabeth? I'm taking you home. Let's go."

Chapter Fifteen

The way ahead had two roads. One diverging to the right into a thicket of weeds and swallow-wort vines, and another branching to the left across a crumbling cliff ledge pebbled with glittery white stones and an ominous red horizon.

Elizabeth Pennybaker stared at the Waysmith with open horror."How should I know which way to go?!"

"It's your house." Somerset Sayer rejoined, idly looking up at the sky and peering at the clouds. "How do we get there?"

"Uhh..." The younger woman looked seasick. "You're asking me like I've ever been here before. I don't even know where I am and you think I'm going to be able to tell you where we're going?"

The folklorist sighed again. "As a matter of fact, yes. That's exactly what I expect."

"You're mental."

"Elizabeth, I've already explained this to you. You are different from most people. When the average person gets lost, they rely on their memories to get them to something familiar. They intuit, navigate, figure out context clues, that sort of thing. Based on what they already know to be true. But that's not how this works for you and I. The paths we take are the ones we make."

"The paths we take are the ones we make. Right."

"Now," Somerset Sayer flicked a lock of blond hair out of her eyes. "Tell me how we get there."

"Okay, well." The younger woman trailed off, glancing nervously from side to side in an attempt to choose a direction that felt logical. Or, at least, plausible. "So, do I just, like, make something up?"

"Sure. You can try that."

"Yeah, alright. That doesn't seem so bad. Make something up. I can do that." Elizabeth Pennybaker nattered to herself before offering a smile to the waiting company (sans Hat Trick and Coat Check, who had remained behind on other matters) that she hoped would instill some measure of confidence.

"Um, so, let's go with that road over there, the white gravel one. That kinda looks like something that you'd find on the East Coast."

"Okay." The Waysmith crossed her arms and waited.

"Yeah." Elizabeth Pennybaker brightened, feeling as though she might finally be getting a sense of this Wayfinding business that Somerset Sayer had been describing, of shaping the Way By by giving it meaning, as one might in weaving a story. "So, we take that road there to, uh, a crossroads. And then we, um, turn left there and go down another road, but that road isn't actually a road, it's a river! And all rivers lead to the ocean, right? So, this river then takes us towards the coast before it turns into the storm run-off on the street which..." She waved her hands about as she tried to think of something more interesting than just waste water flowing down a sewer grate. "...has all kinds of old leaves in it that float on the top like little boats. And the little boats are swept up by the wind where they pile up against the gate in the back garden. I know this because we have this terrible problem with garden slugs all the time but there we go! We're standing in my backyard, on the steps, and the back door is open. Voilà!"

She smiled triumphantly, even raising her arms up to twiddle her fingers in an excited manner. The Waysmith, however, was unimpressed.

"Seriously?"

"What?" She tossed back. "What was wrong with that?"

"Take a left at the fork, follow the river, and then some crumpled paper boat-magic happens and we're all miraculously standing on your porch?"

"Look, you said to give you directions with a story. I gave you directions with a story. Okay, so it's not the most original story in the world but I thought the point was that it works?"

Somerset Sayer sighed. "You're still trying to work from memory, Elizabeth. You're trying to think of directions like a map, like something you've seen before and just need to describe accurately enough for others to follow. But you can't actually do that here. Memory isn't like that in the Way By. It's too erratic, sometimes nonexistent. It won't tell you anything. At least, nothing useful for navigating."

"Ugh." Elizabeth Pennybaker clenched her fists in growing frustration. "Well, as usual, I think I just understood about half of what you said. You want me to give you directions but not like a map, while standing somewhere in a place I've never been that for all I know isn't even on the right planet, so that we can get back to my place where you think my cat is going to help us figure out the problem. I don't know what you want me to do!"

The folklorist uncrossed her arms and stood thoughtfully, hands resting on her hips. "There's a pile of leaves that's constantly building up against your back gate? Where the slugs are, yes?"

"Uh, yeah." The other woman shrugged. "So what? I was just trying to think of something random and noticeable about the house."

"Why does it do that?" Somerset Sayer asked.

Elizabeth Pennybaker regarded the elder scholar as though she'd been rendered insensate. "The wind, I guess?"

The Waysmith nodded. "Alright. Let's try this." She moved to stand a few feet from the younger woman, shifting both her posture and her cadence in an unnerving way.

"A garden is a human thing, written lovingly by hand.
How can we know?
Each flower, every vine, is chosen, planned.
To grow there. As a tended repertory,
Shields against grief.
A garden is a story.
That takes weeks and months and years to tell.
Not made by Nature's bent,
Our own timely verdant carousel.
It stands apart from wild, uncaring things.
It is read, by those who know its tongue.
The walls on whom it clings.
About what it means and where and why.
Without all that is better cut and burned,
This is how we make the world lie.
And it remembers us, in the trees, bulbs, and plot.
That return.
When we do not."

Spoken as poetic verse, in a timbre that seemed so uncharacteristically sentimental for the otherwise reserved and unapproachable Waysmith, Elizabeth Pennybaker and all of the Huntresses of the King found the words to be unexpectedly lovely and continued to listen intently as she continued.

"But the wind comes round the moon,
And trails behind it hail and tide,
Leaving thoughts as tatters strewn.
We once stood watch but never now.
Cut our words into the ground,
So that only a draught will shake this bough.
It never shows itself, although,
Hangs the leaves on crumbling pins,
To mark a path that changes flow,
But shall arrive at the appointed time.
And force all into refuge beneath the rot.
Lest it steal their breath out from behind.
So, with vermin we must share,
In that we follow now the wind,
to the places in its care."

Fiona Guthrie and her mother shivered against the cool gusts suddenly pouring in off of the waterfront. Madam Bel Carmen pulled her jacket closer as she pinched the crackled bits of an autumn leaf from her hair.

"That was pretty good." The teenager spoke up first. "Is it something you wrote?"

Somerset Sayer cocked an eyebrow but did not look away from Elizabeth Pennybaker, who now paled and stared aghast, past the Waysmith and over her shoulder, as a swell of chill wind whipped up the leaves at her feet, pulled them from the twigs and branches in the wood on their right, and dragged the entire mess, bouncing and rustling, through the grass.

"Where are we, Elizabeth?" The folklorist raised her voice against the murmuring.

The younger Waysmith looked around and could hardly hold back the gasp in her throat. "This..." She started. "This can't be right...."

"I said, where are we?"

"It's the creek behind my house. I mean, not where I live. This is where I grew up. There's the hill where my cousins and I used to play and...and the garden my mom put around the big oak tree. That statue, it's Ganesh. The, uh, the one with the elephant head, you know?"

"The Remover of Obstacles. Good choice."

In a daze, Elizabeth Pennybaker could hardly believe her own eyes and with tentative steps, approached the long-forgotten shrine, overgrown as it was with creepers and moss.

"He was always her favorite from the stories my grandparents told about India when she was little. She hid it down here because she was afraid that the neighbors wouldn't like it when she came to pray or give lamps, that they might think it was demonic or something. I...I used to come down here with her to put flowers on him during the holidays. And for her birthday we would..." She stopped and looked behind her, at something else that was no longer there. "But...nobody comes here anymore. Nobody has been here in.... years."

Elizabeth Pennybaker rounded on the Waysmith. "Why are *we* here? We were supposed to go back to the Old Squat. We were supposed to go home!"

"We did." Somerset Sayer replied, with a placid demeanor in the face of the other woman's fury. "*You* followed the wind, Elizabeth."

"What? I didn't follow anything. You were the one with the weird poem and all that."

"And you were the one who knew where it was going."

The younger woman looked around again. Notably, she kept glancing at a large stone opposite the heavy icon with a worried brow. "I really don't want to be here. Can we leave?"

"Of course. Tell me how we get there."

She scrubbed at her forearms for a moment, purposely avoiding the concerned and awestruck gazes of Alice and Fiona Guthrie and Madam Bel Carmen. Who, for their part, seemed to wisely surmise that they should remain quiet as Waysmith and Waysmith worked out their discord.

"I don't know how...."

Somerset Sayer reached out to steady the other woman. "You're not strategizing on the plays, Elizabeth. You're making the rules of the game. But in this way, you have to be prepared to abide by those rules once you've decided what they are. What applies to you here, applies to everyone else as well, human or otherwise. And if you are not careful, the Fae will take your rules and use them, manipulate them, even bring them back against you if they can. You do not own this world. You're only passing through it for a time. That is why, when we, the Waysmiths, speak our thoughts into being we must be mindful of the ways in which we do it, of the world we are setting into motion, because it will affect the outcome.... the.... destination of our path. When you were born, Elizabeth, the world gave you a pen. So, tell me what's inside of it? Words? Lines? A sketch? Musical notes? Schematics and blueprints? Equations? A map? Or would you just prefer to punch holes in the paper with it until you've cut out some paper dolls?"

"But I'm not a poet or an artist or anything like that. I can't do what you just did."

"Yes, you can. Perhaps not in the same way as I've done but that doesn't matter. You *can* do it. You already have once before. The Way By can hear you, Elizabeth. It is listening. Tell it what you need and it will answer."

"I, um, okay." She attempted to rally and re-center herself. "I guess I can..." Somerset Sayer stepped back.

"No, wait." Elizabeth Pennybaker looked at the garden stones with a mournful face. "This is bothering me. I feel like there is something I'm supposed to say but I really don't want to."

"Why is that?" Somerset Sayer continued to encourage her path.

"It's what's obviously missing here. Your poem made me think of it. Like, I got your meaning even if you didn't know what it was or what it means to me."

The elder Waysmith broke into a grin. "What does it mean, Elizabeth?"

"There used to be two statues here, two *murti.*" Elizabeth Pennybaker felt her voice choke up. "Ganesh, he's right here. But also, Kali."

"Destroyer of Evil, the Black Mother, and The One Who Overcomes Death." Somerset Sayer provided for the benefit of the others before returning to the exchange. "She is missing?"

The younger women seemed far away. "She used to be on that rock over there. It was this really pretty statue but one I was always warned to stay away from. Painted all glossy black with red hands and this huge, wide, mouth. She was also posed in a weird way; I mean, not like Kali *murti* typically look. Her left foot stuck out really far and she had this huge sword in her right hand raised straight up in the air. Which was supposed to mean something specific, I guess. I never really understood why my mom kept it because I don't remember her doing much with it most of the time."

"What happened to it?" Madam Bel Carmen asked, inspecting the empty space in question.

"I don't know." Elizabeth Pennybaker replied. "The last time I saw it, it wasn't a...happy moment. My mom had a friend, Drishti I think was her name. More like a sister to her than a friend. She was in a bad situation. I have memories of seeing her when I was little; coming to visit my mom with bruises all over her face and raw fingernails cut off past the quick. I didn't get it at the time but it was pretty clear that someone in her family was doing it. Her husband, or her mother-in-law, or maybe both. Anyway, she and mom would come out here together to the garden to talk and I would see them talking to Kali too. Giving her food and paper prayers mixed in water. I think my mom was telling Kali to protect her or, I don't know, maybe she was trying to convince Drishti to leave. Saying that no one would dare to hit her ever again if the Goddess was looking over her. When we got the news that she'd...taken her own life, mom came out here and smeared the whole statue in ash. From where she got it all I never found out. Just covered her in this thick grey paste from head to toe. After that, Kali was always covered with drapes. I didn't see her again. Just the odd shape where she was standing."

"She must have been heartbroken. Honey, I'm so sorry." Alice Guthrie said, wringing her hands as Madam Bel Carmen continued to pick through the overgrown garden on the off-chance that the icon had simply fallen.

"I used to think that she..." The younger Waysmith trailed off before snapping back to attention. "Dr. Sayer I...I can't go there. I can't talk about this. Not right now. Please."

Somerset Sayer nodded in agreement. "Never a bad choice, Elizabeth. Don't force yourself to undertake a Way you are not well prepared for. You can always revisit it later. Let's try something a bit more optimistic instead then, shall we?"

Elizabeth Pennybaker sighed; she hadn't expected this to be so arduous. Or for the world around her to hang onto each word with weights strung like crepe.

"We'll try a more popular tactic." The elder Waysmith concluded. "Why don't you tell me about your dreams."

"What are you, my therapist now?"

"Ha ha. No." Somerset Sayer laughed a bit sarcastically. "But dreams are often the most immediately accessible avenue for people to understand their interactions with the Way By. Especially dreams that happen more than once. Do you have anything that comes to mind or that has really stood out to you in your life?"

She thought for a while.

"Maybe. When I was a little girl, I did have a recurring dream. I would be walking along a river bank and see this box out in the water. And, for some reason, I always knew that there were kittens in the box and that if no one did anything, they were all going to drown. Because someone had thrown them into the river, obviously. I could even hear them mewing from inside it and it would just break my heart. All I wanted to do was to swim out and grab it and rescue all the kittens. But the water was so fast and the currents were always too strong and I couldn't make it no matter how hard I tried. It was so scary and so bad that I would wake up crying and I would run to my mom's room trying to tell her that we had to go save the kittens and why weren't we saving the kittens? Later on, my mom used to say that cats in dreams symbolized intuition and secret knowledge and that if you saw one, it meant that your subconscious mind was trying to send a message to your conscious mind. All I had to do was figure out what the message was about and then I would know what it all meant."

Elizabeth Pennybaker looked off into the distance, watching as the wind shifted and began to pull the leaves and blades of grass down the creek and into an odd-looking hollow surrounded by an iron-wrought fence.

"And then, one day when I was about sixteen, I heard this sad little noise coming from a gutter in the alleyway next to our house. It was one of those really cool old coastal alleys made from crushed white seashells and I used to pick through it when I was a kid to see if I could find whole shells to collect. I really liked how they glittered when you turned them over. Anyway, it turns out the noise was this tiny, emaciated kitten that, I'm guessing, must have wandered away from his mom and gotten lost. He was, like, this little orange dirt-ball, not much bigger than my hand, with a huge head and most of his teeth missing. But I didn't care, you know? While I was taking care of him, I actually kept remembering my dream and for a really long time I believed that's what it was supposed to be about. That I was supposed to be there, on the shell alley, so that I could save him. That he had purposely gone there to find me as well... and that when he grew up big and strong, he was going to give me the message... from my dream..." As the thoughts coalesced in her mind, Elizabeth Pennybaker began to stutter, tripping over her words as the connections between her childhood dream, the river of white shells, the discovery of the dying kitten, and the oracle of the marmalade cat began to come together. She whirled around. "Dr. Sayer, you don't think that..."

"Mew."

The entire company stopped short and turned to look down the creek bed wherein the sound had first emanated. There, sitting patiently on a rock jutting above the shallow pond water was Noseworthy, whose elongated face and misshapen paws were unmistakable even from this distance.

"Nosey!" Elizabeth Pennybaker exclaimed. "How did you get here? Oh my god, come here, you stupid cat."

Somerset Sayer chuckled as the younger Waysmith went promptly splashing into the muddy green scum to retrieve the otherwise completely passive feline. As she lifted him up and snuggled into his scruff, as one does with large unmoving cats; Noseworthy craned his neck and turned to view the assembled before fixing his lazy golden gaze on the folklorist, who gave a curt nod in response. Elizabeth Pennybaker came slogging back up the bank and onto the grass where she continued to loudly chastise her cat as she did so. "What on earth are you doing all the way out here, dummy?!"

"Hunting for birds, I suspect." Somerset Sayer answered for him.

Knowing this particular cat quite well, Madam Bel Carmen also couldn't resist reaching out to give Noseworthy a few reassuring scratches between the ears. "Well, good thing we came this way, I should say. He certainly has gotten himself lost again then."

"Oh, not at all." The Waysmith laughed, immediately drawing a number of concerned looks. "I imagine he came much the same way we did. I was wondering how long it would take him to show up. May I?" She held out her hands in a gesture that indicated that she would take Noseworthy. Reluctantly, Elizabeth Pennybaker handed him over and watched as the folklorist propped the bony orange cat up on her forearm so his front paws could rest on her shoulder and that he might see everything around them.

"Now, if the lot of you don't mind, I think we should be getting on with things. I will help you all learn as much as I can as we go, but time is sadly, not exactly on our side here. Elizabeth, I need you to do something for me. On the night that the Para-Sprites attacked you, you described seeing a place. Sorry, let me correct myself, you passed into the Way By through a threshold in your kitchen. Yes?"

"I guess. Yeah."

"Fine. Do you think you would recognize the place again if you saw it?"

"I think so. I mean, it was like some kind of museum or museum storage room or something like that. I don't really remember it all that well."

"Not a problem. Recall what I have been telling you about memory here. That whether or not you remember something, or even how accurately, isn't really the point. I don't need you to remember it like that. I need you to tell me about how you got there."

"Right, as in, 'tell me where we are' but not like a map."

"Exactly."

"I was reading your book." She started. "There was this section on fireflies that I really liked."

Somerset Sayer nodded. "The Analogy of Fireflies, yes. Go on."

"Okay. You were talking about how a little girl captures a firefly in a box, like some great magical prize. But when she goes back to look at it later, it's gone. Just the remains of it are left behind. I remember thinking how depressing that sounded. That the remains you were referring to was the actual dried husk of a dead firefly and how that was like this metaphor for lost hopes and dreams. How we cling to bodies, sort of like clinging to the dead, only because we don't know where the light has gone and we can't find it."

"And then?"

"And then two dead birds flew through my window."

"Meow."

"Yes, thank you, Noseworthy." The folklorist picked at her nails absently. "And then you fought with them?"

"Sort of. Nosey here was the one who really went at it right then and there. I remember grabbing the book and trying to fight them off but it wasn't working. I thought the little bastards were going to poke my eyes out with the way they kept coming at my face."

"Most likely they intended precisely that. Continue."

"Well, I ran into the kitchen looking for a pan but I don't think I saw one right away so I was just kind of flailing around looking for a weapon or anything really."

"Alright. Elizabeth, I need you to listen to me very, very, carefully and to concentrate as much as you can on what I'm going to ask you. Answer with whatever comes to mind, okay?"

"Okay."

"Mew."

"Yes, thank you, Noseworthy."

"You keep doing that. Like he's saying something?"

"Never mind that right now. You're in the kitchen, understand?"

Elizabeth Pennybaker sighed, glanced sideways at her aunt who nodded in encouragement, and replied. "Yeah, got it. I'm in the kitchen."

"Now what?"

The younger Waysmith paused as she tried to make her thoughts work for her rather than against her, scrunching up her face as she tended to do when trying to think on things of a complicated or difficult nature. "Blood."

"Blood?"

"I had blood on my hands, from the fight. It got it on the door jamb and then I saw it again later, like in a handprint."

"Hmm, interesting. And where did the blood take you, Elizabeth?" With that question, Somerset Sayer gently placed Noseworthy down on the ground at her feet. "Speak it again like you did before. Tell me about the dream."

"Okay. It's like a graveyard. A place of death with a boring name. I'm walking through rows and rows of specimens. Birds in a glass case. Snakes in jars. Bones mounted on the wall. But everything seems so familiar. I'm starting to think that these are my memories and what I've done to them is like the girl with the fireflies. The light is all gone but I keep coming back here hoping I'm going to find it again."

Without realizing it, Elizabeth took several steps forward, followed by Noseworthy who rubbed up against her ankles reassuringly.

"But it was there once, wasn't it? Where did the light go, Elizabeth? Can you follow it?"

"I...I'm not sure." She laughed suddenly. "But there's a map! Or, it's a globe. I saw it sitting on a shelf. A globe covered in oceans; no land. There's light hidden behind it but the closer I get to it the more restless the dead things are becoming."

Her eyes turned frantic as the memories broke through her defenses and the sensations of that night came flooding back. Brittle nails scraped against ancient displays and a chattering arose out of the darkness. "They're tapping against the glass. They're trying to get out. Oh god, I can hear them!"

Madam Bel Carmen rushed forward, grabbing hold of her niece with a crushing embrace. "Lizzie-bet, calm down! I'm right here!" But Somerset Sayer did not relent.

"Stay with me, Elizabeth, we're almost there. Listen to me!"

A wild gaze met hers, pleading and uncertain.

"The wind comes round the moon and trails behind it hail and tide," The folklorist repeated earnestly and with great emphasis on each beat in the poetic cadence. "We once stood watch but never now. We cut our words into the ground. So with vermin we must share.... Elizabeth.... follow it!"

With that, Noseworthy bit deep into his mistress's thumb, drawing several drops of blood and an angry shriek.

"Ow! What the...!"

She moved to pull away. but the Waysmith was faster and grasped the younger woman's hand in her own, smearing red between their palms as they were plunged into lightlessness. Elizabeth Pennybaker yelled something incoherent and struggled, forcing Madam Bel Carmen to release her and grab onto Alice Guthrie so as not to fall backwards and out of sight.

The world around them vanished.

The creek fell away into nothingness.

Dander and dust fell over them as snow.

Alice Guthrie was the first to regain her footing, her eyes instinctively darting around to find her daughter and then the others. Everything around them had changed so suddenly, it hadn't been possible to right herself immediately. It was as though they had been teleported whole, abruptly and violently, onto some far away platform. As she helped both Fiona and Madam Bel Carmen back to their feet, she spied the Waysmith far afield from the rest of them, appearing to be kneeling, long train-coat spread out around her, in the center of a flagstone hallway.

All was completely still and quiet.

"Dr. Sayer?" She called out hesitantly.

"Shhh." Came the admonishing reply. "Do not speak carelessly here."

Elizabeth Pennybaker slid across the floor to her aunt and carefully stood up.

"Where are we?" She whispered hoarsely.

"Somewhere you've been before." Came the folklorist's quieter response.

The dank, molding, hall outside of Dry Storeroom 1 hadn't changed in the time they had been away. Motes and specks floated amiably through the filtered moonlight, dancing overhead through a skylight of disintegrating lead glass atop walls of mud-shale blocks.

But this time, the old ship's door sat open and a very pleased-with-himself looking marmalade cat sauntered past the company and approached the Waysmith, who remained resting on her knees before the threshold.

Glancing above them, Alice Guthrie noted, with some interest, the sculptured frieze above the archway: a beautiful mess of carved ivy, a lion, and four tall women surrounding a fifth who carried a crown in each hand.

"This...this is it." Elizabeth Pennybaker breathed, her mouth drying as she looked about. "This is where I came. This is the hallway off of the kitchen."

The Waysmith subdued a laugh. "Kitchen Hallway doesn't seem like quite an apt name for it, but it'll do." Slowly, and with great care, Somerset Sayer rose to her feet, not bothering to disturb the dust from her legs or coat. She turned to the assembled and raised a still bloodied hand to beg their silence.

"This is a very dangerous place, so I need you all to be very much on your guard. Don't make any unusually loud noises and don't touch anything unless I tell you to. Understood?"

"Mew."

"I quite agree, Noseworthy."

Elizabeth Pennybaker shook her head in dumbfounded wonder. This was almost starting to feel normal and that was the most abnormal thing about it all yet.

"Elizabeth," Somerset Sayer called out softly. "Where do we go from here?"

The younger Waysmith gestured towards the door and the beeswax resin lettering indicating the open portal to Dry Storeroom 1. The folklorist turned and regarded the doorway with a measure of apprehension.

"It's okay." She replied to her elder's question. "It's just a bunch of junk, mostly. Disturbing though, if you're not used to collections. Formaldehyde preservations, skeleton mock-ups, that kind of thing. But it all looks really old and I'm pretty sure half of it's broken."

"That's not what it is, Elizabeth. You should understand that by now. But thank you for the warning."

The younger Waysmith fell silent, briefly meeting the eyes of Fiona Guthrie, who smiled and shrugged; as if to impart her own familiarity with such chastising words.

Inside the room, everything was grey: colorless, cinereal, and ashen. Grey banners hung on grey walls over dusty grey shelves. Grey fossils in similar rock adorned equally grey boxes whose previously yellowed labels had darkened into an unreadable black stain. Fiona Guthrie did not believe she had ever seen a grey butterfly before, and yet here there were a thousand of them or more; lined up on silvery pins in a grey display case.

Even the birds had lost their carefully conserved luster and looked more like the ghosts of snakes and other creatures suspended, glimmering white, upside-down in their corroded jars. Dried flowers, which never kept their true colors to life anyway, were scattered into the dust; losing everything which rendered them most recognizable. With slow, cautious steps the company dispersed through the storeroom, looking for anything that might be important even if they hadn't the slightest sense of what that might be. Perhaps it simply wouldn't be grey.

Halfway across the room, standing beneath the partially missing remains of a mounted ichthyosaur, Somerset Sayer stared down at the floor. Near her toe, a tattered cloth lay rumpled around a ruined seal and barefoot prints in the dirt.

"What was here?"

"Uh, I'm not really sure." Elizabeth Pennybaker joined her near the archives. "There was this voice I was trying to catch and it led me over to this shelf. There was something here but...I'm sorry, I don't remember what it was."

"That's alright. It can't be far."

"Dr. Sayer? Are...are we in my subconscious or something? Is this my mind?"

"No, Elizabeth. We're not inside your mind. We're in the Way By. Which has taken on a particular character in response to you. In response to what it is holding for you."

"But," looking around in ire, Elizabeth Pennybaker continued. "Where is this place?"

"This is most likely a kind of warren. Somewhere in the outermost encroachment of the Stumble. The place on the edge of sunset where night is forever falling. The line of the raindrop, Elizabeth, where light cannot be."

"Oh."

A gasp alerted the attendant company to Alice Guthrie's distress.

"What is it?" The folklorist whisper-called from over her shoulder.

Pale and trembling, Alice Guthrie raised her hand and pointed to the stuffed and mounted heads and hominids adorning the wall; the gaze of each which in turn followed. The Waysmith tensed imperceptibly. When they had entered the room, she was certain that the wall had contained nothing but the rather droll line-up of Australopithecines native to every museum exhibit storeroom she had ever encountered.

Hunched and battered by more than just geological time, they had hung on bent hooks and twine until such a time as the curators might see fit to reintroduce them to a curious world. But now, their pedestals were empty of bones and clay. Replaced instead by the silhouettes of ethereal spirits who glowered down at them from a modest height. Six, she counted. Six emanations of the Dead and the one that led them; a striking woman with wild hair and a shattered breast.

Blood still appeared to seep endlessly into the remnants of her white burial gown and drip to a vanishing point before it struck the floor, leaving nothing in her wake. For all but Somerset Sayer, this was the very first time they had ever beheld the ghost of Mary Elizabeth Toft. For the Waysmith, however:

"Shit."

Somerset Sayer grabbed ahold of Elizabeth Pennybaker and rather unceremoniously threw her clear into the back shelving, upsetting more than one restless preservation and briefly stunning the younger woman. Once the other was behind her, the folklorist was quick to advance, placing herself between the specters and the rest of the Flidais Venatica, who, for their part, were drawing together and forming a vanguard in place of their previous division. Even Noseworthy himself leapt up onto the nearest display and hissed loudly, swatting at an errant twist of ghostly threads.

"Hold your ground." The folklorist instructed. "The Dead are only memory and it is only memory that they retain. They can't move as we can."

"Somerset Persephone Sayer." The wispy voice emanated from a harrowing place deep in the empty breast, far behind the pinpoint glowing eyes. "Waysmith of the Peerage. Envoy of the Summer King. Justicar of Avenant *Ard Rí de Là-arn-a-Mhàireach*."

"I'll not hear you speak his name again." She seethed in return. "And I'll not see you oppose us. The Hunt has been called on this night, fair and right in the appointed manner, and you face the Flidais Venatica so ordered and ordained. The Name of the King restrains you. The blood of the Bramble Crown humbles you."

The spirits remained unperturbed, drifting lightly in the unfelt breeze. "Ah...yes..." Came the reply, "The Crown That Only He May Wear."

Shivered words from the other spirits followed, "Bramble thicket there.... Once a year.... lash him.... lash him...drain the royal blood...."

Alice Guthrie clenched her fist and exchanged a knowing look with Madam Bel Carmen; a clever witch who, unbeknownst to many, had come better prepared than they could have presumed. Her hand went to her pocket and Alice Guthrie went to shield her daughter as Fiona, from the inside of her coat, produced a weapon of her own; the wooden sword no bigger than a dagger in her hand.

The spirit's voices filled the room, their presence magnifying greater and greater in unjust fury. But Mary Elizabeth Toft silenced them with a growl and met the unwavering gaze of Somerset Sayer.

"But I too serve a Crown of light and thorns which shall sup upon the blood of the worthy, the unworthy, and the vile. The Muse beckons you, Waysmith. Join me here now in this place that I have prepared for you. Your time is now at hand."

Chapter Sixteen

Madam Bel Carmen was no stranger to the Dead. A uniquely clever medium whose extensive training in West African Vodun was beyond reproach, and who had buried a husband and an unnamed child within months of each other, knew the subtleties of relating to lost spirits as few others might. But despite her many ritual experiences and the stories passed on to her by grandmothers and great-grandmothers, she had never actually seen the ghosts or experienced their mischief firsthand, as so many members of her family had often claimed to. Rather, her divinations and practices had been largely academic, intent as she had been on better theorizing the relationships between humankind and the nature of the divine.

For a long while, especially after the desperate and all-consuming loneliness following Eirnin Pennybaker's untimely death, she thought that she might not actually even believe in ghosts at all. The metaphor and the desire, of course, but hardly the actual reality. If ghosts were real, she surmised in her heartache, someone would have come back to her by now. Someone, surely, would have come to haunt the empty spaces in her body where pieces of her soul had been torn out. Now, in less than a week, that had all changed and here she was, face to face, with a literal handful of them. Very real and entirely malevolent.

From her pocket, she produced an object that took both Waysmiths somewhat aback. The rattling fetish, constructed from what might have been a monkey's head, dried dangling chicken feet, and a small bottle of powdered chameleon tied with red knots, clacked with each movement she made. She raised it high so that the colorful beads adorning it in a kind of jouncing skirt could bicker with the bones that made up its arms, legs, and tail. Her body then began to sway in an intentionally serpentine fashion; as a snake-handler might adopt with a particularly cantankerous cobra. Her face set, Madam Bel Carmen stamped her foot loudly against the stone floor.

Mary Elizabeth Toft however, whose blood still seeped into intangible cloth and dripped down along her ethereal tethers and into oblivion, was not to be startled by this; though the others shimmered in apprehension at the snap of the twine and bone talisman. The leading ghost hissed her irritation and observed as Madam Bel Carmen then produced a second object from her pockets and pouches: a twisted knife with a smooth arched blade.

"Fall down, spirits. Fall down!" She bellowed.

"Devoted." The spirits snarled back. "Voodooist." spat another.

"You are not welcome here!" Madam Bel Carmen replied in a loud, authoritative voice. "This is no time for you. I name your boundaries. You may not cross your keepers! Zhango calls for you. Ogu denies you. Lêgba judges you. Go! Now! It is not for you to walk about. Heed my words or I'll bury you twice!"

"A priestess comes to try her hand with the chattering dead, is that it?" Mary Elizabeth Toft chided softly, still wavering in a non-existent breeze. "Come to play possession with the eternally dispossessing?"

Taking a quick swig of water from a flask palmed in her hand, Madam Bel Carmen took the moment to spit an arc of it across the floor at her feet; between the enemy ghost and the rest of the company. "To your graves and stay there!"

"The Stumble *is* my grave, *mambo*. Now, it will be yours."

"Evelyn!" Alice Guthrie screamed.

But Madam Bel Carmen had seen far too much to fear them as deeply as haunts would have it and brought her knife down in a wide sweep. The fetish clacked in time with her stamping feet and the water splattered across the dusty stones bubbled and began to burn up into a wall of steam and fog. The other spirits shrunk back, looking to the enraged Withersmith for guidance.

"Impedimenta!" Mary Elizabeth Toft reared backwards but not far from the obscuring cloud, which seemed to pull and eat away at the wafting threads near her feet. She had no love for the *loa* but nor did she disrespect them. Especially not the name of Ogu, whose dominion over fire and iron struck at the very heart of her railway demise.

With the Dead distracted, Somerset Sayer wasted no time and as soon as the mist rose up to confine the dark manifestations of the Stumble, even if only temporarily, she grabbed ahold of both Alice and Fiona Guthrie where they stood in petrified terror.

"Listen to me. I'll help Madam Bel Carmen. You two get back to Elizabeth and help her find the alicorn. She needs to see where it went and tell us how to get there!"

"The what?!" Alice Guthrie stuttered.

"The alicorn. Tell her that she needs to find the alicorn! The thing that was hidden here. Go! You have to hurry!"

Happy at least to have a task before her, Alice Guthrie staggered awkwardly into a frightfully moldering bird exhibit and shrieked before Fiona was finally able to right her mother, make her way past the elder Waysmith, and into the open room near the shelves where Elizabeth Pennybaker was just regaining her wits. Having ascertained that the others were regrouping, Somerset Sayer then turned and brought herself up well behind Madam Bel Carmen, who continued to admonish the spirits of the house loudly.

"Corrupter of Birds! Red dirt reveals black magic! Water falls and binds you to Earth!" She snapped, the thickening of the fog continuing unabated. The Withersmith struck out at her, clawing at Madam Bel Carmen's face with talons formed out of shadows and hateful slurs. But she arched then and rounded out her movement with a disconcerting rattle to the fetish and a swoop of her knife, and Mary Elizabeth Toft could do little more than leave a few raised lines on her skin as the Benin priestess dodged around her. Again, the vodun turned and twisted her body along the steps of a macabre dance, weaving through the fog just out of sight and then stamping her feet loudly to call out her position to the spirits once more. And when they followed, she would do it all over again.

Somerset Sayer raced to the edge of the ad-hoc ritual circle, grasped the edge of a brass pan on a low Gothic table and flung it to the floor. As soon as Elizabeth Pennybaker could discern their destination, they would need to travel quickly and there were no better ways out of an inescapable room than water. This was largely due to the fact that water, when unable to trace the shortest path outwards from a single point, had a habit of making its own way given time. Even through impenetrable rock.

The Waysmith then snatched a jar from the dusty line-up, one filled with seashells and river stones, as opposed to those filled with serpents and the faunal unborn in a ghost-white glaze. It was part of what she would need; Madam Bel Carmen would no doubt supply the rest. Alice and Fiona Guthrie, on the other hand, wrenched Elizabeth Pennybaker to her feet on the far side of it all and set about to regain her sense of the setting so that she might divine what was to follow.

But as far as diviners went, the younger Waysmith was entirely inexperienced and hadn't the slightest idea where to start. Fiona Guthrie was then the one to point out that Noseworthy had stolen a stuffed bird, more precisely a faded dove, from the glass displays and had dropped it at their feet. Madam Bel Carmen stepped up. The clacking of the monkey-bone fetish had been but a warning, a call to attention more like an orchestral instrument plucked in a minor key. Now, the ensemble began in earnest, with a flurry of activity from all corners of the room.

Madam Bel Carmen had used her toes to draw the cornmeal lines into the water on the floor, admonishing the spirits to tire and to take their sickness back to the mysteries that had made them. Thrumming the dancing fetish against her forearms, she brought the knife to the side of each of her knees, nicking the skin and drawing enough blood to paint her feet in red and spatter the stones below. This allowed the ghosts to follow her in and out the mist, simply by walking in her steps.

The spirits pulled forward and skittered away; one attempting to taste the meager droplets while the others circled menacingly. The call and answer itself was a dance, coy and dangerous but increasingly filled with a kind of pomp and propriety. There were things now to be communicated between vodun and ancestors, and the spirits were taking up their roles accordingly. Madness, however, had gripped the Waysmith, who now flew into a reckless frenzy of gestures over the brass well; setting shells and sand into fantastic designs beneath a few inches of briny water and then wiping the geometric patterns away with a flourish. She seemed to pay little mind to the Dead just an arm's length away.

This was no ordinary Danse Macabre. No dancing plague-man in a shabby suit who inexplicably shows up on floor after floor in a haunted elevator. Nor were these the skeletal kings and knights parading across the frescos of the Holy Innocents, enticing the living to their graves through the painted whorls of a beautiful nightmare. There were five who took their places and a sixth who led them. All but one was nondescript.

Little more than outlines in the fog or impressions in the dust motes, they had no pageantry to define them. Wiped clean of their grave clothes and ornaments, they were faceless and nameless. The empty girl, the Withersmith, who seemed in possession of a sucking void at her center however, was suffocating everyone around her. For her, death had not been a theft of wealth and privilege but relief from a life of stolen labor. She had welcomed the darkness the Unicorn had promised. Now, her form fluttered up and up despite it all; a heaving mass swallowing everything whole, consuming every desperate gasp of breath until one might never know the freedom of their own body ever again. From this, she proclaimed that there would be no escape.

But that which was truly divine was born of filth. Always out of place and unclean; befouling better food with sodden cracker crumbs that soaked up all that was left when the best meat was already taken. And it was with Madam Bel Carmen that day. It seeped into her thoughts and out of her words to permeate as the mist did. Somerset Sayer would later remark that it appeared as if she, rather than they, had become Death Incarnate and who had enticed the ghosts back to their rest with carefully timed rhythms and dance steps like chess moves in a game played against the Grim Reaper. And the fog, the arc of water along the ground, began to wash them clean from the world.

They moved thusly, the living and the dead, between animation and stillness, to become one body and from them Madam Bel Carmen drew lots in an economy of salvation; bidding them back to their tombs at the very least, and then betting them on to Hell when that was necessary.

But Mary Elizabeth Toft would have none of these solemn workings and screamed in fury at the machinations of the vodun. Madam Bel Carmen stretched her knife-wielding hand out towards the enraged spirit now closing in on her.

"You depart without faith!" She accused loudly. "The lament for you shall be the lament for animals."

"I have remembered those whom you have not!" The spirit countered. "My rest was not given but taken. My name was not spoken on the third day nor the thirtieth. My fellowship denied where no place is kept for me."

"No good is done to feed the dead." The fetish snapped and rattled. Madam Bel Carmen stamped her feet and swayed to draw the spirit closer. "When you were born, milk filled your mouth. When you died, your tongue turned to dust. Close your lips! There is no more for you to eat."

"Birth creates not a body but a spirit. Another spirit who hungers and who will never be filled." Mary Toft advanced again.

"Those who sleep do not hunger but dream. They have taken in all they could in their time and now make the world in their reverie." The priestess replied.

"I make the world." The Withersmith wheezed lowly. Madam Bel Carmen again stepped back. Again, the spirit followed. "I *am* that reverie. You think you can send me on?! You're in *my* house, witch!"

"Evelyn! Duck!"

With a desperate heave, Somerset Sayer upended the brass plate, indelicately flinging a wall of water, sand, and detritus into the air in a wide, glittering, wave that flew clear over Madam Bel Carmen's bowed head and landed square onto the Withersmith's fractured shoulders.

"Mary Elizabeth Toft." The Waysmith pronounced. "I now baptize you in the name of the Father and of the Mother, and enter your Name in the siblinghood of all people. Your soul is no longer in exile, your memory restored. Go in peace."

The resultant wail shook the very foundations of the Stumble, throwing the room into chaos as jars fell from their shelves and shattered, dust and mortar tumbled from the flagstones, and moth-eaten animals cracked under their unstable supports. Somerset Sayer barely had time to careen onto her side as she grabbed a hold of Madame Bel Carmen before she too fell to the ground. Scrambling backwards, the two women rolled several times before finally regaining their footing against a bolted-down chest.

"What did you do?" Madam Bel Carmen yelled over the unholy cacophony.

"Vicarious baptism after the fact." The Waysmith hollered back gleefully.

"What?!"

"An impromptu Naming Ceremony from the Baptism for the Dead!"

"What on earth made you think of that?"

"Oh, you know. Restless dead, exorcisms, repelling with holy water; that's how it goes right?"

"And that's going to destroy her?!"

Somerset Sayer snorted. "Oh, hell no. But it's going to screw her night up something fierce! And! Hopefully it will buy us enough time to get out of here! Come on! We need to re-open the Way!"

Madam Bel Carmen fell back beside the Waysmith, out of breath from her efforts. "What can we do?"

"You're the *mambo* here, Ms. Evelyn." The absolutely exuberant folklorist retorted. "What are the four substances that open all gates again?"

A glimmer of understanding crept into Madam Bel Carmen's eye as she glanced about at the jars filled with creatures. "Alcohol." She smiled. "And blood, spit, and milk. Dr. Sayer, hand me that python in glass."

Fiona Guthrie tugged at Elizabeth Pennybaker's sleeves in frustration. Nothing neither she nor her mother had tried so far seemed to be helping her memory, or getting them any closer to where they needed to be, and it was clear from the wanton destruction beginning to take place on the opposite side of the room that they didn't have much time left to figure it out. Noseworthy meowed plaintively, rolling a mummified dove forward again and dropping it onto his mistress's shoe.

"Seriously, Nosey. I've just about had it with the birds." The younger Waysmith huffed, narrowly avoiding a bit of debris sailing past her head from the battle being waged beyond.

"But you said you saw it here?" Alice Guthrie interrupted.

"Ugh, I've already told you all. I don't really remember *what* I saw. There were these shelves here and the jars and then...something. But it's not here anymore and I don't have any idea where it went! I don't even know what it was!"

"It's an alicorn." Fiona Guthrie explained, and not for the first time. "It's a horn, you know? Like on a unicorn."

"Great. That doesn't help me at all."

"Well," Alice Guthrie began. "What if we think of this like a study problem? You're a student, right? How do you recall things when you need to?"

"But that's with things I already know. Or have read, at least. Alice, I don't think I ever knew what it is I'm supposed to know. I can't remember something I never knew in the first place!"

"Okay, what do you know about unicorns?"

"Nothing. I don't know anything about unicorns because unicorns don't exist!"

The ceiling overhead trembled ominously and the trio of women reflexively took cover as a shower of stone chips and splinters rained down around them.

"Well obviously they do!" Fiona Guthrie shot back from beneath a nearby overhang. "And one of them is going to kill us!"

"Hard to believe, but my professors never mentioned anything about being hunted by a crazy unicorn!"

"Yeah, well, no one ever said that the Land of Make Believe was going to look like *this* either!"

"You two!" Alice Guthrie shouted through the din. "Enough! If we don't figure this out now it isn't going to matter what was supposed to happen! All that's going to matter is what's about to happen!"

With another plaintive meow, Noseworthy bit Elizabeth Pennybaker on the shin.

"Ow! Stupid cat!"

"Wait!" Fiona Guthrie left the relative safety of the overhang and skidded to the ground at Elizabeth's feet. "I think he wants us to use this."

Elizabeth Pennybaker had a strong stomach for the grotesque but since her last encounter with the Para-Sprites on the threshold of the Hallway Beside the Kitchen, she was truly developing a visceral distaste for dead birds. The lop-sided dove did not improve her perspective.

"What am I supposed to do with that thing?"

"I don't know!" Fiona Guthrie threw her hands outwards in a gesture of defeat. "But it has to be useful for something!"

The problem was that Elizabeth Pennybaker had always preferred empirical science to interpretive words. Mainly because words were some of the most easily manipulated things she had ever encountered and, at least in her experience, were far too easy to fashion into weapons against those whom one did not care for. But stories still held a special place in her heart and even as a small girl she had been fascinated with all the wonderful technological and mechanical ways in which stories could be told; from parade floats to prayer wheels and Saturday morning cartoons.

She gingerly accepted the bird from Noseworthy's impatient jaws and lifted it up into the meager light as one might inspect an especially loathsome boil. It was actually quite a pretty little thing, though; slate-blue with copper undersides and hints of purple. A tag dangled from its foot.

Passenger Pigeon. *Ectopistes migratorius*
1895
Manistee River
Extinct

"A puzzle! What if I make it into one, big, giant puzzle?" Elizabeth Pennbaker offered.

Alice Guthrie seemed unconvinced. "How is that going to help us?"

"Well," the younger Waysmith continued, "that's how you get knowledge you don't already have, right? We talk about this in school all the time. It's like Morelli's detective!"

"Great. Now you sound like Dr. Sayer. What does that even mean?" Fiona Guthrie dodged another bit of airborne flotsam before scooping Noseworthy up from his precarious place on the floor.

"A couple of years ago I had this English class, right? We read this piece; you know what, I don't even know who it was by but it was about Sigmund Freud and Sherlock Holmes and this art historian called Morelli who basically invented modern investigation methods. And almost every puzzle and mystery story out there is based on his ideas." She held up the tag again to read it against the lantern light.

"Which are?" Alice Guthrie shot a worried look to the far end of the room.

"Okay, it more or less works like this: it's all about the relationship between the clues and the detective. You take every little, tiny clue you can find and those lead you to more clues and so on and so forth until you get to the solution. Just like fingerprints in a crime lead you to the criminal or brushstrokes in a painting tell you who the artist is. It's exactly how Sherlock Holmes was written and how a lot of medicine works. Symptoms lead to tests and tests lead you to the illness. Get it?"

Both mother and daughter nodded.

"So, what if we 'follow' Clarisant in the same way? Like Dr. Sayer keeps saying, 'find the Way.'"

"And a stuffed pigeon is a clue?" Fiona Guthrie was as yet unconvinced. Somerset Sayer's descriptions of Wayfinding had always struck her as more innovative than that; that the Way had to be created rather than found. But she did have to admit that this was one method by which they could tell a fair story, if that's what they needed. And if it worked, then it worked.

"Why not? It's the only thing I've got right now." Elizabeth Pennybaker started them off. "Alright, a passenger pigeon. What can I remember about these things? They're extinct, I know that. I'm pretty sure they were hunted into oblivion. Commercial hunting! Yes, that's right. They would migrate in these huge flocks that completely blacked out the sky and were just wiped out once railroads and telegraphs became a thing. If I remember correctly, they're always held up as this great failure of conservation. The 20th century came roaring in and poof, no more passenger pigeons. Slaughter and destruction on an industrial scale."

"Okay, then..." Alice Guthrie searched her memory for any additional information. "This is a hint at where we need to go next? Where were passenger pigeons from?"

"Uh, the Midwest, I think." Elizabeth Pennybaker turned the bird over in her hand.

"Do you have any connections to the Midwest?"

"Not really."

"To pigeons?"

"I think my 3rd grade teacher raced homing pigeons once."

"To industrial destruction?"

"My family is from India."

Alice Guthrie considered strangling the poor girl and just getting it over with before the Dead inevitably reached them.

"Wait," Elizabeth Pennybaker paused, ruminating on the last time she had been in this place; on what she had felt and why. "I don't think this bird is about where we're supposed to go. I think it's about where we are."

"It's about the dead, you mean?" Fiona Guthrie hugged Noseworthy harder. A concerned meow followed as glass shattered in the background.

"Yes!" Elizabeth Pennybaker nearly bounced out of her shoes. "That's it! Fiona, you're a genius! This isn't about a trail of breadcrumbs to where *we're* going, it's about how *they* got here before us. I'll bet that those ghosts were all murdered by something modern. Industrial accidents. War. Cities and poverty. Invasion. Genocide. That's why they're faceless. They died and no one noticed. The world forgot about them. Just like a mass of passenger pigeons, they all look the same and they all suffered the same way. Chewed up and spit out by an unfeeling machine!"

"I really don't see how this is going to help us right now!" Alice Guthrie shouted.

"Argh, don't you see it?! It's all connected! It's the fireflies in the book! Clarisant surrounds herself with the dead who are just like she is. Who died the same way she did. Who hate the world that was created when people stopped creating and greed just started eating. Eating everything it could reach; food, feelings, land, hope, dreams, happiness, the lives of other people, passenger pigeons! It's a void! The Stumble is the unfillable void! The Hellmouth!"

Lostwith Notes returned to her mind. *When something is missing and we don't know what it is, we can spend our entire lives searching for it. Following hints and clues, scraps of misinformation and belief, we try to fill the emptiness with whatever we can find. We try to redefine happiness and fail. We look for love and never find it. We attempt to fill it with material possessions or unmet promises, and yet remain alone. We waste what little time we have in pursuit of falsehoods, because the uncertainty is worse.* And in that singular moment, Elizabeth Pennybaker understood what a ghost truly was; it was an absence. A place-holder. A reminder that something had once stood in that space and had been taken from it; like rings in the dust on an abandoned mantle. And these ghosts were no different. They were here, to show her what was missing.

When she looked up, the room was gone. There was no hallway or museum door. No exhibits. No birds or jars or flagstone floor. There was nothing but darkness and the unexpected smells of sweat, copper, alcohol and some other preserving spirits wafting away. She called out but heard nothing in reply. She tried again with the names of her companions and was met with silence. She began to panic.

A hand fell onto her shoulder, startling her.

"Don't run." Came the familiar voice of the folklorist, somewhere behind her in the hollow. "You can be afraid but don't turn your back on it and don't run."

"Dr. Sayer? Where are we?"

"Do you hear the wind?"

"No. I...I can't hear anything. Just you."

"Listen again."

"I think that's just the blood roaring in my ears."

A soft chuckle joined the sound. "No, it isn't. It's the wind, Elizabeth."

Alice Guthrie hadn't realized she'd closed her eyes until she opened them again. What greeted her senses then could only be described as a blighted railway graveyard. A twisted, wrecked landscape with equal parts man-made intention and persistent overgrowth that had all the stylishness of an incompetent topiary. Ruined beams jutted up from the ground at all angles.

Shattered glass and stone were piled high, but partially hidden beneath poisonous-looking vines whose thorns might have been rusted nails or stinging nettles. It seemed as though it went on forever, staining the dusky open sky with underlit clouds and a coppery taste. For a moment, she wondered if they'd somehow stepped out onto some destroyed museum exhibits in miniature. All that was missing were the bodies.

Both Madam Bel Carmen and Fiona Guthrie took stock of their surroundings. Neither of them knew when the world around them had changed; they only knew when they had awoken to it. Each now tried to clear the fog of sleep from their eyes and locate the rest of their company. They were all, thankfully, within sight of one another. Except for one.

"Wait, where's Nosey?!" Fiona gestured with empty hands. "I just had him!"

"Cats have their own paths. He'll catch up." Somerset Sayer replied without turning. "Well done, Elizabeth." The Waysmith slid her hand from the other's shoulder as she slowly angled about to face her. "Now you're starting to see."

Rather than acknowledge either place or persons, Elizabeth Pennybaker continued to follow her earlier line of thinking. "Dr. Sayer? I need to ask you something. Why did I see this thing, this alicorn, in the first place? What does all this have to do with me or my life?"

The Waysmith sighed. It had finally come to this. "What do you know about unicorns?"

The younger Waysmith rolled her eyes and sighed. "Oh, for... Nothing. You keep asking me the same questions like you think you're going to get a different answer."

"Even after all this? Nothing?"

"Yeah, I mean, a white horse. One horn. Magical enchanted forest. Storybooks and cute movies."

The elder smiled. "Yeah....that's what I figured." She paused. "But our family has a long history with unicorns, Elizabeth."

"Wait, what? What do you mean *our* family? Are we related?"

"Distantly, we all are. You and I and every Waysmith who has ever lived has one thing in common, Elizabeth. And her name was Eilis. Well, that's probably not what her name actually was but it's what we call her. You see, a very, very long time ago, there was a unicorn who lived in a bog. Okay, more of like a hearth-witch kind of thing, but who danced with spirits every night and commanded the natural world in fantastic ways. You get the idea. She was a creation of the Wild, back when fairies and ghosts and all manner of spectacular things were still sovereign over the unknown Earth. Before we trundled over and dug our fingers into it and never let go."

The Waysmith folded her arms with a low exhale and tried not to let the macabre scenes around her become too distracting. "And then a man came along, as they often do, and decided to claim the land for his own. He brought with him a wife he had no intention of freeing and a few children he had no intention of loving. In fact, he treated his wife in much the same way he treated the land; to be torn up at his whim and planted with seed that only he would be allowed to truly ever enjoy the fruits of. In the tales we tell, her name was Eilis and he was called Pennebrooke; meaning 'hill by the stream' since that's where he decided to cut his homestead. Long story short, Pennebrooke began to notice, after some time, that his wife and daughters were spending more and more time out in the woods and whenever they came back, they would be chattering on with secret words about strange, supernatural happenings and other beautiful things they saw. But, most importantly for our purposes here, they would talk about a woman they sometimes met with, hiding away in the deepest, furthest reaches of the moor. A woman who had taught them magical things."

"The unicorn."

"Yes. She had a different name then as well, but it's not important right now. In any case, Pennebrooke was, by no means, interested in his wife or their children going off to learn about evil, contemptible nonsense from the forest folk, nor was he at all pleased that their escapades took them away from the house and, presumably, from him and his endless wants and needs. So, Pennebrooke, ever the practical fellow, decided to put an end to the whole problem once and for all. He took up his axe and other weapons and headed off into the woods just like so many versions of so many fairy tales remember him. Like you say, repeating themselves. But what they don't seem to remember is the sickening acts that followed. Nobody likes to tell their children about how an angry, hateful man found her in a glade. How he tore apart the thickets and brambles and burned them. How he beat her, and cut her, and defiled her until there wasn't enough blood left to spill. How it was he who severed the alicorn and in so doing, cursed every branch of his lineage to destruction. And not just because of the violence he had perpetrated against the innocent, but because of the rest of the family who saw what he was doing and did nothing to stop him. This is why the sons of the Pennebrooke line are driven to seek out witches and sacred women as wives to stave off the hell that pursues them, even though they all die young anyway. All of them.Each and every one of them will eventually succumb to the melancholy and the despair they can neither identify nor shake, and they will never know why or what caused it. Pennebrooke and his sons were cursed to die the very moment he raised his hand against her; to pay the price of his transgressions over and over until there was nothing left of them and they were all reduced to dust. And their daughters, well, their daughters, you see, were not forgotten in this. The Daughters of Eilis were not absolved in the rape of the unicorn, Elizabeth, and carried on their hands the cast-off bloodstains of her destruction. Because they could have saved her, and they didn't. They could have welcomed her in and healed her, but they turned her away in fear of retribution. They hid their faces and claimed ignorance when she saw them. But that is also how the first of them found the Way. Blood on our hands and therefore attuned to the Way By, we're all a part of this now. You and me, the ghosts in the hall, the stolen children, the forgotten, she will come for all of us, just as she has since that day."

Elizabeth Pennybaker stood in silence as Fiona Guthrie quickly wiped the tears from the corners of her eyes.

Somerset Sayer let her hands fall to her sides. "The alicorn is something every Waysmith sees the first time they enter the Way By. It's a kind of reflection, a point of continuity, that guides us across the threshold. But then, it disappears, gone, somewhere else, never to be seen again. That's why I need you, Elizabeth. That's why I need you to hang on to that image as hard as you possibly can and to help me find it now. I didn't know what it was the day I first crossed into the Near By from my closet. I didn't know what she was yet and I have not met another Waysmith in a very, very, long time because she has seen to it that I wouldn't. Even I have lived most of my life on borrowed time because an elven king took pity on an orphaned girl hiding behind a couch while her parents ripped holes into each other over pointless resentments. So, please, concentrate. Right now, you're the closest person to that first light. Don't turn away from it just yet. Don't turn your back on her."

"But why is she doing this? None of us had anything to do with what happened in the peat bogs of Ireland during, what, the Stone Age?! Not my mom or my dad, not my aunt." Here she indicated the somewhat preoccupied Madame Bel Carmen. "Not my grandparents, not anyone!"

"And yet they do, Elizabeth. They all died because they couldn't bear to be here anymore. Because something pursued them all their lives and then stole the very breath right out of them. And you've felt it too. That room. All those stuffed birds and rotten, empty, mannequins..."

"Stop! Just stop! I've had enough of going around in circles with you. Why are you even doing this?"

"Because this isn't about vengeance, Elizabeth. This is about annihilation. And it's here. That's the injustice that united us. Those who must bear the pain and live with the scars are not the ones who threw the first punch."

A low whistle drew the attention of the assembled company; trembling as it did over the abandoned railyard. But whether it was meant to signal an arrival or merely designed to note the time was unclear. Nothing in this place had ever once moved to the tyranny of a mechanical clock.

Chapter Seventeen

The Kingdom of Lilylit had not been built. Like all true strongholds of the Fae, it had grown; taking on the shape of a castle and halls and streets only through careful fostering. And for this reason, it was constantly in a state of change. New roots spreading out to raise foundations for towers and huts, cottages and villas, ramparts and fortifications. New branches arising into vaults and lattices, new leaves whose wintery veins made for filigree windows and vines lashing timbers together into columns as high as ancient oaks could grow. Each spring, when all the world was in bloom, the gardeners would come to subtly change the angle of the light, or to tame the new growth just so, that the flowers would form grand murals and mosaics that told their stories by the motion of the buds and blossoms as they tracked the sun across the sky. In fact, if an observer was possessed of the requisite amount of patience, they could see the entire tale play out from early morning sunrise to twilight as each new section turned, opened its petals, bowed, and then closed them again.

In the furthest end of the Summer King's antechamber, one such mosaic recounted the events that had led him to his current station. It told the story of a much younger man, possessed of wit and vigor now tempered into quiet intellect; one who had first rejected the determination of his birthright but who had, in the end, taken up the Bramble Crown because there had been none other alive who might do so in his stead. It showed, in progressing creepers and seedlings, how he had ascended the winding stairs to the dais, had placed the wicked crown onto his own head, and how his blood had then enlivened the thicket into a halo of butterfly blooms. At his feet, withered hawthorn sticks lay in the shape of the rival usurper who had come before him. Someone he had once known well and, for a time, even called brother. The Crown, however, had not had mercy on the arrogance of pretenders and the doomed petitioner to the throne had been rendered a corpse just as soon as he had attempted to claim the title.

Much to the terror of all who had been assembled, as the Bramble Crown drained him utterly without ever losing so much as a speck of crystal hoarfrost. The mosaic also crept and seeded itself into other moments and Avenant was not always sure whether they were meant to memorialize him or admonish him. They sprouted and receded throughout the day, sometimes overlapping one another in form and color; much in the way that a dirty paintbrush makes for a better painting.

But one thing that grew and grew again in the patternings of Lilylit's gardens was the outline of a lonely, isolated, figure. Resplendent, but set apart. The King knew this to be a reflection of himself as he was now and his decision, each day, to maintain a solitary rule. He had never taken a mate, nor named a Queen, and had sired no children. But this too was by design; his own this time. He had not passed on the lineage of the Bramble Crown and there was no blood in the world to sustain it now that was not his own.

This was, unsurprisingly of course, a point of great contention in his household. Many of his retainers long wished that he would join with another and produce an heir, but they did not dare chastise him for refusing it. Even the most distant Fae had a worrying sense that their king was protecting them from something in the denial of this duty. The powers of the Summer Crown had always come at a great cost and the true nature of this Bargain was only ever known to the sovereigns themselves.

What is more, Lilylit itself mirrored all the confessions of his heart he could not put into words. It was, and had been for a long time, empty. There were no grand balls and no courtesans. No namings or knighthoods bestowed, no rites of passage to greater ranks or gossip to be parlayed. The halls of the castle were quiet except for the few faceless untold stories that kept the candles trimmed. There was nothing, because he would not allow it to grow from him nor would he feed its roots further.

Rather, he now kept to only a single vow: to maintain his stranglehold on the Crown until either it was no more, or he was. Seeing as it intended to strangle him in return anyway. Thus, Lilylit faded as he did; into a child's fairytale about castles in the sky. It was a barren place, filled with constructs and memories and the uncanny. Something to believe in for a little while, or something to remember fondly, perhaps. But just an edifice.

Pensive, Avenant stood before the Foras Feasa. Its great raised back the cross-section of a tree lain sideways, but though the trunk appeared to be cut down, it was far from dead. Rather, each year the rings added new growth along the outer rim and marked the changing of the seasons in the Way By; showing not the passing of hours but of times of plenty and times of famine. A generation in each line and a dynasty in every forking branch.

As such, the throne of Lilylit had expanded with each new coronation, finally reaching up beyond the king's chamber and into the roof-boughs of the canopy overhead. There, its uppermost edge had become the seat of griffons and other such messengers and sometimes served as an audience to the pageantry below. But if all went as he intended, such heights would be the limit of the throne's reach and there would be no more rings to further raise up an empty roof. Or what should have been an empty roof. Now, a most sudden and unwelcome sound tittered down from the roosts above.

Sparrows. Sparrows had alighted on the rough bark of the archway and now glared down at him from unblinking, accusatory eyes. Fixed and dead, they stared out as the imps mechanizing them chattered back and forth in grim anticipation. He looked back up at them equally unflustered, yet he did not raise an alarm. In truth, he had been expecting this. He had sent Somerset Sayer and the new young Waysmith away, along with their companions. Hat Trick and Coat Check he had busied elsewhere in the Kingdom. And the court was quiet in the late afternoon. There was no one left here as he meant for them not to be. He knew what came next.

Her soft footfalls were the first things he heard. The dark timbre of her voice followed after.

"I'm surprised at you, Avenant." She proclaimed, entering the throne room without so much as a nod. "I at least expected a token resistance. A guard, perhaps. The Octadic at the ready. Instead, here you are. Alone. Nothing and no one at your side as if the whole kingdom were already in exile. If I didn't know you better, I would have said that this was a precursor to suicide."

"Clarisant." He replied, his gaze drifting down from the sparrows to regard the unicorn. "I would say that it is a pleasure to see you again, but you know that I would be lying if I did."

She chuffed benignly. "Well, it's not as if you and I have ever met on good terms exactly, Ard Rí."

"She's not here." He countered the unspoken query.

"No, I suspected not. But that's alright. I'm here for you."

A clatter arose from the enclaves surrounding the Foras Feasa as eight figures suddenly animated throughout the lengthening afternoon shadows. A hand dealt by a deck of cards halfway between a tarot and a gambler's shuffle, the Octadic formed and responded to the played threat in an instant. Aranaugh and Arafin were the first to step forward in defense of the king with Hafath and Mede not far behind. The others lingered in the wings, tense as they awaited the next move. But the unicorn was unconcerned and dismissed their approach with a furtive click of her tongue.

"Come now, Avenant." She chided with a familial tone. "Your time has come and you very well know it. The moment of your death was set the instant you raised that crown to your head. Bleeding your life out with every authoritative word. Every order. Every infallible proclamation. Drinking up your allotted existence every time you dared to impose your will on a defiant world. A king who pays for his dominion with every beat of his heart. And look at you now. Spent. Fading. Already whitened and wizened for the winter sleep."

"And is that what you propose to give me, Clarisant? Sleep?" He deftly sidestepped her aggressive approach before regaining ground at the center of the room. "That there are no more words that I might yet have to speak? That I should now be swept away with the dust? Or is it that you fear what I will say next?"

She could hear the whine of breath through the Bramble Crown, covered on its pedestal, and the sound picked at her. Only a few hundred yards ahead, the trunk of the white tree creaked and groaned at the promise of new edicts from the king. Clarisant surveyed the field. Her view of the Octadic, though, was far different than that of most others. She saw them for what they really were underneath the cultivated veneer; saw the debris from which they grew. Instead of eight named guards, she saw eight corpses jumbled amongst clots of peat, shambling forward encased in mud.

Each bore weapons marking their former stations: A Knight, a Crusader, a Cavalier, an Archer, a Ranger, a Druid, and a Scribe who faced two directions. They may once have been great heroes, and she had no doubt that they likely still were, whatever he called them, but they were all Nameless now; conscripted into the vanguard of the Bramble Crown when it had stolen both their lives and their dreams through the blood of their wounds.

In the remnants of the stolen eye finally decayed enough to drop off, she could also briefly see the remains of horses and dogs scattered about them and the last remnants of a banner snapping angrily on the branches overhead. All this she knew however, because this garden had once been her palace. The Octadic was what remained of the heroes who had once sought her, in service now to the Crown forever. Heroes she had vanquished, heroes she had loved, and most especially, heroes who had thought to tame her. The Hill of Foras Feasa was none other than the bog of her former homeland, grown over in her absence.

"Avenant, of the House and Line of Nuada macBalor," She called out. "Who was called Finn Fáil, Neachtain. Tiarna an Dál nAraidi. He who is Maine Mórgor, I have come to defy you. And to put an end to the last of your lineage."

A shiver passed through the grasses all about them as something deep in the wilds breathed its first in a thousand years. The room around them trembled awake and something in the depths of the unconscious mind of the world rose up to meet her demand. Avenant heard a voice, rasping but somehow sonorous, carried on air, but emanating from grey water and buried roots.

"*You* are not welcome here. *Níl fáilte romhat anseo*." The voice spoke without true words, but she heard them anyway. Formed into the language of her own Gaelic soil by the Way By.

"The medicine never is." She replied. "It brings only pain in the moment, but remedy in time."

"The medicine is poison. *Tá an leigheas nimh*." The voice intoned, shaking the great tree overhead as it rattled the bones of the Octadic ominously.

Clarisant smiled but considered her words carefully, knowing that the riddle could change at the slightest misstep. She spoke now to the Bramble Crown, whose voice she had not heard in an age.

"But only when given too much. What is medicine and what is poison is only a matter of measure." She answered.

"One cannot measure the blood. *Ní féidir an fhuil a thomhas*."

"But only the blood, cleaned, brings healing." Avenant stiffened at this, having sensed a change in the air.

The voice spoke once more but remained an ominous, halting, sound. "If blood is offered then blood will be taken. M*á thairgtear fuil ansin tógfar fuil*."

Clarisant replied quickly. “Only that which was written in blood, can now be made plain.”

The voice sighed, a strangled noise that heaved a dying breath out of the earth. “A Name for a Name brings life. *Tugann Ainm do Ainm an saol.*”

The Unicorn Queen took an excited breath and steadied. The answer to the trial she had set before herself was hidden in the words of the fen. She need now only decipher the meaning of the phrases and begin.

“Now apt, now obscure.” Avenant recited; an admonishment and a warning from his own father from before the wars had split their houses forever. If this was to be a battle of riddles, he knew how to weave his own and stir up the magics of the Way By into the netting. “All those who run in the Hunt know what must follow them. All Hunters remember the Battle of Trees. All Victors must answer the Riddle of the Lady of Achren.”

He thought back to his schooling and to his many teachers, and all the stories he had been raised to remember. If he could set the rules of the Way By to favor his own in their conflict, he might stand against her long enough to help them. But even then Avenant knew that he was the interloper here, as all sovereigns inevitably were.

And as Clarisant had been the one to bring down the heroes of the Octadic in life, she would know how to end them all over again in death. She knew them. She knew their names. For this reason, he attempted to bind his enigma in the rules of the bardic Cad Goddeu, the epic poem within which had been woven the mystic meanings of trees. The Riddle of the Lady of Achren, a section of the poem wherein the secret Names of Heroes were already hidden, came easily to him and he parsed the necessary verses in his mind as quickly as he could.

The tops of the beech tree
Have sprouted of late,
Are changed and renewed
From their withered state.

When the beech prospers
Through spells and litanies
The oak tops entangle,
There is hope for the trees.

I have plundered the fern
Through all secrets I spy,
Old Math ap Mathonwy
Knew no more than I.

For with nine sorts of faculty
God has gifted me:
I am the fruit of fruits gathered
From nine sorts of tree.

Unfortunately, this was what Clarisant could do just as well as he. She would use the hidden names of the Octadic to undo them before turning her wrath to the king. This is what he had been waiting for. The true battle of riddles had begun.

The Knight advanced. In Clarisant's vision, a specter rose up before her, peeling its limbs from the embrace of the swamp with a sickening ingurgitation. The twisted, mummified form clanked loudly in plates of brass and steel armor before raising a rusted claymore with both of its gnarled hands. The armor bore the remnants of etching on the breastplate and she could discern a shape like that of a Great Cross, tree-like with roots below and arms split above. Truly, he seemed quite familiar to her.

The Unicorn Queen raised her hand and brandished a bleeding wound. It was all she had time for as the first sweeping blow came straight at her head. She ducked the swing and parried lightly, testing her opponent's strategy and reading what memories she could in his posture and stance. A second, over-extended arc came at her midsection and she used the opportunity to slant the strike and sink her nails into the Knight's side. When he pulled free, she bit back a snarl in noting that the guardian creature was blithely unaffected.

There was hardly even a mark where she had pierced its ribs. The Knight shambled forward and swung again, this time with more precision, and Clarisant was forced to take a step back and block the sword with the flat of her forearm. The hit was jarringly hard and nearly knocked her to the ground but, by the grace of anticipation, she maintained her footing and responded with a series of forward strikes the Knight knocked sideways. They exchanged more blows, each attempting to unbalance the other. Then, to Clarisant's even greater concern, she heard a noise.

Each in turn, the figures began to rise and close in: a Crusader with a longsword and a shield of iron, a Cavalier whose forearms and chest were bound in thorns, an Archer with an oak and holly bow, a Druid in a hunter's headdress, a Ranger with the head and jaws of a wolf, and a Scribe who could not be flanked given two faces that could peer in all directions. Unhindered by the bog they must have risen from, they began to circle her; closing in on every side until the smell of the moldering grave was overwhelming.

Clarisant, however, did not wait for them to trap her. She was quick to strike the Knight hard enough in the shoulder to turn it so that she could block the first volley from the Archer. At a dead run, she then closed the distance with the Cavalier, avoiding the first blows of thorns, to turn his position about and put a few extra steps between herself and the Huntsman. She was not quite fast enough though. A rotted hound, commanded by druidic magics, caught her hard to the right. She was able to reflexively side-step the worst of it, but, unwittingly, it left her wide open to a full bash from the Crusader's iron shield.

She felt it connect with her shoulder, felt her collarbone break, before the follow-through sent her rolling into the tussocks furrowed up from the living floor. It was a terrible misstep and Clarisant had barely a split-second to right herself before a lash of mistletoe, covered in three-inch thorns, nearly took out her throat. But once on her feet, she cursed at herself and rallied. She had bested them all before, but she would need to be better than this to meet the Crown's challenge.

Clarisant went for the Archer first, catching the tip of the bow in the back-hook of her wrist along the trailing edge. The Archer responded by raising the weapon but before it could fire, the Unicorn Queen lunged past the string and stabbed her hand directly into the Archer's upper chest and then straight on through its first ribs to the scapula behind; effectively breaking the bones and rendering the bow arm useless. Pulling herself free, she then turned on her heels to meet the expected blow to her back, parrying the Cavalier's buffeting strikes with her forearms. She shifted then, avoiding the claymore now on her left and slashed her talons low against the Knight's legs.

The heavily-weighted corpse buckled and landed on the grassy floor with a wet slap. The Cavalier engaged her again and through multiple traded clouts; Clarisant managed to cut the thorns from both its forearms and was about to snap the vines from its torso when a searing pain lanced through her neck. She withered and lurched to the side, barely avoiding a second strike. An unseen blade wielded by the Scribe had gone partially into her chest, just beneath her right arm, with a wound to join the others. It was bleeding. Badly.

She dodged the next round of oncoming strikes with a tumble and then stumbled backwards towards the outer edge of the Hill to regroup. To her consternation, she observed as each of the Octadic shook off their injuries, set their bones, and rose up again. They hardly seemed bothered by her. Clarisant growled, low in her throat, in part from uncertainty and partly from pain. She had missed something.

She thought back again to Achren's Riddle; the one that Avenant had been so keen to mention in his orders to the Way By. The last of the great Heroes to have used it was none other than Gwydion himself; the very first to have called the Trees into battle against the forces of Annwn; the Otherworld of both Fae and the Dead.

From there, Gwydion had come to the realization that no warrior of the Otherworld could be vanquished unless his opponent could guess his Name. Such a thing Gwydion had then done; using the Ogham Tree rhymes to deduce the name of Brân Fendigaidd, the Blessed Crow, who was both a giant and once a king. In the end, he had accomplished this feat by discerning the marks of the Alder branches on his shield and knowing him to be the Vanguard of Annwn.

The alder leads the attack,
while the aspen falls in battle,
and heaven and earth tremble before the oak,
a "valiant door keeper against the enemy."

Clarisant paused. So, that was it. Avenant had set the rules of their game by invoking the verses of Gwydion, Brân, and Annwn and had, therefore, attempted to hide the path to victory in the meter of an old bardic rhyme. Fae certainly did love their word conjury and the spells cast in the Way By through them. But therein was her answer. Seeing as she presumed herself to be the Crow in this story and Avenant in the role of Gwydion, that meant that the Octadic she faced now had been remade in recitation as the Nameless of Annwn; consumed utterly by service as heroes under the Crown but held fast to it even in death.

That way, her knowledge of their former lives would be of no use. She would no longer be able to simply break them as she had once done. To defeat them, she would have to Name them and in Naming them, reveal the riddle's method of their undoing.

She turned and studied each of the guardians as they bore down on her position. The Knight came ahead first, raising the claymore high in the start of another devastating sweep. But what more could she see? The creature charged her outright; never flinching or feinting and coming directly at her with nothing in its soulless eyes but the intent to kill by command of the Bramble Crown.

Uncouth and savage was the fir,
Cruel the ash tree
Turns not aside a foot-breath,
Straight at the heart runs he.

Clarisant set her heels and stood her ground. If she was wrong in her reading, this was about to end very badly for her. A full attack from the Knight, even partially blocked, would still likely result in at least a few more broken bones and she could not afford the detriment at this point. She still had a king to deal with.

The Knight reached her and swung, the blade screaming downwards towards the unicorn's neck, but Clarisant was ready and dropped to one knee just as the blade completed the arc. As it hurtled overhead, she called upon the ashen alchemy of the Stumble, raising a surreptitious handful of the burning embers she still carried.

And with that, she struck directly beneath the heavy breastplate and shouldered the powdered remains into the moldy flesh and matter she found there. With a flick of her hand, she released oblivion directly into its heart.

"Nuin, the Ash." Clarisant whispered, still bearing most of her opponent's weight as the corpse suddenly stilled.

A moment passed and Clarisant recoiled, allowing the now restful Knight to slide limply to the ground as her hand came away stained black and grey. As the body fell, the tussocks of grass nearest them reached out and spread around it, water rose up to meet it, and in seconds, the figure was gone. Vanished; back into the mire the throne room had now become.

At last, the truth of Lilylit was revealed. That it was the very same bog wherein she had once reigned supreme before the Way By had been shattered and the Crown given leave to grow untended, writhing beneath the wilting flower mosaics. But Clarisant did not have long to celebrate her victory before an arrow landed squarely in the moss between her feet. The rest of the Octadic had reached her.

Several more arrows nearly made their mark as Clarisant dashed for cover in the now taller grasses. The Cavalier caught her there and a pitched battle between claw and thorn-wrapped fists ensued. Twice she was forced to take the hit or be shot through by the clothyard bolts whistling past her. And once, thankfully only once, she was glanced by the longsword, leaving a searing new cut from the rise of her cheekbone to the curve of her jaw and nearly taking off her ear. But three times she was able to force both the Cavalier and the Crusader back onto lower ground, keeping them at bay while still managing to dodge the incoming volley.

Their battle ranged all over. Each of the Nameless Octadic was clearly skilled in their own discipline and Clarisant was forced to change tactics and strategy repeatedly just to keep ahead of the blades and points constantly seeking to lay her low. During one particularly tense exchange, the wolf-headed Ranger had managed to bite down onto her left arm, and had it not been for the fact that the creature had chosen to throw her rather than attempt to swallow her, she was left with two additional broken ribs and several lacerations rather than a missing arm.

With foot beat of the swift oak
Heaven and earth rung;
'Stout Guardian of the Door'
His name on every tongue.

But the toss and tumble gave Clarisant an opening and she was quickly on it before the others could rejoin. The Wolf Trees of her birthplace were the names given to White Oaks, called Dair. When the Ranger turned to snap at her again, she did what the creature did not expect and leapt from the hillock onto the top of the wolf's head.

It was a bit of a struggle, but Clarisant managed to wrap her legs around the Ranger's neck just as it attempted to scrape her off, used one hand to grasp onto its stout left ear, and yanked its head back with as much strength as she could manage without leverage. The Ranger yowled with a terrifying, hollow, sound but Clarisant did not hesitate and plunged her fingers into the wolf's mouth, severing its tongue. And then, it too fell into the bog.

The Unicorn Queen took a pained breath as she hovered over the vanishing corpse of the Ranger. The battle had gone on for nearly half an hour. She was tiring and was already a little light-headed from her injuries. The wound beneath her right arm was continuing to bleed and if she wasn't careful, one or both of her broken ribs could move and run her through. And she still had a long way to go.

The holly, dark green,
Made a resolute stand;
He is armed with many spear points
Wounding the hand.

The dower-scattering yew
Stood glum at the fight's fringe,
With the elder slow to burn
Amid fires that singe.

By now, however, she had remembered their first deaths and from that divine the likely Names of the others approaching. She had only a moment to rest though, and then the fight was again upon her. The Cavalier she would take next, having figured out that she needed to cut off the creature's hands to defeat it. The Archer fell several minutes later, as Clarisant first fought it back onto the edge of the Hill and then took out its eyes as the bones of its feet became tangled in the exposed roots.

The Scribe went down similarly, with a twisted neck and its own hands stuffed into its mouths. The Druid was then consumed by shadows when the moon was out of view. The Crusader took her the longest, raining blow upon blow down on her as she set her forearms against the iron shield, over and over again, dragging metal against burning Fae skin until the sparks of their battle at last lit the straw hair and cracked fibers of the corpse's threadbare tabard on fire. As it burned, the armor and shield melted away and were snuffed in the blackened water around her feet.

Clarisant spit a mouthful of blood into the grass and watched them go. Finally, only the Summer King now remained. Clarisant turned and regarded the last of them, standing near the center of the Hill, graced in fine clothes of muted red, purple, and gold. Her eyes glinted with the images the Way By supplied to her. Like everything else, Avenant was something to her he was not to others, and she saw him through battered eyes and a shattered face.

She saw him as a trespasser, whose life could only be sustained by theft. His skin was the same color of dark brown possessed by all the bog dead and his hair was long, pale, and bright. His eyes were white and empty, his mouth twisted into a grimace just showing a hint of yellowed teeth and congealed black gums. Around his head, stretching nearly from pointed ear to pointed ear, an open and weeping gash that leaked muck and lichen. He raised a blade, still a pristine shard of glittering light, unmarred by age or battle. Undoubtedly, he could wield a sword just as easily as he could wield his words.

The birch, though very noble,
Armed himself but late:
A sign not of cowardice
But of high estate.

The heath gave consolation
To the toil-spent folk,
The long-enduring poplars
In battle much broke.

It was clear that the Unicorn Queen was profoundly wounded. Though she stood with her right hand at the ready, her left was clasped around the deep cut beneath her arm. Her breathing came in a strained wheeze and the stridor of blood in her lungs could be heard with each labored breath. But she observed as the king advanced, though he did not find her to be yielding.

"It comes now to this, little one." Clarisant spoke out. The king hesitated and canted his head thoughtfully as she straightened to address him. "I should have called on you earlier, if not for the caprice of the Way By and the needs of the Stumble."

"I know what they did to you." Avenant replied, noting only in passing a trickle of blood that was now slowly staining the rags at her back. "I know that Men came and they took everything from you. They broke you and there was nothing you could do. They ruined the world and it crushed your soul so deeply that you still wear the cracks on your skin. But I cannot give back what they took, Clarisant. It is from their spoils that I and all of this was born."

The Unicorn Queen seemed almost pleased at his confession. "Ah, yes." She breathed deeply of the cooling air. "Who is the Summer King? What is the Kingdom but that which grew from fields and gardens planted over the wilds? The day that Pennebrooke subjugated the earth and from it, the tilled soil obeyed and yielded fruit to new masters. Pennebrooke, who grew the Bramble Crown as he made the fences that marked his territory. The boundaries between homes, between worlds. And whose sons became the heirs and stewards to this very Court. Whose daughters had to find their Way alone."

It was the unspoken truth; that the blood of the Unicorn had watered the Bramble Crown and from whose deterioration the Kingdoms had grown. That the children born of violent unions had themselves founded lineages and whose Houses were ever consumed by the sins of their ancestors. Because it was from these materials that they were first created and that fed them still. And so, Avenant had vowed to end it. He had vowed that there should never be another Sovereign who made the world in his own image.

Clarisant took another pained breath and continued. "And for that reason, I take back from you what they took from me. All that was planted inside of me and that which grew from me. All of the memory I did not cede, the names which I did not bestow, and everything that has been all but almost forgotten. You are Aos Sí, are you not? Descended of the Houses of Men and Fae? Poisoned fruit of a poisoned tree? You are the last of a doomed line that never should have been. An abomination of worlds. You gave to others what did not belong to you. You were the ones who first wrote Ogham into books so that the Druids might learn it and are likely the very reason Mankind knows of our stories at all. You painted tomes that, under the light of the moon, come to life and tell their stories without need of a storyteller. And then you dare to call the last Hunt, because she came to you. Because you thought you could save her instead. Now she is gone and you are alone. Though she may yet come 'round, it shall be that you are never seen or heard from again." The true implications of the threat were not lost on him.

"But she knows you, doesn't she?" Clarisant chided mockingly. "She has known about you from the very beginning. When I met her, she mumbled about stories and fables beyond her and that's how I knew it had to be you. You were the one who told her. You must be the reason that she loves the old tales so very much. It is all because of her knowledge of you and the secrets that you chanced to share with such wretched ears. But if it is any consolation to you, Avenant, I promise that she will remember you for all the time that she has left."

The king looked sad, his gaze drifting off into the moor as it continued to spread out from the Hill upon which Foras Feasa sat; as though he were contemplating something of unspeakable sorrow. There were great and wondrous stories here that most people still did not know, and soon there would be no one to tell them. And, possibly, no Waysmith to find them again.

With care born of both injury and caution, Clarisant pulled the cloth bundle from her waist sash, flipped the tie free of it, and let the linen fall away to reveal a piled handful of oil-slicked ash. Walking carefully over the shuddering remains of the Octadic and their battle, she approached the gnarled roots of the throne with her fingers slowly opening. Threads of soot and charcoal slithered down to the ground where its destructive work immediately began.

It ate away at the flowering galleries, wiping out the tales told in their blossoming heads and verdant blades of grass and heather. It then devoured the mosses and lichens that tiled the floor, moving up along the vines in the walls, until patches of sickly light began to appear in the boughs overhead and a starless sky fell across the firmament. Soon enough, the rot arrived at the base of the ringed throne and was seen to begin the task of wiping out all evidence of time itself.

Avenant steeled himself and rounded on the approaching Queen. "Lilylit may fall." He snarled. "But even the Stumble cannot undo the binding Geas of the Bramble Crown. Reduce the Foras Feasa to driftwood and you will still be left with the shrine of his transgressions. Still the Crown will grow. Blood has quickened it; blood again will restore it."

"Oh, yes." Her mood darkened with malicious glee. "Oh, yes Avenant. Blood is the lifeforce which imbues all things with the temporal nature of their existence. My blood. And now your blood, specifically. Which is why I am going to feed it, gorge it...with every last drop I wring out of you."

Chapter Eighteen

When writing of literary men, historians often describe them as being before their times. When writing of women, they instead rather marvel at how they've set their times aside and done great works despite expectations and certainly not because of them. Somerset Sayer was just the kind of woman to be thusly memorialized. Born two centuries too late; a figure indentured to the Enlightenment with little other option, a pub-house pamphleteer, a ready orator, an incomparable duelist, and a most unreasonable provocateur, who would no more take to spousehood alongside a man than she would to God himself. Or, at least, that is how Elizabeth Pennybaker would later describe her.

Somerset Sayer looked out across the Way By Stumble. In the intervening years between her own initiation and that of Elizabeth's, it had grown exponentially and now appeared without beginning or end. Once the mien of a fairy-tale woodland, filled with storied trees and roots of history deeper than a ground well, it was now a desolate horror; annihilation given form, the paradox of absence and emptiness shown in fire and dingy reflections. The small part that surrounded them, the Railyard, was a meager offset patch sewn onto the larger fabric; dissolving where it ended just beyond a ruined train-car half-buried in rocks.

Madam Bel Carmen spit another curse at the uneven ground that seemed intent on gashing and cutting her feet no matter where she tried to step. She then levied a curse at the sky as well, for good measure. The thick, ashy, wind that kept the barren landscape just so never let up, though it had led them all out of the remains of the dry museum storeroom and into something far less familiar. What sort of hell had the Waysmith managed to trap them in? She had to hand it to the folklorist. She never did anything by half measure. Not even eternal damnation.

"Withersmith!" Somerset Sayer yelled, trying as much as she could to be heard over the constant howl of an iron-red gale that could not be felt, only tasted. There was no response.

"Mary Toft!" She tried again. "I know you're here, so let's get on with it." They were all on the home ground of the dead now, and in such places, she knew that no one is ever truly abandoned. Even if they'd rather be.

"The ghost? Are you mad?" Alice Guthrie called out. "We only just escaped that horrid thing!"

Elizabeth Pennybaker, however, was more circumspect. "You actually know who she is?"

"I know who she was. Mary Elizabeth Toft. She was a Waysmith, more than a century ago..."

"And then?"

"And then Clarisant."

"I suppose I should have figured that. But why train tracks?" She gestured about.

Somerset Sayer answered as quickly as she could, still keeping her eyes trained for any potential movement. "Clarisant didn't kill her outright. That's not how she usually works. Instead, she dragged her down, ate away at her from the inside. Took her time with it, really. Years, in fact. Finally, when Mary Toft had nothing left, she jumped in front of a train."

"And now she's trapped there forever." Alice Guthrie stated, taking particular note of the wreckage and the themes it adhered to.

"Hn. And if we're not careful, we will be too." The folklorist replied.

Getting their bearings was no easy task. The Stumble had not been made by or for the presence of living minds and was both in a constant state of flux and oppressively still. It weighed on all those who traversed it in ways few could describe afterwards. Its limitless void drawing in all sense of order and meaning until the traveler had little choice but to give up and surrender to it. Because, by then, all that remained seemed worthless. But like the Way By from which it emanated, the Stumble responded to the words and deeds that took place within it. Anyone could shape it and it give it form, even the most innocent. Especially the most innocent.

"Dr. Sayer?" It was a sound that the wind made and Somerset Sayer froze, cocking her head to try and get a better bead on its direction.

"Fiona?"

“I’m.... I’m so sorry....” It was indeed Fiona Guthrie, but where were the words coming from? They sounded like they were being carried on the desolate gusts; dropped down from a great height and landing all around them with no sense of their origin.

“Alice, where is Fiona?”

“What? She...she was here! I just had her with me!”

Indeed, the young woman, despite having been at her mother’s side seconds before, was nowhere to be found and instantly the company was in a panic.

“...I’m so sorry...” Her voice was saying. “I wanted to help. I wanted to make it better...I thought I could fight it....”

The folklorist spinned around, looking above and below for any clue as to where she should turn. “Fiona, I know!” She called back. “We all know! Where are you?”

“What is happening?” Elizabeth Pennybaker yelled, very nearly grasping onto the Waysmith’s coat to force her around again.

“It’s the Stumble.” She snapped back. “It’s trying to take Fiona. Damn it all to Hell, of course it is. I should have known she would be the most vulnerable to it.”

“...I’m so sorry I failed.... that you had to leave me....”

“Leave you?” Alice Guthrie whirled about. “I didn’t leave you. I would never leave you...” But the thought caught in her throat. What manner of lie was this? Or...

She felt her stomach drop.

Somerset Sayer had warned them of this, in a time that seemed like a thousand years ago. Was this what her daughter feared the most? Was this how Despair trapped the unwilling; how the Stumble consumed? Just as the folklorist had said, it eventually made everyone a prisoner to the terrors they couldn’t admit to. The Chirurgeon should have taught her this. He had been the form the Way By gave to a young woman’s turmoil within and his defeat had only sent him back here. This was the maw she had seen in the gallery.

Alice Guthrie felt a sudden influx of shame. How many times had she awoken in the middle of the night to Fiona's crushing grip on her arm or to her sudden shouts down the hall as a violent nightmare roused her from sleep? How many times had her daughter come wandering into the same room as she, only to take a moment to look at her and then walk out again? How many times had she stopped whatever she was doing to ask Fiona if she was alright? If she needed or wanted anything? How had she not noticed what was happening beneath that jovial exterior? How had she not noticed that her children feared loss and from a belief in their own fault most of all? The Stumble truly did whisper terrible things and though it whispered them to her as well, there was a more pressing problem at hand. She grimaced.

"Fiona!"

The voice on the wind floated through again. "I tried, mom...I just couldn't...I don't know how..."

"No, NO! Fiona Guthrie, you come back here this instant!"

Alice Guthrie was turning frantic but the landscape seemed to follow her; offering up new rocky paths as she sought the voice high and low. In a flash of insight, Elizabeth Pennybaker stopped; planted her feet and shouted into the expanse. "Fiona! Didn't your mother ever teach you not to wander off? Don't you dare walk out on us. I will never forgive you if you do!"

"Elizabeth?"

"Didn't you hear me?" She was keeping her tone intentionally unsympathetic because, for some reason, it always seemed to endear people to her even more. As her own mother had once noted, bland hostility was apparently Pennybaker-creole for familial affection and no one wanted to disappoint a Waysmith. "We can't finish this without you. And now you've left! You just left us all standing here! I mean, what would the King say?! Which means that I have to come all the way here, to whatever pit Dr. Sayer has gotten us into, and drag you back home! I hope you're happy!"

Alice Guthrie stared back at the younger Waysmith anxiously. But whatever she was doing, it seemed to be working. The voice was getting louder.

"Is someone...are you...there?"

"I'm here!" She squinted through a blast of scouring dust. "I'm here. Where are you?"

From beneath a pile of shale slabs and cracked flagstones, Somerset Sayer spied something working to get out. She sprinted to the mound, Huntresses in tow, leaving smears of blood and sanguine footprints behind them all as they did so. But what she came upon was more than just a washout of debris, it was some kind of cairn. 'A tomb,' the folklorist thought but didn't say. Beneath which Fiona Guthrie had been slowly piling massive rocks on top of her own chest, burying herself in her own grave at the foot of another massive, burned out tree.

Madam Bel Carmen dropped to the ashen dirt and quickly began to pull the larger stones away. The rocks were jagged though, and cut her even more, until rivulets of blood began to flow freely over her hands and down her forearms. But she wouldn't have cared either way. Soon, Alice Guthrie joined her, tearing into the mound with cracked fingers and throwing detritus in every direction. As she dug and clawed, scooping out handfuls of pebbles and mud, she could see Fiona's form revealed. Both women nearly sobbed in relief and elation. Not only would neither of them be burying another child, they were literally digging her back up.

To Elizabeth Pennybaker's surprise, the girl was pale and peaked. As though she had been engaged in her own demise for rather a long time. Her eyes were open, however, and she was still breathing. Albeit slowly and painfully. She didn't seem to see them though, and even as the others continued to free her from her self-imposed catacomb, the teenager would reach out absently to drag heavy stones back onto herself almost as soon as they were set aside. Madam Bel Carmen snarled and snatched a particularly nasty piece of sharp granite out of her grasp before grabbing onto Fiona's wrists and shaking her.

"Stop!" She yelled. "Stop doing that and, hey, look at me!"

Dazed, Fiona looked down at their hands, at the splatters of blood and dust turning into a macabre kind of tempera paint and paste, and then up at the assembled coven. She seemed confused, as though she didn't quite understand what she was seeing. With a shaking touch, she then reached up to run her fingers through her own grey-powdered hair.

"Fiona, it's me. Evelyn."

Slowly, she nodded, but the answer in response wasn't encouraging.

"Don't tell Mom." She said, barely above a whisper. "Don't tell her that I did this. Don't tell her I'm dead."

Madam Bel Carmen flinched but didn't let go. Alice Guthrie entwined a worried hand into her daughter's shirt.

"Fiona." She said again gently. "You're not dead. None of us are." She did not see the Waysmith's furtive look about their surroundings.

"I...saw..." Fiona stared past her and into the roiling sky. "Headstones covered in marigolds. Brightly colored crypts but everyone is dead inside. There are no more pictures to put up on the mantle. My family is all gone...whatever I do, I just make it worse."

Alice Guthrie folded her legs underneath herself and hauled Fiona, as much as she could given her still partial interment, into her lap. Lying there, half in and half out of her daughter's own grave, Alice Guthrie understood what the Stumble was doing. This place, this dark, desperate, despairing place, had taken ahold of her just as much as it had attempted to take hold of each of them with the nightmares of the storeroom. Fiona was a prisoner and it would use her to claim them all.

"I'm still making it worse aren't I?"

"Fiona, listen to me, I..." Alice Guthrie took a deep breath and tried to swallow. "You haven't made anything worse. In fact, that would be impossible at this point, I think. Even if everything falls apart, even if the both of us die right here and right now, it still wouldn't be your fault. Don't you see? Becoming who you are rather than living up to an image of something you thought you might be, isn't something bad you do to someone else. It's your path. That's what this is, don't you see? You got lost because you didn't know the way and I...I couldn't show it to you. But that doesn't mean that the time you spent looking or getting turned around wasn't worth it. We wouldn't have traded any of that time with you for anything. Not Madam Bel Carmen, not Elizabeth nor, you know, that goblin fellow. Well, maybe Dr. Sayer would; but we all know she's a snide bit of a saucebox."

When no response was then immediately forthcoming, Alice Guthrie chanced a look back down at Fiona resting in her arms. To her surprise, both Fiona and everyone else was staring at her.

"Alice? Did..." The folklorist coughed through parched lips. "Was that you calling me...a smart-ass?"

Alice Guthrie couldn't help herself but laugh. She'd usually kept the more colorful words she used to describe some of her experiences with the Waysmith out of her hearing range, even if she did find her otherwise amenable.

"I.... yes. I believe I did." She smiled. "I fear I'm having quite a time of it at the moment and I have said something out loud I probably shouldn't have."

"Well," The folklorist actually offered her a wry smirk "I won't tell if you won't."

"Fiona? What happened?" Elizabeth Pennybaker moved to help the other women to their feet, reflexively clutching Madam Bel Carmen's arm as she leaned in.

Unsure fingers came up to trace the tear tracks on Alice Guthrie's cheek. "Are we dead?"

"No." The younger Waysmith chuckled through a hitched breath. "No, Fiona, we're not dead, but we are in danger. Do you remember what's going on?"

"Remember? Yes. Wait. Yes. We came through into the Way By to...to...something?" The girl tried to sit up a little but was, ultimately, unsuccessful. Falling back into her mother's embrace, she grimaced slightly. "A unicorn. We came to fight the unicorn. But...it went wrong. I..."

"Hush." Alice Guthrie smoothed the hair from Fiona's face. "It doesn't matter what happened. I've got you now. We need to get out of here. Can you walk?"

She pondered the question for a moment. "I think so? Get me out this hole."

With much scrabbling and stumbling, they all managed to pull each other upright, with Fiona's arm thrown over Alice Guthrie's shoulders and the rest of her supported by an attentive Madam Bel Carmen, who also seemed grateful for the added support as she took stock of the mess that had been made of the soles of her feet. Once balanced, they turned to regard their dual Waysmiths. It was pretty obvious that arrival in the Stumble had hit them all harder than anyone had been expecting, but they were at least mobile for the moment. Limping and faltering as they went, but moving.

That was when they felt the ground shake.

Somerset Sayer cringed and dropped her head as Elizabeth Pennybaker nearly lost her footing.

"What was that?" She asked, noting with some chagrin the hard look on the folklorist's face.

"It's her." The Waysmith replied. "She's coming. She'll protect the graves with every advantage the Stumble affords her. Elizabeth, let me deal with the Withersmith. I want you to keep the others on the Way and keep going."

"What?!" She snarled in response. "Haven't you been paying attention to anything that's gone on so far?"

"I have." The folklorist said. "But we're not alone out here and I'm the only one who really knows how this works. She's not going to just let us leave. I have fought the Stumble for as long as I have been alive but I was never strong enough to destroy it. I never will be. I'm not strong enough, Elizabeth...to save you. There's no deliverance from this place, only the passage through it."

Elizabeth Pennybaker raised her head and met Somerset Sayer's eyes, but there was no flicker of angst or dismay this time. Just hard mettle that begged the world to make the wrong move. Dared the Way By to test her again.

"You know, this isn't exactly how I pictured a Great Hunt."

Somerset Sayer tipped her chin in agreement. "Well, that's because neither side is running yet."

Just as Alice Guthrie finally allowed Fiona to part from her, the young woman slumped to the ground, sitting heavily on a high, flat, rock a few feet from the now empty cairn. She was exhausted; every movement was stiff and sent shooting pains through her joints. She didn't know how long she had been here but it felt like an eternity. For a moment, she even considered the possibility that she actually had been buried in the Stumble several weeks ago and had simply dreamed the rest. Madam Bel Carmen's hand steadied her until she was solid.

"What is it, Dr. Sayer? What's out there?"

It was such a simple question, really, and yet the answer was so achingly complicated.

"A demon." She answered. "But not like what we've fought before. She gets into your head when you're out here. Turns the world upside down. Makes everything seem real and imaginary all at the same time. And then you get punched in the face by, oh, I don't know, a giant spider or something."

The ground shook again and the folklorist turned around and about, trying to get a sense of where the creature was.

"I don't see anything." Was Elizabeth Pennybaker's reply.

"Yeah, she does that. She's going to come at us with something nightmarish first. Something she can craft and draw from our fears."

The younger Waysmith nodded but didn't answer. There were any number of doubts and horrors she harbored that she definitely was in no mood to see physically personified. She was a little amused by the giant spider comment, though. Apparently, Somerset Sayer had a particularly unique distaste for arachnids. Maybe she was even phobic. What things the Stumble could do with that.

Rocks tumbled down from an escarpment and the Waysmith called them to ready. But what came to them first was a voice.

"So good of you to come, Somer." It rasped. "Too afraid to be separated, so you come here to see to it that your separation will, at last, be permanent."

The Waysmith remained silent for the rules of their engagement to be read.

"Look at them." The creature continued. "Tired. Weak. Spent. They have nothing left to give you. You've taken it all and now they're going to die."

The folklorist bristled. She knew that what the darkness was whispering to her was a lie, but it didn't mean that the words didn't sting. She knew she feared isolation and she knew she feared the loneliness that followed almost as much as she feared being manipulated by anyone she dared to trust.

But she hadn't ever faced the nagging part of herself that also believed that she asked too much of others and gave too little, that her presence was too much of a burden, and that most others found her to be barely tolerable and would prefer to gather without her. What had stayed her in that regard, however, was that she knew almost everyone shared the same fear.

"Come out and fight, demon!" The Waysmith called out to the maelstrom. "You'll need to wield more than just toxic words if you want to face me. I can do that well enough on my own."

More rocks shifted and collapsed. More of the ground shook, rattling the broken tracks. Whatever it was, it was moving towards them and it was big. Shadows flitted about and Somerset Sayer glanced back to check on the others. Fiona had remained seated on the table stone with Madam Bel Carmen leaning onto her for support but with eyes resolute. Alice Guthrie stood close. She clearly intended to fight, even if it took the last of her strength. But the Waysmith vowed to make sure that it didn't. Elizabeth Pennybaker gasped.

Finally, they saw it. A leviathan rather than a spider-thing, swimming through the air on arms and tentacles of ink-and-water smoke. It nearly blacked out the sky, floating across the barren expanse with one great eye turned to see them all. One-part Kraken and one-part devil crustacean, it came through the clouded murk with dripping mouth agape and rows upon rows of grasping teeth. Even worse, its body seemed only partially tangible, mutating in and out of material existence like a squid pulsing with camouflaging colors. But instead of iridescent reds, blues, and greens, it was an oscillation of flesh, slime, and ether.

Somerset Sayer immediately dropped into a defensive stance and called upon a bit of balladry to set her mind at the ready. It wasn't that she had a tremendous amount of experience with this particular sort of thing, but she knew that the Stumble worked on similar laws to that of the rest of the Way By. And if monstrous horror was the Withersmith's opening salvo, then so be it. What she couldn't possibly know however, was how their battle here simultaneously mirrored another elsewhere, not always rhyming in words but in actions.

Fiona heaved a pained breath and carefully stood up, sliding her curiously small wooden dagger back into her hand; as though she obviously intended to fight a monster with a toy sword in the manner of a quaint storybook illustration. Elizabeth Pennybaker actually smiled as she raised it. Today, she thought, bravery wore the face of one who had already despaired but who was still willing to beat back the darkness with a stick.

The leviathan bore down on them, whipping and lashing from above. None of the strikes were serious, however, and the Huntresses of the King were easily able to dodge the higher blows while still protecting each other from the more grounded ones. The demon was testing them. It knew the more inexperienced members weren't as adept and seemed to be gauging just how good the folklorist was going to be at shielding them from harm while still trying to fight offensively. The Waysmith's skills were certainly impressive, it noted, but it was a stretch even for someone so practiced.

A shadow flogged the ground, becoming tangible just long enough to batter the combatants into a momentary retreat. Fiona actually countered, sliding the flat of her blade between the two halves of an immaterial tentacle with enough patience that the beast was forced to take the wound if it wanted to also take form and hit her in return. This was how they all traded blows for several minutes. Each time the demon would charge them, a Huntress would thrust an arm or a weapon into the shapeless morass, keeping it steadied until the creature had no choice but to pull the blow or be cut in its own attack.

Some it took, some it retreated from. Both Somerset Sayer and Elizabeth Pennybaker knew, however, that they wouldn't be able to keep up this strategy for long. The demon would simply outlast them if they did. And that is precisely what it intended to do. Demons of Fear and Despair didn't generally make a habit of engaging in open warfare. Rather, it was their tactic to pick away at their prey piecemeal, until there was nothing left of them to fight. It pressed down, like a heavy, constricting, weight all around, suffocating, and murmuring spiteful words of worthlessness, meaninglessness, and pain.

This monstrosity that floated in the air was the embodiment of all of those terrible things. It would strike at them; flay them and thrash at them but it would never really face them. It would besiege their minds, lap at their thoughts, and feed on their love for one another until none existed. It wasn't in a hurry about it, either. It would happily keep this up for years if they lasted that long; growing ever stronger as it devoured them. Just as the Waysmith had said when they arrived. In the end, it meant that there would be no heroic battles here or glorious triumphant returns with swords and streamers held aloft.

That simply wasn't how such beings were ever defeated. But fear, despair, and hate were something that each woman knew in her own way and these facets were the weapons they readied. As the creature drew back to consider them again, they regrouped.

Elizabeth Pennybaker bolstered her position and shouted to the elder Waysmith.

"We can't keep this up forever. There has to be a better way. Can we reach some kind of bodily mass and discorporate it?"

Somerset Sayer nodded, her mouth set in a line as she came to a decision.

"A brilliant idea." The folklorist answered. "One I think I should have gone with from the start. And maybe I would have if I were a better person. Unfortunately, I believe this means that this is the point where I must leave you to take care of things for a bit. So, perhaps you'll excuse me and step aside. I need to have it out with a murdering ghost."

"What are you on about?" Elizabeth Pennybaker hissed, watching the leviathan carefully as it began to move back into striking position.

"Something I wish I had done a long time ago. Don't worry about me, Elizabeth. I'll see you on the other side."

The younger Waysmith looked worriedly over at the demon. "What? Where do you think you're going? You're not serious about leaving us out here!"

From beneath the folds and lining of her impossible train-coat, Elizabeth Pennybaker observed as the Waysmith produced a strange trinket on a cheap necklace chain. The ornament, a plastic unicorn's head with a stained white face, blue resin hair, and a broken yellow horn, was so old it could barely keep its shape and looked as if it had been kept at the bottom of her pocket for going on twenty-five years. Without hesitation, she pressed the child's jewelry into the younger woman's palm.

"This was mine, all the way back at the beginning. It's how she found me. The first time I crossed that threshold and saw that shard of light. This is how you will find her, Elizabeth. Through the memory that's kept in here. This is how you're also going to find me in return when the Stumble takes me."

Elizabeth Pennybaker blanched, growing frantic. "No, no, no, no. Don't do this to me, Somerset. Please don't do this! I'm not ready yet!"

"I know." She replied gently. "But this is the only way. Mary Elizabeth Toft is nothing if not a memory of outrage and a demand for revenge. She is wielding a truth against me that I have to face. It's not something you or anyone else can do for me. Hold this tightly, keep your wits about you, get to the Hill, and then come find me."

"The Hill? What Hill? What's there?!"

"The unicorn's grave, Elizabeth. The last parts of her that remain. That's where you're going. Don't stop. Not for anything. I've told you the same things in as many different ways as I know. You have what you need. Now you just have to take the memory and make it yours. The first lesson, Elizabeth. It's the hardest one."

Leaving the stupefied woman with the pendant dangling from her hand, the Waysmith turned and leapt up onto a spire of rock, the sickly greenish sky against her back and the tempest of hate bearing down on her. With a cry, she spit her riddle to taunt oblivion.

Summer dons a holy crown, as flowers in her hair.
Even when they're picked and bowed, there is merit in their care.

Winter waits but cannot last, nor change the child to crone.
It is only when the black beast comes, she believes she is alone.

But with each breath it comes again, she cannot fear its claw.
Her ancient head is not abed, and the dreaming must withdraw.

The crown she wears belongs to all; and all who keep it reign.
Their souls defy and are abandoned by a narrow life of pain.

She held both hands out at her sides, clicking her fingers together as ashes wafted up into the air. Her form soon became indistinct; wavering and haunting, almost like a ghost herself. Shimmering lines of white bled into one another until the Waysmith had nearly ceased to be and the gathered women could only see a specter of her. The demon leviathan shrieked merrily into the void and lashed out at her; drawn by the sudden influx of energy and the challenge shouted at the world.

"SOMERSET!"

For a second, Elizabeth Pennybaker saw the scholar turn back.

"It's time, my friend. You know the Way and the Way By knows you. Go."

The mouth of the creature opened wide and it dove; a stygian monstrosity plunging down through the clouds to swallow her whole. It was not despair that came but chaos that descended. A white, hot, explosion of light and power that burned like an inferno at the center of a star. The assembled Huntresses were blinded almost immediately.

Rocks and debris rained down onto their faces. Everything was burning; it seemed like the entire expanse of the sky overhead was wailing in anguish. Black tar splattered everywhere, bubbling, hissing, and boiling onto the stone. Elizabeth Pennybaker meant to leap backwards to shelter with the others, unable to see anything or hear anything beyond the din of weeping voices and enraged howling. But she slipped and then, the necklace chain wrapped around her wrist and she was falling.

Falling. Into the silent, endless abyss.

Quiet, like sleep. Cold, like death. But filled with overwhelming sadness.

And then bright! A sliver of light splitting the grief.

Stretching out before her, a vision leaked out of the trite child's necklace she grasped onto for dear life. She saw a cobblestone path in a moor. Winding, almost completely obscured by overgrowth, towards the gnarled morass of a tree blasted white by winds and far too much time. A tree that was older than cities but had not grown in just as long. It sat at the foot of a makeshift stone wall of roots and boulders.

And there, wedged into the roots, an exposed skull, equine and delicate, balanced into the spaces where two granite lodestones were split apart by the taproot. The mosses had overtaken the bridge of the nose and the curve of the empty sockets, and rocks now served to hold the rest of the skeleton in the suspended semblance of motion.

But at its forehead, the jagged splinters of horn still attached to the center of the skull were already animate; shifting and chattering together as they seemed to anxiously and angrily give testimony to their violation. An insult, an alicorn, lay in crackled glittering pieces shattered on the rocks below.

Somerset Sayer was sitting on her bed. In her childhood home. In a painted pink room with fairy posters and clipped cartoons tacked to the walls. A bookshelf, filled with worn-out paperbacks, slumped in the corner where the sounds of anger knocked at the walls; flicking clumps of horse-hair plaster onto the carpet. Ugly words, screamed back and forth, brought the memory into focus. She leapt to her feet, nearly tumbling over as she caught her toe on a hideous, imitation fur rug she had insisted on keeping as a child. It had been her "Yeti skin" despite serving no other purpose than catching lint and looking like roadkill.

The folklorist huffed bitterly. She had no illusions that this was still the Stumble but she wasn't about to lose her wits to something as banal as a change of scenery. And while she didn't lament being momentarily out of reach of the aerial demon, it would be too easy to get lost in the labyrinth of dreaming that Mary Elizabeth Toft deigned to make for her. Again. She knew all too well the danger they were all still in, but this was the only way to ensure Elizabeth's unbarred path to the Hill. The Way By may have quite a few tricks yet to try, but this memory was hers. And hers alone.

Sharp voices from downstairs roused her from her distraction but as she stepped out into the hallway, a curious fog began to fill the rooms. Grey and heavy, almost like smoke, but it smelled of sea water and salt. The sense of foreboding was palpable and the Waysmith figured it best if she didn't tarry overlong.

The Stumble was already attempting to entrap her again of its own accord, its insidious designs woven into this image by none other than an old and talented Withersmith with a long history of deadly hauntings. She looked around the bedroom doorways and herself. She had retained her coat and immediate garments but had nothing else to recommend her. Nor could she see anything immediately useful around her.

'Fine. If that's what you want.' She thought. 'I can do this the hard way.'

Somerset Sayer noticed only in passing, but she was aware that she now had a rather surprising sort of clarity. The vagaries of the Stumble felt like they were retreating and she didn't have to fight the influence of the memories and emotions that came unbidden into her mind quite as intentionally. When she had first learned of the Way By, she had been completely at the mercy of the dream; unaware of her own sense of self and unable to discern fantasy from reality. Much like Fiona, who had been intent on burying herself in her own grave, she had been despairing long before her thoughts were made manifest.

The Waysmith set out from the comforts of her bedroom and into the mire outside her door. Still heavier banks of fog rolled in and she could feel the cold, damp mist settling into her clothes and skin with the kind of chill she generally associated with the coast. She stopped. Is that where this was? Why did she feel as though she were arriving on the banks of Lilylit once more? The Way By shuddered and seemed to fold in on itself.

"I'm...I'm sorry..." She heard her mother's voice repeating the words this time. It sounded so bleak. So heart-broken.

She trudged forward, almost batting at the greyness in an attempt to clear enough of a path that she could see where the sound was coming from. The roar of the living room fireplace had already given way to the roar of the ocean far in the distance. Then, an unpleasant squelch beneath the heel of her boot forced her to pause. She looked down but it was just more of nothing.

With a few tentative steps, Somerset Sayer tested the ground ahead of her. More slick squelching and something crunchy. She felt, with a toe, along a hard beam or rod a few inches away, and then something like curved, parallel bars. The Waysmith recoiled slightly. Ribs. She was walking on corpses. But she couldn't see them, only feel them. The Stumble certainly did not disappoint when it came to the macabre. But it was more than just gratuitous horror this time. She grit her teeth. This is what the Stumble was made of.

"I didn't mean to..." Her mother's voice again.

Layer upon layer, the memory and the Stumble bled together. This was her last real memory of her parents before the fateful night when they both had died. One by the hand of the other, the latter by the hand of a monster; hellion against fiend until the entire structure of her life had collapsed. They'd just been battling a demon of Fear and Despair, a form taken by a vengeful spirit; so it almost made perfect sense that Mary Elizabeth Toft would choose to show her this. But the worst part, as Somerset Sayer well knew, was that she had no idea how long the others would be missing her. For the Waysmith, they'd been parted for mere minutes, but the Stumble played with time in frustrating ways. From the others' perspectives, she might be gone for days, even weeks. All that stood between her and escape now was a little trinket in the hands of a reluctant coed.

"If you weren't so stupid, we wouldn't have this problem..."

"I'm sorry! It was an accident! You know I would never..."

"And you're making that girl just as bad. She has a mouth on her..."

"Don't talk about your daughter that way!"

"If you don't shut up..."

There it was. That voice. That malevolent, wet, gravelly voice that felt like the vocal equivalent of cold sand and mushy paper. It was her father's voice. A man whose story was too much like that of the tales the Summer King had told her of Clarisant. How comfort and protection had been promised before the dream of freedom had vanished before her eyes and all that had replaced it was cynicism. She had felt such pity for the unicorn in those days, before the worst of it had come.

She continued forward, but slowly and with as much care as she could manage. Instead of a hazy, smoldering reminiscence of a Great Old One filling the air, she had to contend with a choking fog. Instead of knifelike stones cutting at her hands and feet as she struggled to walk, she had to deal with the cracked bones and shattered skulls of generations of the unnamed and the forgotten that had filled this place for years. But she was definitely getting closer; two figures were just now beginning to take shape up ahead. One, a tall, imposing silhouette and the second, kneeling on the ground staring at her hands.

"You know," Her father was saying. "I would have thought you'd have gotten the hint by now. No one can stand you. Why do you think no one talks to you anymore? You're not really of much use when you're like this. Maybe you'll finally start listening better."

"Yes." Her mother answered, her voice subdued and morose.

"Then get up. I'm tired of the whining."

Somerset Sayer tapped her resolve. There was something she had wanted to do since the very beginning and this being the Stumble, it was as good a time as any to do it.

Without preamble she bull-rushed the overbearing figure; taking off at a run and then utterly, unceremoniously, slamming into the man with the full weight of her momentum. In any other circumstance, it might almost have been comical. But as it was, both of them went down in a heap, crashing into a pile of bones and gore with an unsettling racket. The folklorist ended up on top, as she had planned, pinning the form of her own father to the ground by straddling his midsection. She reeled back and then punched that sneering face once and then twice more until she got the satisfying crack of teeth. In the real world, she'd only been a child when her parents had died, but here, she could finally take out her anger on at least one of the monsters in her life.

With a yell, both Waysmith and apparition began to struggle, but Somerset Sayer wasn't about to let this go down without as much blood and injury as she could inflict. Her father continued to bite and flail at her but the memory, the form, wasn't strong. With a satisfied grin, the folklorist wrapped both hands around the man's throat and began to squeeze as hard as she could. She would strangle the life out of this nightmare with her bare hands if it took every ounce of force she had left.

"Somer!" It shrieked. "You can't! Please!"

It was at that moment that the Waysmith had a terrible thought. Trapped in the hallucination, manacled by the feelings and recollections of one of the most painful moments in her life, why was the face of this terror still obscured? She knew the countenance of the man who had destroyed her life and that of her family with inescapable clarity, so why hide it in cloud and haze when the full-on likeness would be so much more infuriating? For what reason would the Withersmith make this man faceless?

He thrashed and struggled. "It's a lie! It's all a lie!"

Somerset Sayer slammed her palm directly into the side of the blanked face and tore the caul from its features; a mask it seemed, fashioned from an ideal rage that made it only somewhat like the face of her father. But beneath it, another form. There was *someone* laying there for certain, but it was not her father.

Beloved, but not a man.

Avenant.

Chapter Nineteen

How many times had she returned to this place? It was impossible to tell. There was no present or future. Only the past, echoing back again and again.

The house on Trowbridge Street didn't exist.

There was no *Lostwith Notes*.

The Flidais Venatica had never been.

She was home. In the prison generations before her had built. Right where she belonged.

'It is because most people never go there.' She had once written of the Stumble. 'Which does not mean that they don't suffer or that they don't know pain or sorrow, but this is the place that makes agony real. It's the place where nothing ever leaves. It solidifies it in your memory, it makes it a part of your story, a part of who you are. Once that happens, there's no escaping it.'

But that it was Avenant who struggled beneath her bespoke of a hellish sensibility to the Stumble's designs.

Despite the common presumption, she had never thought of the Summer King as a paternal replacement. Her father had only ever been a figure of briers and rage with thorns embedded in his heart and growing entwined throughout every attached organ; where Avenant wore his thorns solely on his skin. And despite the blood of his sovereignty, he'd never allowed them to reach beyond the superficial. Psychoanalysis had long told her that these two men must be the same; archetypes of childhood terror and separation where one had simply replaced the other by guilt of association. But the revelation of a Waysmith's reading revealed that this was not the truth.

Still his visage spoke. "Is this what I am to you then? Is this what you've always desired?"

Somerset Sayer pulled on the remnants of another memory. The pointed words began to fade and the pain of rejection diffused. Her body relaxed and her fear liquified as it was wicked away by a flashback. She was in the Kingdom of Lilylit, in the far rooms of the King's chambers on a treetop cataract not many years ago. The hearth was burning brightly and the room was warm and quiet. She buried her face into the rumpled sheets and took a deep breath of the scent of sandalwood and pine smoke. It was the perfect smell, native to cotton, and it always reminded her of comfortable nights in his arms; laid against his chest and snuggled into his neck as he tickled at the scars near her collar bone. Listening to her lover's slow, deep breaths as he slept. The soft fabric ghosted over her cheek and across the ridge of his ear as he turned his head and smiled. A familiar chuckle drifted over her as wide, warm hands kneaded into her lower back.

This was a memory the Withersmith did not possess. No one did. As it had never been confessed and thus never been given true shape.

The figure below her shifted. No more cockled skin or twisted shoulders but stronger features; a lean, elegant, sinuous body curved at the middle to arc away from her. She did not give in to the suggestion however and instead, held the worthier image in complete concentration. It was Avenant who had relented at her approach but she had known he would. The king was leaving in the morning, though he would not say where. And yet, there were many roads to Perdition. What would his liege or his subjects say of their company? She never knew.

Most Fae viewed the breadth of humanity rather poorly and as those who simply did not know the implications of their actions. Or worse, humans merely abused the noblest institutions of intellect by trying to peer into the mysteries of existence through the knot-holes they'd managed to secure for themselves as a child secures a hole in the fence for a popgun. Some thought them interesting, certainly, but only to the point that an immortal could temporarily lodge with one and not live among them.

In the end, the Fae had all sorts of metaphors by which they described their relationships to humanity: as sovereign to subject, noble to peasant, and master to pet but certainly not as friend or comrade. And never as a lover. At least, until him. The Waysmith threw herself against the chains of her own perception; the bonds of trauma that imprisoned her and allowed the Withersmith to twist her experience. She tensed and snarled a vulgar oath. This world, this vision, belonged to *her*e and she would no more allow this demon to claim it, to steal what little was precious, than she would allow her life to be claimed again by cruelty.

And then, insight. A storyteller cannot help but be included in the stories they tell. Teller and tale are, in the end, the same thing.

The folklorist's calloused hands wrenched the simulacrum upwards, forcing him into a sitting position with ungainly imprecision. She had already regained her foothold on rationality and instead of railing against the agony and the confusion of his presence here, she denied them. She denied everything about them. Her past and her present were not the same. And she would split them apart if it took her last breath. Because this memory held no pain, no terror... no Despair...the demon had nothing to cling to. But she did.

"You are not him." She spat in its face. "You cannot possibly be him. Veil yourself in whatever cloaks you can find, Mary Elizabeth Toft. Whatever false faces you can conjure. The story reveals you."

Her transformation came in a flash; without preamble or contortion. The Withersmith's proclivities for deception had come upon her early in life, of course, but even the most entrenched preferences must eventually change their key now and then, on penalty of monotony or getting out of tune. The Waysmith blinked. The ghostly form that appeared before her seemed to reflect a trick of complementary colors.

Wherein the prolonged exposure to any one hue on a person's vision might result in the appearance of the opposing shade: that staring too long at a *blue* object would be a *yellow* image. But then as her eyes sharpened, the figure could manage little more than an ethereally white outline that had the effect of being complementary only to itself, and the folklorist was quite pleased with the way she remained exactly as she was whether the Waysmith had her eyes open or closed. Her mind could now see her enemy in no other way than this one.

"The Stumble is never going to let you leave, Somerset Sayer." That stereophonic voice intoned. "Not you. Not any of them. Not ever."

"The Stumble lies." The folklorist rejoined. "To you and through you. But do you want to know how I know that, Mary? Do you want to know how I learned that I had the power to control it? It was the day my grandmother told me that my nightmares were mine."

She fed the spirit with her thoughts, with the brilliant sounds and words of a child's remembrance. Of a night when she had been awoken by terrifying and bizarre dreams of abandonment, falling, and torment, as was common for her in those days. A night she had only happened to be spending with the one person in her life who had always stood between her and the brutality hidden behind plaster walls and domestic bliss. Her grandmother, who had sat down at the side of the trundle bed, late in the night, as she sobbed and had asked her about the nightmares.

Had asked her if she could still remember the story that was in her mind. When she did, spilling out the words as only small children can, her grandmother had then reminded her that just because she was now awake, didn't mean that the story had ended. Rather, it only meant that they could finish it together. And so, they did; taking all the elements of the dream and telling one another what was going to happen next. And next again after that. Until the night terror was played out and its tale was done. A tale which, in the end, didn't seem quite as bad anymore. Perhaps frightening at first, but one that gave way to pride. This, she gave back to the Withersmith. Sitting down now at her side to finish this nightmare.

"There was once a Waysmith who could speak with animals." She began. "But she never used words as such; at least not in the way that books like to tell it now. Rather, she would sing to them. Using the notes of her well-practiced scales to endear them in their own language. Like birds, who utter no syllables and communicate only in the relationship between melodies. But when industry came, her songs were drowned out by the screeching of railway bars and geared wheels. Great, big machines that blacked out the bird-skies with smoke and made it impossible to hear the whispers of the green world. The Way By was broken then, wasn't it? She found you in its fractures?"

A wail shook her. Splinters of their thoughts burst outwards in every direction as Somerset Sayer felt herself knocked backwards and to the ground. But she didn't stay there long. A second, infuriated, sound roused her and she cracked her eyelids to peer over at what had made it. It was Avenant. Or...it was the thing that was clearly attempting to wear his face again.

"Wherein we encounter such monsters inclined more to simply cut out and devour a man's heart than discuss the exegesis of Scripture," The folklorist read the Withersmith's own words back to her. *"Should we chance to meet the fiends whose evil is so cleverly masked by pious declarations of virtue, we cannot but see the hands of the duplicitous Faire at work.* Your work, Mary Toft! The very work that carried your story forward. That inspired a young girl hiding in her local town library so that she didn't have to go home! Too old to join the preschool story hour and too well read for the elementary sections. You were the Virgil who led me out of Purgatory. My story is yours continued!"

The gnarled ghost crouched in the corner of a charred but unremarkable room. It glared at her, wheezing and spitting, its face morphing and contorting into all manner of reminiscent shapes. Her father. Her king. Her friends. Everything and everyone that had fettered her life. But its form had clearly become unstable and the creature, the specter, could no longer hold a single shape. Despair didn't know what it was anymore.

"And now," the folklorist said. "I see that it's time for another storyteller to help me finish. Just as I will help you."

With deliberate intent, Somerset Sayer rose to her feet. She was herself again. Whole and armored; the Way By blazing to life in her anger. The demon cowered in its malevolent light, skittering backwards as a warrior's furious silhouette closed in on it.

"Sleep." The Waysmith growled. "It is time for you to sleep. You've confessed all you need to. Justified all that was necessary. Now, the dream takes you. We will carry you, your myth, from now on. Your names become our names. Until we pass it to the next one."

The blow landed devastatingly hard, tearing a ragged sob from the decaying form. Cracks of light shredded the creature, piercing through its façade with refracted power. Rags of shadow began to fall away from the prone body and just as they did, the voice also drained out of it as dribbles of ichor. But it had one last thing to say.

"I didn't choose him." It hissed. "She did. It was not as I saw him, but as she does. The Queen goes now to conceive of his destruction. And the end of her succession. She goes now, to sit at his side, and bring it all to ruin."

These words were her last and Mary Elizabeth Toft finally discorporated; her consciousness abandoning the Stumble while rolling, lingering threads of her memory seeped back into the Way By. Until, at last, oblivion rose up to drain the last few fleeting attachments away. In seconds, Despair was nothing but ashes.

Somerset Sayer furrowed her brow. The ghost was no more and everything around her had gone eerily quiet. She was standing alone in the ruin of a burned down house. The remaining support struts that still stood looked like ribs jutted up into a fiery sky with the rest of the architectural skeleton scattered through piles of dust and refuse.

A fallen chimney for a spine; floorboards for decomposing fingers. Desolate windows for teeth and nails. For a brief moment, the Waysmith started to think that this might be some kind of metaphorical embodiment of what was left of her life. Sometimes it seemed that all she had in her wake was soot and cinders. But then she realized that the structure, or what remained of it, still looked familiar.

Lilylit. Destroyed.

She stepped forward, wary, and stared at the debris. The choice, she reasoned, for the Withersmith to have crafted such a place before her demise was not as evident as one might suspect. It might be read, most obviously, as a lie. A threat: that this would be the inevitable future and that all would come to naught. But the pain growing in her heart at Mary Elizabeth Toft's parting words told her that, for once, the Stumble spoke the truth. She had seen Avenant in this place, not because he was a weapon against her, but because he was reaching out to her. And he was saying goodbye.

The Summer King was dying.

The elder Waysmith clenched her hands tightly and prepared the words that would braid the Way into hold-fast tethers. This was Hell, but in Hell, no one is forsaken. She was meant to feel alone, but she didn't. His mind was strained to breaking; she could hear him in the depths of torment and in his anguish, he had called out. And she would not abandon him. She would not abandon any of them.

"Hold on, everyone." She said. "I'm coming."

The Way By continued to flow through the folklorist's necklace but what Elizabeth Pennybaker saw was hers alone. She raced along a forgotten path; through a backwoods boscage that could have been the garden behind her house, which was also the hills and valleys of the Dandakaranya and the Khandavaprastha in her mother's favorite Hindu books, and the wooded and overgrown church playground lots she had been abandoned in as a rebellious Sunday School child.

They were the back alleys of an Indian village she had never been to, filled with roadside shrines she had only ever imagined visiting. She ran her fingers along the nubbled protrusions of plaster worn off by swipes of red kumkum and yellow turmeric and heard the clay Krishna deity say that he was so very happy to see her again and how much he had missed her. The palanquins of Durga and the Buddha were piled high with flower petals that floated down to become shreds of plastic and brightly dyed litter as they tumbled off of the edges and onto the pavement.

The colors were then washed away by pure waterfalls down into sewer drains where they were mixed into uniform brown mud. But the filth had only been made filth by the people who dug it out; uprooted from its home in the meadows to be thrown as unwanted dirt into the streets. She passed graffiti on every wall in moss and mushrooms and votive candle wax. Soda cans and cigarette filters were the confetti that celebrated her return to the swing sets and spring-horses as she cut ravines through the sandbox with broken toys and built castles from toilet paper tubes.

She could see it all. Every connection in her mind alighted in one long, continuous string of wrapped and woven threads that formed the edge of a greater tapestry; entwining themselves together as she went, just as vines overgrow a forsaken loom and roots split through the seams. The paths of her life converged and divided, trees became libraries became palaces on clouds that were mists in an ocean on a shore that wrote out the words of change and transformation on a beach erased by tides that predictably come again at the same time every day. The day she turned away from story books to take up math and medicine, only to find that they said the same things in different ways.

When she learned that the body was not like a palimpsest to be scraped clean but rather a life history inked on stolen pages of time, that revealed its knowledge in the languages of pain, pleasure, joy, and dread. Every choice she had ever made became loops of cotton and sinew knit together and spun around a drop-spindle ever spiraling upwards and away to treetops that were the crowns of royalty bestowed by the sun; one who lent its golden light for just long enough to set a maze of rivers in motion and not a minute more.

Her soul rode through canyons trailing a knightly coat of arms that could summon every creature supine, sinister, and ascendant. And everywhere within and without, there were those who had taken her as far as they could. Mother, father, friend, teacher, sibling, ally, adversary, uncle, aunt, grands and greats. Names bestowed more names which linked together with other names until the kinship of the world was revealed. And through those ties she saw it. The threads of the Way were spun.

Elizabeth Pennybaker was humbled by the vastness of the Way By's unseen but unyielding power. How it could transform anything given the right word and the right direction. She gasped at a sudden revelation: given the right Name. Stolen names could corrupt, dead names could destroy, but names given as gifts or earned in tribulation could change the course of life itself. So too the nameless could be forgotten or made to have never existed at all. A name was form turned into meaning at the very beginning. It was the last remnant left in memories at the end; with an entire life lived out in the spaces between letters and sounds. But no name existed by chance or alone, rather in relation to everything around it, before it, and after it.

She watched as the Way By poured through every one of them shimmering into existence; just as water poured through the starred holes of her vision's cloak of night. They did not define the light any more than a lantern could be said to contain it; only making it momentarily visible to others. She felt then that so much of what she could now understand was coming to her through the new name Somerset Sayer had bestowed upon her: Waysmith. The old name, Elizabeth Pennybaker, had so often felt as if it didn't belong to her and it was silent now. The secret other name she did not yet have the courage to call herself was also still unspoken.

Away she saw it all turn, around and around on itself, into a great spire disappearing into a vanishing point on the furthest reaches of a low horizon. Like a single horn, wide at the beginning and stretching on into an unseen end. She smiled as the vision of it dropped down and lengthened. The horn ceased then to be just a horn and transformed in her eyes to become the road before her in the Way ahead. At last, she saw the alicorn for all that it was, all that Somerset Sayer had been trying to tell her it could be on the first day a new Waysmith dared to cross the threshold. It was the point of view of one who happened to be standing at the beginning of everything. It was the name, the form, and the path, and they all were on it.

Noseworthy yowled suddenly out of nowhere, popping up out of a makeshift tunnel in a pile of debris. The Waysmith whirled around to face the gathered women but spoke, initially, to her cat.

"We're almost there!" She exclaimed breathlessly. "I know where it is! Nosey! Alice, Fiona, Evelyn, I know *what* it is!"

Madam Bel Carmen huffed a concerned noise as she pulled up to a halt. The Stumble had not forgotten their presence and already the anemic sky threatened to fall around them as a glass bowl shatters on the creatures inside of it. Embers tumbled from the crackling trunks of eternally burning oaks, sending small deluges of ashes and torrents of bones clattering towards their feet.

"Well, how do we get there then?" The Vodoun asked. "I don't think we have a lot of time here, lovely. Something seems to be taking this place apart."

Elizabeth Pennybaker turned with an unnerving grin. "I've seen my own Way on. Now, tell me how you got here."

Alice Guthrie was nonplussed. In a moment, the young woman both looked and sounded almost exactly like the folklorist. And about as nonsensical.

"What?" She replied.

"What led you to where you are now?" The younger Waysmith shook her head at the resulting expressions of her companions. "No, no, I don't mean this, the Stumble. What was it that made you curious? What started you on the Way By? Where was the beginning? Because that's how we get to the end. We begin. We Name ourselves."

Alice Guthrie was the most unsure. "Name ourselves? Isn't that what the Summer King already did? Name us Huntresses to make this all possible?"

Elizabeth Pennybaker couldn't help but marvel at the rapidly shifting world around her and it made for more than a little distraction. There was so much she could see and so little she could describe, but she knew without question that the others could not make sense of their surroundings as she was starting to. They did not know their place in it yet; but only because they had not made one.

"He named *us, yes.*" She finally replied. "All of us together. However, that is only our Way forward as we are together. But I don't yet know who each of you are, what *your* Way is. I need you to Name it so that we can weave our strands together. The alicorn is what we find because it is what we become! Therefore, who are you in this place? Who are you...to me?"

She still seemed irrational but to each of the Flidais Venatica it was all becoming rather this side of normal. Fiona Guthrie, however, puffed up her chest, as though she had been waiting for just such an opportunity. She was the quickest to understand the absurdity and the jumbles of folly that seemed so characteristic of the Waysmiths. It was the perfect absent-minded logic: there was no need to search for a beginning when one was already present. Or that the answer to their current confusion would be to tame the chaos within the rigid boundaries of names and build out from there. With special glee at the elder women's surprise, she loudly announced herself.

"Night Light!" She nearly squealed. A most inappropriate kind of enthusiasm for the situation, it would seem, but Fiona Guthrie was newly undaunted after her ordeal and continued her explanation with remarkable poise even as the others turned in surprise. "You know, like Hat Trick and Coat Check? For me, it was a Night Light. That's what I secretly called my teddy bear when I was a kid. If I had a nightmare, I would wake up and still be able to see him no matter how dark it was. So, he was my protector. I would imagine him taking up his sword and chasing the monsters away while everyone else was asleep! And then having all kinds of adventures with my brother's toys. And with the Chirurgeon and everything, it continues to be true. It just started to make more sense the longer we were out here. Night Light! Always there for the lonely and alone, the light left on underneath the door for the frightened, and slayer of closet dragons. Also, great at tea parties but hey, I was six, okay? Anyway, that's how I got here. I know that's me."

Elizabeth Pennybaker laughed out loud and hugged the girl as hard as she could. "You've really been thinking about this, haven't you?" She giggled.

"Well, yeah." Fiona Guthrie blinked. "Ever since the king said that we were his vanguard. I mean, haven't you all? He named us knights. Knights are supposed to have fun names, you know."

The Waysmith shook her head. "Night Light. It's perfect. Madam Bel Carmen?"

"I...well." She stammered in response. "I certainly don't think anything quite so colorful as that."

"Whatever it is." Elizabeth Pennybaker confided. "It's exactly as it should be. I mean, look at me. My answer to the question of how I got here is 'attacked by a bird with a cocktail sword and saved by a cat.' Imagine how I'm going to make that sound later on!"

Noseworthy purred loudly in approval.

Madam Bel Carmen chuckled. "Yes, I suppose so. Well then, let's see. If I am to follow Fiona's example, then I should say that I am Evelyn. Whom others named Chanton-Pennybaker, yes? But as I call her, Bel Carmen. Song Master. An old name for story-keepers. I think it all started when I didn't have anywhere to go but up. I needed to make my own way in life since all the other ways I was told to take...well." She paused to recover herself. "I've carried too many names with me that I can never let go of. The living, the dead, the not-yet born, and the should-have-been. I've held them all. I still hold them. And it was they who showed me that I could stay behind or start again. Think of me as a kind of madam scribe then, if you will. A ruined archivist if there ever was one!"

"Song Master it is!" The Waysmith acknowledged with a sly smile, reaching out to grasp her aunt's hand and pull her in.

"It works!" She exclaimed to the amused eye roll that followed. "We have the Teddy Bear Knight-Errant, nurturing and abiding. Myself, a Waysmith so distracted with birdwatching that I have a cat for a helmsman! And you, the Song Master, to remember it all and recount it later. So! Ms. Alice? Have you considered how you'll be joining this ridiculous crew?"

Alice Guthrie nodded, but her face was downcast. "Yes, well, see... the thing is." She started. "I'm just not that interesting." {wnd-do not join}

Elizabeth Pennybaker scowled. The Stumble truly never relented. "Oh, I doubt that very much." She answered. "Look around you, Alice Guthrie. No one gets to where you are by dint of being boring, even if the road that led you here was a bland and scenic one."

"That's right!" Fiona Guthrie agreed. "Mom. You're a rock! An immovable, steadfast boulder in a tsunami. Yeah, sure, maybe it's not all crystals and gold but when everyone runs for shelter, let me tell you, they don't run underneath a pile of gemstones. They'd get washed away."

Madam Bel Carmen raised an eyebrow at the girl on her right. That had been remarkably poetic of her. "And furthermore!" She added. "It lasts beyond all other things. A true legacy, never forgotten."

Alice Guthrie smiled. "I suppose I never quite thought of it that way. I always just did what needed to be done."

"That's why," the Waysmith replied, "You're a cornerstone to all of this, Alice. The one from which anything can be made. They don't call some people pillars of the community for nothing, you know?"

"I guess that makes me a good old sod." She motioned around herself.

"More like the Megalith." Madam Bel Carmen supplied. "After all, wasn't it you who first saw Stonehenge on the horizon that morning? Who knows...maybe that had more to do with you than you know? I've often wondered since that day if Somerset Sayer intended for all of us to go there or just followed us there. Maybe you were in the lead all along?"

Alice Guthrie nodded. "Yes." She stated decisively. "I can be a Sarsen. For now, anyway. And it's fun to say. Well then. That's enough of that. Elizabeth? We know how it all started. We know who we are, for the moment I should say. Where do we go from here?"

But that was what Elizabeth Pennybaker had been trying to tell them. They were already there. On a Hill. Where everything had ended the day that everything had begun. But such a horrid place as this one defied explanation.

As a child, the younger Waysmith had once spent long summers walking in the fields behind her home. One particularly cloudless day, she had come upon a large, flat stone, which lay, half buried, in the center of the pasture with the grass forming a little hedge, as it were, all around it. She had then, in obedience to the kind of whims typical of childhood, pressed her foot under the highest rim and overturned it as easily as a mudcake. Blades of grass flattened down, colorless, matted together, as if bleached and ironed.

Frightening, crawling creatures scattering out of their hidden community; scarabaeus and pill-bugs, they had been called. Dermestids and millipedes, accompanying. Black, glossy crickets, with their long filaments sticking out like the bannerets on a battering ram and motionless, slug-like things.

Larva; perhaps even more horrifying to her in their fleshy stillness than if they had leapt out fully armored in chitinous plates. But no sooner was the stone turned and the wholesome light of day let upon the oppressed society than each and every member fled wildly in a panic to retreat from everywhere that was defiled by sunshine. She saw it all again now as if having returned to a place she was certain had long been plowed under. But she couldn't grasp its meaning, since she wasn't convinced it ever had one.

That stone was little more than some glacial forgetfulness dropped by a passing ice giant; the grass not crushed but merely misfortunate for having fallen there and attempting to grow where it was not wanted. The shapes which were found beneath were all the craftier things that sought out and thrived in darkness rather than anything made helpless by it.

Turning the stone was therefore the only real act of malice because the creatures that lived beneath it were not the kind to change in the manner of more sunlit mortals. None would ever find themselves sprouting gossamer wings by virtue of the stone having been lifted.

But it was on this Hill that Elizabeth Pennybaker perceived herself, not the child, but the worm. The Way By then rose up to answer her and began to remake their surroundings to meet the change in her awareness. To reach the top of the hill, she felt as though she must withdraw from the light and go aground to walk through the insect paths in the soil, now transformed into a cistern before them.

This bricked-up pit, built long ago of the same such cobbles as had been scattered as stepping stones throughout the back countryside of her youth, writhed into being up and around the gathered company. Water flowed past their feet and trickled down scarred walls to feed the mosses and algae that anchored there. Roots dangled from the arches, swaying in an unseen breeze.

The sounds of wind above and streams below made up the bellows that breathed stale air into the rock-lined throat of the tunnel that moved past them of its own accord, and with each exhalation, it murmured things that all children loathe to hear. That they do not belong.

The Waysmith shouted a warning for the Huntresses to stay close and stay together. And then, they were unceremoniously spat out. Or, at least, that's what it had felt like. The Hill upon which they all now stood was a desolate mound that held but a shallow central well covered with underbrush. Out of which whispered thoughts and feelings that permeated the very air around it.

How to describe a voice such as the one Elizabeth Pennybaker could feel resonating throughout her chest and echoing in the tympanics of her skull. How it reduced her utterly, from a woman to a nursling; her flashing grin to milk-teeth; her youthful strength to senescence a thousand leagues from sunset. It was St. Thomas trying to interpret the Leviathan and painting only a Hellmouth, into whose maw the damned must walk on the Last Judgment.

"I know you." The intonation made the very stones themselves lament and shudder; grinding like bones on their crumbled mortars. "I tasted your soul in the crypt of your mother's womb, your tears weeping into the ground all around the tomb that held you. Where I held you. Now, you come to me again. Bringing me your pain and your fear; all of the terrors in the night that remind you of the fact that your grandest accomplishments, and all that you are or ever will be, will go unnoticed. You are Unnamed. You are...empty. And if not, is it rather that now and forever the people of your imagined homelands will believe that your kith and kin are nothing more than vomited debris cast off from the spittle of detestable gods? Tell me, Elizabeth Pennybaker, does this frighten you or do you embrace it?"

The Flidais Venatica approached at the ready. The Waysmith grimaced and tried to focus. "Who are you?" She growled.

"What a benignly pompous question."

She shuddered. Such a rich, deep, sound that wasn't really sound at all but the vibrations of a carillon ringing only its largest and most sonorous bells. At the lead, she forced herself to press on, up the side of the thick tussocks that wrapped around her feet and threatened to pull her down, towards the top of the summit just meters away.

"Of course, you must think me very dull as well." It continued. "The theater is never what it promises to be, is it? Yes, it is pleasant to see real gentlemen and ladies who do not think it necessary to over-mouth, and rant, and stride, like most of our stage heroes, but wouldn't we rather see the characters show their good graces and talents than announce them from the limelight? So, you must forgive me in that it has been so long since I have seen a fresh, unrouged understudy such as yourself. With a lissome figure and an alluring voice; acting out a melodrama to make us all young again. Have you come to play for me, little one?"

Madam Bel Carmen muttered her own warnings to the assembled. She did not want to even begin speculating as to what the last part might be in reference to. Something here had been listening to them, watching them, and, dare she say, waiting on their inevitable arrival.

"You didn't answer my question." Elizabeth Pennybaker replied instead.

"True. I did not."

By all rights, however, it hardly needed to. The Stumble had shown them already and the obvious became plain enough when the rings of thorns around the mouth of the endless well began to thicken, grow, and twist themselves into rising tines.

"Oh, my God." The Waysmith exclaimed. "It's the..."

"Yes." Madam Bel Carmen finished.

"Oh no." Alice Guthrie breathed.

But then the Way By trembled around them; almost palpable in the sensations of drifting, floating, and then...falling. The well seemed to widen, a hole in the earth with no bottom, gaping and gulping; as if to swallow them all up in turn.

They were each unsure as to what exactly it was that they saw then. A figure, for certain. An anthropomorphic shape forming out of the shadows as it crawled upwards towards them. At first, it appeared to be a noble; a great cloak swirling around an obscured form as it became clearer against the black abyss. But it was with a gasp that the Waysmith realized that it was no velvet or wool that made the garment, but rather that the mantle worn was a cascade of blood!

It flowed downwards from its neck and shoulders, enveloping the indistinct silhouette and obscuring its true outline but it moved as fabric would: fastened and folded in every way as to be the recognizable guise of an aristocrat. And out from its head, a familiar bracken wreath that grew outwards from its skull; a rooted Bramble Crown that was all at once the rim of the well, the band and tines of a coronet, and the gaping jaws of a Hellmouth opening a wound at the creature's pate that seeped and wept.

The thing reached out as if to catch them. Claws; deadly coils of nightshade thorns curling out from knotted, oaken, hands. A mouth, ringed with sharpened teeth to receive them.

"Don't be afraid, little ones." It said, "What I would do to you... isn't half of what *he* will. I can give you peace..."

But the Grave of the Unicorn also now lay before them; bare and exposed on the hillside Stumble and out from which the rot, the ruin, and the blackened tendrils of sorrow and hopelessness had grown. They spread out all around the Huntresses of the King, as blue-black veins carrying infected blood just beneath the skin of the flowering earth. Draining it and killing it in a drought of misery. They were just like the roots of a downed tree, threading into the Wound in a desperate attempt to stanch the flow and stitch the ragged gash together again, but themselves diseased by the effort.

Carrying not healing but choking purulence and pus ever further outwards. And at the center of it all, a single rent skeleton folded in on itself, lying at the bottom of the shallow well. A ridge of thoracic vertebra sat atop a rounded ribcage, four long bones arranged lengthwise beneath it, with four split hooves in four squares at the center; as though she had only just lain down to rest with her legs bent beneath her and had never been able to get up again.

And then her skull. The long, flat, face of it turned upwards. Empty eye sockets filled with sparse grasses and lichens to limn them. Shattered teeth where she had been struck. And a devastating crack to the center of the forehead where splintered bits of horn and bone were all that was left of an alicorn that had once grown there. But it was here that the Waysmith and all of her attendant company noticed a most revealing thing. The horn that had once sat upon the Unicorn's head had not simply fragmented to scatter in the dirt, nor had it remained a single fallen piece.

Rather, it had, in the way that Elizabeth Pennybaker could best describe it, unraveled. Its entwined threads had unspiraled and unspooled to part like locks of hair as it fell. These golden-white braids had then lain over her body as it decayed into nothingness, and as her blood had fed the great thorn bush that now grew up from the center over her heart, through the spine and ribs, and up beneath the sodden head to form a crown like antlers made of thistle leaves, they had risen up with it. There they remained, woven throughout the barbed branches in glittering strands, as if cut by the Fates themselves, into the necessary life-lines of destiny.

"You three!" Elizabeth Pennybaker yelled to her compatriots. "Climb down! Cut the threads! Do you understand me? Gather them all up! Break the thorns with your bare hands if you have to. But you need to get them out of the Bramble! You need to free the alicorn!"

Madam Bel Carmen cast a glance between Waysmith and royal-looking shade; still looming in on them and emerging from the depths as a devouring void.

"Elizabeth!" Alice Guthrie called out. "Can you even fight that thing?"

The younger Waysmith rolled her shoulders and cracked her knuckles with an air of false morale.

"You know what? We're about to find out."

Chapter Twenty

Enemies can have many faces, but the Bramble Crown could wear any one it wanted. Fears and memories were its palette, and it could compose any portrait from what it found therein. But an enemy fully personified is always the weaker one. A nemesis seen can be taken head on; contained, dismantled, and set aside. Caricatures were even less effective. It could have chosen any such stereotype and portrayed for her all manner of loathsome characters as the subconscious might conjure. But Waysmiths were not known to traffic in the obvious. The illusion would be too superficial, too easy to dismiss.

Then again, the Bramble Crown had no interest in weaving costumes for a performance of terror, or mixing monsters together to frighten a few children, but rather, that it should resist the forms she might try to give to it and remain unknowable: to further their descent into a listless void by withholding everything and being nothing. The Undefinable. The Unknown. The Nameless. The Crown had grown, after all, from much deeper clays, and the memories of the trees from which it bloomed were, just as the king had proclaimed in his riddles, ultimately indecipherable.

Madam Bel Carmen and Alice Guthrie rounded behind the well and skidded to a mutual stop, barely in time to avoid Fiona striding determinedly up the margins. Alice Guthrie yanked her daughter back harshly, just as the mists parted on the threshold of a drop further forward than the girl had seen. The hollow wasn't all that deep, but far enough that a fall would be disastrous, and at its bottom, a spike trap of thorns and splintered bones. What was more, the Bramble creature that had emerged from the mouth of the cavern, and that which was now closing in on Elizabeth Pennybaker, appeared as something different to their eyes.

The subliminal collective mind of the Flidais Venatica gave a form to their fear and the Way By made it real. The creature itself, however, didn't seem as if it cared to pay them much mind, but Alice Guthrie wasn't taking any chances and pressed her daughter behind her as it moved beyond them. A second later, Fiona Guthrie's jaw dropped in terror and astonishment at the great beast rising up before them. It was both dog- and wolf-like, balanced on four massive legs tapering to wide paws with thick, yellowish talons.

A covering of shaggy grey-green fur obscured most of its discernible features but did nothing to cover its steady, terrifying gaze. Eyes as wide as the moon hanging in the sky behind it panned back and forth as the hound took shape. Its tail, a versatile whip-like mass of overlapping weave, flicked around in a kind of circular motion as the creature stalked forward. They heard as Elizabeth Pennybaker drew in scream and held it. Everything seemed to slow and there was a momentary stillness as all awaited the next move. It came when the Hound huffed once before raising its cumbersome head and bayed loud and long into the darkness.

"Now!" The Waysmith cried. "Go!"

Like a white hart facing Death itself on horseback, Elizabeth Pennybaker darted forward. Tearing away from the others, who for her sake, leapt into the cavern as she taunted the Great Hound and led it astray. She bolted down the Hill and into the nearby mire filled with stone fences less than half finished. Ash and smoke still choked the escape routes to her right, but she pressed forward into the twilight of the Stumble. Having little else to go on, she made for the taller shapes in the background and hoped that she could reach a hiding place before the emptiness she felt behind her came breathing down her neck.

For a moment, Elizabeth Pennybaker wondered if this was what madness truly felt like. A thing, which no two people ever saw the same way, but that which pursued on the heels of desperation so closely that stopping to turn around and get a look at it would only ensure capture and an abrupt end. And if that were true, how then was she to fight such a thing? Elder gods and giant spiders were, to her, almost preferable. Panic began to set in.

But then, a sharp and familiar feline yowl forced her to look up.

The wisest of cats, from what the Waysmith could tell, all seemed to have one of two things in common. A sense of when to go high and a notable distaste for unseen frights. Noseworthy was no different and as the marmalade cat leapt up across gnarled branches hanging overhead, he squawked such a yammer she worried that the snapping jaws of her pursuer would find him first. But instead of quieting, he mewled and wailed, pawing at the rough bark beneath his feet and flicking his tail into all sorts of esoteric symbols. Again and again, he turned his mistress's attention back to the trees littering the beaten ground. In the strangest way, Elizabeth Pennybaker had the sense they were waiting for her. Dormant perhaps, but vigilant. They twitched when Noseworthy clawed them and batted him away with their smallest twigs.

She was thinking of the King's words then. What had he said of the Hunt?

"But our quarry is swift and clever. She will not be taken easily. We must therefore use all that we have at our disposal: our cunning must be brought to bear on the riddles presented, our strength on the battles to come, and our wit on the strategies of our prey."

Noseworthy howled again and scratched a bit of clean wood with unreadable lines. She could no longer see the Hill or tell from which direction the voices of her company had come. She was lost. She had gotten off track. Though, she hoped, that if she could not tell which way was the correct one, neither could the thing that followed. But how then to find the way onwards? Had not the King himself spoken to the trees that made up the Bramble Crown that set them on this path to begin with?

Were they not now fighting the very thing that had started this journey? How was she supposed to untangle meanings layered upon meanings when no one seemed to speak their intent plainly, or perhaps that was the problem? The simplest answer may be the most comforting, but it held within it all of the unsaid possibilities that might yet come to pass. Just as the King's Geas had been straightforward, all that he might have meant by it was still unfolding.

The marmalade cat was growing frantic and swatted the younger Waysmith impatiently from overhead. When she returned her attention, he once again clawed his concerns into the nearest branch. When the same such branch then waved him off as an ox might an irritating fly, Elizabeth Pennybaker had a peculiar idea. There had been three rules to traversing the Way By back when they first took the road to Lilylit but then there had been a fourth rule just for her. It was an idea that seemed to emanate from something that Somerset Sayer had already told her.

If you are lost in the woods, ask the trees.

And so, that's precisely what she did.

"Where?" she asked. "Where do I go now? Can your branches show the Way?"

When a great crack of thunder shook the ashes, Elizabeth Pennybaker looked up. The Stumble moved on an axis as the world below broke through the world above. Everywhere was suddenly alive and the Waysmith's eyes widened in awe. The entire forest was rejoicing! A forest of death now dancing wildly, roots tearing up from the ground as elms, willows, and ash trees, hundreds of years old, swayed and rolled in their utter elation.

Cremation ground was turned over and a scattered mess of snowdrops and crocuses burst out from the soil as leafy buds split through winter-darkened branches to wash the world green. They also hid her from the encroaching darkness in an instant and from the tides and ebb, a new passage appeared.

Despite herself, Elizabeth Pennybaker laughed and smiled at the antics playing out before her. It was like a grand performance, a kind of welcoming gambol, for a prodigal child they were completely overjoyed to see return. Several of the trees even approached, reaching out their lowest branches to touch her hair and then her face. When she responded by running her fingers over their rough edges, they trembled and shook, the sounds of their voices emanating from deep within the heartwood at their centers. She heard them then, she heard and understood everything they said.

Not in talk, so much, but in images and tastes and scents carried in on a cool, spring, breeze. Sentences formed out of emerging buds and wafts of pollen, ideas expressed in the insects hiding along the bark, and words tapped out in the rustlings and murmurings of leaves overhead. An ancient and bent oak rambled up to her and, without fear, she stepped into it and wrapped her arms around its knotted base.

"Jenny's Has More Leaves." She laughed warmly. "That is your name, isn't it? It was given to you by a little girl a very long time ago."

But then her face fell and she gently laid her cheek against the heaving trunk. "You miss her. You wonder why she didn't come back. I don't know the answer to that, I wish I did. But you have all these wonderful memories of her, don't you?"

The wood shifted and groaned in sad repose.

"Well, that's all we can do. Keep our memories with us. The parts of you she touched are now safe inside your rings. She's always with you. When you're ready to leave your acorns again, you can scatter them in her honor."

But, despite all this and the moment's respite, the nothingness had not yet relented and, though seemingly confused by the sudden din, was moving quickly on open ground. Thorns and briars sprung up at her feet where sickly vines were already creeping up newly enraged trunks. As quickly as the Way By changed, the Stumble churned over to meet it.

"Which Way do I go?" She yelled out to them. "How do I lead them out?! Please! How do I do this?"

Oak raised its voices first: "Upon the legacy of rage has every great king been crowned, but it cries out in joy when the Sovereign returns to his own. See, in all ways, and not just one."

Followed by Birch and Willow in time: "Before it can be revealed, the past must illuminate. But tarry not in pain and go into the reflections that hold and protect wonder."

Then Ash, to add its own distinction: "Because anguish is always revealed, but joy stays where we hide it."

And Elm, entwined with Mistletoe: "Upon such stepping stones as these, begin the path anew and consider carefully where it may take you. Just as a path behind bodes knowledge for the path ahead, you must still choose how you will walk it."

Finally, Holly, hidden in the mire: "Do this, and with anticipation. A path of regret is to be abandoned, a path of providence is not one to follow, but that which will follow you."

That's what the folklorist had meant when she said that memory worked differently here. That it was, by no means, a recollection of something gone but a revisitation of what might have been; not a static memorial to an indelible event, but a remaking, a restoration, of what was not yet finished. By moving through her memories, she moved through the trees, and in so doing she appeared to dance as they did. She walked their branches as paths and their divisions as crossroads. Up and down, over and above, meeting a dead end and continuing on anyway, always just out of reach of the thicket racing along below her. As she strode and wandered, time and place ceased to be separate from one another; blending and blurring into movement and flow.

The teapot her mother placed on the stove the day she was home sick from school was the teapot on the stove every day afterward. And every day afterwards was any day the teapot had sat there and steamed ready with chai. The same chai that had boiled up and stained a book her father had given her years before that. The brown mottling then marking the page where her favorite quotes were outlined. Quotes that she had read, over and over, to a mangy kitten rescued from an alleyway until he knew their cadence so well that he came running just as soon as the first words were uttered.

Words that had inspired her to pursue a life dedicated to healing and study, and those which had bookended the night where she, in tears, had told her mother of her heretical dreams for the future over the same simmering teapot of chai. They had then walked their cups out to the back garden together and left them at the feet of deities who tended it all. Her mother, to Ganesh. Her, to Kali. And just as easily as the sights and smells returned, Elizabeth Pennybaker was moving through the Way By, all along the boughs of the Stumble, traded from tree to tree, as though pacing the solid rise of a field road; with the shadows far below.

She wound her way further, into the memories of her back garden. She greeted Ganesh, sitting on his mound of flowers and waving at her with glee, even as he ate up the offerings of fruit and rice her mother had left there from the meal at her father's funeral. But her Kali was, again, missing. The trees then handed her across a great chasm to a time when Padma Pennybaker was deathly ill. She sensed the darkened room with the broken lamp, cotton bedcovers piled high over a form that withered into dust so that no one would be forced to watch the inevitable dissolution.

It would then become the shroud that covered her always afterwards and whose folds lead her daughter to this identical place over and over again in her mind. The place of death, the storeroom, she couldn't let go of. Noseworthy, of course, immediately leapt from the Waysmith's arms and onto the edge of her mother's bed: to a spot where he had sat for days and nights watching over her and as Elizabeth Pennybaker now understood, to keep the monstrous vermin of the Stumble at bay.

This night was also every night after it, having metastasized in the darkness and taken ahold of everything around it. The offerings of food were only now ever made to the cat and the back garden overgrew with the flowers that would have adorned the altars and windowsills and the kitchen table whose emptiness was a thing itself now. The same as the open pedestal where a goddess should have presided. Which was why, when she heard a voice, she very nearly startled herself into an unfathomable fall.

"You're finally here."

She had never been so happy in all her life to see the edges of that wind-whipped train coat or the pensive frown that always sat above its smoothed-out collar. Or the long, blonde hair let loose to the elements and the silhouette that was always some bizarre hodgepodge of styles from a dozen different eras. In fact, there was some part of her that wondered if Somerset Sayer actually just accumulated her trappings and attire as she traversed the Way By; appearing therefore as a kind of hand-me-down mélange of pointless regalia wherever she went, depending on what stuck. Or, perhaps, not so pointless, as the folklorist herself strode in as a patchwork monarch and took command of the roiling Stumble.

"Somerset!" The younger Waysmith couldn't help but exclaim. "I found you! I mean, you found me!"

"Of course." She replied, in that ever so characteristic deadpan. "It doesn't take a Waysmith to figure out where the Stumble will always take you. It's predictable like that. It only goes one direction."

Elizabeth Pennybaker glanced back; the threshold of her mother's sickroom slowly beginning to pull away from her and down into an endless hallway getting longer as she watched it and did not move to react. She thought then that she could hear plaintive calls from somewhere in the distance. It was telling her the last story she could remember in her mother's voice.

My sister was once possessed by the Goddess Kali. She came down to her because her husband beat her. Her mother-in-law screamed at her. She was hurt and miserable all the time. She wanted to kill herself. But she also wanted someone else to do it for her first. What a horrible place to be. Contemplating death every night because the alternative seemed worse and worse all the time. She opened her spirit to Kali, the Black Goddess who is death, who is life, who is destruction, and who is protection. No one would dare touch her when Kali was upon her; when she was possessed by the Divine Wrath. No man would dare strike the Goddess and risk the terror she would rain down. And then Death took her anyway, my love. She took her away anyway. I was so angry. I could never forgive her for that. But the funny thing is, I've come to the same place myself now. This sickness is eating me from the inside, little one. So, I've decided to open my soul as well. Kali will come for me. She is the arbiter of death in this family, Elizabeth. Only she decides, and I'm ready. Are you?

"Elizabeth." Somerset Sayer prompted. "That's not a place you want to go. There's nothing for you down there. Just more of what it already is. That's not your mother and that's not her house. It's just the place where the pain dwells. We have to keep going. If we don't, we're both stuck here. Forever."

Slowly, the young woman nodded. It would be a place to return to, but only at the proper time. Right now, her friends needed her more than the grief did. She picked up Noseworthy from his spot at her feet. "Yeah, I know. Let's go."

"You ready?"

"Lead the way."

Alice Guthrie swore in a way that was most unbecoming, and yet quite appropriate for the circumstances. They were each entangled in a morass of thorns, filling the depths of the well to all sides. Though, at their center, the Huntresses could see the suspended corpse, arched and snarled in the mix. If Madam Bel Carmen hadn't been party to the nuance of the situation, she might also have said that the brambles were puppeteers to the bones; hanging them in full view to tremble and clatter as they cut their way through.

That the remnant threads of the alicorn also wrapped around the remains and into the Bramble only further crystallized the image of a strange, macabre marionette with unseeing eyes and a rictus grin. Fiona raised her wooden sword to break the thorns off at the base while Alice Guthrie preferred to meander around and through them.

All the while, Madam Bel Carmen took up the worst of the briars in her calloused hands and crushed them before they could harm anyone. She was also the first to reach the relic, though her task was a far more literal one. With concentration born of urgent panic, she began to unravel the turmoil and confusion.

She pulled the first threads free just as Alice Guthrie reached her and took up the middle mess. When Fiona arrived at the furthest end, it was then the three of them in triunity working steadily to unmake everything that had knotted and aged in the unkempt grave of the Unicorn. It made for a sight that was less the Fates now than the Charities, or the metamorphosis of the Seasons.

Fiona Guthrie wrapped her hand in a rope of golden hair and twisted it free.

"So, when we get it out, we fix it, right?" She called out to the other two. "Give her back the horn they took? Put her back together?"

But Madam Bel Carmen shook her head, peeling another lock free. "No. There is no restoring this. We can't save her."

"Wait, what?"

The elder Vodoun gave a resigned sigh. "One day, you're going to learn that some things in this world can't be fixed, Fiona. That they won't be what they were before and, in truth, they shouldn't be. What was has become what is, and what is must become what will be. What you have to do is take the pieces that are left and use them to make something new. That's what we're going to do. That's what I believe the Waysmith has been preparing us for. Clarisant can never be what she was because of what she is. There is only now what she will be."

Alice Guthrie undid the bindings all around herself, raising her handfuls over her head before rolling them together. As she did so, she could feel the threads strengthening; tightening through her hands until the entire length began to petrify. The more each of them added to it, the more it twisted into the familiar shape of the alicorn; recomposing itself through entwining threads and a shimmer of light just beyond.

"What becomes of her then?" She asked, though she didn't truly expect either Madam Bel Carmen or her daughter to have a real answer.

"I don't know." Madam Bel Carmen replied. "But it will be unjust. Whatever it is."

Fiona Guthrie started to respond but realized she had nothing to add. She may have said similar things of her own life, and yet here she was on a macabre adventure none could have predicted! What road had she not taken that the Unicorn had? But no more had she just formed the thought than Elizabeth Pennybaker and Somerset Sayer came abruptly crashing out of the woods and, with more dignity than it seemed like either deserved to wield, marched up the side of the Hill and turned towards the baying on the moor. The Waysmiths had returned but moreover, they had been pursued, it seemed, along a path of their own intent. And having now guided the Bramble back to the center, they loosed a squirming cat back into the reeds and took up their positions on either side of the well together.

"Do you have it?" The folklorist shouted down to the three.

"Dr. Sayer! You've found us! Yes! Yes! We have it!" Came the voice of Madam Bel Carmen.

"Good. Make ready! Each of you, take an end of the threads. Pull it out, like a rope. Trust me, the strands will not break. When I tell you, draw it taut. We'll have one good chance at this and likely not another."

"Chance?" Alice Guthrie queried, struggling to once again wrench at the twists of the alicorn to loosen it again.

"To tie it." Somerset Sayer replied, exhaustion beginning to strain her voice. "As the Bramble binds her we must bind it in turn. She's already gotten further than I thought she would. I know it. She's reached Lilylit. We have to get to her before she's through. It's the only way to free Avenant."

"Free him?" Madam Bel Carmen heaved a section of the uncoiling tether and looped it over her arm. "Waysmith! What has happened to the King?"

She turned, as much as she could, to each of them. "He's dying, Evelyn. She's killing him."

A mournful and angry sound echoed from every corner of the Stumble. During the Hunt, the thorns had only continued to spread and now overtook everything beyond the Hill. It writhed, like a living thing seized by shock and pain. Even the trees seemed to thrash as they were bent and pulled to the ground. They fought, they tried to protect the Huntresses for as long as they could, but to no avail. Their creaks and groans filled the sky.

"Where is it?" Elizabeth Pennybaker growled, squinting into the bluster and dismissing her anxious thoughts.

"Not far." The folklorist replied. "Do you remember what I told you?"

"I think so." She answered. "But I've never attempted anything like this before."

"Well, think of it like an impromptu quiz, then. Except getting a bad grade really is the end of the world." The Waysmith continued to pick through their surroundings with an attentive gaze. "I mean, that should resonate at least a little."

"Somerset." She bantered back good-naturedly. "Never refer to taking on a nightmare like that ever again, okay?"

Blithely, the elder Waysmith actually chanced a smile. "Fair enough. But I am trusting you to remain steadfast, Elizabeth. The Bramble Crown will not untangle easily."

"Yeah, I figured." She chuffed in response. "But when it's done, you're going to explain to me exactly how all this happened. Again, I mean. We were sent to hunt a unicorn; a crazed monstrosity out to annihilate all of imagined existence, and now I'm apparently, for the second time, standing in front of the very thing that sent me on this quest to begin with realizing that I have to take *it* down first! So, once more, professor. But in plain detail this time!"

"Hardly necessary. You already know. You just have yet to accept it."

The Huntresses fell silent.

"There." Somerset Sayer finally concluded, pointing to a break in a small copse of trees near their return road. "It's not far. Just beyond the rise. It's coming."

Madam Bel Carmen coiled more of the threads through her fingers and straightened her tunic. "Alright. We're ready when you are. Fiona, you stay to that far side so that as soon as something, anything, drops down here, you get that snare over it. Got it?"

"Got it." She sniffed.

The three of them waited in a tense hush. It was up to the Waysmiths now.

When a sudden upheaval in the woods ended with an uproarious clamor and more shattered branches, Somerset Sayer wheeled about and grabbed Elizabeth Pennybaker by the hand.

"Tell me, Elizabeth. Did you ever play at blood oaths when you were a kid?"

"I...what?"

"You know, where you and your best friend cut your fingers on the playground or something and then mix the droplets together to declare your eternal loyalty?"

"Are you insane? No, of course not! What kind of childhood friends did you have?!"

Up ahead, a howl caught their attention.

"This kind, I'm afraid." The Waysmith interjected just seconds before producing a small razor that dangled from a woven friendship bracelet in the pocket of her coat and neatly sliced into her companion's scabbed thumb. Elizabeth Pennybaker made to pull back with a shout but was held in place as the Waysmith turned the blade to her own hand for a similar gash before grasping their fingers together tightly.

"What are you doing?!"

But the slow dash of blood pressed between their palms had already spattered into the dirt. "If there is one thing, Elizabeth," Somerset Sayer raised her voice above the racket of the Stumble. "That powers like the Bramble Crown cannot abide, it is the flow of blood it does not command."

Through shadows in the trees, they could barely make out the delirious shape. A nightmare and a monster, it barreled across the expanse with a wide, ravenous, mouth. Intent on devouring the two women, it loped along on the legs of a wolf-hound, dug into the land with the talons of an eagle, wrapped itself in the countenance of an aristocrat on horseback, and made to appear as a hybrid of man and beast if not for everywhere it was rife with thorns that jutted out in every direction, including into its own body.

The eyes that then regarded them from beneath lawless locks of auburn-green hair were inhuman. Golden irises with an ovoid pupil bespoke an animal, a shimmer of reflected light at the retina told of a predator, but a glimmer of sable and blue indicated the possibility of a soul. There was no fear in it as it bore down on them, only a curious sort of focus, and when it lunged, it met them head-on at the summit of the Hill.

Somerset Sayer and Elizabeth Pennybaker did not part as the Bramble slammed into them, raging and shrieking as it tried to gorge on the proffered blood and flesh it could immediately taste and on the insult it left on its lips. Whips of briar lashed out everywhere but the Waysmiths only set their heels deeper as the void wrapped around them. Each holding tight to the other, even when they could not hear anything above the roar of the Bramble as it screamed their unworthiness to the Crown.

It bellowed out their unchosen-ness, their uselessness, and wailed in anger at their hubris for ever having attempted to ascend above the bottom stair. But these were words that every one of them had heard before. From a hundred different mouths that the Bramble Crown now spoke with. Dishonorable. Dirty. Shameful. Unfit. Undeserving. Out of place.... Meaningless.

Madam Bel Carmen, Alice, and Fiona Guthrie winced at the force of it. How it warped around the Waysmiths as unending waves of cloth or hair or skin to suffocate them beneath a steep deluge. How the mass became formless and without structure as it slavered and chewed until the two figures within began to dwindle and to dissipate. But suddenly, a guttural noise, and a wet handful of fetid mud slopped to the ground. It was thick with decay and dissolved almost as soon as it landed. Then, there was another and quickly another after that.

The morass burbled something incoherent but as the Waysmiths emerged, the three Huntresses below could make out the sights and sounds of a hideous fight. To the shock of everyone, Somerset Sayer and Elizabeth Pennybaker were, quite literally, tearing the thing apart, piece by torn off piece. And each time they dug their hands into it, they came away with mud and sludge that smeared across the ashen soil. But again and again they returned and did not, for a second, relent.

They wrenched and broke it, even as the Bramble faltered. More mud, more moss and swamp, fell away from it to reveal a skeleton of thickets beneath. They were not silent either and answered each of the accusations the terror subjected them to. They recounted sorrows and retold parts of their lives, remade the sharp edges of themselves that had been broken off, and reclaimed words that wouldn't fit. They were cut by it but fought anyway; breaking through their cage and sundering their way into freedom inch by bloody inch as the Way By twisted their disjointed stories together into a familiar metrical form.

"My words are not big enough, to not fall through the cracks..."

"...They fall there in a jumble, discarded nails and tacks."

"Mixed with mud they try to grow, but scorn has crushed them down..."

"...With each step it tramples up the counsel to the crown."

"And so they wait another year, to spring up from the roots..."

"...That rest deep in the soil for a time of fewer boots."

"With no one left to injure them, and no one there to see..."

"...They rise up high into the sun, unexceptionally free ."

"No footprints, no hints, no reminiscent strains..."

"...All that will be there, exists. All that once was there remains."

"What is kept in an empty room? Why presume what was has left?..."

"...If what I will make of it is still unknown, is the loss of silence theft?"

"Or is this my admission, my sole chance to submit, that I have intentionally made it blank, for you to fill the writ."

"If that is what you have to give, I'll take the page from you, and with this breath, thread and wreath, carry them onward through."

Whatever it was that was actually said, no one knew. Because that's what the Huntresses heard. But then, the folklorist called out and everything stopped. With a heave, she and Elizabeth Pennybaker wrapped their arms into the Bramble, locked eyes, and fell as one into the maw of the well.

"Wrap it! Wrap it quickly!" Madam Bel Carmen yelled. "Alice! Tie the end!"

"Evelyn, behind you! It's going to...!"

"Oh, no it won't! I see it!"

"Wait, how did you do that?!"

"I've got it!" Fiona Guthrie cried.

"There's nettles everywhere!" Alice Guthrie shouted. "Watch out!"

"I've just about done it. Fiona! Help your mother to secure the back!"

"I tied this side! It's trapped!"

"I've got Elizabeth! Someone help Dr. Sayer!"

"I can't see her! Can anyone see her?"

"Alice! Brace to your right! It's breaking free!"

"Oh, no, it isn't! You're not going anywhere!"

"Aunt Evelyn! Look! The threads are tightening around it! It's working! It's binding up!"

"Look out, Fiona! Dear girl, are you alright?!"

"I'm alright! Just scratched me, it's fine."

"You're bleeding!"

"Evelyn! Your arm!"

"Everyone! Get back! Get out of here!"

"Dr. Sayer!"

"Go! I've got it. You've got to get out!"

"We're not leaving you!"

"Of course not! You couldn't if you tried! Now go!"

Alice and Fiona scrambled up the embankment with Madam Bel Carmen close behind, towing Elizabeth Pennybaker up as she went. The cacophony of the Stumble was deafening as the very fabric of the world seemed to be on the verge of rending. And even as they turned back, they could not make out the difference between Waysmith and Bramble, perceiving only chaos at the summit of the Hill. The quagmire bubbled up from everywhere, and from everywhere the thorns bit into the ground loosening painful screams from the entombed bodies that lay beneath.

Fonts of brackish water erupted from the well and poured the same stinking marsh out into the jagged rushes until the Stumble began to sink. It was all sinking! Even the trees around them too slid into the muddle and began to submerge. It was then that Madam Bel Carmen spied a curious thing. From the top of the void of thorns, the first rounded leaves of a lily pad began to unfurl from deep in the well. Carefully drifting up between the jagged Bramble, great big heads of lotus flowers emerged and began to open, littering the fen with slivers of white and pink.

But they were only the beginning and more followed; a hedgerow of underbrush burst outwards, trailed by wildflowers. Sprouts and saplings soon climbed out in turn, sloshing through the mud until finding a suitable place to set down roots and bud. Out it grew, and kept growing, until the rot and the refuse were obscured. Until the Stumble vanished beneath carpets of flowers and gentle grasses, until the ancient, shattered trees had become the hidden scaffolding on whose backs a splendid and breath-taking castle in a kingdom by the sea was built.

Within minutes, the whole oasis grew to maturity and the world around them transformed as if waking from a dream where the mundane bedroom and magical realm were always the same place. The Huntresses stood back stunned as their world changed from the place they had ended to the one in which they had begun. And as the ashes fell away to be churned up in the soil that fed the expansion of ever more gardens and hedge groves and pathways, the darkness receded into the corners and seams; kept, as it were, contained, behind a curtain of flourishing prosperity. The carrion tucked away, so that the scent of the bouquet that grew out of it masked its presence.

They all knew it to be the truth. Lilylit and the Stumble were one.

Alice Guthrie leapt back as the mire vanished beneath a covering of hyacinth stalks and the great burning trees circling the Hill became the columns of a familiar rotunda; the well, a concentric ring at the center of a cross-sected trunk upon which a throne had been built to cover the innumerable graves beneath its roots. Clouds and soot arching overhead turned to a glittering snowfall and, at last, the painted mural of new life overtook the ruined canvas beneath, and the court of the Summer King once again surrounded them.

It was as if they had never left, despite how far they had gone. But they did not see the High King returning to greet them nor the Octadic making to welcome them. To the wrenching heartache of Somerset Sayer, now revealed to be sitting in the middle of it all, they did not immediately see him anywhere. But the Hill was no longer empty. It had a new regent already turning to acknowledge them upon their expected arrival.

A Unicorn Queen, ravaged and desolate, stood on a pedestal, itself worshipped by the bowed and defeated bodies of the old guard. Acknowledged by a King who was nowhere and for whom the Waysmith feared the worst; whose command of the Bramble Crown had once been all that had stood between her and the hate that would come to gnaw her clean. He was all that had kept the truth from destroying what remained by sheer dint of the fact that his blood could not be drained to dust in its roots when it was placed on his sovereign head. But Clarisant had subverted his crown by stepping into it.

It had then entangled not her head, but her feet. And now, it consumed her entire form in the briar as it grew from her body, her open wounds, and her blood. Its tines snaked up her back to form a radiant halo of burrs from her shoulders to the top of her head, entwining her silver-white hair in the tangle as it had the alicorn before it. The blood that seeped from the wound in her forehead was, to it, the most precious of all however, and the apex of her crown twisted into the broken flesh there to gnarl together as a new kind of jeweled antlers that ascended high above her. The Bramble thrived and swelled, and reached with splayed, knotted fingers ever further towards the Sun.

Chapter Twenty-One

Sparrows alighted en masse and filled the Bramble with chattering and delighted shrieks of triumph; their jerky, mechanistic movements making the antler-boughs over Clarisant's head blink like a thousand eyes hovering within and above the pulsing, branched veins against the sky. Even then there were twice more than that; the tiny, unblinking eyes of the dead birds themselves staring fixed and unwavering to the women below. The Unicorn Queen turned to face them, and as she did, revealed more of the pedestal on which she stood.

To the horror of all assembled, it was undoubtedly the resting place of the Bramble Crown which they had already seen, but now run through with fissures that made it appear as a discontinuity of carelessly stacked pieces. And crumpled to the ground beneath her feet was none other than what the folklorist had feared the most. The Summer King lay as lifeless as the skeletal guards that surrounded him. He was also now as white as she, with only a few flecks of golden brown at his temples, and bore the wounds and bruises that she had traded to him.

Where her flesh was now whole, save for the void yawning at her forehead and where run through with briars, his was broken and bleeding. He did not respond when his name was called and was so still that not even the gentle breeze of Lilylit's passing wake could stir him. Somerset Sayer nearly screamed with the weight of her sorrow.

"Unnecessary lament for an irrelevant death." Clarisant sighed. "Your world no more knew him than it will mourn him. His name is all but unknown to them. And with your end, nothing of consequence is lost. Is that not yet clear to you, Waysmith? The housewives will dismiss you. The scholars ignore you. The whores will no longer pray to you and thieves will have better things to do. The preachers cannot hear you. Refined ladies cannot see you. There is nothing here but what festers in your own mind."

"You cruel, hateful, thing!" Somerset Sayer hissed. "Depraved wretch! If there was anything in this place not worth saving it would be you."

A fault in the wind brought the scent of smoke to the garden. Clarisant appeared to sway with its strange calling while her eyes darkened with sudden yearning. As though thinking back to a time before the essence of all things had not yet grown so old and tired.

"You could have saved me."

Elizabeth Pennybaker tilted her head at the tenderness of the words. But Clarisant paid neither her, nor the Huntresses of the King, any mind; as she approached on graceful, unencumbered feet towards the folklorist crouching in the tussocks.

"You could have stood up. You could have stayed." She said again, with such a mild, lilting tone as to imply her gentility. "You didn't. Did you? None of them did. Waysmiths and Withersmiths and all manner of trespassers into a world that was never theirs to claim. Knowledge that never belonged to you. Forgotten ghosts littered behind you. All of it stolen and its rightful heirs left to rot." She leaned in to emphasize her point. "You could have given it back and consigned yourself to death instead of us! Now, I deny you. I deny you the possibility of imagining a life better than this one."

"Clarisant." Somerset Sayer rose to her feet, clumps of dirt falling from her knee and the gussets of her coat. "I told you then, and I am telling you now, it was never the injustice that any of us denied. Not me. Not Mary Toft. Not Elizabeth Pennybaker who follows us both. Not Avenant, no matter what you believe of him. We know what *he* did. We know what *they* did. It's as inescapable to us as it is to you."

The Unicorn Queen curled her lip in abject scorn and growled her refusal of such benign comforts. "No, it isn't. You turn your heads and walk away. You marvel up at the stars and pretend not to see what is below them. You run away from the fire because it burns you and because you are not the one trapped inside it. But the shame follows you and it is that which makes your stomach turn and your heart stutter. Not the inequity, only the dread of it. The Bramble grows everywhere you try so hard not to look."

"Only because you were the one who fed it. Gave to it more than it was ever due in your vengeance!"

"I am the testament to your transgressions! The remnants of virtue!"

"There are many bits and pieces of us that survive, Clarisant." The Waysmith countered without rancor. "Usually the worst ones. And out of everything, *virtue* is the worst of all."

It was an unholy scream that replied. An enraged, incensed outcry that echoed out of the obscurity of time and into the present; as though it had never stopped from the moment it was first loosed. Clouds boiled in the sky and wisps of ash chewed at the veneer of beauty still thriving all around them. The birds that clung to her branches burst upwards as they scattered into the rising winds; chattering with ruined beaks and dried-out feathers as she gnashed her teeth at the circling Hunt.

"And now," the Unicorn Queen trailed into words again. "You think you're going to save him, don't you? Save your precious illusion? Prop it back up, tell them it's alright? Go back to how it was and tell all the same stories you did before? How..." She paused to cock her head and sneer. ".... uninspiring of you."

"I didn't come here to save Kingdom or Crown." Somerset Sayer took another step forward, her feet sliding through the flowering grass stalks as one who knows how to turn with the blades when the tempest changes direction. "I didn't come here to save you or to save myself. Destroy it, if you have to. Destroy this place. Tear the Bramble into pieces and Lilylit with it. Bury the Stumble and everything that has rooted above it as poisoned fruit of a poisoned tree. It's yours to sever and we deserve your wrath. Let it rage."

But Clarisant was unconvinced and scowled at the approaching Waysmith with misgiving. What she had set into motion was becoming disobedient to her recitation. Somerset Sayer, however, continued her story.

"I knew it the moment I saw the dry store room in the museum that the Way By brought for Elizabeth when she first crossed its threshold. Everything in that room. Everything in those display cases and jars and on racks. The snakes we pickled in formaldehyde and lined up on a shelf. The globes we scribbled with our own lines. The birds we stuffed and mounted. So many things that were beautiful and fragile in this world, and we killed them. We broke their necks and cracked their skulls for our glass exhibits. We stole them from their lands and stared at them as they wasted away in cages. We took away their beautiful things and gave them *our* names and *our* page numbers in archives we never return to. I get it. I have seen it all just as you did. So spread your annihilation and burn it down. I didn't come here to stop that."

A great and agile form twisted, readied for any deception to come. "And why are you here then.... Waysmith?"

"You can take your vengeance on the past, Clarisant. But you can't take the future. I won't let you hurt them. You and I? We're done. They go on."

At last, Elizabeth Pennybaker, Madam Bel Carmen, Alice and Fiona Guthrie, understood something that had eluded them until now. Something about the stories that Somerset Sayer had told them, something that had always been there but left unsaid. Left incoherent and without substance. That every journey not only will end, but should, so that what comes after might be freed from it. That some things exist only to be retold and never relived. And if there was anything left to write, it would come from another's pen.

This had been her plan all along. But as serious as it was, Elizabeth Pennybaker did miss the moment when all attention had been drawn away. A younger Waysmith, unschooled in the formalities of fiction, looked around and saw the gaps in the world open as the Stumble continued to bleed through and eat away at Lilylit's grandeur. So, on a whim, she reached through them when no one was looking. As she raised a handful of ashes, she bowed her head and touched a portion of them to swipe lines and symbols across her forehead. No one yet felt the change brought about by the unfamiliar language she used to call out to the Way By though, and did not hear the words that she barely remembered herself.

In the open and bleeding rifts all around her, Elizabeth Pennybaker saw something more than ashes. The mass below churned; writhing with intent. Without question, it felt to her like a macabre dance, pulsing to a rhythm stamped out in bare, kicking feet. In the momentary shapes formed in the currents, she saw a cremation ground filled with wailing.

The image did not surprise her, given the nature of the exchange now passing between Waysmith and Unicorn up ahead. In fact, it was all quite satisfying to see the raw truth behind the façades she had been taught to revere all her life. It felt real in the way that only loathsome honesty could. But that's not all it was. She glanced back up at the folklorist, who continued the steps of her own beat in keeping her body between them and the Bramble. Time once more stretched out and slowed. Her vision shifted.

Two statues stood on flattened stone pedestals in an overgrown wood. Padma Pennybaker sat before the icon of Ganesh, imploring him with lamps and cut fruit to help her daughter find a better way; to guide her when her mother was inevitably gone too soon. She was thin to her bones, ravaged by illness, but in her collapsed frame, Elizabeth Pennybaker saw not the desperation for a way forward but rather the refusal to turn and see what was looming behind her. There, the goddess Kali stood tall and beckoning, grinding the reddened soles of her feet into the jagged rocks of the pillar.

She crushed and ate the food that was left for her, spitting the remnants into the dirt, and drank the fire from the candles at each corner. But whenever Padma Pennybaker begged for peace and mundanity, Kali answered with shock and wonder. Whenever her mother pleaded for her daughter to follow in the same path as her grandmothers and great-grandmothers, Kali pointed in another direction. She would not look, though.

She refused to acknowledge what was plain enough. Instead, she only further descended into the gloom rising up from the memory. In reaching out into the ashes however, Elizabeth Pennybaker also reached out to the Black Goddess in her garden; realizing then that the figure seemed to be trying to tell the ghost of her mother to turn and look. Not to where she wanted her daughter to be but to where she now stood overlooking them. The young Waysmith gasped. That's why the statue had been hidden. Kali would not remove the obstacles in the desired path, she would instead raise hell itself to send them down a new one entirely.

Somerset Sayer continued to close in on the Unicorn Queen. She dodged the occasional swiped branch and was mindful of the murmurations of the cadaverous sparrows above. Face to face at last, she stared down at her life-long nemesis but this time the Waysmith had no intention of fighting alone. Not anymore.

"This is where it ends, Clarisant. It's done."

Elizabeth Pennybaker pulled herself from the chasm. When she stamped her foot into the ground, she felt it reverberate in response. When she did it again, the Bramble seemed to tilt away from her and careen about. Remembering just such similar motions that Madam Bel Carmen herself had enacted in her fight with the Withersmith, Elizabeth Pennybaker could not help but think of the Divine Mother's dance of time, creation, destruction, and rebirth. She who destroys to protect the innocent and judges the corrupt. It was now or never. The ashes on her body prickled with blackening wrath as the Way By possessed her. The fight for liberation had begun.

The younger Waysmith came up quickly on Somerset Sayer's right, joining with her erstwhile mentor as the two of them formed a united front. Madam Bel Carmen and Alice Guthrie stepped up and into the flank; both paying their solemnities to the horrors around them while Fiona, on the other hand, was, at first, nowhere to be found. Not one to lose sight of the younger girl however, the Huntresses were quick to follow the bounding movements of one rather homely marmalade cat as he swatted a number of diving sparrows away from the place where she now sat, hunched as she raised her hand to gingerly touch the brow of the bloodless Summer King. She also wielded her wooden sword with equal impunity, and cut away the imps who clung to him, feeding on all that was left of his soul. For a moment, her shoulders shook but as her fingers met the smooth line of his jaw, she suddenly raised her head and called out to the others.

"Dr. Sayer! He's breathing! The King lives!"

In that moment, the fulcrum of the Way By moved on its axis. Light, where light had never been, broke the horizon and turned it upside down. Whether her words were true or a compassionate lie meant only to bolster her companions didn't matter. The Summer King was both alive and dead in that same single moment and Somerset Sayer knew where her circle would close.

What had begun on one terrifying night to a desolate girl behind a floral couch would end with the same destruction, the same failures, that had dogged her everywhere. The same roles would be fulfilled, the same words screamed across unchanging space, and the same wounds cut and healed and cut again. Clarisant could only repeat this violation because she existed at a single moment in time.

Over and over, she would bring the Waysmith to this point; just as she had promised. But though her father had died, Avenant was not her father any more than he was Pennybrooke, any more than he could have been King. And though her mother had succumbed to the violence of the circle, the Unicorn was not her mirror. That she made it appear so was a lie. And a Waysmith must know the difference.

"It's the one thing you never understood, Clarisant." Somerset Sayer pronounced. "The Way By listens. It hears you. It hears all of us. It becomes what we give to it and gives back to us what it becomes. If you cannot see anything less than what is before you, the Way will never show you more."

The Unicorn Queen bristled, the Bramble shuddering and scoring deep, painful, lines into the sky.

"Nothing is rewritten." The Waysmith continued. "Only written again. A forest over a grave."

"A tattoo over a scar." Madam Bel Carmen furthered.

"Gold bonding a crack." Alice Guthrie added. "A mural on a crumbling wall."

"A thrown-away teddy bear, picked up again!" Fiona Guthrie rejoined, her tears dropping down onto the hand of the Summer King. "Dirty and damaged...but my best friend!"

"Putting flowers in an empty vase." Elizabeth Pennybaker said. "And seeds in an empty pot."

"It's time, Clarisant."

The Unicorn Queen breathed deeply of their verse. "Indeed, it is."

The Flidais Venatica had no time to react. No sooner had the final exchange passed between them when Clarisant seized the folklorist in the Bramble, which had continued to root and spread even as the Stumble sank beneath them. Instantly, Somerset Sayer was overcome, thorned lashes curling around her limbs and biting wounds everywhere they reached. But though the pain was blinding she did not struggle to free herself.

With dawning horror, Elizabeth Pennybaker watched as the Waysmith took up the threads they had used to bind the Bramble Crown in the well, only entangling herself further and further into a writhing mass impossibly knotted with ribbons of bale light and strangling creepers. She then began to drag herself and the Unicorn into oblivion.

She stepped down and the Stumble allowed her, opening its mouth once again to reveal the wastes beneath. Tightening her fingers into the frayed remnants of the alicorn, the Waysmith stepped down again and was welcomed into the mire where the mosaic had moldered away. Mud bubbled up around her to her knees and washed in to pull Clarisant further into drowning. With satisfaction, however, she only followed her haughty adversary; sending out stronger Brambles to tear into unresisting flesh and feed on more of the blood she had been denied.

She would consume the Waysmith as she had consumed the King, and enshrine her bones in the sepulcher below with all that was left of her kin. There were cries of terror and resistance from the others, but neither could hear it. The world had narrowed to the diminishing spaces between them and the inevitable descent into the abyss. Clawed hands scrabbled at her and Somerset Sayer threw all of her weight into the tow lines. For each draining gulp the Bramble took, the Unicorn Queen took a step further back into the bog and to the grave she had escaped; from the place where she had given life and been given death and from whose rage at both called forth the vengeful ghosts.

One step in and the other would match it, around again to retrace their steps in the spiral that went all the way back to the beginning. The oldest shape revered, remains of it found and not made; moving forever outwards and inwards at the same time. Spirals in the first petroglyphs and in the logarithms of the first mathematicians; too precise, they would claim, to be animal. Too profound, they would say, to be Man. But it was, as it had always been, their shared unending Way.

At last, Clarisant reached the Waysmith and snatched her up in a cold embrace. The Stumble had risen to the folklorist's waist and now flowed easily over the form of the transfigured Unicorn Queen. Her limbs had lengthened and her chest grew thick. A ratted mane stuck to the flat of her neck and to where her face began to pull forward into a ghastly, haggish, beast-like shape. Once, it may have been equine but now corrupted, the Bramble molding her into a nightmare beyond reckoning.

Hound and Unicorn, Queen and Aristocrat, Corpse and Demon; she was all that she had devoured and a monster born of its decay. The Bramble flogged the ground and gave her hooved feet with which to resist being dragged further, the great rack of leafless boughs rattling around them as bones, chimes, and branches. The abomination raised its head to reveal a gaping maw of teeth thrashing on bursting wet vines, spittling blood and black water. Soon, her skin began to rip and sag as the creature outgrew its own natural form and it hung as gossamer on the skeleton crackling at its core.

The Unicorn Queen reared back, laughing with the joy of retribution and the lust of exsanguination. But the Waysmith did not flinch. If enmity was the last thing she would ever see, she would repay the favor in kind and go into their entwined fates defiantly. A sound then unsettled the cacophony. A high-pitched squeal and a shriek. The noise of splintering and a shout of confidence. Somerset Sayer twisted in the salivating grip only to perceive a most unexpected object sailing past her head. Orange and white, with a bit of feathers still stuck to his face, Noseworthy bounded through the Bramble. A swat and a bite, and down went another sparrow sniping its complaints to nothingness.

He spit it out, bound up again, and snatched another from its perch, crunching tiny, brittle, bones until the homunculus had nothing with which to move. In a flash, off he went again, taking on a horde of imps as they rushed through the branches in defense of their mistress. But despite their winged maneuvers and slashing weapons, they were no match for the marmalade cat and as the Waysmith watched stunned, he cleared the chittering devils from the monstrosity's crown. Cleared them, because up behind him came four earnest figures, moving as those who had spent their youth climbing trees and discovering the mysteries atop them.

Madam Bel Carmen and Alice Guthrie may have been less practiced than the younger Fiona but they each took hold of one side of the fork that split the Queen's skull and pulled the massive branches down; anchoring themselves as counterweights so that the nightmare could not throw its head and could not immediately reach the folklorist. Clarisant wailed with indignation and tried to thrash them off but to no avail. Fiona Guthrie had already taken the stepping stones up the column of her decrepit spine, wooden sword in her teeth, and had taken hold of the braided twine in her mane in time to throw it over her nose and clamp the snapping jaws shut.

Clouded eyes rolled in fury and the sheer force of her flailing nearly sent them all flying, but before she could complete the arch of her enormous body and crush the Huntresses of the King into the mire of the Stumble, she loomed back to bring down the full charge of her malice onto the folklorist and end the Waysmith at last. In this, she would not be stopped. She would feast on the death of Somerset Sayer even if all the world fell to pieces around her.

It was to her shock and utter confusion then, that she did not round on the trapped Waysmith, submerging in mud. Her widened jaws did not meet pale flesh or golden hair, or sup more on stolen lifeblood. She stared down, momentarily transfixed, at the untapped outrage of a different face. Long, black, hair loose to the wild, amber skin beneath the patina of soot, and eyes set in the same resolute line as her mouth. When Elizabeth Pennybaker raised up both of her arms as if in supplication, the Unicorn Queen derided her determination with a taunt.

"Little girl." She spoke with the vibrating filaments of light tying her pieces together. "Forget all this. It is not for you to decide. What happens now has always happened and will again for all the time that is to come. This will all pass through you as a half-remembered dream. This is the Way."

"No. Not anymore. Not for me." Elizabeth Pennybaker replied, drawing in a breath and tightening her fingers on two clenched hands raised high. "So get out of *my* Way!"

An Octadic in arms swirled out around her; eight hands drenched in red striking the creature in a hail of beats drummed out by her heels. But here she charted her own steps, to her own songs, as she began to dance. An ally to destruction, she used the sounds to mark out the passage of time as the slayer of all things. As Black Mother, she called upon the goddess in the garden; the one who devours her own children to protect the flower that is born by itself. But also the incarnation that Elizabeth knew more intimately than that, as the divine protector of transformation and the one who bestows *moksha*.

She spoke her names as lyrics and recited her *mantras* on the appointed time of death and as a result, the Waysmith's eyes shone red, gold bangles jingled ominously on every arm as she continued to dance, while something in her palms began to shimmer. All this she did to draw Clarisant's swaying head down to her, to meet her eyes as the great monstrous Queen dipped low with a malicious grin. She meant to eat her, of that there was little doubt.

"So be it." Clarisant sighed. "I will settle for you then, for now. A sad and sorry little sacrifice you have made that will serve you no purpose but the continuation of my endless revolution. Of *my* Hunt."

"A sacrifice, yes. But not for you." The Goddess agreed. "For me! *Om Sri Maha Kalikayai Namaha.*"

She brought both arms down hard, slamming her elbows directly into the open flat on the bridge of the Unicorn's nose. When the blow caused the monstrous head to dip, she did not hesitate for a second and opened her palms to pour the ashen contents directly into the wound where the alicorn once grew. Ashes, that she taken from the Stumble beneath the burning Hill and smeared across her own face.

The cry that came of it would, for every day after, weigh on her heart. Sorrow the world could not comfort and despair too deep to fathom. It echoed there and would echo for an eon yet to come. But the ashes from Elizabeth Pennybaker's hands clotted in the wound and as the Bramble drew more and more for its sustenance, it was taken up into the Crown. It pulsed once, shivered, and then split. Feasting now on embers and burning ruins, the Bramble began to wither before their eyes. Faster and faster, its boughs wilted and dried, and its roots began to atrophy.

Once the cascade had begun there was simply no stopping it, no matter how much the Queen railed or thrashed or clung to the dying briar. It consumed itself and the lines of succession it had created along with it, from the moment of a woodman's violating axe to the fall of a king in his prime. Moments later, the Crown broke and began to scatter its thorns as thistledown into the wind. And as it did, the nightmare faded, drifting away into the unseen distance on spritely diadems of white fleece.

More ashes fell away and the behemoth quietly crumbled, until Clarisant was little more than a frail figure waning against the muck. She did not look up at the Huntresses of the King, now circled around her, nor the Waysmiths, one on either side of her. All she knew was how very worn she felt. Exhausted and prostrate, she looked down at her own hands curiously as colorless seams began to open up everywhere. She watched as her body too began to disintegrate.

The last dried sparrows fell from the sky and, much to Noseworthy's irritation, broke apart into specks of fluff and sand. And to all assembled, the Bramble Crown and its flocks of birds became no more than a cloud of newly windblown seeds and tumbles meandering indifferently away on a caravan of embers. Clarisant was, at last, undone. Listless, she diminished and went weakly to the ground. Somerset Sayer, however, approached her and knelt down.

"My Lady?" She queried softly.

Madam Bel Carmen and Alice Guthrie looked on with unease. But slowly, Clarisant raised her head, and as though through great effort, met the Waysmith's gaze.

"Yes, child?' She replied.

"Death has come and wishes to speak with you." The folklorist said.

"Does he now?" She wheezed. "It must be early morning then."

"Yes." Somerset Sayer agreed. "But before you go, will you do one thing?"

Clarisant wavered, her eyes growing dim. "If you shall ask."

"Take it with you." The Waysmith touched her fingers to the fading profile. "Take it all with you. Bequeath nothing."

The Unicorn almost smiled then and gently nodded. "And then the mortal toll was paid, and all alone this pretty maid, by Death so cruelly was betrayed...and we all come stumbling after."

The Waysmith stepped back as the last remnants of the unicorn unraveled. Traces of her outline falling onto the Hill and then disrupting what the women thought they could see. It was disorienting at first, but then Elizabeth Pennybaker shouted in alarm. Clarisant was nothing now but the void, and from where she had fallen, darkness coursed outwards.

The last of the grand hall of Lilylit fell into it, the remains of the Octadic were overtaken and vanished, and soon, even the Stumble beneath began to flow into the center as the top chamber of an hourglass marks out the last bit of remaining time. But where it was going, none of them could guess. The Way By was disappearing into it and leaving no clue as to its destination.

"We have to get out of here!" Fiona Guthrie grabbed onto Elizabeth Pennybaker. "It's falling apart!"

But Elizabeth Pennybaker had a somewhat different sense of things. "It's not falling apart, Fiona. It's...turning over. We're capsizing! Somerset?!"

But the elder Waysmith had rushed to the side of the fallen King just as soon as the Unicorn Queen's final touch had begun the inevitable. They could see her, folding her legs beneath herself in the grass, her coat billowing out to cover them, as she cradled his face and wiped a stray lock from his forehead. To Alice Guthrie's delight, she could see that Avenant was, in fact, breathing.

Shallowly, and with shaking pain, but her daughter had spoken what was true. Or, had made it true in her exclamations. She still wasn't exactly sure how it worked. For a moment, Waysmith and King appeared to exchange words and though Alice Guthrie was not near enough to hear them, she felt that she already knew what they were saying.

"There you are, my love." Somerset Sayer said, touching the back of her hand to his.

"Never elsewhere." Avenant replied.

"But always somewhere." The Waysmith bantered back.

"As you would have it no other way."

Frantic, Madam Bel Carmen hurried to where they were, to help bring him up, but the folklorist did not appear terribly pressed to move, despite the victorious downfall all around her. Rather, she simply sat, holding the beaten man tenderly, as the others quickly gathered.

Madam Bel Carmen gesticulated wildly. "We must leave, Dr. Sayer! We must leave now! Quickly! Let us get him up. We have to run!"

Somerset Sayer chuckled and shook her head. “Yes. I know. We need to get back. It is, after all, time to wake up.”

“Yes! AND!” Alice Guthrie flailed. But Somerset Sayer only tilted her head and looked to Elizabeth Pennybaker.

“What do you say, Waysmith?” She smiled. “Can you get us home?”

“You know what?.” Elizabeth Pennybaker huffed as she stepped up and flicked the yellow and red flakes from her hand. “I think I know just the Way. Nosey? Here boy! Here kitty kitty!”

Chapter Twenty-Two

Hat Trick and Coat Check were arguing over some such problem as a misuse of stationery and the lack of proper postage. But in the house on Trowbridge Street, these minor aggravations were easy to ignore. That was because the clatter of teacups and bright conversation filled the quiet rooms with a rare liveliness. The attendants were, in fact, quite pleased about it all since Somerset Sayer almost never entertained guests and certainly wasn't in the habit of doing so for an entire afternoon. They also usually weren't laughing when she did it either. But today, Madam Bel Carmen had arrived with her niece, Elizabeth Pennybaker and Ms. Alice Guthrie of Tappan Street had come with her daughter, Fiona. As a result, the two dwarfish Fae had their hands full with kettles, napkins, a tray of bitter cookies, and the occasional request for a book or other obscurity from the back of the house.

"You know," Alice Guthrie was saying. "I think that this is going to be an excellent project for the Hearthcraft Society. This kind of documentation takes years to master and I know of at least a few quite skilled calligraphers and painters among them who would love to do something like this."

"You mean if Ms. Amelia Cosmos doesn't take over and redirect things before we even get it going?" Madam Bel Carmen interjected jovially.

"Well, that's what we have you for, Ms. Evelyn. I seem to recall something about an experienced scribe or a story-keeper that you may have mentioned?"

"Oh, if you insist. I suppose I shall have words with Ceres Warren. She's always had a calm head about this sort of thing."

"Quite." Alice Guthrie sipped at the very edge of her cup. "But this new study library is exactly what we need! We can invite authors, artists, and poets, maybe even open to the public one day! I have plans for everything, just you wait and see. It's been years since I worked in a charitable foundation but my brain still has the knack for it, it would seem."

"Aren't you a cornerstone, indeed!" Her friend teased. "But I did notice that one member of their governing council specifically requested no puppet-making. Did you see that? What an odd thing to be concerned about, don't you think?"

"Puppets? Hm, no. But that is strange. I don't think anyone has even suggested such a thing."

"Hey!" Fiona Guthrie replied. "Can I join the Hearthcraft Society?"

"I don't see why not?" Madam Bel Carmen shrugged. "You may have to wait until you've graduated from school though, dear. I don't know if they accept youths."

The girl laughed. "Maybe not normally. But I have parental permission! See?"

Alice Guthrie returned a coy expression but did not dispute her daughter's announcement.

Somerset Sayer, however, stood at the threshold between the front parlor and the furthest room. A threshold that she found herself in more often than anything else. But this time, she hardly felt as torn as she once had between the trees in the windows out back and the burst of conversation before her. Hat Trick wandered past and bobbed deferentially, balancing a very precarious plate of papers on his way to the desk behind her.

"So," Elizabeth Pennybaker strolled up and stood next to the elder. "How's Avenant lately?"

The Waysmith smiled. "He's fine. Or, at least, he will be. There's a lot left to come to terms with and now, he has an entirely new life to build for himself. The first time he's ever been offered the chance, I dare say. No noblesse oblige, no duty, no titles, no destiny...no captivity. He's kin to no one and nothing claims him. What happens now is entirely up to him. Not something he was prepared for."

"You mean, not since he was expecting to die."

"That. Or the end of his meaningful conscious existence."

"He's still Sovereign though, right?"

Somerset Sayer chuckled. "Well, no. Lilylit is gone. The Stumble, the Bramble, and the Crown. Every block and stair stacked upon every other has fallen. The Way By is undefined, unordered. Or is it just disordered? Either way, it's chaos now and bodes for some truly interesting times ahead. The dust hasn't settled, so to speak. But it will and then we'll have to start again."

"What do you mean?"

"Well, first of all," The folklorist sniffed, "You need training."

"Hey! I seem to recall that it was I who got us out of there in the nick of time. I've got this! I mean, I'm still figuring out the details but you've shown me the Way."

"I've shown you a Way, Elizabeth, but that's only a fraction of what you'll need before you can master the path."

"Thanks, *guru.*" The younger woman chided with mild sarcasm.

"I mean it. We've barely scratched the surface of what is still to come. I haven't even mentioned the Lore."

"Lore? You mean *Lostwith Notes?*"

"No, *Lostwith Notes* was just one of my commentaries on the Lore. The Alia Aenor: the collected knowledge and experiences of every Waysmith that has come before us. Which, you should know, is where it gets its name. Alia Aenor means 'a daughter differentiated but having the same name as her mother,' and in that sense, we teach one another the Lore as a way to both pass on what we know and to make it possible for our own knowledge to change and grow. Through names and heirlooms and fairy tales and bad allegory, everything that carries with it the parts of us we value the most. It is a method through which we are distilled, like a symbol, into our essence, so that we may gift it to others."

"Hmm." The younger Waysmith palmed her face thoughtfully. "Is it complicated? I mean, my mother told me all kinds of stories from her childhood and..."

"...And they will become a part of your journey as Waysmith. You will learn how the Way By manifests and how it appears in everyday lives. You will learn to see its machinations when people tell you about their dreams, or how they are revealed through trials when people face up to their flaws. How their choices become links along paths and then how the Way By offers up possibilities. How meaning becomes reality; which is made and not simply...stumbled upon. You will come to know its denizens, the Fae, as friends, foes, and occasionally, allies. In the end, you will learn how to tell a story that is true, false, could be, and will be all at once. Then, when you're ready, the Way By will show you how that story becomes real." She shrugged at that. "Or not, as the case may be."

Elizabeth Pennybaker didn't bother hiding her annoyed twitch. "Ambiguity really isn't my strong suit, though. In my world, things are or they aren't. You can prove it or you can't."

Somerset Sayer nodded. "I know. But it's that or some bliss-ninny fortune-cookie motto like: 'imagine imagination imagined.'"

"Imagination imagined?" She seemed incredulous. "What about imagination?"

"It's the answer to suffering. Always was."

"Well, that's not exactly what they teach you in medical school."

"Piffle. There have been plenty of fantastical and visionary doctors in the past. In literature too."

"Yeah, and I believe they call him Frankenstein! No thank you. Think I'll come up with something, I don't know, a little less Promethean maybe. Gods truthfully aren't so bad if you know how to work with them."

She did not see the smile that followed her pronouncement when a burst of merriment from the front room momentarily distracted the two Waysmiths.

"So, Ms. Guthrie says that you've agreed to do the keynote opening for the Hearthcraft Society tomorrow." Elizabeth Pennybaker rejoined. "About the library project?"

"Keynote? Not exactly what I would call it."

"I didn't think so. Either way, what has possibly inspired you to give a public lecture? Not really your approach these days, or have you turned over a new leaf?"

"At some point, I need to discuss with them the choice of the books." The Waysmith replied, ignoring the second question entirely. "They haven't set aside nearly enough room for the number of copies they'll need."

Elizabeth sighed, though she was starting to get used to this. "As in, you think a lot of people will want the same book at the same time?"

"Oh, goodness no. But tearing pages out of them for Way use eventually means that you run out of the pages that you need. With time, it just turns into an archive of half-stuffed covers and a mishmash of out-of-sequence papers that are missing so much that they start telling the wrong story. And the older and more loved a volume, the stronger its presence becomes, the faster it gets used up. I mean, I've gone through almost a dozen of my favorite poetry books in just the last three years. Having several copies of the same thing on hand, Elizabeth, is going to be essential."

"A library of dismantled books. I guess I'm not surprised. And here I thought you were just eccentric."

Somerset Sayer nodded. "Well, you're not wrong. Elizabeth, may I ask you something?"

"About the fight?"

"Yes. What made you choose Kali? At that moment in particular."

"I don't think I did, actually." She replied. "If I can echo you for a moment, it was more like I suddenly realized that I had somehow missed the obvious. That I was just catching up on something that everyone else already knew, what with the graves, the ash, the destruction and everything else trying to come out of it. Her presence felt like common sense. To be completely honest, I was thinking back to when my aunt, my mom's sister, was possessed by the goddess. She was getting beaten up by her husband and it was, all around, an awful situation. I don't actually remember it clearly though since I was pretty little; I just remember the stories mom used to tell about it. Even back then, I didn't believe that goddess possession was what had really happened but I could see that it was important that everyone told the story like it was. Like she told Drishti. And it worked. Things changed, for a while at least. But I never quite got over the paradox in my mind. Whether Kali was real or not, telling her story like they did meant that the line between real and not real didn't actually need to exist. She *was* real, she stopped the violence. She protected my aunt. Whether she was objectively a spirit or a god or a story or a person, or even some combination of those things, didn't make a difference. That's how I just suddenly knew she'd come for me too. She would stand between me and Clarisant, and defend us. Because she was already there and had been since the beginning."

"And here I thought you were all, what was it, scientific?"

The younger Waysmith returned her attention to the gathering in the opposite room, letting the elder blur in her peripheral vision and thus appear to inhabit multiple worlds at once. "All in how you look at it, right? Just like how the fairy-tale castle always falls apart in the end."

With a reassuring knock on the door jamb, Elizabeth Pennybaker then happily rejoined her companions now plotting a rather nefarious scheme involving the strategic placement of potted plants. They had long past come to the conclusion that the Victorian language of flowers had dialects in both succulents and broad-leaves, but the problem remained as to whether one was further predisposed towards spell-work than another; given the complexity of thus having to arrange an incantation on a shelf.

Madame Bel Carmen was of the opinion that creeping vines were the better solution while Alice Guthrie put in her vote for a good Ficus tree. Elizabeth could offer no further thoughts though other than that she would like something that wasn't easy to kill.

It was then, however, as the conversations continued, that Fiona Guthrie took her chance to steal up alongside the meditative Waysmith still hanging back.

"Hey."

"Hello again. Something on your mind?"

"No, not really. I just wanted to say thanks, for everything. I'm still working through a lot of it but I just wanted you to know that I don't have any regrets."

"Even if you did, Fiona. It would still be alright."

"I know. And maybe they'll show up one day but I'm not going to wait around for them. That's what my mom says, 'don't wait around for grief if it's not there on time.' But I am curious, do you? Have any regrets?"

The folklorist crossed her arms. "About a great many things but that will always be true. Not about you, though. Or your mother, or Madame and Elizabeth. You don't need to be worrying about that."

"And Avenant?"

"Ah, the real concern shows itself." Somerset Sayer's tone was playful and she winked mischievously at the girl's embarrassed blush. "You can be assured, my friend, that he is as he can be. In a sense, he's almost exactly where you are right now. For the first time in his life, he doesn't know what happens next or what the path of his life is going to be. He only knows what he doesn't want and what he will not become."

"Will he stay here? In, um, our world?"

"Well, he's not human but he can pass for one sometimes. So, I don't know. He might. Maybe you'll see him again where you least expect it."

The girl huffed and rolled her eyes. "Let me guess, he'll get a job in an antique store or something. He'll become some weird old guy who never seems to leave the building and is probably a wizard because he speaks in riddles and wears funky vintage clothes."

"Oh, Heavens no. Avenant is many things, but I promise you that he is not a cliché. I think he might even be contemplating an apprenticeship under Madam Bel Carmen or something of that nature. Now that she's accepted the director position for the Council of Heritage Arts and Folklore, she'll be named Esteemed High Witch by the congregations within a season. She's on the cusp of something truly great I suspect and there's a lot he can offer. In any case, whatever he decides, he'll find his Way. It just won't be the one he came from."

"Really"? Fiona replied. "He'd be her student? Shouldn't he be the one teaching her, and us? I mean he is..."

"Fiona." Somerset Sayer replied amiably. "Did you happen to notice anything peculiar about Madam Bel Carmen while we were on the Hunt? Anything about the Hill or the Stumble?"

"Um, no, I don't think so? Like what?"

"That no matter how hard the darkness tried to reach her, it could never quite seem to get a real purchase. Like it couldn't grab on to her, even when it was able to hook into us. It tried to twist her. It showed her the same terrors and all the same deceits that it showed us, but she brushed off the Stumble's lies like she was swatting gnats."

"Huh. I guess you're right. So what that mean then?"

The Waysmith, for all her doleful appearances, genuinely smiled. "That's not for me, or anyone, to say. But I think, in time, that we'll see. Just like Avenant. When she's ready to tell that story, she will. In the words that belong to her alone and to no one else."

Fiona Guthrie wished that she could express all the myriad thoughts sticking together in her throat but they wedged in her voice every time she tried to get them out. It was a confounding experience, to not have any sense of what one's future was, but it was even worse to feel like she'd once known, been proven wrong, and then been sent back around to try it again.

"Where are you off to after this?" The Waysmith asked.

"I honestly don't know." Fiona Guthrie said. "I was thinking about school further up the coast, but my brother's heading off to college soon and I don't really want to leave mom all by herself. She kind of needs someone to get between her and the world sometimes."

"That doesn't have to be you, Fi."

"Yeah, but it's good for now. For a few years at least, you know?"

"Hm. Ever and always the bright defender." Somerset Sayer scanned the stouthearted form for any sign of a wooden weapon. "Without her sword though?"

"I, uh, heh, yeah. I gave it back to teddy. He's better with it than me anyway. Wouldn't want to leave him defenseless against the nightmares, right? It's fine though. I've got plenty of other ideas for my arsenal."

"Fiona dear!" Madame Bel Carmen called from the table. "We need your help on this decision! We are at an impasse!" The girl cheekily saluted and moved to go. "Anyway, thanks."

"Oh," Somerset Sayer said, patting her pockets. "Before I forget, I have something for you."

"Okay?"

"Here." From her hand to Fiona's dropped a curious stone; a small, black ammonite fossil with a clear spiral and a surface as smooth as a pool of untouched ink. It seemed to vibrate with a strange energy and the younger woman scowled down at it thoughtfully.

"Wait. Isn't this *the* fossil?"

"Well, that's one name for it. It has others, as you might recall."

Fiona Guthrie stared down at it, almost as if it were a dangerous thing. It wasn't that she did not remember the first time she had seen the spirals of this particular ammonite but more that she had not anticipated ever seeing it again. In truth, she had convinced herself that it, and everything it held, didn't actually exist.

"I...What am I supposed to do with it? I mean...I..." She paused to finally voice her disinterred thoughts succinctly. "Was all that weird ritual stuff you did in the living room just for pretend? To make me feel better? Am I, like, actually, I mean, pregnant for real?"

With a heave and a cough, Somerset Sayer pushed back from the threshold and turned to walk into the parlor. "There's...a lot... between sixteen and forever, Fiona. And I can't tell you for certain what's going to happen. But I *can* give you the choice, the chance, to figure it out for yourself. It's here. The answer to that question is suspended inside the perpetual mystery of this stone and will remain so, for whatever you decide. You can keep it. Leave it. Throw it in a lake. Put it in a drawer. Give it to someone else who needs it. The choice is in your hands now. As in, literally. I trust you. You'll make the right call."

She nodded, still considerably awed by the answer. "But Clarisant. She's gone though right? Finally gone?"

Somerset Sayer shook her head. "Nothing is ever truly gone in the Way By. It can't be, if you think about it. So no, not completely. Just until her story is told again. I only hope that we've made a better one possible by then though. If not? Well, the Way By may forget but it never forgives and we'll have to tell it all over for someone else. Just with different words I suspect. In the end, Fiona, it's not what the story is about. It's about what it does after it's finished."

Fiona Guthrie then watched her go. She really was a strange sort of person, this folklorist. The kind of person who believed in better possibilities, even if she hadn't lived them. She was, Fiona realized, ultimately as good as she had ever been allowed to be. Barring that, she went with what she knew. Hence the inaccessible demeanor, the aloof responses, and the feigned arrogance. There was safety in resentment but it constantly cracked and when it did, something marvelous was briefly revealed beneath. She rolled the stone in her hand and sighed. Maybe she would just keep it in her pocket for now.

Alice Guthrie, however, was not yet done with the whole ordeal. And as the Waysmith returned to tea out of the mists of the back library, she decided to finally make her peace. It felt like as good a time as any.

"Dr. Sayer, there is something I still don't quite understand that I want to ask you."

"Yes, Ms. Guthrie?"

"On that day, when we walked across the sea to Stonehenge, I heard the poem. The one about the King and the Crown. It appeared at the same moment you did. Now I was thinking it must have been some kind of prophecy, or a warning, though I do not know where it came from. But if it was, what does it mean now that there is no Summer King? No Bramble? Not even a waiting castle. It's all gone."

Somerset Sayer sat down carefully in the furthest chair to the head of the table, now occupied, at everyone's insistence, by Madame Bel Carmen. She had wondered when this question would come up and now she decided it was time to pull out the last remaining thread in this particularly tenacious tapestry.

"Do you know what a poem is, Ms. Alice?"

"As in, a dictionary definition?"

The folklorist laughed. "No. But it's not a prophecy and it isn't precisely a warning. My favorite explanation comes from Dickinson, when she described the feeling of being so cold that no fire could warm her and that's how she knew that what she had read was truly poetry. Because of all that it had taken with it when the book was closed and the emptiness that was left in its wake. It's because what poetry actually is, are words unwilling to be defined, refusing to be labeled or categorized just so. Even, from time to time, transcending the notion of what language is. But the Way By, like poets themselves, is unrelentingly miserly in how it doles out words. So, it takes a great outpouring of emotion for it to pay up and even then, it offers words in a shape and cadence that has more than one meaning and can be understood in all kinds of ways."

"How does that explain the poem we heard?"

"You didn't hear a poem, Ms. Guthrie. You wrote a poem because of what you heard."

Alice Guthrie contorted her face almost comically. What the Waysmith was saying felt right to her, but she remained convinced that she had listened to the stanzas spoken by the wind and had not, as Somerset Sayer was suggesting, composed them herself.

"Are you to mean that it was all in our heads?" She tried again.

"Of course it's all in our heads." The folklorist admonished. "Kingship and villainy and love and fear have always only ever been all in our heads. But for every new poet there is a new poem, writing along with a story of their own making. Heard, re-heard, taken up, and told a different way to reach a different conclusion. People have been pouring out the emotions too intense to know what to do with in this way since it was possible for us to speak. We simply aren't capable of not doing it. You created that poem, and then it created you. rending significance and defining your experiences right out of thin air. Right out of the Way By. This was your journey, all of your journeys; I was just reciting it for you."

"So, there is no poem about a Summer King?"

"Alice, there is no Summer King."

Alice Guthrie would think on that single question and answer for the rest of her life.

The following morning, the gathered members of the Hearthcraft Society of Massachusetts sat around a misshapen table. Ceres Warren, still one to occasionally level her gaze at the pompous posture of Amelia Cosmos, sat in counterpoint to Cyrus Lowell, who could not look anywhere but the floor. Elfriede Davies of Salem then continued the line around the conference seat, with Heath Laney and Noelle Seward of Gloucester taking up their usual positions at the foot of the proceedings.

With nametags properly placed, the rest of the company was fulfilled by Keenan Burroughs and Gayle Esparza of Beverly, Timothy Flores and Chris Campbell of Essex, and finally, Nyla Cromer, Emelina Huang, and Hugh Dickinson of Boston. All of whom had arrived, by summons, with bags of talismans and amulets, along with bottles of water and preserved lunches: on the misgivings that this meeting would end up in some terrifying elsewhere. This would not be the first time, after all, that they had met in one place only to unexpectedly find themselves in quite another, and no one was taking any chances where the invited speaker was concerned.

A scattered round of the more casual members ringed the walls on all sides. They had been told next to nothing about the nature of the meeting but, as was their habits, didn't seem overly concerned. Each contributed to the Society as they were able or so inclined, in a bricolage of skills and life-long talents that were incorporated just as they were offered. Hence, none felt much of a pressing need to know more than the brief letters that had been circulated about rekindling studies in the esoteric had already explained. They were now here to see who might be engaged in such a project though and what they might say about it.

Amelia Cosmos banged her crystal globe against its stand and called the Hearthcraft Society to order. Very few paid her much attention however. All eyes, as it were, remained fixed on the panel of guests happily chatting amongst themselves, with little care for the solemnity of the space that the erstwhile headwoman was typically embroiled in trying to increase. One Madame Bel Carmen and her dearest companion, Ms. Alice Guthrie, the Society already recognized.

But the third woman, with pinned-up hair, a mehndi-patterned kameez, and a very smug-looking marmalade cat in her lap was entirely new. Before her sat a folded paper, with old printing obvious on the back of it, and the hand-written name: Elizabeth Pennybaker. Beneath that was a stained cigar box whose label had been taped over more times than was hopefully necessary. She was the only one to acknowledge the gavel that was meant to signal the need for everyone's attention.

Rising to quiet the group, Amelia Cosmos rapped the crystal again. "Alright now. Bring it down everyone, bring it down. We've been called today to hear a proposal. Ms. Guthrie and Madame Bel Carmen have submitted their designs but I do believe that discussion is warranted on the particulars. We also have..." She swallowed involuntarily. "We are also to hear an opening statement by Dr. Somerset Sayer. Whom we've...met."

The immediately silenced table glanced around nervously, though there did not appear to be a folklorist in sight. Amelia Cosmos noted this openly.

"Ms. Guthrie? Has Dr. Sayer not yet arrived?"

Alice Guthrie beamed with a gentle smile. "Oh, no, I believe she is quite ready whenever you are."

Amelia Cosmos turned about again, thinking that she might witness the taciturn scholar making her entrance through the side door, but failing to locate her anywhere in the room she looked back to Alice Guthrie. She could also not keep all of the sarcasm out of her reply.

"Well, where is she then?"

"Right here, Ms. Cosmos. On your podium, as requested."

And there, indeed, she was, where she clearly had not been before; blonde hair rolled up into a bun and black train coat impeccably centered. A murmur rippled through the assembled and, for a moment, it appeared as if poor Cyrus Lowell would fall straight off his chair in a dead faint. Ceres Warren, however, was the first to find her voice again.

"Welcome back, Dr. Sayer. We're all very excited to hear what you have for us today."

"Of that, Ms. Warren, I have absolutely no doubt. Shall I?" The latter question she had directed to Amelia Cosmos, who nodded her assent and took her seat without further comment.

The Waysmith glanced down to the companions on her right, who clasped their hands in joyful anticipation. To her left, she recognized Hat Trick and Coat Check; both of whom were laden with string-sewn pamphlets they were eager to begin distributing. Hat Trick in particular had also dressed for the occasion and was quite keen on the reaction he'd get to the new heraldry he'd drawn on their tunics. As the result of which, he and Coat Check bore the signet of a unicorn, rearing back, its body rendered in vine-like filigree that could have been flames, with a shattered chain encircling her feet. Behind her, a sun and shield, the end of which bore the faint mark of a broken spiral.

Somerset Sayer then regarded her audience.

"My Ladies, my Lords, Naughts, Crosses, Gentlepersons, and the Royal We." She began, with a broad and expansive tone. "My name is Doctor Somerset Persephone Sayer, and I am a Waysmith. The first among you but not to be the last."

The crowd murmured and shifted, though attentive and stern. In truth, they were not used to being addressed by anyone such as this or with these terms. But the folklorist didn't flinch. Rather, she quietly placed a penny at the edge of the podium, turned her lantern-head lapel pin over three times at her collar, and slid a small glass square directly in front of her where it would catch the light and split it into a rainbow of colors through her fingers.

"Let me begin," She breathed deeply and looked out over the gallery of upturned faces as she tapped a torn-out, though blank, page against her palm. "By reading for you, a poem."

Biography

Holly Walters originally hails from a small, rural, town in Minnesota. A life-long storyteller, Holly is also a cultural anthropologist with a PhD from Brandeis University working in the high Himalayas of Nepal. While her ethnographic work focuses on fossil folklores and sacred ammonites in South Asia, her creative work pays homage to the dragons, unicorns, and fairy tales of her youth. When not writing, she can be found perfecting her Medieval archery skills, theorizing about movie plots, and forgetting where she left her tea cup. Today, she makes her home in Boston, Massachusetts, with a very unruly garden, a few equally cantankerous pets, a clever spouse, and a resident house ghost. And since her creepy sculpture hobby hasn't panned out thus far, she is looking forward to the publication of her first novel and the writing of many more.

The Three Little Sisters

The Three Little Sisters is an indie publisher that puts authors first. We specalize in the strange and unusual. From titles about pagan and heathen spirituality to traditional fiction we bring books to life.

https://the3littlesisters.com

Printed in the USA
CPSIA information can be obtained
at www.ICGtesting.com
JSHW012344180124
55538JS00010B/82